THE ANONYMOUS LETTERS OF C FORESTIER

FELICIA DAVIN

PRAISE FOR FELICIA DAVIN

Davin's book feels genuinely, shockingly rebellious in its insistence on the beauty of transformation. If over-hyped books are plastic necklaces, [*The Scandalous Letters of V and J*] is a string of natural pearls, each a luminous gem on its own but even more exquisite in sequence.

— THE NEW YORK TIMES

But bodies and identity are never a space for trauma in [*The Scandalous Letters of V and J*]—only for joy, attraction, experimentation, and play. Within their sexual and romantic relationship, Victor and Julien are perpetually trying on different roles, different acts, even different bodily configurations, unfettered by the constraints of what's allowable to a person of this or that gender.

— REACTOR

CONTENT GUIDANCE

This series takes place in a violent, unjust world, and there are some abominable villains in it. I wanted to write fantasy that wasn't about armies or the fate of nations, but with more individual stakes. In practice, that means the villains here deal in intimate violence. There is abuse in this book. There is also violent vengeance against the abusers.

Here is a more specific list of what you will find in this book. If you don't need to be forewarned and would rather avoid spoilers, skip it.

- Violence (blood, stabbing, murder).
- Copious discussion of death and mortality.
- Suicidal ideation (an immortal character wishes for death).
- Death of loved ones from contagious illness.
- Magical violations of bodily autonomy.
- Mild gender dysphoria (a shapeshifter is unable to change form).
- Explicit sex.

For the ones whose half of the correspondence never got published

Chiron refusa l'immortalité, informé des conditions d'icelle, par le Dieu même du temps, et de la durée, Saturne son père : Imaginez de vrai, combien serait une vie perdurable, moins supportable à l'homme, et plus pénible, que n'est la vie que je lui ai donnée. Si vous n'aviez pas la mort, vous me maudiriez sans cesse de vous en avoir privé.

Chiron refused immortality when his father Saturn, god of time and duration, told him of its conditions: "Imagine, in truth, how much less bearable and how much more painful an everlasting life would be, compared to the life I have given you. If you did not have death, you would curse me forever for depriving you of it."

— MICHEL DE MONTAIGNE, *ESSAIS*, I, 19,
"QUE PHILOSOPHER, C'EST APPRENDRE À
MOURIR" (TO PHILOSOPHIZE IS TO LEARN
TO DIE), 1595

I never travel without my diary. One should always have something sensational to read in the train.

— OSCAR WILDE, *THE IMPORTANCE OF
BEING EARNEST*, 1895

❧ I ❧

PARIS

1825

PRIVATE DIARY OF ISABELLE DE TOURZIN, APRIL 11, 1825
WRITTEN ON ENCRYPTED PAPER

I have survived everyone who has ever loved me.

I have also survived Jean-Louis-Alphonse Malbosc, a man whose rapacious love became indistinguishable from hatred. He will not survive me. I have never written that down before. What need is there for paper when the vow is carved on my heart?

Granted, this paper is special. It reveals my words only to readers I permit.

The paper's magic encryption was devised by Sophie's ward Victor Beauchêne, a horrible child of twenty or thirty years of age, useful for their zeal in studying magical artifacts and for impersonating their dead brother, but otherwise a little blond pest. Like their aunt Sophie, they make tiresome daily attempts to befriend me. They share opinions with wild abandon. For the past year of our work together, I have been subjected to Victor's judgments of my home ("spooky, but I'm so concerned about the mess that I've stopped noticing") and my behavior ("it's very unsettling how little you sleep," "what if you went to the theater or for a walk in the park," "I've heard needlework can be soothing"). I have learned, against my will, their preferences regarding food, drink, clothing, literature, art, and whether they should organize their catalogue of enchanted artifacts alphabetically, chronologically, or by type. Worst of all, I have endured endless rhapsodizing about their lover, the young artist Morère, and how happy the two of them are.

I refuse to respond in kind. My preferences are of no importance and I have no happiness to speak of. They remain undeterred.

Victor explained how they like to be referred to as "they," in addition to "he," to reflect their status as something other than a man. I told them I didn't wish to be referred to by them or anyone else. They mistook it for humor. After much badgering, I relented and said if they must speak of me with Sophie or Morère, "she" is acceptable. They smiled. They have done that to me on several occasions. Unthinkable.

Enough of these annoyances. That is not why I am writing.

Victor is a gadfly, but there is a reason I tolerate them. This encrypted paper will serve as a record. I have survived too long for memory—Victor's quest to catalogue all the artifacts in my home is often accompanied by exclamations over my stores of knowledge, but I can no longer picture my mother's face. There are things I need to remember.

Last night's events, for instance.

I was hunting Malbosc. I'd been on my feet for hours. Days. The enchanted compass needle flicked wildly, following my discomposed thoughts as I trudged through the darkened streets of an ostentatious Right Bank neighborhood. Finding and killing Malbosc is the sole purpose of my interminable life, so my lack of focus was inexcusable. The compass had guided me faultlessly on my long slog of a journey to Toulon and back. Its magic requires nothing more than concentration. I did not have enough.

It was a mistake to go in search of Malbosc as soon as I'd returned to Paris, taking no rest after my weeks of travel, but I had no chance of sitting still at home. I could not wait. Once I'd secured the compass, its small brass case had a weight in my pocket far beyond what it should. When I gripped it in my palm, I swear my pulse made it vibrate. At last I had a way to find Malbosc for certain.

In retrospect, that was a foolish hope, as hope often is.

I circled the house. It belonged to Renard Bertin. I am not as quick with the names and addresses of all of Malbosc's disciples as young Victor, who spent so many months hidden among them. Bertin, a forty-something man of enormous wealth and the same insatiable grasping as all the rest of them, had not featured in Victor's reports as one of Malbosc's intimates. But there remains much I do not know.

A brief observation from the shadows was all I needed to determine that a ground-floor window on the left side of the front door would be the best entry. It was unlatched.

Too easy, I thought, and had no idea how right I was.

I was armed, though only lightly. I did not intend to engage Malbosc unless I was sure of my kill. He should have died months ago when Victor cut his head off, but through the intervention of some unknown person or artifact (likely both), his head had disappeared from the room by the time I arrived to burn his body. Ever since, I have fruitlessly observed everyone I knew to be acquainted with him. Has his head become a gruesome relic, or has he contrived some other embodiment? His cunning makes me suspect the latter. I cannot stop until I know for sure. What condition Malbosc is in, and how I might transmute it into death, remain mysteries.

First I have to find him.

The compass pointed the way. If I could confirm that he was in Bertin's house, I could study its plan, watch his movements, and perfect my approach. Before his failed decapitation, Malbosc was in and out of Paris, hiding in the spare bedrooms—or sometimes the beds—of his most devoted followers, people who believe he'll grant them riches and magic and everlasting life.

Malbosc has clung to life for an extra century, but he possesses no immortality. Only a few caches of my blood, taken by force. Victor and I have discovered and retrieved all the ones we knew of. It gave me no peace. Malbosc is an inveterate secret keeper; I know because I was one of his secrets.

The stone was rough under my fingers, the windowpane cool. The hinges swung silently. I dropped into a crouch inside what I suspected was a parlor. Heavy drapes blocked most of my view. I pulled one over myself, crept to the side, and rose.

Someone slammed me against the wall.

The drape was between us, but I knew it could not be Malbosc. My assailant was too large in all dimensions, and Malbosc would never stoop to using his body if he could use a weapon instead.

I brought my knee up as hard as I could. My body is a perfectly serviceable weapon.

My assailant grunted. Hurt, but not debilitated. I'd missed the point of greatest pain. Their forearm remained pinned across my collarbones. I could still breathe. Their whole weight pressed into me. We were so close that the heat of their body through the drape contrasted with the chill of the wall at my back.

My pulse ought to have been racing, but instead it was my mind. My knee to the groin had accomplished nothing. My assailant must be accustomed to violence. They'd taken me by surprise, moving noiselessly and effortlessly in the dark. A member of the household would have no reason to eschew light—or leave the window unlatched. My assailant was an intruder.

I can hear Victor's voice in my head saying "a _fellow_ intruder"—what a curse, to hear them even when they are not present—but I feel no fellowship with anyone.

If my assailant intended to steal cursed artifacts from Bertin's collection, they were greedy, cruel, or both. If they'd come to find Malbosc, nothing good could result. Either way, we'd have to fight.

They ripped the drape away. It happened in the space of a second with no time for me to escape. They pushed me into the wall again, neither covering my mouth nor cutting off my air, but trapping my arms. Without the curtain between us, my suspicion of their height was confirmed. My face was level with the top of their chest, or it would have been if their arm wasn't between us. When I inhaled, it was the mingled scents of sweat and caustic laundry soap.

In the slant of light from the window, they squinted at me. I was in trousers with my hair braided and pinned up under a battered hat. It was how I'd dressed to ride into the city earlier in the day. I was still begrimed from my travels. Before breaking in, I'd tied a kerchief over my face.

They might as well have covered their own face for all I could see of it.

"Who are you and what are you doing here?"

Their voice was a low rumble. Based on that and the hard, flat plane of their chest, they might have been a man, but such things aren't always evident. I do hate to be wrong.

I hate to answer questions, too. Their forearm still barred my collarbones, and their other hand was on my shoulder. I brought my hands together, palms flat against each other, and speared them toward my assailant's chin. They jerked to avoid my sudden movement, allowing me to elbow them in the face instead. I wrapped my arms around theirs, twisted our position, and rammed them into the wall. They gasped.

I thought I'd won then. I should have climbed out the window and come back another night. Unfortunately, the fight had roused something in me. My fatigue inverted into vigor.

I pulled a knife from my boot and brought it to their throat. "You first. Who are you and what are you doing here?"

In this position, with the advantage of the window, I could see the scruff of a beard on their face. The light was insufficient to determine whether it was brown or black. They were dressed in dark clothes, a shapeless coat and trousers.

"You're armed," said the stranger. Yet the point of my knife might as well have been the tip of a feather for all they noticed it. "Maybe you have another little knife somewhere on you, but I'd guess not much else, so I don't think you came to do violence. No bag, so you can't be planning to steal more than what will fit in your pockets."

I had three other knives on my person, and I don't wear my sword when I plan to climb through a window. "'Little' doesn't preclude 'lethal.'"

They huffed through their nose. It must have been frustration; it couldn't possibly have been amusement. "You came here same as I did. You want a look around. I'd be happy to let you."

"Let me?" I dragged the point lightly over their skin.

"You're a criminal, I'm a criminal, no need for trouble unless we're after the same thing."

"We are not."

There is no one on Earth who needs to kill Malbosc as badly as I do, not even Victor, who nearly succeeded. I let Victor and their lover try, but I refuse to share my project with any strange interloper who comes along. I will find and end Malbosc alone.

"I don't think so either," they said. "Would be funny, though."

The alleged humor eluded me.

"Then you'll let me go? If Malbosc is here, I'd like a word with him," they said.

"You're... working with him?" The thought that I'd been touching someone who would willingly ally themself with Malbosc made me recoil.

An instant's error, but the instant sufficed.

They seized my wrist and wrenched the blade away from their neck. My reactions lagged with fatigue. Before I knew it, my knife was in their hand. I jumped back from a slash. Reaching for the knife in my other boot cost me precious seconds. Once it was in my grip, I lunged. They dodged. They were as agile as they were silent.

In the fight, I had no time for begrudging admiration, but now that I am recording it and forced to reckon with my own defeat, I must acknowledge it. They bested me. I was exhausted and unprepared. Anyone else would be dead.

I doubt they meant their slash to cut my abdomen quite so deeply. My footing slipped and I fell toward the knife. There was the usual blaze of pain that accompanies a stab to the gut. I crumpled to my knees and then to my face.

I wish I were not so well acquainted with the gore and humiliation of stabbings, but I prefer them to poisonings. Pain always narrows my focus regrettably, but I do remember a further detail from this portion of the night. The stranger muttered "fuck" after my collapse, and then several more times, quietly but with increasing panic, as they opened the window and slid over the ledge.

What they did after that, I don't know. I'll have to return to Bertin's house to determine if Malbosc is or was there. All

I could manage last night was to extract myself, bundle my coat over my abdomen to stanch the flow of blood, and drag myself home.

I lay down on the foyer carpet. It's ruined.

Victor found me this morning. They dropped to their knees. Their bag hit the floor and exploded into a flutter of loose papers. "Jesus fucking Christ, Isabelle."

They sounded distraught. They shouldn't have. I am, as always, unharmed.

Victor attempted to check me for wounds, remembered that there wouldn't be any despite all the blood, and then went in search of a glass of water. I determined that prone on the carpet was an acceptable position and remained there.

Victor called me Isabelle. I can't remember when they started using my first name. I shouldn't have let them. It breeds familiarity. Working together was unavoidable, but I've been lax. They should find me both disgusting and terrifying. That arrangement is safest for everyone.

Unhappily for both of us, it's hard to be afraid of the half-conscious, blood-soaked woman you're pulling into your lap and forcing to drink water. Of course I didn't plan to arrive home in such a condition, or be witnessed, but I will have to take more care in the future—and not encounter that stranger again.

Went to Louise's tonight.

She grabbed a fringed silk pillow from her enormous bed and chucked it at my head. I deserved that. Louise meant to be playful. I snatched it from the air and threw it back at her too hard. She still caught it—I didn't raise her to miss—but she was seated at her vanity and her elbow knocked over a vase of tulips and a bottle of perfume. Nothing broke, thank fuck. I would have bought her replacements and still never heard the end of it.

"Oh, I see," she said. She righted the vase and the perfume and blotted the spilled water with a kerchief. "You only call on me when you've had a bad night. Is that how it is now?"

"I was here..." I tried to count the days, but my blood was still pounding from the fight—the kill, maybe. Gut wounds are slow, ugly things. Hell. I hate to do something like that, and by accident, too. "Last week."

"Two weeks ago, you ne'er-do-well." Louise clasped her peignoir closed with a little brass filigree clip and gestured at her round, absurdly luxurious bed. "People pay handsomely to arrive there and I let you sit on it for free, yet here you are, looming in your greatcoat and glowering at me. I have an appointment in an hour, so you'd better get to your point quickly. Sit down. Take your hat off. What have I done to merit such a visit, since you never come see me anymore?"

I shouldn't have gone tonight, but the thought of tossing and turning in my boarding house room until dawn had made me want to tear my hair out. I was angry at the stranger and angry at myself. That fight had annihilated my chance to search Bertin's house. Robbery takes careful preparation. There's not much else to do in the small hours now that I've given up sex. Louise was a better choice than drinking. I don't have to be careful around her.

I shouldn't piss her off. She's my favorite person in the whole world.

It's hard to go see her at Florine's, though. On my way up I have to pass through the parlor. It's always a froth of lace and giggles. I used to love it in there. Who doesn't want to be surrounded by card cheats and cleavage? Now it makes me feel like an elephant in a porcelain shop. Florine, Catherine, and Apolline are always perfectly welcoming, naturally. Tonight they all got up from their lounging to greet me—or the false name I've given them—and tease me about going to see Louise. Apolline might have her suspicions about who I am, but Florine and Catherine have no idea. Who knows what Louise has told them about our relationship. I left that up to her. She's good with my secrets.

In the old days, if I came here in disguise, I'd use a password with her. I'd mention something about Les Feuillantines or Hermès, or one of my tree names. Something only we knew. These days, we don't bother.

"You know I hate to come here like this," I said to Louise.

"What, like a cop?" she asked. "You look far too disreputable for anyone to recognize you, and if you think you're the only cop who frequents Florine's, then you don't know nearly as much as you pretend to."

"You <u>know</u> what I meant." I tossed my hat and greatcoat on the floor and sat on the edge of her bed. I put my elbows on my spread knees. I managed not to put my face in my hands, but only just.

Louise said, "It's been four years of this, Cheat. Are you going to be angry about it forever?"

"Yes," I said.

"You always liked it before," she said. "Why don't you like it now? And even if you don't like it, it's your life. You're alive to live it. Half of what you want is better than nothing."

I was too tired to explain myself again.

"If posing as a cop makes you miserable, quit," she said, though that wasn't the problem and she knew it. "Go back to your roots."

"I've lost my talent for crime."

"Ha," she said. "Can a fish lose her talent for swimming?"

I didn't tell her about the house I'd broken into, or the fight I'd won, or the bloody scene I'd fled. I slumped backward onto her bed to stare at her sky-painted ceiling and the gilt-framed mirror hung there. When it showed me my stubbled, scowling face, I turned my head to look instead at Louise, twenty-four years old and resplendently fat, happy, and beautiful in her printed silk robe with chestnut curls cascading down her back. That Louise survived our childhood after Les Feuillantines is the only good thing I've ever done in my life, and I like to see her thriving.

"Ah, Cheat," she said on a sigh.

"Nobody calls me that but you."

"Cheat, darling, <u>everybody</u> calls you that. Cheats Death, master of disguise, legend of the underworld, undetectable thief. The cops couldn't catch you or kill you. Nobody's seen you in four years and people still talk about you.

Besides, everybody calls me Butterball and that's not <u>my</u> name."

"Do you like it?" I wasn't sure how I'd get all of Paris to stop saying it, but that didn't matter. If Louise didn't like it, I would make it go away.

"I love it," she said. "Fame requires a memorable nickname. You taught me that. And look at us! We could have starved after the Sisters died, and now I've made these"—she pushed her breasts together—"entirely out of pastry, which I can afford to eat whenever I want. What could be better than that?"

"Fame for you," I corrected. "Infamy for me."

Louise swept a fan-shaped brush through a pot of powder, then tapped the handle, clouding the air with a shimmer of excess. She flicked the brush expertly, letting the bristles kiss her pale cheeks. "You and your words."

A memory intruded from earlier in the night: the stranger saying "'little' doesn't preclude 'lethal'" in that low, serious voice. Enunciation like the tip of their knife against my throat.

Not quite their last words, but close enough.

My head swam. The sweet, perfumed air of Louise's room turned sickly.

It had been a long time since I'd killed anybody, and I didn't like to kill a thief if I didn't have to. It hadn't even really been self-defense. The stranger had moved in a way I hadn't expected, and the blade had gone deep.

I wondered who they were, what their corpse would look like when the morning light came through the drapes. If they were a man or a woman or something else.

My money was on "woman," though they'd been dressed in trousers. Then again, people thought I was a man and half the time they were wrong.

I didn't want to think about that. To Louise, I said, "We could work on your letters while I'm here."

"You're having a bad night so you want to ruin mine?" She was pulling one eyelid closed to draw a line of black along her lashes. "I told you I have an appointment. And I don't need to work on my letters. I can read what I need to, I just don't enjoy it. I don't understand why you do, or why people are fanatical about it. One of my clients tried to help me with my letters last year, you know."

"Oh?" I propped myself up on my elbows.

"Stop that," she said, lining her other lashes. "You always want me to snitch. I won't do it."

"Not on the ones you like, anyway," I said. Florine and her bouncers were pretty good about kicking out men who misbehaved, but for Louise, I was always ready to step in.

"I did like that one," she said. "As peculiar as he was, I liked him a lot. He stopped coming. He sent me flowers and a very flattering sum about a month ago and that was goodbye forever, I suppose. I heard he sold his house and gave away his fortune and retired to the countryside. Can't imagine. Not even if my whole family died, which is what happened to him. Of course, you're my whole family, and I don't have a house to sell. I've never been to the countryside. Is it nice?"

"Louise," I said, sitting up fully. A rich man giving away a fortune was a rare and notable thing. "Are you talking about Horace Faucheux?"

"Oh, here we go," she said. "I shouldn't have told you that."

Faucheux's connection to Malbosc was all I could think about, but Louise wouldn't talk to me if she thought I wanted information about Horace Faucheux as a collector of magical artifacts and an associate of the man I was looking for. My approach had to be more nonchalant. So I said, "I'm surprised you liked him. Faucheux had a reputation as a cruel and thoughtless man—that is to say, before his change of heart and move to the countryside. You know if you ever have a concern, even the slightest worry…"

"I didn't. He wasn't anything like his reputation."

And wasn't that interesting? I prompted, "He sent you farewell flowers and tried to teach you to read."

"Get over here and do my hair."

I washed my hands with the ewer of water she had at her washbasin before I touched the silk of her brown hair or any of her delicate hairpins. Already set in pristine ringlets by nature and devoted care, her curls needed nothing. I gathered a mass of them to twist into a bun at the crown of her head. Each of her pins was tipped with a little paste gem, worth no more than its sparkle. I slid them in without jabbing her scalp, more gentle than I would have been with myself. Here and there, I let one tendril escape to loll against her neck.

I worked in pleasant, silent concentration for a time—I've always liked using my hands, long-fingered and dextrous in all my forms, good for arranging hair or picking locks—until I judged it safe to say, "You were telling me about Horace Faucheux."

"And you care too much about him," she said with finality. "It must have something to do with your obsession. I don't want to tell you any more and I don't know anything, anyway. Go home and rest and maybe go for a walk in the sunshine tomorrow. Stop working yourself to the bone chasing a ghost."

"Louise," I said, not quite a plea.

"What you need is to fuck somebody new," she opined. "Find somebody to fall in love with so you can forget all this."

I grunted in response. There was no chance of that. But if I argued, she'd really get going. I finished her hair and retreated to the bed.

She continued, "And before you say anything about how I

have a lot of opinions for somebody who doesn't fall in love, we're not the same. I'm not made for love, but you are. That man broke your heart."

"My heart?" I said incredulously. "Louise, he ruined my life."

"No, you did that," she said. She's brutal when she wants to be. "Plenty of people suffer a heartbreak and pick themselves back up. You didn't. You can't stand that you're Cheats Death, legendary thief, and he stole from you. Who are you if some halfway handsome stranger can sweet talk his way into your bed and steal your most precious possession? It's like he stole your whole self."

Malbosc had been more than halfway handsome, and I don't care much for sweetness, but she'd grasped the betrayal and the loss. My heart wasn't broken. It was the theft that hurt. "Now you understand."

"I don't, really. Why have you been living like this for years?"

"You know what he stole from me."

"You made yourself. Just do it again." Louise pulled an enameled metal comb out of the top drawer of her vanity and tossed it at me.

I caught it out of the air and ran the pad of my index finger along the edge. "The teeth on this are too fine. They'll break your curls."

"Do you give your cop friends hair advice?"

There was a note of genuine curiosity in her voice. I rolled my eyes. "I don't have friends."

"That's not a good thing, Cheat. And I see you trying to change the subject. I'm serious. Stop living like this. Make a new comb—or whatever. Fuck a new man—or whoever."

"You think I haven't tried?"

"The combs, sure. I saw you eyeing mine every time you came over here. I bet every surface in your little rat-infested boarding house cell was littered with combs. I bet you spent every spare centime on new ones. I bet you fell asleep with your sweaty hands clenched around a different comb every night and woke up with teeth marks in your palms."

The only thing worse than having a sister—somebody who knows me well enough to be fucking mean about it—would be not having a sister. I raised Louise to observe people and go for the throat in a fight, but Jesus.

She was right. I couldn't let her know that, though.

"I can't just make another one," I said. "Magic isn't bound by rules. Doing it once doesn't mean you can do it again. Maybe you can, maybe you can't. What I did to that comb, how I made it, I'll never know exactly. It was just the right moment."

Every other moment had been the wrong one. I tried enough times to know. I might get lucky if I spent the rest of my life working on it, but it's a surer bet to steal the one I already made. It's mine by rights.

And if I have to kill Malbosc to get my life back, that's fine by me.

WRITTEN IN AN INVENTED
SHORTHAND

Couldn't sleep after visiting Louise so I went through all my notes again. Each time I rearrange everything I've gathered from police records, old and new contacts, my own skulking and eavesdropping, and this city's appetite for gossip, I learn something new. There is a hole in the middle of all this. Malbosc is crouched at the bottom, lying in wait.

- Horace Faucheux, shitty rich boy who spends all his excess banking wealth on magical artifacts to impress a circle of similarly shitty collectors (Taillefer, Bertin, Duret, etc., most notably Malbosc), current whereabouts unknown, might be dead
- parents deceased, probably murdered with magic
- brother: Victor Beauchêne, see below
- In March of this year, Horace Faucheux sent Louise a generous farewell gift, dispersed his family fortune, and retired to the country. He was one of Louise's favorites, though her glowing

account of his personality contradicts everything else I've ever heard about him.

- Based on Louise's comments, he must have been seeing her since roughly March 1824.

- Victor Beauchêne, né Victorine Faucheux, definitely meddling in these affairs, former resident of the Maison Laval, current whereabouts unknown, might be dead

- It was no trouble to connect Beauchêne's two names, but his identity isn't my affair. I only care because I <u>know</u> magic is involved in the Faucheux family's misfortunes. I'm sick of solving unrelated mysteries. I just want to know where the fuck Malbosc went.

- In February 1824, I saw Beauchêne leaving Aveux's shop on the Quai de Voltaire with a purchase bundled awkwardly under his coat, which confirms that he knows about magic.

- In February 1824, Horace Faucheux broke into Beauchêne's room at the Maison Laval and tried to steal something. In the ensuing chaos, a resident named Julien Morère (Beauchêne's lover) was hurt. Stabbed, I think, although I didn't see it happen. Beauchêne strenuously assured me it wasn't a matter for the police.

- In March 1824, Beauchêne faked his own death— Mme Laval and all the residents received a letter stating that <u>Victorine</u> was dead—in a way that briefly, magically convinced me. My notes cured me of any confusion. There is no such person as Victorine. There is only Victor.

- Did Beauchêne pose as his brother between March 1824 and March of this year? To what end?

- Louise might know more, but she will throw a fit and bash me in the face with a pillow if I ask.
- Jean-Louis-Alphonse Malbosc, motherfucker, current whereabouts unknown, alive??
- His house was abruptly emptied and quietly sold in late February of this year and he has not been seen since. Not in his usual shape, anyway.
- None of his friends/rivals/fellow collectors seem to have come into possession of the huge amount of artifacts I know were in his home. Neither has Aveux's curio shop.
- Recently dead or disappeared associates: Horace Faucheux ("retired to the countryside") and the Marquis de Quennetière (found dead in his study in January, no wounds)
- I have watched his other associates' houses and chatted with their servants, and only Bertin and Duret have guests staying with them.
- Stranger, encountered in Bertin's house tonight, dead
- The stranger recoiled at the mention of Malbosc's name.

If someone is killing Malbosc's associates (Faucheux, the Marquis), I wish them well. But if Malbosc himself is dead, I may never see my comb again.

My dear Isabelle,

When Victor comes home, they occasionally let slip the most distressing details about you. I'd ask if you're well, but we both know the answer.

Won't you come see Béatrix and me? Let's have dinner. Or we could do something else. Dominique has a new Pleyel, and we could go over there and listen to him accompany Béatrix. They make lovely music together, and the sofa is very comfortable. You don't have to smile or chat. I won't permit anyone to ask you any questions, not even me.

Your friend,
Sophie

ISABELLE DE TOURZIN TO SOPHIE BEAUCHÊNE, APRIL 12, 1825

WRITTEN AT THE BOTTOM OF THE PREVIOUS LETTER, SENT BY PRIVATE COURIER

No. Stop this at once.

SOPHIE BEAUCHÊNE TO ISABELLE DE TOURZIN, APRIL 12, 1825

WRITTEN AT THE BOTTOM OF THE PREVIOUS LETTER, SENT BY PRIVATE COURIER

Stop what, darling? Caring about you? We're decades past that. You're not the only one who can be stubborn.

Sophie is the love of my life and therefore I respect her wish to care for you even when you refuse to receive care. I respect you as well, though you baffle me. I cannot imagine refusing Sophie's affection—refusing the most precious thing on Earth!

You and I both know what it is to have a magic that sets us apart from the rest of the world, and how attentively one must shepherd that power. You will twitch and grimace that I have recorded the word "magic" in violation of your cherished secrecy, but take it as a sign of how serious I am.

If I did not respect you, I would shove aside the strict code and vocal control that I have developed for myself over fifty years, and I would look you in the eye and say, in that voice which everyone obeys, "<u>Stop being rude to my wife</u>."

Alas, the irritating truth is that I care for you as Sophie does. I know your hatred and fear of compulsion. I will never make you do anything against your will. Consider repaying this act of friendship by <u>not being rude to my wife.</u>

PRIVATE DIARY OF ISABELLE DE TOURZIN, APRIL 13, 1825
WRITTEN ON ENCRYPTED PAPER

The compass led me to a different mansion last night, that of César Duret, Baron de Sainte-Claire, where I made another ill-fated attempt to find Malbosc.

The compass needle pointed toward a bed with two entangled lovers, deep in sleep, neither of whom had the right face. A man and a young woman, probably. Perhaps even the Baron de Sainte-Claire himself and a wife or a lover, but there was only the thinnest stripe of moonlight, and what do I know?

It was too hard to determine which person was the one I sought. I want to kill Malbosc very badly, but not enough to murder sleeping people at random. I need to be certain it's him.

A magical disguise is possible, though a disguise that maintains itself through sleep is a rare power. Not impossible. I must consider it. But how can I attain certainty if Malbosc no longer looks like himself?

The presence of two people in the bed kept me from the risk of waking them, though I think I would know Malbosc in any form, awake. Time will tell. As long as he remains unaware of my intrusion into the Baron de Sainte-Claire's mansion, I can return to observe.

I checked every other room of that house for good measure. Malbosc wasn't there.

That damn stranger was, though.

I ran into them in the servants' stair as I was leaving. They must have intended to search the second floor. I opened the door to slip into the landing and failed to detect their presence. As soon as I closed the door, what should have been my smooth and soundless exit became a scuffle. They grabbed me by the arm and pulled hard when I tried to escape. When I stopped resisting, the force of their pull slammed me into them. By feel, we were chest to chest. Their proportions struck me as familiar, but I couldn't be sure.

In the hall outside the door, a voice said, in quiet alarm, "Did you hear something?"

The stranger and I were silent.

"You heard something?" asked a second voice. "Where?"

"In the stair."

In one cunning movement, the stranger swept me into an embrace and spun us away from the door. Our sudden closeness made their scent more evident, which confirmed for me that this was the same person I'd met previously. The salt and musk of their body was faint, but the cheap, sharp detergent that emanated from their clothes stung my nose.

A warm, broad hand covered my lips. An arm banded my waist. The tightness was unnecessary. An insult. I'd lost our previous fight and stumbled into them tonight. They thought me incapable of silence and stillness.

The landing of the servants' staircase was not large, yet we didn't block the door as it swung open. The flat plane of wood came perilously close to my back, but neither servant pushed it further.

There was no sound. I could see nothing. I assume the two of them peered into the landing.

I could feel the stranger's chest and belly, as breathless as carved marble, but pressed too hot and close against my own. I was thinking, quite practically, of the movement I would make to free the knife from its sheath at my hip, and then the one in my left boot, when we were caught and had to escape. Less practically, I was overtaken with bizarre gratitude that I had bathed and changed after Victor had found me passed out in the foyer, covered in blood and filth. I would not venture so far as to say the stranger smells good, but between criminal exploits, they clearly find time to bathe and have their clothes laundered. I wouldn't want them to think any less of me.

"It's empty," said the second servant. "You satisfied?"

The first servant made a reluctant noise. They nudged the door.

The wood brushed my back. I shrank from it. The door forced me into deeper, fuller, much worse contact with the stranger in our soundless scramble to make space. We generated an unfortunate friction. One of their thighs, disagreeably thick, parted my own. The toes of my boots hardly touched the floor; they'd used their leg to lift me. This foolish act gained us not one centimeter of extra space. The stranger was an impudent rascal. I don't wish to credit them with anything, but they managed their recklessness in silence. Not the slightest grunt of exertion passed their lips, and I am no dainty little thing. The arm around my waist constricted. Their fingers dug into the flesh of my hip.

Though the stranger was taller than me, our wriggling confinement had hitched me up their body and brought our faces nearly level, separated only by the hand smothering my mouth. They wore no gloves. I'd tied a kerchief over my face again. If not for that thin cloth, I could have sunk my teeth into their palm.

Everywhere we touched, I could feel the thump of their pulse, as slow as my own. The stranger wasn't fearful.

If our positions were reversed, my hand on their mouth, their lips would curve against my palm. A smile. Almost a kiss. As it was, suppressed laughter and unseemly enjoyment of our circumstances quivered in their chest, vibrating me as well.

I did not like it, of course.

The pressure against my back vanished. The door shut. The two servants pattered up the stairs. I waited an agonizing age for the sound of them to be subsumed into the whisper and creak of the house, then disentangled myself and leapt back from the stranger, grabbing a fistful of their cloak. It offered less surety than grasping their shirt or anything more firmly attached to their body, but I genuinely did not know what would happen if I touched them.

Not, I suspected, a conversation. And we needed to speak.

So I clenched that thick, scratchy wool in my fingers and gambled that it was enough to keep them from fleeing.

The absence of their warmth and closeness was a relief. The heat dissipated from my body. I stood on my own and pressed my feet firmly into my boots, into the floor, and let my thighs touch with no intrusion, as it should be. Nothing stirred between them. I was at peace.

Or rather, I was not at peace, but it was because I was confronting a stranger who had recently stabbed me and was determined to interfere in my hunt for Malbosc. Nothing more.

"You seem in... robust health," the stranger said.

"Why did you hide me?" I demanded.

"Why aren't you dead?"

"Your ineptitude at murder."

A soft huff of amusement. "Murder? You fell on my knife. If I wanted to kill you, I'd do it right."

Would that you could, I thought to myself. Years of practice silenced it. "You're free to make a second attempt."

"You want another go." Their tone was, to my disappointment, incredulous rather than inciting. "You're a sore loser."

"I do not have time for this," I said.

When I say that to Victor, sometimes they reply "technically, what you don't have is patience." Why can I not banish the echo of their voice from inside my head? And if I did lack for patience, standing a mere hand's breadth from that infuriating stranger, overheated and itching and hating every stitch of my clothing and barely restraining a dire need to wrap my hand around their throat and snarl in their face, I cannot be blamed.

With ferocious urgency, I asked, "Where is Malbosc?"

"If I knew that, I'd have what I wanted and be warm in my bed right now," the stranger said.

"Warm" and "bed" were irrelevant and intrusive details. I began to form my next question, but the stranger interrupted me.

"He owe you money or something?"

"I am going to kill him," I said, reaching for a knife. "And if you pose an obstacle, then I am going to kill you, too."

"First part sounds good. Second part's maybe a little bloodthirsty, but it won't be a problem," the stranger said. "What if instead of getting into a second, even more wasteful knife fight, the two of us work together to find him?"

I made a sound of disgust and dropped the handful of their cloak I'd been gripping. The scents of wool and sweat threaded the air. I departed in haste.

They could have stopped me from slipping out of the

house. I expected an attack, but my furtive, wandering path through the city suffered no disruption.

This morning, Victor observed that while I hadn't stained any more carpets with my blood, I was in as foul a mood as if I'd been stabbed a second time. I relented and told them about my assailant. Despite their incomprehensible youth and vast inexperience, Victor occasionally offers useful insight. Today was not one of those days.

"Why not work with this person?" Victor asked. "What do you lose if you say yes?"

"They stabbed me," I said.

"You're fine." Victor flapped a hand, hardly looking up from their copious notes.

But I remembered them pale and trembling as they dropped to their knees in the pool of blood I'd made. My condition has done ruinous harm to my heart; Victor's foolhardy, unstoppable caring has reminded me that my condition also harms any short-lived people with the misfortune to know me.

Blithely, Victor continued, "And by your own admission, the stabbing was your fault and you attacked them first. Besides, even if they try to stab you again, you'll be fine. Why not find out what they know?"

Victor had posed a good question, and I did not have a good answer, so I said nothing. Fortunately, I was spared any need to raise my opinion of Victor by the next absurdity that emerged from their naïve mouth, which they had the audacity to accompany with eye contact and twinkling amusement.

"Is the stranger handsome? They sound handsome."

Memory acts as touch sometimes. My body carries the imprint of the stranger's. Their hand on my lips. The thick thrust of their thigh between mine. Their swallowed, soundless laughter. I think I would know them by feel if we met again.

I would die before I said any of that to Victor, and I cannot die.

My withering glare failed to make them cower. A contemptuous silence congealed between us.

I said, "It was dark."

Victor said, "You're four thousand years old and can't see in the dark?"

"An unsubtle attempt even for you."

I left. I shut the door with a satisfying finality, but did not descend the stairs quickly enough to miss Victor calling "Three thousand! Two thousand?" after me.

PRIVATE DIARY OF C. F., APRIL 13, 1825

WRITTEN IN AN INVENTED SHORTHAND

Ran into the same stranger—alive.

What an exciting little mystery my new enemy (?) presents. Who is this stranger? How did they survive? Why do they want to kill Malbosc so badly? It's not hard to come up with reasons, but I'd like to know the specific one.

Anyway, our encounter was more fun this time. I told them we should work together, but clearly I'll have to ask again.

Had time to go through a few rooms before I got diverted. Some interesting findings. One of the secondary bedrooms had dresses hanging in the wardrobe, and one of those dresses had papers tucked into its pockets. Haven't had time to read those yet.

I also went through César Duret's desk. There was only one letter of interest, an unsent one from June. The handwriting matches Duret's, and I'm almost certain it's addressed to Malbosc. Their names don't appear—life would be so dull if they made it that easy—but it mentions the Rue des Grands Augustins, where Malbosc had a townhouse, and a number of Malbosc's other associates. No idea who this Mademoiselle Reynaud is, though. Maybe the dresses in that secondary bedroom are hers?

I didn't realize Malbosc and Duret were fucking. Wonder if that went as badly for Duret as it did for me.

CÉSAR DURET, BARON DE SAINTE-CLAIRE TO JEAN-LOUIS-ALPHONSE MALBOSC, JUNE 2, 1824

UNSIGNED, UNSENT, FOUND IN A DESK DRAWER

I know you don't like letters, my love, but myself, what I don't like is being forced into the abhorrent company of Mlle Reynaud. Consider this page quid pro quo.

Must you marry that spoiled brat? I understand it's only for her money—and that rundown old ruin of a house you want for some reason—but surely there's a better way.

Why on Earth did you think it was a good idea to have us both over last night? And why did I drag myself all the way to the Rue des Grands Augustins to be subjected to that? If I have to spend any more time in her presence, she won't live to see her wedding day.

I know you said it was important, but I'm having trouble remembering why. In fact, I can't remember anything after our excruciating dinner with your would-be queen and her vicious little face. Her head would look so much better detached from her neck. <u>How</u> are you going to tolerate your marriage? How am <u>I</u> going to tolerate your marriage? Just one evening with her and I'm left with a pounding headache this morning. It makes perfect sense that I would have drunk a cellar of wine to survive her company, though I don't remember doing that, either.

What was the important thing you wanted to tell me? You said you needed to tell both of us, but I can't imagine why you'd entrust that nasty girl with even the most trivial of secrets. You've all but told her that we're lovers, and I don't know why you did that, either. She hates me for it, as I hate her. All of that would be fine if only you'd let me lord it over the others, too. I want those pompous old blowhards Taillefer and Bertin and the Marquis de Quennetière to know they discount me at their own peril. I want brick-dull Horace Faucheux to know that he'll <u>never</u> have what I have with you.

Why haven't you made <u>them</u> suffer the presence of your betrothed? I understand why you keep me a secret, but usually a man parades his rich fiancée all around. Is all this secrecy because you're worried she'd cuckold you with handsome blond Horace before you even got her to the altar? I wouldn't worry about it; his lechery was his only interesting quality, so naturally he's shed it. He's basically a gelding.

You're better-looking, besides.

Speaking of Horace and geldings, I'm going riding with him today. He simply would not take no for an answer. That's why I'm writing you this note instead of scolding you in person. I have to expel some of this bile before I get on a horse.

Horace is a terrible rider, did you know? At least I'll have that to amuse me. Maybe he'll fall off his horse and break his neck. Don't worry, I won't push him. I know you think he's "useful," whatever that means. You remain a most alluring mystery, my darling.

FIRST NOTE, POSSIBLY BY MADEMOISELLE REYNAUD

UNSIGNED, UNSENT, FOUND IN A DRESS POCKET

[Front of page. All the tightly written text below is crossed out and very difficult to read.]

You would think me pathetic if I ever confessed this, but I am so crushingly lonely in your absence. I wish you would let me live in your house so I could at least have your things to keep me company. No. Your enemies would find me, I know, and that cannot happen.

I know you are occupied. It is all part of your plan. I must endure. Missing you is not fatal, though it feels like it.

Boredom will not kill me, either. Bertin's daughter and her friends and indeed all the other girls my age—they are girls, you understand; I am a young woman—are empty-headed cows obsessing over trifles and tittering about glances from equally dull and worthless men. A hundred times a day they trill "Marie, look at this!" as though I could possibly care about anything that interests them. Some of them were only recently ennobled, and others are merely rich. They disgust me. Spending time with them is so lowering.

I steel myself with thoughts of you—and the passion and devotion and protection you have offered me all my life, and my family's powerful lineage, and the home we will return to once we are wed, and the magnificent future that awaits us— but I do have moments of weakness. I try to keep them confined to the privacy of these notes.

I know you are hard at work hunting that demon bitch and laying traps for your enemies and gathering the resources we will need to go home to Songecreux, but all this waiting weighs heavy on my heart. I wish I could help you. Instead I exorcise my sentiments into this private writing. Otherwise I would scream.

[A second note on the back of the same page. This text is also crossed out.]

No matter how bored or isolated I feel, the cure will <u>never</u> be the society of the odious Baron de Sainte-Claire. I would do anything for you, so I tolerate that sneering little rat of a man on the occasion that you charm us into the same room, but his existence makes me boil with rage. And to hear you call him "César" and gaze at him with affection—even false affection, as I know it is—scrapes at my nerves. I can hardly remember our dinner last night, which I must ascribe to the effort I expended in keeping my seething hatred contained.

I do recall that he tried to look down his nose at me, but I am taller—and more beautiful, and younger, and have a greater claim on your heart, but you know all this—so he failed, and there is, at least, some enjoyment to be found in that.

And some day you will wed me, and take me home to

Songecreux, and discard him, and there will be joy in that, too.

For now, you want me to associate with him, for his servants to know me, so I am doing as you ask.

ANONYMOUS LETTER, APRIL 13, 1825
LEFT OUTSIDE THE DOOR TO 9, RUE BRANOUX

I don't know your name, and you don't know mine, but you know who I am. We should work together.

We're going to keep running into each other and fucking up each other's plans if we don't coordinate. You know it's true. Think how much it'll slow you down if you have to hide my corpse. I promise I'm more useful to you alive.

Leave a response outside your door if you agree.

Victor presented me with a foolish little note they'd brought inside by saying, with far too much excitement and without making the least attempt to pretend they hadn't read it, "The stranger wrote you a love letter."

"Throw it away," I said.

"No," Victor said. "Read it first. If you want to dispose of it, you have to do that yourself. I won't do it for you."

I sighed, held out my hand for the page, and read the short, unaddressed, unsigned letter. I would never have guessed that the stranger was literate. The handwriting stole across the page in a curious, halting slant, like a slouching child being reprimanded to stand straight. The spelling and punctuation were scrupulously correct.

"Either a lack of education trying to disguise itself, or years of being rapped across the knuckles with a ruler for writing left-handed," I said, mostly to myself and to no end, since I will not be working with the stranger and thus all knowledge of their life and temperament is useless to me. "The thickness of the paper is a surprise. A wasted expense, of course, but still a surprise."

"It's marvelous how you do that," Victor said. "You love knowing about people. You can't help yourself. Was the stranger attempting to impress you, or does the paper represent a wealthy person's oblivious attitude toward luxury goods?"

I suspected the former, but refrained from being drawn into Victor's enthusiasm. Still, the words passed under my eyes a second time; the letter was so short that I could hardly stop once I'd started.

The stranger avoided any grammar that might reveal a masculine or feminine nature. That could have been an accident. A man might write such a note with no concern for how it would be read. Then again, a person such as Victor might write it with careful consideration for each word, each ending.

The stranger's identity meant nothing to me. I folded the note roughly, ignoring the fine paper, and shoved it into my skirt pocket.

Victor gazed at my curled hand in my pocket and said, "What are you going to write in response?"

I should have thrown the note in the hearth. "Nothing."

"Of course," they said.

I said, "If you leave a note for the stranger pretending to be me, you will suffer for it."

"No need to worry about that. I'd much rather see what happens when you write your own letter," Victor said, though they know my aversion to correspondence.

I watched the door at every opportunity for the rest of the day, but I never saw the stranger check for a reply.

PRIVATE DIARY OF ISABELLE DE TOURZIN, APRIL 14, 1825
WRITTEN ON ENCRYPTED PAPER

When I entered the storage room this morning, Victor rushed toward me in excitement and pressed a book into my hands. I suppose I should call that room the study, since Victor's various inquiries have disturbed all the dust and transformed its purpose. It was even more of a whirlwind of chaos than usual; the same applied to Victor. They were vibrating.

I recognized the slim, worn volume as one with deadly ink. "I am not going to poison myself for your amusement."

"Oh, don't worry, I already touched it," Victor said.

"You're poisoning yourself for your own amusement?" I asked, exerting all of my considerable control to keep my expression indifferent. Victor is so, so young. Sophie would be devastated, and she's already lost too much. "There are more pleasant ways to die."

"But I'm not dead, and I'm not going to die," they said, nearly bouncing. "Not from the book, at least. I nullified it. The ink is only ink now. Touch it. You won't feel a thing."

"If you need to test something dangerous, you should ask me."

"I thought you'd be less severe about everything after a little sleep," Victor said. "You're always up all night and I didn't want to wake you. Besides, I knew it was going to work."

"I will terminate your employment and banish you from the premises if you experiment with your own life again—assuming you live."

"Could you revive me?" they asked, their insatiable curiosity already caught by another hook. "If I really died, I mean. Have you ever brought someone back from the dead?"

"Do not attempt to devise an experiment."

"That's not a 'no.'"

"It is possible Malbosc survived decapitation through the use of my blood, if he had some secret cache," I said. "And he may have had some spark of life left in him. We don't know. I do know that if too much time has passed, I cannot heal an injury."

Victor contemplated me for a piercing blue moment and then concluded, "You mean when the Vicomte de Savigny lost his eye. You couldn't fix that."

Their perspicacity alarms me sometimes. I regretted even my oblique allusion to Dominique losing his eye. Though we worked together most of the time, he'd gone off by himself in search of an artifact. We'd both thought the retrieval would be an easy one, and we'd both been wrong. He came back to me in bandages. By then it was too late. Dominique had masked all his distress with jokes about how he'd been too beautiful, and too good of a shot, and the universe had been forced to even the balance. When I'd failed to laugh, he'd said "I forbid you to be sadder than I am about something that happened to me, Isabelle. Unspeakably boorish behavior. To make amends, you must tell me how dashing I will look with an eye patch."

I had, but not well.

"You tried to fix it, though," Victor guessed. They stepped toward their desk and searched for a blank page and a writing implement. "When was that, exactly? How much time had passed since his injury? What did you try?"

"Victor," I said, lifting the volume in my hands. "Stop trying to catalogue me. Explain what you did to this book. And I'm going to tell Sophie about the risk you took. Morère, too."

At last, they stilled. "That—isn't necessary."

"I'd rather tell your aunt and your lover about your foolish experiment today than inform them of your death from the same next week," I said, and then added, with cold indifference, "It will be tiresome if they blame me for something that is so obviously your fault."

"I wouldn't want my death to be tiresome for you," Victor said, like we were sharing a joke, which was not the effect I sought.

"The book," I said, shaking it a little. "Explain what you did to the book."

"The Vicomte de Savigny delivered something this morning. Or actually, Quang delivered it, wrapped in layers of sacking and stuffed into a wooden box, and said neither of us should touch it."

Though I myself shun other people's affections, I do notice them, and I have observed that Victor is usually in high spirits after encountering Dominique's companion Quang, a kind-hearted man whose broad shoulders and muscular arms make themselves visible regardless of how many layers of clothing he wears. Victor has the misfortune of being easily swayed by both attractions and tender sentiments; one might think they would exhaust these feelings by spending time with Morère, but their stores never empty. They are so profligate with warmth that they even like _me_. A pitiable condition. Long life has relieved me of any such inclination.

However, today Quang's visit had rattled Victor, not cheered them.

"What is it?" I asked.

"Quang said it's a sponge," Victor said, staring at the box on the table as though a snake might pop out to strike them. "Savigny had it in his coat pocket last night while they played chess. He lost."

"I have known Dominique for thirty years and he has never lost at chess except on purpose," I said. The poor man has an uncanny aptitude for patterns, especially the disturbances that tend to pile up around magical artifacts. Thus he's perfectly suited to finding them, which, for any decent person, makes life miserable. If Dominique were not a decent man, he'd have made life miserable for everyone around him as well, but instead of using all the powerful artifacts he's hunted down, he simply brings them to this house. I keep them locked away. It's a bad solution, but until recently, it's been our best one.

Dominique is also unbearable as an opponent in any card or board game one might care to play. Luckily, I don't care for games, and he's never managed to change my mind. I don't understand what amusement he finds in winning so predictably.

"Not this time," Victor said. "He was testing it. Quang said he didn't know why Savigny—Dominique, I'm permitted to call him Dominique, though it feels strange—anyway, he kept touching something in his pocket while they played."

"The sponge caused Dominique to lose at chess?"

"The sponge caused him to lose his ability," Victor said. "It undoes magic."

"Permanently?"

Victor nodded. "They played this morning without it, and

Dominique lost again. And I tested it on the book, so I know it works on artifacts as well as people. It's an incredible tool, or it could be. We could empty this room. We wouldn't even need to call Julien."

Victor's lover helps us on occasion by destroying some of the more malevolent objects in the collection. They have a particular talent for transforming the world through painting. Their method is the safest, most reliable way to nullify an artifact, but it takes a great deal of labor and time.

Victor plucked an envelope from their desk and handed it to me. "Dominique wrote you a note."

DOMINIQUE GALMICHE-VUILLEMIN, VICOMTE DE SAVIGNY TO ISABELLE DE TOURZIN, APRIL 14, 1825

WRITTEN IN PLAIN TEXT

Isabelle—

Excuse the letter. I would have said this to your face, only I don't feel at all myself and will require some time to become accustomed.

We've never had a formal arrangement, so it's strange to pronounce our partnership officially finished, but it is. This letter begins my retirement.

I offer you my apologies, as I had hoped to work alongside you until you terminated your project, though I am not sorry for myself. There are things I will miss—the triumph of capturing some cursed object at last, so satisfying that it could sometimes even elicit a smile from you—and things I will not miss. Various injuries, plans going awry, all the times we had to hide in hedgerows or crawl through muck, or, God forbid, both at once.

Do you remember the night we infiltrated that house in Bourges and my stomach gurgled so ferociously from hunger that a servant nearly caught us? It was the first time we'd traveled out of the city together. 1798, I think. (How strange to have lost the exact date.) And on every excursion after that, you brought me food and insisted I eat first—and insisted, equally, that you didn't give a fig for my comfort and only wanted things to run smoothly. I was touched; this irritated you profoundly, and likely still does, which is of course why I mention it.

Anyway, enough reminiscing. I've learned to live without one eye, and without the full function of my right knee, so I have no doubt I'll learn to live without my magic. Life will be different, but it will go on. This time, the first difference is that without my ability, I cannot trust myself to detect or retrieve artifacts safely, and must cease working. The second difference is that I anticipate with great pleasure having more time to practice defeating Quang at chess now that we are more evenly matched.

Though I cannot see your project through to the end, I know you will end it. I offer you this parcel as a parting gift. If you refrain from touching it with your bare hands, it shouldn't affect you. Do contrive to make it affect <u>him</u>.

I know you don't like to speak of anything so frivolous, and insist that our thirty years of working together don't constitute a friendship, so I will only say that perhaps we can begin one now. If "friendship" is too lofty an aspiration, let us settle for "habit," and say you will still deign to see me from time to time though our affairs are concluded.

Dominique

PRIVATE DIARY OF ISABELLE DE TOURZIN, APRIL 15, 1825
WRITTEN ON ENCRYPTED PAPER

Dominique dealing himself a magical injury and then abandoning me with a house stuffed full of cursed artifacts put me in a foul mood.

The damned compass led me back to the Baron de Sainte-Claire's house and the damned stranger ruined another damned search.

ANONYMOUS LETTER, APRIL 15, 1825

LEFT INSIDE THE FOYER OF 9, RUE BRANOUX

Here we are again, nameless stranger.

I killed you and you didn't die, and last night I was sure I was killed—yet I didn't die.

Instead I awoke in a bedroom inside what I can only assume is your house, and was healthy enough not only to steal this paper, but to slip down the stairs and leave this note for you. (You keep pencils! How modern. I like this one very much.)

Surely you've brought me here because you see now that I'm right about working together. If you need me, I'll be back in that lovely bed.

The stranger continues to be a menace.

Victor found a note from the stranger—in plain text and not even folded, left where anyone could read it! the nerve— and knocked on my bedroom door to demand an explanation, which is audacious behavior even for them.

"Isabelle," they said tightly. "This was in the foyer. What is it?"

They did not apologize for disturbing my rest—I was not sleeping, but I could have been—or breaching my private space.

"It looks like a note," I said. I did not rise from my bed, where I had been contemplating the ceiling plaster and longing for unconsciousness.

Victor thrust their clenched fist toward my face. That same harried handwriting crossed the page, though the contents gave it a smug aspect. The stranger had woken and gone downstairs while I'd been lying here. I must have slept for a moment after all.

Two thoughts arrived simultaneously, conflicted and entangled. Descending and then ascending the stairs must have cost the bastard, and it served them right. Yet a curious relief washed over me that the stranger was alive and undaunted.

The relief was because I needed to exploit their knowledge, and if they were dead then the truth would be lost to me and all my disgusting, exhausting efforts wasted. That was all.

"I deserve to know if there is someone else in this house," Victor said. "Especially if it's a person who tried to kill you, Isabelle. I work here. I come here every day. For fuck's sake, tell me what you're doing. Did you—did you kidnap someone?"

Victor turns a little pink when angered. It's like being scolded by a kitten.

I said, "The word is 'rescue.'"

Someone at the Baron's house last night had gutted the stranger in a fight. I'd missed the violence, but arrived in time to follow the servant tasked with driving a cart to the river-bank to dispose of the body.

The stranger was still alive—barely—when I fished them out. The rest of the night was extraordinarily unpleasant. Every room I'd dragged us through still carried the scent of blood and river muck. I had, at least, discarded my clothes, washed, and put on a clean dressing gown.

"You... saved the person who stabbed you?" Victor asked, agog. "You brought them home?"

"_You_ told me to work with them," I said. "I want to ask them some questions."

"I didn't mean you should give them free run of the house! Where did you put them? What 'lovely bed' are they talking about?"

I lifted a hand to point behind my head. The room next door was the mirror image of my own, with the beds pushed against the same wall. I should have heard the stranger make their earlier excursion.

"Jesus," Victor muttered and abruptly left.

The floor creaked. They did their best not to make a sound when opening the door, but I could still hear it swing. I expected them to enter the neighboring room, but no footsteps fell and no voices rose. The stranger was either absent or asleep.

The door swung shut a moment later and Victor reappeared.

"Isabelle," they said. "I know that man. His name is Forestier and he's a police officer."

I should have thought with alarm: the stranger is a police officer. In this private writing, I will confess that I thought, with some distant feeling that defies description: the stranger is a man. In either case, the stranger has ceased to be a stranger. I ought to think of him as Forestier.

None of it felt right; I'd learned it from Victor rather than the stranger.

How bizarre to feel such regret over acquiring precious new intelligence.

I discarded that useless feeling, concentrated on the information, and said, "Perhaps he changed careers. Every time I've encountered him, he has been pursuing a life of crime. Vigorously."

"He was a police officer when we both lived at the Maison Laval," Victor insisted. "Actually, he was there the night you came to save Julien. And in Delphine's house investigating the death of the Marquis de Quennetière—you overheard him."

I hadn't recognized his voice. The police officer had spoken every word gravely. The criminal wasn't like that.

Victor said, "Shit—Isabelle, he thinks I'm dead."

"He thinks a young woman named Victorine Faucheux is

dead, and he thinks a formerly wealthy young man named Horace Faucheux has given up his fortune and retired to the country," I said. "He should not have any opinion about Victor Beauchêne."

"Still, I'd rather avoid him," Victor said. "We never liked each other, anyway. I can't believe <u>Forestier</u> is your mysterious stranger. He's not even good-looking."

"I was too concerned with dragging him from the river and the brink of death to notice his appearance."

Forestier is redheaded, a shade so dark it's nearly brown. The color didn't reveal itself until I dumped him in the guest bed while the light of dawn jammed its meddling fingers under the curtains.

Last night all I knew was that his hair, like his clothes, had served as a catch for the filth of the Seine. Sodden hanks flung muck all over both of us when I heaved him out of the river. He's ungainly, angular, and too large—a size that makes it inconvenient to prevent him from drowning and impossible to cart him around the city unconscious unless one secures an actual cart, which I did.

He has a scruffy beard, rugged features, and thick brows. By dawn, his face was relaxed in painless sleep, his lips slightly parted. Time has sketched a few faint lines across his forehead and around his eyes, but they're only noticeable on long inspection. A little silver glints in his hair, too, but it's easy to miss.

As for the rest of him, the fight must have gone spectacularly badly. Even after I'd ensured his survival, an ugly constellation of cuts and bruises arced over his skin. His clothes and shoes were unsalvageable. I spared us both the removal of his shirt, though the bed linens will suffer for it. I left a dressing gown in the room; he took it as an invitation to steal my stationery and leave an absurd little note where anyone could read it.

Taking the stairs must have been painful. Though magical, my healing requires time and rest. What could possibly have motivated him to sneak out of bed to do something so ridiculous?

He must have collapsed afterward, if he didn't even wake when Victor opened the door. Forestier probably looked just as I left him at dawn—still but for the slight rise of his breath and occasional flutter of his lashes, unbearably young and vulnerable in sleep.

Victor said, affecting a sort of weary, parental dismay, "I can't believe you're one thousand years old and beside yourself about a man."

Irritated, I raised myself from the bed. I cinched my dressing gown closed, retrieved these pages and a pencil, and pushed past Victor. "Why does it matter to you how old I am?"

"It seems only fair. You know I'm twenty-three—well, almost."

"I do not know that."

"You do now. I just told you. My birthday is the sixteenth of May."

"No," I said, appalled. "I will continue not knowing it, thank you."

They did not follow me into Forestier's room. My intrusion did not wake Forestier, so I sat at the desk, where I found the stolen pencil and a stack of blank pages. I cleared a space for my own diary and began to write, and have been writing ever since. Forestier has not so much as twitched.

PRIVATE DIARY OF C. F.,
APRIL 15, 1825
WRITTEN IN AN INVENTED
SHORTHAND

I woke up in the home of my stranger, mysteriously not dead.

I don't remember anything after losing the fight and getting loaded into a cart, but I'm smart enough to draw a line connecting the stranger not dying when stabbed and me not dying when stabbed. I got up to steal this paper and leave a note about it. Probably shouldn't have—my insides don't feel right—but it was satisfying.

Fell back asleep. Next thing I knew, the stranger was in the room with me, wearing a grey silk peignoir. From the light and how ravenous I was, it was mid-afternoon.

Funny to see, for the first time, the body I'd already held twice. "See" is an exaggeration. The robe was loose and the stranger's back was turned. Still, there was nothing to stop me from staring, so I did. A long dark braid, heavy and messy and threaded with silver, pointed toward their bottom. Even sitting, the stranger had rigid posture. The back of the chair didn't touch them. The curve of their hips overflowed the narrow wooden seat. A little twitch ran through my hands, hidden under the covers. I measured against my memories. I'm a damn good judge of the size of things. Thieves spend a lot of time in the dark, sliding through little openings or crammed into small spaces. The stranger was one of the more pleasant surfaces I'd been thrust against.

Writing this, I can imagine Louise asking, "Cheat, are you seriously thinking about fucking somebody you nearly stabbed to death?" Before I could even tell her no, never, I just appreciate a nice pair of hips, she'd be halfway through her speech about how it's bad for my health to be horny for four years without fucking anyone about it, and then she'd give up and say, "Fine, go ahead, it wouldn't be your worst decision." Even when I don't tell Louise anything, she still gives me unwanted advice.

I'm not going to fuck the stranger. I like a risky gamble every now and then, but that's too much for me. Still, it's been a long time since anybody clamped their thighs around me like that. If it's a crime to enjoy it, I'll get away undetected like I always do.

Without turning from the desk or ceasing the soft scratch of writing, the stranger said, "There is a plate next to you."

Christ, hunger was a saw in my gut. I could smell the food, though the cheese wasn't particularly fragrant. A little pile of cornichons scented the air with briny vinegar. I grabbed the plate and hacked at the wedge of firm, pale yellow cheese with its thin, ridged grey-brown rind, amazed that the stranger had given me even the dullest of knives. It was a good cheese, not too sharp or strong, just a little nutty, and an even better bread, fresh and fluffy inside with a chewy golden crust. Not stale at all. When I set the plate on my lap, a little bowl of some fruit preserve clinked against another of mustard. Richly red slices of saucisson were stacked next to them, and then three bright orange ovals, thumbprint-sized, wrinkled like raisins.

Apricots.

The stranger has money. I knew from the soft bed and the

huge house and the whole room to myself, but the food was more proof. That I was permitted to handle those fine dishes and scatter breadcrumbs over the bed while devouring everything offered was even more proof.

"I prefer creamy cheeses, for future reference," I teased.

"My name is Madame de Tourzin," she said. "They tell me you're called Forestier."

Who could have told her that? I'll find out. My mouth was too full for words, but I nodded.

She hesitated. "Monsieur?"

Laughing would probably disturb whatever was happening to the former wound in my gut, so I didn't. "Forestier's good enough."

At last, she turned. An unusual face, not delicate and soft, but with a kind of stony, rough-hewn symmetry that I liked. Louise always tells me I don't have good sense, and she's right, since the last person I slept with robbed me of my whole damn life. It's one thing to ogle a nice round bottom that could belong to anyone and something else entirely to gaze at someone's face. So I don't care about Madame de Tourzin's nose or her eyebrows. If her eyes are dark and deep and her mouth is surprisingly luscious, that's not my affair.

I waited for her to tell me what the fuck she wanted, why she'd saved my life and brought me here, but instead she said, "It's an apricot. The thing you're examining. Fresh ones aren't in season yet."

"I know what an apricot is." She'd seen through me. I didn't like that. I popped it into my mouth with nonchalance, or maybe spite, and chewed like I ate one every day. I don't, though. It was so sweet. It tasted as bright as its color. The fresh ones are probably even better.

They meant so little to her that she'd given three of them to me, her—hostage? rival? I don't know what we are to each other, but if she's giving away fancy food, I'm staying.

"You saved my life," I said.

"I am exploiting you," she replied. "Don't confuse yourself with sentimental absurdities."

"No, I meant—why? What do you want? But since you brought up sentimental absurdities, you're the one who tucked me into bed and fed me breakfast."

"You are of no use to me dead, or sleepless, or hungry," she snapped.

It was easy to provoke her. Fun, too. "Exploit me any time."

"If you continue to be disgusting, I will dump your body back into the river."

It was too late; I knew she wouldn't. Not yet—and if she wanted to try later, she was welcome to. I picked up the cup of coffee she'd set next to the bed and luxuriated in the scent. It was fresher and richer than anything I could afford myself, and she hadn't stinted on the milk. The first sip made me sigh with pleasure. I didn't even do it to make her mad. That was just a little extra gift.

She glared and then turned away sharply like me and my coffee were too filthy to watch.

A flush of heat ran through me. Winning always makes me hot. As the victor, I decided to grant mercy. "Seriously, what do you want?"

She seized my olive branch, but acted like nothing had passed between us. "Tell me what happened last night. What you found in the house, who you fought, anything you noticed."

"It was a bad idea to go back." I hated to admit it, but if I didn't say so, she might think I didn't know I'd done a damn fool thing. That was something, at least, to have enough awareness to say it myself before she could tell me. "I didn't have time to find or notice anything in the house. After our near-miss in the stairs the night before last, they were waiting for me—or waiting for you, I bet."

I'm just someone Malbosc once fucked and robbed. She can survive a stabbing and revive another person. It's not hard to figure out which of us is the important one.

Madame de Tourzin said, "Who is 'they'?"

"It's the Baron de Sainte-Claire's house. César Duret. You must know that—you broke in. Duret was there, and so was a woman. Mademoiselle Reynaud, I suspect. She's taller than Duret, but he's a small man. They were both armed. Rapiers. Couldn't fight off both of them at once, not when they ambushed me like that."

Her expression was unreadable. Not one flicker of interest or emotion.

"Rapiers," she repeated.

"Yes," I said, irritated. Why ask me anything if she wasn't going to listen?

"How old is Duret? Twenty? Thirty? Even if he had a military career, which he doesn't, to my knowledge, wouldn't his weapon of choice be a saber? Or a pistol, for that matter. He doesn't have a reputation as a duellist."

"This is rich-people shit," I said. "I like a knife or bashing a man's head in with whatever stone I can pry loose from the street."

"The woman didn't appear old, either," she murmured, and that was how I knew she'd seen the woman.

We'd only been talking for a few minutes and she'd already annoyed me, asking what I knew without offering anything in return. Her insistence on the swords interested me, though I didn't know much about swords, because she seemed to suspect —as I suspected—that the man who looked like Duret might not be Duret. But she didn't know about my comb and she hadn't read the letters I'd found, so how had she arrived at that idea?

Maybe because I was half-sure Duret himself didn't matter, I decided to be generous with my information. "Duret's twenty-eight. He became the Baron de Sainte-Claire last year after his father and two older brothers all died of a sudden, inexplicable illness. Not married, no children, no mistresses that I know of—other than the woman last night, if that's what she is. He's a bad gambler, but a habitual one. Prefers horse races to card tables. Handsome, vain, loves a fancy waistcoat, always late to pay his bills. Short-tempered and cruel to his staff."

I expected—hoped for—astonishment. I wanted to see that pretty mouth drop open, incredulous. Maybe she'd ask how I could possibly know all that, and I could shrug like it was nothing, like I hadn't spent years cultivating a network of informants, months combing through police files, and countless hours spying on Duret and his household. Maybe she'd snap her fingers and come to some crucial realization because of what I'd given her.

She asked, "Was he good with the sword?"

"Answer your own damn question. I lost."

"You were surprised and outnumbered. They might have defeated you through luck rather than skill."

"A sly compliment," I said. "You think I'm good in a fight."

Flatly, she said, "Or it might have been the other person, and not Duret, who humiliated you."

Humiliated. That was some choice of word. Honest, but not necessary. I picked at the crumbs on my plate. "They both attacked. If my memory can be trusted, it was Duret who landed what should have been the fatal blow."

"He's good with the rapier, then," she said like she'd solved some private equation. Then she called through the closed door, "Victor. Are you occupied with anything life-threatening? You shouldn't be. I need you to bring the portrait in here."

The floor creaked outside the room, and a familiar voice that I couldn't place said, "Isabelle. You know I can't—"

"Forestier," said Madame de Tourzin who was also called Isabelle, addressing me and brusquely interrupting whoever was in the hall. "My associate Victor believes you work for the police. If you attempt to arrest Victor, or do him any harm, or cause him the slightest of inconveniences, or even briefly contemplate any of those things, you'll be dead before you leave this room."

The name "Victor" and the voice I'd heard in the hall came together in my mind. Madame de Tourzin was working with Victor Beauchêne.

He'd seen me while I was unconscious and recognized me. That rankled. He must have been the one to tell her my name. I examined some filth under my fingernails. There was plenty, so I took my time. "Seems wasteful to kill me after you went to all that trouble to save me last night."

"Are you an agent of the police?" she asked.

"You think a cop would be breaking into houses and getting into knife fights?"

Her silence endured so completely that I heard Victor shift his weight from one foot to the other and back, like the floorboard was a saggy fiddle string he was coaxing back into tune.

When it became clear that her patience could bludgeon mine to death, I relented. "I wear that uniform like I wear any other disguise, to find what I'm looking for. I have no interest in policing."

"You've been posing as a police officer," she said. It wasn't a question, so her tone mystified me. Writing this now, maybe I'm flattering myself, but I think she might've been impressed.

I shrugged. "It's not hard."

Not technically, anyway. Most of what the police do is put starving people in chains. If I can't slip in some piss and twist my ankle to get out of that, I usually manage to fumble the key. It's not true that I'm posing as an officer. I am an officer. There is somebody named Forestier earning a salary from the prefecture. That person is more or less me, and he's remarkably bad at his very easy (cruel, brutish) job.

I wasn't always. In the early days, when I was still riding high from swindling my way in, occasionally I'd throw myself into a puzzle. I couldn't help it. My mind spins even when there's nothing to make into yarn, so when I find fiber, I have to twist it. The others noticed I was good at stringing things together, so I started to show them—the shape of footprints in the mud that we could compare to suspects' boots, the drops of blood we could look for on suspects' cuffs. They'd never thought of that. No wonder they never solve anything. Once I realized I was getting my hardworking criminal associates in trouble, I stopped explaining which walls were scalable and which features were easiest to disguise. My colleagues think I had a bad fall and hit my head, or that I've taken up drinking too much. They murmur sadly about how inept I've become. Some day they'll fire me, but I've already abused my position to interrogate a lot of rich assholes and rifle through the prefecture's records. The work has been dull since then.

Louise is always telling me it's hard on my heart. Whatever that means. I'd open up my gut wound and jump back into the Seine before I admitted thinking about those words to her _or_ Madame Isabelle de Mysteriously Not Dead and Keeping Me Hostage.

"You came to ask questions after the Marquis de Quennetière was found dead in his home," she said. "When the household staff provided a laughably bad alibi for the

Marquise, you let it go. You didn't care if it was murder—you were looking for Malbosc."

She'd been present and I hadn't known. An oversight on my part, but an interesting glimpse into her.

"Victor," she called.

Another oversight—I'd forgotten him. She'd been raising her voice for his benefit when she recounted my non-investigation of the Marquise. I'd only been thinking about Madame de Tourzin, hiding somewhere in that house, pinning herself to a wall without me.

"Bring the portrait in here."

The slender young man who'd once lived alongside me in the Maison Laval sidled into the room carrying a painting. It was unfinished, blank at the edges and with sketchy brown stuff behind the head and shoulders of the person it depicted.

Malbosc. I recognized him as much by my feeling of dread as by his golden-brown hair and blue eyes. Thirty or so, still youthful, smooth and symmetrical. The kind of cheekbones and lips that can trick an unsuspecting thief into revealing her most precious secret. A serious, pensive expression.

A treacherous wet shit smear of a soul.

"No need to ask if you recognize him," Madame de Tourzin said. "Your flinch is answer enough."

"Why do you have that?" I asked. "Why are you making me look at it?"

"I find it useful. I would like to know if it elicits anything new in your memories of your attackers."

"No," I said, though of course I knew what she was getting at—whether Malbosc had changed shape. She suspected, but wasn't sure. That was why she'd thought so hard about the swords. Malbosc must fight with a rapier.

Victor turned the painting to face the wall and I met his gaze. He averted his eyes immediately, but I kept staring.

He looked almost the same. Under his cap of blond curls,

he had sharp, delicate features, accentuated with a fashionable little goatee. High-class speech, expensive clothes. Whatever had happened to him in the year since he faked his death, he'd still never gone hungry or worked outdoors. There's a kind of cosseted glow people only get from growing up rich.

Isabelle doesn't have it.

Victor hadn't wanted to be in the room with me. Faking one's death is a lot of trouble, and he thought he was undoing all his hard work.

"We lived together in the Maison Laval," I said, which startled him. "Don't worry, I doubt anyone else there saw through your trick with the letter about Victorine being dead. Were you posing as Horace this past year?"

He gaped. Isabelle didn't, but I thought her eyes might have widened a little.

I said, "Horace Faucheux's withdrawal to the country makes much more sense if it wasn't a rich man having a change of heart, but an impostor retiring a false identity. So I'm asking again. Were you pretending to be him?"

"You're pretending to be a cop," Victor said, in a tone like an animal baring its fangs.

I'd been right about his fraud, then. Victor, in disguise as his brother Horace, had visited my sister at Florine's—and tried to teach her to read. She'd liked him despite that. That was worth something.

"And you stabbed Isabelle," Victor said.

"Victor," she said, more tired than scolding.

This diminutive youth defending the older, sturdier, meaner Madame de Tourzin—who'd dismissed a stab wound like a flea bite and must possess incomprehensible power— made some useless little flutter tremble in my chest. I didn't laugh.

It's no good to feel this kind of affection for people I can't trust. It always ends in disaster.

In a different tone, Madame de Tourzin asked Victor, "What do you know about the Baron de Sainte-Claire?"

"He wasn't like Taillefer or the Marquis de Quennetière—always at Malbosc's side," Victor said. "I wondered, actually, if Malbosc and the Baron had some reason for keeping such a careful distance at every social gathering. Anyone who wasn't grasping for more of Malbosc's attention stood out to me. Maybe the Baron wasn't grasping because he already had what he wanted."

"Do you think they were lovers?" Madame de Tourzin asked.

"They were," I interrupted, eager to demonstrate that I had useful information—and to imply that I had a great deal more. Both of them stared at me in disbelief. "I found an unsent letter in Duret's desk. It was dated June 1824. Things might have changed, but they were lovers once."

"It's possible," Victor said to Madame de Tourzin. "I suspect the Baron prefers men. He always had some excuse for not joining us at Florine's, and only women work there. Malbosc has no preferences."

"Not true. He prefers people he can exploit." She sounded like a schoolmistress tapping her chalk against a slate where she'd already written the answer, not like someone relating her own experience.

It was the same word she'd used with me. "I am exploiting you," she'd said. A weird thing to confess. People who want to manipulate you and suck you dry don't usually say so.

I still don't know what's between her and Malbosc, but I bet it's personal. As one of the people Malbosc exploited, I think she and I might have something in common.

"The Baron de Sainte-Claire seems to be sleeping with a woman," Madame de Tourzin said to Victor.

"Are you sure his lover is a woman?" Victor asked. "Oh. I see. You think it's Malbosc."

"May I ask what you two know about why Malbosc has suddenly gone into hiding after spending months flitting around the city as himself?" I asked. "And does it have to do with whatever happened in February when his townhouse was sold?"

From the notes I'd found, I had my own gruesome idea of what had happened, but I wanted their answers before I mentioned that.

They exchanged speaking glances. Madame de Tourzin nodded minutely.

"Yes," Victor said. "I cut his head off."

"You—what?"

He told me a story of posing as Horace Faucheux for months, infiltrating Malbosc's circle of followers, trying to learn his weaknesses.

"Malbosc has a way to heal from almost any wound," Victor said, eyeing Madame de Tourzin.

She must have something similar, since I was alive when I shouldn't be. Obviously neither of them was going to tell me what it was.

Victor continued, "Maybe _any_ wound. We both thought decapitation would kill him, but it didn't. I separated his head from his body by some distance, but when Madame de Tourzin came to burn the body and empty the house, his head was missing."

"How could his head have gone anywhere?" I asked.

"I don't know," Victor said just as Madame de Tourzin said, "César Duret."

Victor said, "I was in that house for hours and I didn't see or hear anyone except Malbosc's two servants, both of whom you spoke with afterward. What makes you think the Baron de Sainte-Claire rescued Malbosc?"

"The woman in his bed that none of us know, even though we've all made extensive study of the people who surround Malbosc," she said. It was <u>almost</u> an acknowledgement of my usefulness. "Certainty is impossible, but this is my best guess. Duret was in the house unbeknownst to you, Victor. In your absence, but before I arrived, he recovered Malbosc's head. I cannot say what artifact he used to revive—and re-embody—Malbosc. As for why Malbosc no longer looks like himself, that seems an obvious tactic when he knows I'm hunting him, though again, I don't know how he's achieving it."

I was pretty sure I did, but I didn't say so.

"Shit," Victor said, scrubbing a hand over his face. "While I had him trapped, I asked him about servants in the house, but it didn't occur to me that anyone else was there. If Duret was—is—his lover, they kept it secret."

"There's no need to blame yourself, Victor. You dealt him a blow, and we've found him again," Madame de Tourzin said.

Her kind remark surprised Victor—and me, though I didn't make it quite so plain. I said, casually shifting the topic, "You emptied the townhouse? What did you find there?"

"Nothing I'd give to you," Madame de Tourzin said.

"Not even if it was mine in the first place?"

"If you describe the artifact to me, I'll check my catalogue," Victor said. "If it's dangerous…"

"Never mind," I said. The comb <u>wouldn't</u> be dangerous if Malbosc wasn't using it to hide. If it was mine again. But it's not mine, and it's not in this house, because that would be too easy. Malbosc took it from me and he still has it and if I let Isabelle de Tourzin kill him without me, I'll never get it back. "What's the plan for Malbosc?"

"You have no need to know it because you won't be involved," she said. "I have all I needed from you. You're free to go."

"That's... not right," I said. "You saved my life and revealed the extent of your power to me. I know your name and where you live. Your actions only make sense if we work together from now on."

"Oh," she said. "It seemed gauche to mention it, but Victor is going to make you forget me and this place."

"What?" said Victor.

I said, "You're worried about seeming <u>gauche</u>? It hasn't even been an hour since you threatened my life."

To Victor, she said, "I have no doubt it's within your ability."

"You <u>should</u> have doubts. He fucking recognized me!" Victor stuck out his arm in my direction and waved it. "And even if I could do it, I wouldn't. Last time was life or death. I didn't agree to this time. He wants to help."

This unexpected solidarity made me consider Victor in a new light. I'd always found him irritating before, a troublesome little rich boy with no real problems, messing with magic he didn't understand. But he'd undertaken a difficult and dangerous task, posing as his brother to get closer to Malbosc, and that earned him my respect. His failure and Malbosc's disappearance made my life a hell of a lot harder, but I forgave him that. It touched me that he was taking my side against Madame de Tourzin.

And we have something else in common. Victor is like me. Maybe not in the details, but in the broad strokes. We both picked the locks on our cages. The world imprisoned us in one category, and we escaped.

Before, Victor's identity had been an irrelevant detail to me, something I'd discovered almost by accident while searching for more important answers. Now he was a person instead of a mystery to be solved, so our similarity made me like him.

I know plenty of people like us—some born in the underworld, some who ended up there by exile or by choice—but it never gets old to meet another. Women with cocks, men with cunts, people who are both or neither, people who have chosen to change themselves with clothes and haircuts and new names, and those like me who use magic.

Used, in my case.

And Isabelle knows Victor's nature and works with him, likes him—or at least, doesn't hate him. I seized that information with an eagerness I don't want to investigate. Neither of them noticed my revelation. I was too careful for that. I'm not ready to explain my nature yet. Luckily, they were still in the middle of their disagreement.

"He's right, Isabelle. You should work together to kill Malbosc."

I said, "That letter I mentioned finding—I have more like it, and other information that could be useful to you. You'll never get it unless you work with me."

"What information?" she asked sharply.

"If I tell you now, you'll leave me behind," I said, wagging my finger at her. "I'll tell you some when we're halfway there, and the rest right before we find him, how about that? Besides, you don't have to like me. Just believe that I hate him."

She cast me a long-suffering glance and said, "I suppose I can believe that."

PRIVATE DIARY OF C. F., APRIL 16, 1825

WRITTEN IN AN INVENTED SHORTHAND

The first thing I did after I was well enough to leave that bed —and free to leave Isabelle's—was to dart home so I could revisit the papers I'd found at Duret's.

I didn't really understand Mlle Reynaud's second note when I first read it, but I think now I do.

Isabelle will want this knowledge. I can use that.

SECOND NOTE, PROBABLY BY MARIE REYNAUD
UNSIGNED, UNSENT, FOUND IN A DRESS POCKET

[The text is difficult to read, not because it was crossed out as in the previous note, but because the writing is unsteady. A scatter of dark brown stains mars the page.]

My God, you brilliant man. The schemes you devise amaze me. As soon as you were injured—I will not say killed—I remembered all the secrets you put into my mind on that obscure night so many months ago, and so did the Baron. That locked chest you'd left in my room, everything you'd hidden in his house... We saved you. We used every last drop, but we saved you.

I saved you, I should say. I understand now why we needed him. I understand everything.

I was and am terrified. Despite my exhilaration at your cleverness, exhaustion threatens to overtake me. The task itself was horrible. I struck quickly, took the knife right to his neck, but the mess and the work of it disgusted me. You had the foresight to choose a small man. I don't think I could have lifted a larger body, not even with the power of my love driving me.

That bathtub will never be the same. I had to leave you soaking in the blood quite a long time to be sure you were healed. Once whole, you were easy enough to wash. There was much less blood by then.

I fear that I have failed you, as you have not yet woken, but you will find these sentiments unworthy. I should have faith in your plan. By the time you wake, I will have wiped myself clean of them.

You must wake. You must. Otherwise it will all have been for nothing, and I will weep. You would find that unworthy as well. I am relieved you cannot see me in this state, and hope this writing will serve to extract the worry from my mind.

I have much to do.

I should never have relented. Victor clearly has some naïve plot to make me talk to more people, as in addition to entangling me with Forestier, this afternoon they mentioned Dominique and how I ought to call on him.

When I asked why, they abandoned their methodical note-taking and passing the sponge over cursed artifacts to disarm them. They screeched their chair legs across the wooden floor to turn their unbearably guileless young eyes on me. They said, in puzzlement, "You're friends."

"No."

"Colleagues, then. Former colleagues," they said before I could correct them, and then explained in a slow and patronizing tone, "Something bad happened to him. He'd probably like to see you."

Dominique can now spend his idle time in the company of his beloved, a cheerful and handsome young man. It is patently absurd to assert that he would like to see the cantankerous old monster whose only use to him is as a deathless guardian of malevolent objects, whatever noises he might have made about friendship in his last letter. I did not see the point in addressing that. I said, "Nothing bad happened to him. He retired."

Victor stared at me. "Isabelle. He gave up his magic. For you."

"You understand nothing of what is between us. He suffered an accident, certainly, but the result is not so dire—he left a self-imposed and arduous career that repeatedly endangered his life and injured his body. He set down a burden. As his last act, he gave me an artifact that might help me in my quest to kill Malbosc, something we have been seeking for decades."

"'Suffered an accident'? The same Vicomte de Savigny who never lost at chess for thirty years? He knew what he was doing. He did it on purpose." They held up the sponge, clenched between their gloved fingers. "This is your way out, Isabelle. You don't have to live alone and tormented in this house forever, surrounded by all this fatal shit. The Vicomte de Savigny gave you a gift—a fucking expensive one. A decent person would say thank you."

"You have mistaken me for someone I am not," I said.

I don't know why I let that insolent child come into this house and roll their eyes at me. They said, "Look, maybe you really think he doesn't matter to you, but <u>you</u> matter to <u>him</u>. It's too late not to. Tell yourself you're a heartless murderer if you want to, but don't be shitty to Dominique. I don't even like the man, but he deserves better than that. He fell on a sword for you."

"He's alive," I said. "And I didn't ask him to."

"Oh my God," they muttered. "I have work to do, cataloguing and destroying the thousands of hateful and dangerous artifacts you two sequestered in this room over the past thirty years. Get out of here and let me do it."

I left and went to skulk at the Baron de Sainte-Claire's house for a few hours. Some inconvenient sentimentality forces me to confirm whether that unknown woman really is Malbosc before I take action. Forestier took a shift watching the house for four hours this afternoon. It was likely unwise for him to undertake so soon after his injury, but he ignored my warning.

Our arrangement of trading shifts had the happy outcome that we spent little time together. We conferred for a brief moment when I relieved him—he had not seen Duret or the woman.

This brevity was a relief to me. There is an undercurrent of suppressed amusement to all my exchanges with Forestier. I cannot crush it without implicitly acknowledging that I have noticed him enjoying himself, which he will doubtless revel in and take as proof that I also enjoy myself in his company, which I do not.

I have grown to hate the sight of his smirk, the corners of his mouth just barely upturned. He needs to shave. His face carries the bristling trace of a beard—auburn in the fading light of evening, redder than the dark shade of his hair—and an attendant air of roguish impropriety that makes me want to smother him.

It is nearly eleven o'clock at night now. I slunk all around the house and immersed myself in its eerie quiet. I write this in a wine shop, my appointed meeting place with Forestier. I will have to tell him that Duret and the woman are gone. The compass needle points to some distant elsewhere. They have left Paris.

PRIVATE DIARY OF C. F.,
APRIL 17, 1825
WRITTEN IN AN INVENTED
SHORTHAND

I deliberately chose a wine shop I never frequented as a meeting place, and still two people I recognized were drinking there. One was an old man who used to play cards at Brasserie La Fortune. The other was a groom I'd once bought secrets from—not in this shape, thankfully. Neither of them would know me. Paris is a big city, but not sometimes it's not big enough.

The first thing Isabelle said to me, in a barely audible grumble, was "I don't wish to discuss it here," and then louder, in what I suppose was an imitation of a man, "Have a drink with me."

She hasn't given me permission to call her Isabelle, and I haven't dared, but these papers are private. It's how I think of her.

Isabelle hasn't asked for my given name and I haven't offered it.

I got myself a glass. No one in that crowd of wilted drunks was watching us, but I humored her. Slumped in a corner in her dark trousers, wrinkled coat, shapeless hat, and general air of dismay, she fit right in. I sat opposite her at the little round table, which tipped as soon as I touched it. It took me five minutes to filch a grimy handkerchief from the nearest person and shove it under the offending table leg. Most of that time was waiting for the opportunity and coming up with a suitably innocuous topic for public conversation. Isabelle answered my questions about Victor in sullen, short sentences, and pretended to be very interested in the glass of red vinegar she was barely drinking.

As I was adjusting my handiwork, she said in a low voice, "Why are you doing that?"

"Asking you questions? Because I want to know more about your friend," I said.

"Victor isn't—I meant the table."

I shrugged. "Passes the time. That's what you want to do, isn't it?"

"That man might have noticed you taking his handkerchief. Someone else could have seen."

"But they didn't," I said. "I'll give it back if it outrages your sense of justice."

The brim of her hat obscured my view of the extraordinarily aggrieved grimace she made. Too bad. I would've liked to enjoy it fully, and especially to revel in how much worse it got when I removed the handkerchief, refolded it, and surreptitiously replaced it in the man's pocket.

The table wobbled again when I picked up my wine. I felt light, absurd. I haven't done anything like that—a little bit of showy-not-showy pickpocketing, just for the pleasure of it—in ages. Before I woke up in her house, before she pressed herself against me in that stairwell, this awful, unchanging face of mine had gone stiff from not smiling. She brings something out in me. She's so serious, I have to provoke her.

"So," I said. "Victor. You trust him with your secrets. He tells you to work with me and you listen. He must be good at what he does—what is it, exactly?"

"Nothing I'd discuss here, or with you."

"He can't have much experience. How old is he, nineteen?"

"Twenty-three next month," she said and pulled her hat to cover her face entirely.

She couldn't see me, so I smiled. I risked one last secret question, folded up in a comment and slid nimbly into the conversation. "A little younger than you, then."

Isabelle straightened her hat, gave me the full force of those heavy brows and the flattened, unimpressed set of her mouth, and stood. "Let's go. I've finished my wine."

Her lips had barely touched it. The full glass was still posed on our precarious table, but I didn't want any more, either.

I walked with her toward Rue Branoux, the night air humid and chill after the eye-stinging smoke of the wine shop. I was ambling, because we were two people leaving a wine shop in the middle of the night who shouldn't have any urgent business, and because my tired feet were dragging. I was more tired than I should have been—I'd only infiltrated Duret's house for a few hours this afternoon and I hadn't even had to scale a wall—but also definitively more alive than I should have been after losing that sword fight. I couldn't complain.

Isabelle wasn't ambling. I don't think she knows how. But she matched my pace a moment after I lagged behind. She didn't push me to go faster. It was the smallest drop of decency, but I was thirsty enough to savor it.

We approached her neighborhood, new enough that the street wasn't yet illuminated by lamps. She picked her way through the shadows and I followed the soft drop of her boots on the cobblestones. Beside me, she was only a rustle and a whiff of wine-shop smoke until she said, "They're gone from the house, Duret and the woman."

"I know," I said. "The stables are missing a carriage and a team of four horses."

"Duret has an estate. They might have gone there."

"They might have. Big risk to travel that far if we're not sure." She didn't protest my use of "we," which I took as a victory. I continued, "Give me a few hours tomorrow and I can find out where they went."

She didn't demand any details or tell me no, so I'll ask around and go back to the house. I want to search their rooms again anyway. But I should have known then that her long silence didn't mean she had nothing to say.

"I... have a suspicion about where Malbosc went," she said. "But I don't want to rely on suspicion, and I don't want to incline you one way or another if you're going to investigate tomorrow."

A confession and a tacit admission of trust. I preened, but didn't comment.

We arrived at the hedge that hides her house from the street. She unlatched the gate and stepped through, then said, "Are you coming?"

"Didn't realize I was invited."

"As you said, it would be a waste of my efforts to save your life if you died now," she said. "You're insensible with fatigue and probably also with that disgusting wine you deigned to drink for reasons I cannot discern."

"Had to make it look real," I said. And I can't waste what I paid good money for. No need to get into that. "And I'm not insensible with anything. You love to exaggerate if it lets you use a big word. I'm what normal people call 'tired.'"

Maybe she was right. Maybe sloshing my blood onto the ground last night and then replacing it with that thin, sour, wine-colored stuff tonight hadn't been my best idea.

She crossed the threshold, planted herself behind me, pressed her palm right between my shoulders, and steered me down the path. I'm taller than her, at least in this shape. Strong enough to resist, too, which didn't even occur to me. I was too surprised. I just let her drive me forward. It would've been comical if anyone had seen us.

We reached the bottom of the entry stairs and she removed her hand. A damn shame. It was the first time she'd touched me so purposefully—without violence, that is. Though it was abrupt and forceful enough that it almost doesn't qualify. What a strange, brusque person she is. I can't stop smiling.

Louise would laugh herself breathless. Maybe if I live through this, I'll tell her.

Isabelle unlocked the door herself, didn't light so much as a spill, grabbed me by the wrist and led me tripping up the stairs to the same bed where I'd stayed before. I dropped down onto the mattress, unspeakably grateful to be sitting.

She said, "This means nothing, do you understand? Your death would inconvenience me."

"Naturally," I said. "And I'm very close to dying. So close. If you just touched me, the barest little brush—"

"Stop," she said. "You are an absurd and unbearable creature. The sound of your voice infuriates me. You talk entirely too much."

Maybe it's the wine, but I am beginning to suspect that Isabelle de Tourzin is a liar. I gambled that she couldn't see me and smiled to myself again.

WRITTEN IN AN INVENTED
SHORTHAND

It took me all morning to find Jacques and convince him to do a little job for me—for Cheats Death, rather. Jacques used to love me as Marianne, used to flirt brazenly and try to buy me drinks at La Fortune and prolong every conversation as much as he could, but our rapport is drastically different now.

He hates cops and has never liked this form of mine. He made me give him the last two years' worth of passwords just to be contrary. Telling him where his payment was hidden before he completed the job didn't earn me any good will.

"Never been sure why our mutual friend would rely on you," he grumbled.

"You questioning our mutual friend's judgment?"

"No. You seen him lately?"

"No," I said, which was true. "I do what I'm told and I get paid. You should try it."

Being Cheats Death used to pay well, but I live off my salary these days. I haven't stolen anything except information in a long time. It hasn't sounded fun. Louise takes care of herself, and my room at the Maison Laval is cheap. Still, I have enough put away to buy help from Jacques when I need it.

Jacques grunted and went off to chat with one of Duret's scullery maids. He must have done it with his usual verve. He was in much better humor for our second meeting. I think he'll go back with a posy of violets for her this evening, but never mind that. He found what I needed. Duret and the woman, whose name is, as I suspected, Marie Reynaud, have gone southeast toward Ardèche.

Duret's letter mentioned a Mademoiselle Reynaud. Malbosc's fiancée, supposedly. He hated her. If she's the one who wrote the other notes I found, as I think she is, then she hated him too. The two of them together doesn't make any sense. One of them must be Malbosc.

If I'm interpreting the second note right, it's Duret, but I'm wary of assumptions.

The maid couldn't remember the name of the village or the estate they're visiting, and was helpless to name any nearby towns, but she thought the estate belonged to someone in Reynaud's family.

As I explained all this to Isabelle, I said, "I wish I'd thought to have my man mention Songecreux to the maid. I bet her reaction would have been useful."

Isabelle made a face like she'd eaten something rotten. It was a rare unguarded moment, and it passed quickly. She asked, "Where did you hear that name?"

"One of the papers I found."

Victor, who'd joined us in the library for our mid-day conference, said to her, "That means something to you. You think they're going to Malbosc's estate in Ardèche." He flipped through the pages of a notebook he'd laid on the table. "Yes, that's it. Songecreux."

"Malbosc was making trips there on occasion during your

acquaintance," Isabelle said to him. "He must have been making arrangements to rebuild."

"Why does it need rebuilding? What happened?" I asked.

When Isabelle failed to answer, Victor said, "A mob set it on fire in 1794. It's been in ruins since then. I can't imagine it's habitable yet."

"That is of little consequence," Isabelle said. "It's his house."

She put a strange emphasis on that last phrase. "He also owned a townhouse in Paris for years," I pointed out.

"Songecreux is his ancestral family home, and it's belonged to Malbosc for a long, long time. It's taken on a certain character. He would go there if he wanted a fortress."

Victor, as keen as a bloodhound, leaned over the table with his pen poised to write. He said to her, "You mean the whole house is magic."

"How long is 'a long, long time'?" I asked.

I expected her to ignore me in favor of Victor, but she turned that dark, solemn gaze on me. "Are you unaware of Malbosc's age?"

"I must be," I said. "I thought he was about the same age as me—thirty or so."

Victor shuffled his papers again and handed me a slim book, so well-read that the text on the outside of the binding was nearly worn away. The title page inside was intact, however: <u>A Catalogue of Artifacts</u> by J. L. A. Malbosc. 1623.

Two hundred years ago.

"You're saying he wrote this? Not an ancestor?" I asked Victor, and he nodded in response. "So when you two told me Malbosc could heal from almost any wound, you also meant he could live without growing older?"

"It is not <u>his</u> nature that makes it possible," Isabelle said. "But yes."

She didn't die from our knife fight, I didn't die after she

rescued me, Malbosc is nearly impervious to death, and she hates him so much she's dedicated her life to killing him. There's an absence at the center of those facts, but I'm starting to think I can fill it in. Her bitter accent on "it is not <u>his</u> nature" was familiar to me.

It's not Malbosc's nature to change his shape, either. It's <u>mine</u>. He took it from me.

He took something from Isabelle, too.

"Can you elaborate on the house?" Victor asked Isabelle.

"<u>No</u>."

I'd never seen her look like that.

I don't know what possessed me. It was so clear that something terrible had happened to her in that house—so terrible that she couldn't talk about it—and she was pretending to be forgetful or stubborn or cranky. Maybe she says no like that all the time. Victor reacted as though she did. But I wasn't accustomed then and I don't think I ever will be. If I see someone get run over by a carriage, I have to pull them out of the road and yell for help, even if it's too late. I can't just walk by.

We were seated at a round table, and I was between Isabelle and Victor, so she was within easy reach. I put my hand on her shoulder.

Victor's eyes got big and he turned to his notes like he needed to memorize every word he'd ever written.

Isabelle knocked my hand away, shoved her chair aside, and hauled me out of mine. I let her slam me into a bookshelf. The spines pressed rows of tally marks into my back. The violence wasn't a surprise—we met in a knife fight. If it would help her to hit something, I didn't mind being the something. What do I care what this face looks like, anyway? I'm tired of it. A black eye would be a refreshing change. So I braced.

She didn't hit me.

Her fingers clawed my chest. She'd spread her hands there when she'd pushed me. My heart was beating under her palm. Isabelle probably thought my pulse was jumping from fear. That was some part of the truth.

She was slow to meet my gaze, but when she did, hers was burning.

"Do not touch me," she said, so close a little puff of breath hit my neck for every word.

Our legs were brushing. She'd put us here. We weren't avoiding discovery by Duret's servants, or hiding behind a door, or engaged in a genuine fight. Any time she wanted, she could break contact with me. She was free to go.

I, on the other hand, was pinned against the bookshelf and couldn't move until she let me.

"Stop smiling," she said, low and quick like she didn't want Victor to hear.

That made me smile more. I've missed being short, but Isabelle shoving me against that shelf and glaring up at me rekindled the joy of being tall. I'm bigger than her in this shape, and I think I could have fought my way out if I'd wanted to. That made it even better to stay there, helpless— or at least pretending to be.

She rocked back on her heels, pulling her hands away and then dusting them like she'd touched something dirty. A person with thinner skin might've been insulted, but one thought kept me serene: she could've just hit me.

I rolled my shoulders and stepped away from the shelf in a leisurely fashion. When the two of us sat at the table again, she wouldn't look at me or Victor, who darted a glance at us— even more shocked than he had been—and then returned to his notes.

"So we're going to Songecreux," I said. "How do we get there?"

While staring into the distance, Isabelle said crisply, "I am aware that I cannot stop you from following me, but you should not go anywhere near that place. You will die."

"And you won't?" I asked.

"With luck," she answered.

Victor's grimace made me think maybe she meant "with luck, I will," and I didn't like that idea. Besides, Isabelle saying "I cannot stop you from following me" is more or less a promise not to kill me herself, which might as well be an invitation. I would've gone anyway—I want my goddamn life back—but it's nice to be invited.

I said, "I'm not dead yet. Let's go."

PRIVATE DIARY OF ISABELLE DE TOURZIN, APRIL 18, 1825
WRITTEN ON ENCRYPTED PAPER

I should have killed Forestier before we ever spoke. How dare he lay a hand on my shoulder—for no purpose! The imprint still lingers, almost as though he burned me. I cannot seem to stop tracing the scorch mark that isn't there. An absurd notion. I was wearing two layers of fabric at the time, a frock coat and a shirt, and he is no warmer than anyone else.

He may not have harmed my skin, but he certainly harmed my reason. It is the audacity that burns. I had neither said nor done anything to suggest such a touch was needed. Indeed, immediately prior to his attack, I had said "No," which captures all of my sentiments. His unbridled insolence—

To <u>presume</u> to offer me solace, as though I need anything in this world other than to kill Malbosc with my bare hands—

And in front of Victor—

Unbearable. It is beyond me to form a full sentence. I am still fuming. The rest of me might well go up in smoke.

And now we intend to travel hundreds of kilometers together, trapped inside a diligence coach with strangers because Forestier does not know how to ride a horse. We will all be a pile of cinders before we even exit the city.

A terrible idea that I should never have agreed to.

And yet there are reasons to try it. Forestier knows something, certainly, and could be useful beyond that. Songecreux might well refuse me entry, but the house has never met him and might let him pass the threshold. He could perhaps flush Malbosc out, and then I would be spared returning to my prison.

Still, I balk at the idea of feeding a stranger—even a meddlesome one with no regard for his own life—to that place. If he lives, the nightmares will haunt him. And using Forestier to gain entry to Songecreux, if it is possible, requires both tolerating him and keeping him alive for the entire journey.

There is another concern. If Forestier were to follow me to Songecreux without my knowledge, he might well die. I already carry the burden of too many of Malbosc's evil deeds. This way I can, at least, lessen the likelihood of Malbosc slaughtering Forestier.

If anyone is going to kill Forestier for his transgressions, it will be me.

Victor drew me into their study this afternoon on the pretense of a question about an artifact. I knew it for a lie as soon as they parted their lips and took an instant to consider their words; Victor's artifact-related questions emerge like water from a burst pipe.

"If you inquire about my wellbeing, or anything that happened in the library earlier, you will regret it." I crossed my arms.

"I would never," they said, which is also a lie, but I let it pass. "I was going to ask if you needed false papers for the stage coach."

"We're not crossing a border," I said.

"A passport isn't the only kind of identifying paper. I could write letters to relatives in the country, or notes of credit, or a marriage license, or anything at all. You must have thought about what name you'll give people," they said. "It's a long journey and you might be with the same few travelers. You'll need some details prepared. You and Forestier might want to... coordinate your stories."

"No one has ever needed a marriage license to take a stage coach," I said sharply.

Victor lifted and dropped one shoulder, but made no excuse for the useless suggestion.

"I will give my own name, and any details that please me in the moment, and I will treat Forestier as a stranger, which he is," I said. "There is no need for us to pose as something we are not, and no need for you to act as though I've never done any subterfuge."

Victor nodded. "You are, after all, nine hundred years old."

I rolled my eyes and turned to leave.

"Old enough not to panic when a decent person is kind to you," Victor said, unfazed when I whipped around to glare at them. "Or to get violent when a man you like touches your shoulder."

In my iciest, most sepulchral tone, I said, "You take your position here for granted, and I would advise you not to."

"My apologies," they said, not nearly as contrite or as frightened as they ought to be. "Don't forget to pack the sponge."

"Victor—" I snapped, and then stopped myself as they lifted a canvas-wrapped item from their desk.

The sponge. The cursed artifact that Dominique had destroyed himself to retrieve for me. The thing that might help me kill Malbosc at last.

Not a contraceptive device.

I have not blushed since the early seventeenth century and would rather be shot than do so in front of Victor. I fixed my gaze on a corner of the ceiling. They placed the canvas-wrapped sponge into a small wooden box and handed it to me. I took my leave without a word.

Victor found me in the library a few hours after we'd worked out a travel plan. He took one look at the map of France I'd spread on the table, and the stage coach itinerary next to it, and said, "You've never left Paris."

"I don't even know where Ardèche is," I agreed. I tapped the name of the province, not all the way south to the coast or east to the Alps, but in some mountainous terrain with very few cities. "Now I do."

"It's funny outside the city. A lot of trees and cows."

"Not to your taste?" I asked.

Victor shook his blond head. He came closer, pulled out one of the chairs, and sat down. "You were different when we knew each other at the Maison Laval. Always watching me—at first I thought it was lechery, but that wasn't it. You thought I was up to something."

"You <u>were</u> up to something," I said. "The only reason I'm not looking at you that way anymore is that now I know for sure."

"I was convinced you didn't like me," Victor said.

"Maybe I didn't." The past few years, I'd kept up with my

colleagues, my informants, and Louise. Everyone else had been either an obstacle or a potential tool. Victor had been closer to the former, and irritating, besides.

"To be honest, I didn't like you, though I don't feel that way now," Victor said. "You seem less unhappy. Back then, you were so... severe. Dour, even."

"I think your standards for 'severe' have changed." I nodded toward the library door and somewhere beyond it, Isabelle.

"Be careful with her," he said.

At the time it struck me as a warning to fear her, which makes sense because she's basically a witch and it's easy to piss her off, but writing this now, thinking about how tenderly he said it, I think maybe he meant "don't hurt her," which is the most ridiculous possible interpretation. I stabbed her and she didn't die. What else could I possibly do to her?

Anyway, I left the house this evening to write a resignation letter, quit my lodgings at the Maison Laval, and pack for the journey. Everything else I took to Louise's. There wasn't much. My papers and some clothes that might fit me again some day.

It was early enough that she didn't have any visitors yet, and she was surprised to see me again so soon. She and Victor must indulge in the same hallucinatory drugs, because the first thing she said was, "You're in a good mood. I haven't seen you smile like that in a long time."

"I'm going out of town," I said. "I think I'm close to finding him."

"Oh," she said.

"You're disappointed?"

"I was hoping you'd made a friend or fucked someone," she said. "Not gone further down this bleak path that's isolated you for years. But if this is what you need to be happy, then I'll do my best to be happy for you."

"I don't know when I'll be back," I said. "If you don't hear from me for weeks, it's not because I'm dead. Probably."

She blinked. "Well."

"If I wrote you a letter, could you read it? Or is there someone here you'd trust to read it to you? One of the other women?"

"You'll write me a letter, will you?" she asked. "While you're going to some secret place for some secret amount of time to do some secret crime, and you might die?"

I shrugged. "I'll try."

She punched me in the shoulder and then we played cards until she had to get ready for work. She's ruthless at piquet. I bet she doesn't play like that with the men who come to see her. I bet she titters and loses on purpose. She took me for everything I had, so I had to steal it back. She laughed when she noticed.

It was nice to make her laugh. I used to do that a lot more.

"You gonna look different when you come back?" she asked.

"If I live, yeah," I said.

She quietly shuffled her cards and slid them back into their case. "You know you could be pretty like this, right? If it's just the long hair and the dresses and the rouge, you can have that now. You don't have to go off and risk death for it. I'll help. We know so many great seamstresses. And you know I have more creams and powders here than I'll ever wear in my life. You wouldn't be the only woman like that, Cheat. Or not woman, I know that's not exactly right. But Apolline was—"

"Until I lent her the comb," I said.

Apolline, who lives and works with Louise, doesn't know it was me who gave her the comb. She knows Louise has some connections to Cheats Death, and that she made some arrangements in exchange for Apolline occasionally passing along a secret or two. One day a rangy, underfed adolescent—just the type of desperate, sly youth Apolline expected as Cheat's messenger—showed up at Florine's with a comb. He told her to use it while imagining the changes she wanted, and then to give it right back. She'd needed about two minutes.

I'd gawked. It worked as part of my teenage-boy act, because of course Apolline is beautiful, but it was genuine, too. I swear she barely got the teeth of the comb into her thick black hair before she was done. Totally transformed and she hadn't even looked tired afterward. It was that effortless to her. Even when I used to switch between my most familiar shapes, it took a good five minutes of work. Apolline pressed the comb back into my palm with a thank you and laughed when I told her she could borrow it again any time. I can still hear her saying "What would I need it for?" in my head, like a line from a song. That was more than four years ago, before Malbosc robbed me, and she's stayed in that shape happily ever since.

To Louise, I said, "Apolline is a woman all the time. I'm only a woman sometimes."

"My point is that she was one before she ever touched your comb. You can be a woman on Tuesday and a man on Wednesday and anything you like on Thursday, and all of that with the same body you have now."

"I know," I said. I'd never managed to explain myself to her any time she'd made this offer, but I thought tonight was the night. "And you're right. But it's not only about that for me. You know the ability I had, Louise. The power. Would you give that up?"

"Well, no, I suppose not," she said after a hesitation. "But to me, it was only ever playing around—getting a little taller, having blond hair or freckles for a few days. It's different for you."

"Imagine something else, then, something that's yours. Something you always wanted and poured your heart into and finally got. Something you cherish. Then somebody takes it from you. Seduces you and betrays you and robs you of part of your self. What would you do?"

Louise set the cards aside and stood from her chair. She grabbed me by the shoulders. Sometimes we're about the same height, but tonight she had to lift her chin to stare me down. "Fuck him up, Cheat."

She wrapped me in a soft, perfumed embrace, and I realized it had been a long time since we'd hugged. I should be better to my only sister—she's right about that, too.

Louise said, "I love you, you know that? Don't die."

"That's my name, isn't it?" I kissed her hair and said, "I'll try."

PRIVATE DIARY OF ISABELLE DE TOURZIN, APRIL 19, 1825
WRITTEN ON ENCRYPTED PAPER

I went to Dominique's tonight. Unannounced. I was hoping he'd be elsewhere. Then I could tell Victor that I'd tried and to stop nagging me, without having to impose on Dominique.

Unfortunately, there was music coming from the house. The tinkling, faltering melody almost made me turn around, but I chastised myself for cowardice and forged ahead.

Dominique was at home with his lover Quang and two friends. One was Béatrix Chevreuil and the other was her lover, Victor's aunt Sophie Beauchêne. I began to suspect entrapment by the Beauchêne family, but everyone seemed genuinely surprised to see me. Dominique was seated at the piano and Béatrix was standing near him, but they'd stopped playing and commenced chattering when I arrived.

"She's in her only nice dress, so you know it's a special occasion," Béatrix teased. Though she is in her fifties and near the end of her career as one of Paris's most celebrated opera singers, her voice can still silence a crowd. In her youth, they called her the Black soprano, and she once said she'd know she'd arrived when they simply called her the soprano, as though there were no others. These days, they call her La Chevreuil.

My red dress is nothing compared to the finery that Béatrix and Sophie prefer. Béatrix was a column of orange flame tonight, with even the tight spirals of her black hair wrapped in fiery silk, the color flattering her dark brown skin. In contrast, Sophie had her skirts spread on the sofa like an ocean of stormy grey. She's of an age with Béatrix, but with more silver in her blond hair and more wrinkles creasing the pale skin of her face. When we first met, her hair was golden and her face was round and unlined. I suppose I look younger than Sophie now, but that doesn't bear thinking about. I am forced to admit that she and Béatrix are lovely together.

In such company, my dress was unremarkable, but I grant that it is an improvement upon my usual rags. I spend most of my time spying and thieving. Wine-colored silk is too noticeable and too delicate for such pursuits.

"It's always a special occasion to see Isabelle," said Sophie, softly enough that we all might have missed it, had Béatrix not cut through the noise for her. Sophie was seated next to Quang, both of them positioned to appreciate the music.

Sophie has always liked me too much for her own good, though I've offered her nothing but suffering in return. She's an older, slightly less reckless Victor. I have entangled myself with two generations of Beauchênes when I really ought to have excised them from my life for their own safety. At least Sophie has survived long enough to find love with Béatrix.

Their presence, along with Quang's, meant I could not discuss Dominique's plight as bluntly and openly as I needed to. They have all retired from our world in their own way, and Dominique has unwavering respect for their desire not to know anything of the trade in dangerous artifacts.

"I came to offer my condolences," I said to Dominique with a nod.

"Condolences?" he asked. "Did you not get my letter? And… the package Quang delivered?"

"I received them."

"Then you should know that I'm happy." He beamed a besotted smile in Quang's direction. "I think we can enjoy a great many years together. I would prefer to accept your congratulations, Isabelle."

"Congratulations." I meant it as a question, but everyone cheered as though I'd exclaimed it wholeheartedly.

"Thank you," he said. "Do you have time to sit with us? I am accompanying Béatrix and she is valiantly overcoming my flaws."

She laid a hand on his shoulder. "You're just a little out of sorts since your… injury. Soon enough you and this magnificent Pleyel will be in harmony again." She tapped a key on the piano to demonstrate its magnificence.

Béatrix and Dominique have known each other about the same length of time as I've known each of them—it was Dominique who rescued me from Malbosc's hold in 1794, and I met Béatrix some time in 1796. The two of them were already close by then, brought together by a shared love of music and scheming to make the world a more just place. Rumor falsely connects them as lovers, perhaps because of the ease and affection with which they touch each other.

Thirty years wasn't enough for either of them to try it with me. They fear me, and I have let them. In my youth—I should call it my first life—I was touched like that, but never since. Witnessing casual touch is like hearing a language I've forgotten, but in which I can sometimes grasp a word or two.

Right after my rescue in 1794, when I was at my worst, Sophie would occasionally dare to lay her hand on mine, always with great caution. Following in her brave footsteps, Victor had drawn me into their lap after finding me wounded in the foyer. That is my only recent memory of a friendly touch, and while it was untainted by fear _of_ me, it was driven by fear _for_ me.

It has to be this way. I survive without it.

I thought of Forestier hiding me in the stairwell, pressing against me, laughing. Sitting with me in the wine shop, not touching, but not afraid. These are useless pieces of flotsam across my consciousness; we are neither friends nor lovers.

I became aware that I was staring at Béatrix and Dominique. Everyone was awaiting my reply to the invitation to sit and appreciate the music. I turned toward the window, where the drapes were not fully drawn, a long vertical gap of darkness separating them.

"I have no time to stay," I said. All four of them experienced an identical shift in their expressions; I suppose they thought it polite to express dismay at my leaving, though they would doubtless enjoy themselves more without my silent, brooding presence troubling the room. "May I speak with you, Dominique?"

He stood slowly, took hold of his cane, and then exercised his bad knee a few times before coming to my side. At his pace, we exited the parlor and adjourned to his study. Neither of us sat.

"I found him—or almost. He went back to Songecreux," I said without preamble. "I leave tomorrow to follow him."

"Tomorrow? Not tonight?"

"For reasons not worth explaining, I need to take the diligence and depart tomorrow."

His eyebrows climbed toward his silver hairline. Dominique was a young man with chestnut hair when I met him. He had both his eyes then, too, though his eye patch did not prevent him from expressing wide-eyed surprise tonight. Our decades of working in concert have been hard on him. He said, "I think your reasons sound worth explaining. But you keep your secrets. You haven't returned to Songecreux since we met, have you? Are you afraid?"

What an absurd question. Dominique's magical injury has rendered him befuddled or maudlin.

"I cannot die," I said. "Malbosc no longer has the emerald necklace; it's been destroyed."

He examined me and I examined the dull, tidy surface of his desk. "You're allowed to be afraid, Isabelle."

The books in his study were all bound in the same tan leather and organized alphabetically by the author's surname. Not a single one was out of place or at an angle. This private library, so meticulously organized, was how I had always envisioned the inside of Dominique's mind. Before he'd touched the sponge and lost his magic, his recall had been eerie.

I said, "It was César Duret who helped Malbosc survive. I found Duret in the company of a woman going by the name of Marie Reynaud. I think it's Malbosc in another shape."

"Marie Reynaud," he repeated in the tone that had once meant he was tracing some impossible connection in his mind.

It was habit for both of us, I suppose, that I let him think in silence and waited as though he would provide me with an immaculate answer.

A long time later, he shook his head. "I thought the name meant something, but it's gone now. Like trying to cup river water in my hands. My thoughts just come and go and slip away meaninglessly. Is this how everyone lives? You forget what's important and remember trivial details at random?"

"Yes." Were it not so, I would not need these pages.

"How chaotic," he said. "Do you know, we played whist earlier and I couldn't keep track of all the cards? Béatrix and Sophie trounced us."

"Béatrix has been waiting a long time to do that," I said.

"She has." He smiled and gestured toward the study door.

"If you're not leaving until tomorrow, you could stay with us for a few songs."

I shook my head.

"Next time, then. If I remember anything about Marie Reynaud, I'll tell Victor. He has a way to contact you while you're traveling, yes?"

"Yes," I said. "Thank you for your help."

"Thank you for coming, Isabelle. It's a pleasure to see you."

This politeness concluded, there was a pause in which other people might have embraced or touched hands. We did neither. I walked home alone.

Last night I returned to Isabelle's house at a late hour and nearly crossed paths with her. She had her head down and didn't see me, so I hung back for a moment to observe her as she entered her house.

She lit a lamp in the foyer, so I could see her easily through the uncovered window. I almost gasped when she took off her cloak—underneath was a dark red dress, one with a low décolletage and a tightly fitted waist. It gave me a shock to see her in something other than the soot-colored trousers and coats she wears for housebreaking. All that red silk, with luster rippling over its skirts and shadows sliding down its folds. Gorgeous. I let out a soundless breath.

The dress was expensive, but simple. Isabelle must not have a taste for frills and ribbons. She wasn't wearing any jewelry, either. I wouldn't dress that plainly if I had money. I'd drape myself in diamonds. Even without adornments, I couldn't stop looking at her.

She raised a bare arm to hang her cloak in the wardrobe, moving like she was lost in thought. Her dark hair was piled on top of her head, exposing the long line of her neck. The lamplight warmed her tan skin. A little shadow pooled in the hollow of her throat and between her breasts.

Isabelle de Tourzin has an enviable figure. I knew that from touching her. Still, what a dream to see her in that dress.

To stop myself from thinking further, I knocked on the door. She was puzzled to see me. "Forestier. You're... staying here?"

"I only left to make a few arrangements." I lifted my valise. "We're departing together in the morning, aren't we?"

She flattened her lush mouth into a tense line. "I would prefer that we board the coach separately."

"Of course," I said, blithely pretending not to be disappointed. "You look lovely, by the way."

Her brows drew together. She glanced down at herself, seemed to remember the dress, and then scowled at me. "This has nothing to do with you. There is no need for politeness, and certainly no need for mockery, so let us discard both. I will walk you to your room."

"You don't really think I was mocking you, do you?" I asked.

"I don't think of it at all," she said firmly.

"I know you're just walking with me to make sure I don't wander through your house and steal any more of your stationery," I said, "but thank you all the same. And thank you for your hospitality. I hope your evening went well."

This flummoxed her. She didn't say anything, so I turned and gave a little bow. The last thing I saw before closing the door was her thoroughly perplexed stare. I wish I'd been wearing something worthy of it.

Maybe someday it will be me in the dress.

II
EN ROUTE
1825

PRIVATE DIARY OF ISABELLE DE TOURZIN, APRIL 20, 1825

WRITTEN ON ENCRYPTED PAPER

I am writing this while caged between strangers inside the diligence, unpleasantly jolted every few minutes, listening to their idle chatter and smelling the tobacco smoke clinging to their clothes. I could be riding, free and blessedly alone under the sky, if not for Forestier, whom I cannot murder because he is currently hiding his face behind his hands to entertain a fat, giggling baby. The child keeps pointing at Forestier to request he do it again. They have repeated this game twenty-seven times in a row. The baby's mother is gazing at Forestier with almost as much admiration as the baby.

Unbearable.

We left Paris in the middle of the day and have made several stops already. We are currently approaching Mormant. Only a handful of hours have passed and already everyone loves Forestier—even the man next to me with the abundant grey sideburns who complains vociferously every time a carriage wheel goes over a bump (Louis-Frédéric Desbordes, he runs a printing business and has three sons, facts I wish I did not know), and the woman on my other side who never covers her loud and frequent coughs though she has a perfectly good kerchief sitting on her lap (Hortense Verville, another name I have learned against my will). She has asked me and every other person in this coach two dozen prying questions apiece. Even now she keeps trying to read what I am writing and has had the temerity to criticize what she perceives as my illegible handwriting.

My handwriting, even in this coach, is perfectly readable. It is the encrypted paper at work. Madame Verville is crossing her eyes.

We have passed Mormant and the next stop, Nangis, and are now en route to Provins. With the fading of the light, writing grows difficult, but I continue because it keeps people from addressing me, and because a record of what just passed may help me make sense of it.

After the stop at Mormant, I resumed sitting between my two unfortunate companions, Monsieur Desbordes and Madame Verville, irritated that neither of them disembarked for good. Forestier sat directly across from me, flanked on one side by the young mother. (Véronique Lachance, and the baby is Raphaël. Mme Lachance just happened to mention that her elderly husband is no longer alive, and she just happened to flutter her pretty brown eyelashes in an appropriately sad but still appealing way while she said it.) On Forestier's other side was a clean-shaven, bespectacled lawyer, Monsieur Dejean. He has repeatedly attempted to win Mme Lachance's attention from Forestier, who hasn't noticed her at all, only the baby.

Mme Lachance indicated to Forestier that the baby needed to sleep, not to play more games, and Forestier nearly offered to hold the child. I saw his hands twitch. It is for the best that he refrained, as young Mme Lachance might have proposed marriage on the spot. While I would be happy to abandon Forestier in one of these little villages to raise a stranger's child—to be free of his nonsense—it would be such a waste for me to have come this far in the diligence coach only to find myself in need of a horse out here.

"You certainly seem to know a lot about children," Mme Verville said to Forestier in a chastising tone. "Do you have some?"

"Yes, in a manner of speaking," Forestier answered. "I raised my sister, and we were always surrounded by little ones. She's grown now."

That had the ring of truth to it.

"What became of your parents, that you were forced into raising your sister?"

It was such a bold, rude question that for an instant I lost control of my face. Fortunately, I was still pretending to be engrossed in my writing, so my reaction was not as evident as it might have been.

"Oh," Forestier said wearily. He cast a sad glance at Mme Verville and then fixed a melancholy stare upon the middle distance. "They died in a stage coach accident."

This provoked a silence in the coach.

I lifted my head slowly in awe and disbelief. Forestier caught my eye. Nothing moved in his expression.

Everything would be ruined if I laughed.

"My goodness," said Mme Verville without a hint of an apology and, I thought, with unseemly glee at having learned something she could repeat as gossip.

"You have no idea the terror these things inspire in me. It's only just today that I've found the courage to travel again," he continued solemnly. "I was doing my best not to think of the past, but I suppose it was inevitable."

Young Mme Lachance let out a little cry of pity and put a hand on Forestier's arm. M Dejean and M Desbordes were both condemning Mme Verville with their expressions. All of this went unnoticed by her.

"Let us speak of something more pleasant," said M Desbordes.

Mme Verville said to Forestier, "Tell us of your sister. Where is she now?"

"Oh, she's very happy and successful in Paris," he answered. "She loves her work."

"Hmph," Mme Verville said. "<u>My</u> daughters are all married. And what of you, Madame de Tourzin? You must have children."

"No," I said.

"How terrible for you," she said, and I wanted to laugh or hit her, but did neither.

"We can't know what another life holds," Forestier said. "Perhaps it is terrible and perhaps it isn't."

I am unaccustomed to being defended—if, indeed, Forestier meant to defend me—and did not know what to say. My lack of children both is and isn't terrible. I only ever idly wondered about motherhood, and never with any great longing, but over my life it has become clear that pregnancy is impossible for me. The nature of my blood is the likely cause; my courses have not come since Laura died. Some rare and secret poetic sentiment of mine understands my body's inability to bear children as the world balancing itself. Other people carry on after death through their children; for me, there is no need. Still, I would have liked to make the choice myself, even if my choice was to decline.

I thought, unbidden, of the canvas-wrapped sponge in my skirt pocket.

"Regardless," Forestier continued, "it isn't our affair, and we can't expect to be invited into such intimacy with strangers until we have traveled at least a few hundred more kilometers together."

Pretty young Mme Lachance and the two other men made noises of agreement. Mme Lachance even offered me a sympathetic nod. How strange.

The diligence stopped at Nangis. We exited to stretch our legs, and when we returned, Forestier claimed Mme Verville's seat next to me. When she complained, as of course she did, he told her he was offering her his old place as he thought it more comfortable, and she deserved to ride in comfort. She could find no response to this.

Forestier occupies a great deal more space than Mme Verville. She and I, both being in skirts, had many more layers of protection between us if our legs ever did touch, an event we took pains to avoid. Forestier, in contrast, made himself at ease with both his arm and his leg in full contact with mine. I ascribe our position to the small space and his size—an accident, and not, as I initially suspected, an attempt by Forestier to read these pages.

I do not know by what contortion he, being taller than me, contrived to fall asleep on my shoulder. His hair is brushing my cheek. It is softer and more perfumed than I would have expected. He ought to reek of sweat and smoke and road dust as the rest of us do. He ought to snore, as most of the others—even the baby, in his tiny way—are doing. Instead Forestier is breathing evenly, having found some inexplicable peace.

As everyone else is asleep, I cannot shove him away without potentially waking them and needing to explain myself, and must continue to suffer his presence.

PRIVATE DIARY OF C. F.,
APRIL 21, 1825

WRITTEN IN AN INVENTED
SHORTHAND

I should've taken a coach long before this. It's delightfully easy to go through everyone's pockets and baggage. Everyone except Isabelle, that is. She never seems to sleep.

Anyway, hateful old Mme Verville got off at Dijon without any of the cash she was carrying, and when Mme Lachance takes her baby home to her family in Lyon later, she'll find it tucked into her things. I thought about robbing the men for sweet little Raphaël as well, but that would have been for sport, not spite. Neither of them had much and they also hadn't said anything vicious to Isabelle. I judged it not worth the risk. Isabelle has been tolerating me and I want her to continue. One traveler losing all their money is simple misfortune, but three starts to look like crime.

I'm riding on top of the coach for this stretch. It's terrifically windy. I tried to get Isabelle to come with me and she gave me the most incredulous look. At least when she's not here I can write in private.

She writes all the time, too. I've tried to read it, but I think she's using some kind of magic to make that impossible. What is she putting in those pages? I hope it's about me.

"Forestier is too charming and handsome to live. I should have tenderly wrapped my hands around his throat and erotically murdered him already."

Ha! As long as I am imagining fantastical things, might as well add "if I ever found out that Forestier is sometimes a woman, I would feel exactly the same."

More likely she's furiously recording a list of ways to kill Malbosc. I can't honestly say I find that any less appealing.

It is dawn. I am writing this from the back of a farmer's cart next to the world's most infuriating and disruptive creature, who I ought never to have saved or brought into my home or made even the loosest of plans with, and who should by rights be in a roadside ditch twenty minutes behind me, screaming in agony from a broken leg.

As soon as Forestier wakes up healed, <u>I will have his hide</u>.

I knew that the coach was going too fast. Darkness and a sharp turn are a fatal combination at such speed. Forestier would have been thrown far and probably snapped his neck if he'd still been seated on the roof, but he'd returned to the interior to sleep. All six passengers, five adults and the infant, were inside. Everyone else was jolted from their rest by the clattering wheels and, soon enough, the baby's wails.

Forestier, the fool, positioned himself to protect Mme Lachance and her baby as soon as we tilted. We careened, the coach breaking free of the harnessed horses and then tumbling down a hillside.

It is a miracle no one died.

I could not have helped in that case. It was by the skin of my teeth that I helped in this one.

How I would have healed anyone other than Forestier, I do not know. Preserving my secret might have required ignoring any such problems, though it would have bothered me. But it did not come up. No one was seriously injured except the gallant, self-sacrificing clod I have mistakenly permitted to accompany me. I am going to wring his charming neck.

I did not see Forestier's fall in the darkness, nor hear the telltale crunch of bone in the shattering of the coach and the shouting of the passengers, but it was a bad break. He was grey and nearly silent by the time I found him in the grass. I've always found that the worst pain forces a sort of impenetrable inwardness.

It took me too much time and a great deal of frustration to arrange privacy to heal him. Though I'd yanked the lantern from M Dejean's hand, shoved M Desbordes, and snarled at everyone, the others refused to leave us alone. They were frenzied and useless. When shouting failed, I resorted to icy tones, and this veneer of calm control startled them into listening. I concealed the severity of Forestier's injury and convinced them that I had the necessary medical expertise and equipment. At last they withdrew.

The vials of my blood in my luggage had thankfully not shattered, so I was not burdened with the difficulty of giving myself a cut that neither sprayed an excess of blood nor healed too quickly to provide enough. Forestier was barely conscious. I had to hold his head up and stroke his throat to get him to swallow. He collapsed after that.

I knew he would heal, and live, and still my heart rioted inside my chest. Fear never listens to reason. Forestier was fine, and besides, it should hardly matter to me if he was injured or dead, as he is nothing more to me than an inconvenience. The tightness in my lungs and the unpleasant prickle of sweat on my skin remained.

Bodies are so, so fragile.

The weight of his head in my lap and the warmth of his skin should not have been comforts. I did not need comfort. I did not need to cradle him or stroke his hair. I don't know why I did that. Certainly not to reassure him, as he was insensate.

I sat with him and the others while we waited for night to recede and more traffic to pass along the road. Our driver and the postilion had chased after the horses to collect them. I told everyone to ride ahead to the next post and send someone for us. As there were four horses, they were able to provide one to M Desbordes and another to M Dejean, who took Mme Lachance and her baby with him so they might arrive more quickly at the coaching inn.

I could have insisted we all wait together for a cart, that they might help me lift Forestier and lay him flat. Then he could have stayed with Mme Lachance and her baby and married her and had a nice life with the family he so courageously saved. Forestier won't thank me for having chosen otherwise. There was no way to get him on a horse, and I could not leave him alone with the others lest any of them notice the unnatural quickness of his healing. So the two of us stayed behind until this cart arrived and I was able to plead with the driver for help.

PRIVATE DIARY OF C. F., APRIL 23, 1825

WRITTEN IN AN INVENTED SHORTHAND

Woke up in an unfamiliar bed with no idea what town this might be. The last thing I remember is the carriage wreck, not counting a strange, disappointingly un-erotic dream where I had my head in Isabelle's lap and she ran her fingers through my hair. If my mind is going to compose such fantasies, they should have kisses, at the very least.

That dream was just me misremembering a moment from a visit to Louise a few years ago. She was caring for Catherine's daughter Zélie. Most of the women at Florine's have children, but not Louise—she'd rather be an aunt than a mother, a sentiment we share. Zélie, probably four years old, had a fever and was curled miserably in Louise's lap. Louise was stroking her sweaty curls. I could hardly look. All I could think was how I used to do that for Louise when she was sick at the orphanage. The touch was instinct, since I couldn't remember Sister Angélique or Sister Marie-Agnès ever doing that for me. I don't think anyone ever will, unless I survive to old age and Louise takes pity on me.

Isabelle de Tourzin wouldn't comfort me if I was dying.

Last night felt close enough. My whole body hurt in that dream.

My whole body hurts now, so that part's not hard to interpret. I should probably be in worse pain, given what I remember. There's a throbbing ache in my leg, and when I peeked under the sheets, the length of it was swollen and hideously bruised.

All of this is eerily like when I woke up in Isabelle's house after she dragged me from the river.

There's a note on the bed next to me—along with a plate of food, thank fuck—that just says DON'T LEAVE THE ROOM.

I'm pretty sure it's Isabelle's handwriting, though it doesn't look anything like the chickenscratch I read over her shoulder. I can't imagine who else would leave me alone with only a rude, uninformative, and unnecessary note. I think I can get out of bed to use the chamber pot, but I'm dreading it. Leaving the room is impossible.

Is this a coaching inn? What happened to the other passengers?

~

I must have fallen asleep for a few hours. She's still not here.

I ate all the food and I wish there was more. It's silly to notice this detail because I'm sure it was an accident, but the cheese was creamy—almost as though she remembered that I told her I liked it better.

I do, but I only said that to tease her. I grew up in the gutter. I eat what I'm given.

Still, it's worth a try to tell her I like capons and truffles and hot chocolate and cognac.

~

Isabelle was in the room at last when I woke up next. She arranged a tray over my lap, propped on two stacks of books so it's not touching me, and then set it with cutlery like I was about to dine with royalty. Where she got the books, I have no idea.

I don't know what they normally serve at this coaching inn, but she brought me a shallow dish of pike quenelles in the most fragrant cream sauce, a carafe of white wine, and a demi-baguette. I nearly cried. She didn't even seem to notice when I didn't offer to share and ate the whole loaf of bread like an animal.

She sat near my feet, careful not to disturb my injury. She's been wearing dresses since we left Paris. Modest, practical ones. Not colorful or stylish or interesting. Suitable for travel and a woman of her age. You can't see her marvelous ass for the all skirts, there's not a hint of bare skin at her throat, and whatever corsetry she's got undergirding everything is doing a lot more smashing down than lifting up. They're not that different from the shapeless coats and trousers she wore before. Clearly, no one is supposed to spend any time looking at those dresses, or at the woman underneath them.

They don't work on me.

They wouldn't work even if she stopped saving my life and bringing me food while being surly about it, but Christ, the combination is lethal.

"I've made travel arrangements," she said. "You may remain here if you wish."

"I don't know where 'here' is."

"A coaching inn. The city is Chalon-sur-Saône."

So we weren't to Lyon yet. That wasn't our destination, just a city I'd marked in my mind as important because we had to switch coach routes there. I wish I'd stolen that big map of France from her library. It would be of limited use, since only she knows how to get to Songecreux, but stealing always makes me feel better.

"I think it wisest if you rest for another day before attempting to go anywhere, but you could likely still catch up to Mme Lachance if you took the coach after that. The others departed this morning, but she left this afternoon."

"Who? Oh—Raphaël's mother," I said, still puzzled even after I identified her. "Why would I want to catch up to her?"

Isabelle stared at me, mirroring my own incomprehension. "You risked your life to save her."

"Well... yeah. She had a baby."

"Exactly," she said. "You loved her child. She's young and sweet and pretty. Widowed. You could have a good life together."

I laughed and then winced when I jostled my leg. "Did you forget that I'm a thief and a fraud and I stabbed you? And also we're here to track down and murder someone much worse?"

"I'm unharmed," she said, touching her abdomen where my knife had gone in. "Had you let _me_ save them, I would still be unharmed. You know this."

"Uh."

"You _would_ have let me save them if you had two thoughts in your head to rub together. Since you didn't, and you don't, and you fractured your bones to prove it, I can only assume young love has rendered you brainless."

"Fractured?" I repeated. I hadn't known that, not for sure, and it made a thread of nausea wind through my gut. "What did you do to me?"

"All that matters is that you can rest here until you're well enough to find her."

"You know I'm thirty-two, not nineteen, right?" I asked. "And also not in love with some woman whose baby I smiled at in a stage coach. I like other people's babies. They're cute and I don't have to be responsible for them."

"You are still young enough to have decades with her—"

"I don't want her," I interrupted. "I did my best to protect her and the baby because it was the right thing to do, not because I'm harboring some secret passion. It was a split-second decision. Also, you haven't ever told me how you're doing these life-saving miracles of yours, so how would I know?"

"I suppose that's... true."

Slyly, I added, "And I've never wanted anyone 'young and sweet' in my whole damn life. I like a woman who will slam me into a bookshelf and kiss me like I've pissed her off."

"Forestier," she said impatiently. "Your sexual preferences will be irrelevant when you are dead. I am trying to delay that."

My flirtation passed over her with no effect. For days I've been staring at her like I want to shred her clothes with my bare hands and she hasn't even noticed. It's frustrating, but there's a certain safety in it. We'll just continue on this way, and she won't break my heart or realize all the things I'm not telling her.

"You want me to give up and I'm not going to do it," I said. "I'm definitely not going to go chasing after some stranger just because you wrote yourself a little story about how I'd fit right into her family. You don't know the first fucking thing about me. Write this one down so you'll remember it next time: I am here to rob Malbosc."

She studied me like she was peering through cloudy water at some bottom-feeding fish. It made me squirm, but not in the way I want. A terrible thought occurred to me: she was in a hurry to kill Malbosc and I was slowing her down.

"Don't you fucking dare leave without me," I said. "I will heave myself out of this bed and hobble after you and undo whatever you did to heal me. I will make a big scene and everyone at this coaching inn will take pity on me, a poor wounded man chasing after his..."

I let the sentence dangle. She barely deigned to roll her eyes. "You and Victor spend too much time reading novels. I didn't tell them we were married. I didn't tell them anything. I paid for a room and they accepted my money."

"And they made certain assumptions."

"That is of no importance to me. They can assume you pay me for sex if they like."

"Absolutely no one is assuming that," I said.

"This whole discussion is irrelevant. My only concern is not being memorable. Your..." She gestured a vague circle around my face and body. "<u>You</u> make remaining unnoticed very difficult simply by... being yourself, and exceedingly difficult when you perform heroics and break your leg."

I hid my surprise. Her unfinished sentence and frustrated gesture had <u>almost</u> expressed that she found me attractive. As tired as I am of this form, I still appreciate a compliment.

Louise once asked, in a very slantwise, nosy way, why I didn't make myself a more conventionally handsome man or beautiful woman, if I could look however I wanted. Then and now, it's almost impossible to explain. What I need is to look like myself. My shape changes, but some things stay the same.

I'm never ugly, but I'm never stunning, either. I've tried both and in both cases, people only pay attention to your outside. Easier to be stunning, of course, but still not for me. I prefer a face that's alluring, but just to the left of beauty. I think of it like cinnamon or licorice. Unusual. Not everyone has a taste for it, but some people love it. The people who really look will see me.

Isabelle might be one of those people. I drank that up like wine, and then said grandly, "Please elaborate on which parts of my personage you find most noticeable and memorable."

"You endanger your life with senseless risks," she snapped. "I will leave you in this coaching inn and continue my travels alone unless you stop."

"Wait. Were you <u>worried</u> about me?"

"No," she said with crushing swiftness. Too crushing, too swift. She was lying. And then, "Stop doing that with your face."

"Smiling?"

"It is crucial that we not draw attention to ourselves," she said, ignoring my question and my continued smiling. "If you repeatedly court death and require miraculous healing, word will travel."

"Sure, sure. Whatever you want. I don't expect we'll get into too many more coach accidents. Honestly, 'courting death' is you exaggerating again." I wondered idly what Isabelle de Tourzin knew of the underworld. If the legendary criminal Cheats Death had ever crossed her mind. If she'd picked that phrase on purpose. If she would ever ask me about that name, or my given name, or anything at all.

She gave me a stern look. Probably normal people quail at that look. Probably they tremble and stutter apologies instead of feeling all warm in their chests while their cheeks ache from smiling.

"This is a serious matter. You were badly hurt. Next time I might not be able to save you." She stood, searched her luggage, and then came beside the bed and pressed a leather case into my hand. Inside were two small glass vials.

That shocked me speechless for a moment. "Is this blood?"

"As you know from your current injury, and from the fight you lost in Paris, the healing is not instantaneous. It's best to rest for as long as possible afterward. Most likely, you only need one vial to heal from a wound, so two vials should help you survive two incidents. If you come close to death, take both at once."

"Isabelle," I said, and she looked up sharply. I'd never called her that to her face. "Is this your blood?"

"I thought that was evident."

"Well, it's not! Fuck, Isabelle. This is how you saved me before? And last night, too." I paused. As I've just recently discovered, it's hard to think when a woman gives you two vials of her blood. The strange letter I'd found in Duret's house—"I had to leave you soaking in the blood quite a long time"—began to make more sense. "This is how Malbosc has lived so long and become so difficult to kill?"

"I thought that was evident as well."

"I'm sorry to be slow to guess that you're immortal because your fucking blood has healing properties, and also that Malbosc fucking—what? Stole it from you? Held you captive and bled you? What the fuck! I want to kill him."

She caught my hand in its wild arc of gesticulating and calmly removed the leather case from my grip. She closed it and placed it on the table next to the bed. Her silent actions made me realize I'd shouted, but I couldn't feel ashamed.

"He's mine," she said, quiet and decisive, like she was scraping a line in the earth with the tip of her sword and she'd kill me if I crossed it.

"Fine, fine, I want to help you kill him."

"And I don't like that word. Immortal."

"Why not?"

She hesitated and couldn't look at me when she spoke. "Because I don't wish to be, I suppose. It sounds so permanent. Unchangeable. This is not the condition I would have chosen for myself, had I the choice."

I'm not eager to die, but I know something about not choosing my own permanent, unchangeable condition. "What would you have chosen?"

"What does that matter? Whatever finite life I might have lived, I am beyond it now. My failures are as deathless as I am. Malbosc would have died long before he hurt you, if not for me."

The last time I'd offered her a comforting touch, she'd slammed me into a bookshelf (and declined to kiss me for my troubles). But it was like the carriage accident all over again: I couldn't not do it. She might re-break my leg, but I had to. I grabbed her hand. Her warm, broad hand.

She frowned, but didn't slap me or hurl herself away. "Please don't do that."

"I've never heard you say 'please.'" Confused and disappointed, I withdrew my hand.

Isabelle stood. "You should sleep."

"What about you? Don't you also need sleep? I never saw you do it on the stage coach, but you must have. You'd be a mess otherwise. Take the other half of the bed. I'm not using it. Unless you booked two rooms and that's where you were all day?"

She shook her head. "I told you, I was making travel arrangements. There is no need for you to worry. A lack of sleep won't kill me. Nothing does."

"Was that a joke?" I demanded. "Did you just make a joke?"

She turned to walk out the door. Where she could possibly go to pass several hours outside our room at the coaching inn, I have no idea.

"Isabelle," I said. I love saying her name. Every time could be the time she lectures me to stop taking such inappropriate intimacies. A delicious little frisson of risk. She hasn't yet. "Don't you think it's more noticeable and memorable if you refuse to spend time inside the room you booked? Isn't it senselessly courting danger to leave me alone here? I might try to follow you. If I don't sleep, I won't heal, or I might even die, and then you'll never find out what I know <u>and</u> you'll be delayed. That would be very inconvenient."

At the threshold, framed by the closed door, she sighed. In her dress that could never stop me from admiring her, even though it would look better as rags on the floor, she stood there and dropped her hand from the door knob. She gazed at me, with her serious brows and her luscious mouth, and said, in a voice as dry as week-old bread, "A waste of all my efforts."

Then she took her shoes off and came and sat in bed, fully clothed, not touching any part of me, and I closed my eyes and went to sleep beaming like she'd kissed me on the lips.

PRIVATE DIARY OF ISABELLE DE TOURZIN, APRIL 24, 1825

WRITTEN ON ENCRYPTED PAPER

Forestier is in good spirits after breaking his leg; I am the one who is fracturing. I know what comes of telling my secrets. I know what comes of admiring someone's skill and good humor and heroics. The last man who charmed me locked a collar around my neck and carved into me until there was nothing left of love.

I never saw Malbosc make faces at a baby or injure himself to protect someone he hardly knew.

No. I must stop thinking such thoughts.

Even if Forestier would never purposefully hurt me—and I begin, foolishly, to believe that he wouldn't—there can be nothing between us. I will never let another lover live beyond a single human lifespan the way I did with Malbosc. I thought our love would last forever, like the two of us, and instead what lasted was his dependence on my blood to sustain him. Imagine if I had been first to stop loving him instead of the other way around. Would I have become his executioner then, as I will be now?

People are built for finitude. Living too long broke something inside of him as it broke something inside of me. To know that every stranger we meet will age and die without us is to stand outside of time and humanity both. Everyone dies but me. Everyone I allow myself to love is another grief in waiting. I have accumulated too many already. The heart is only meant to bear so much.

In trying to protect myself from grief's teeth and claws, I trapped myself in the whirlpool of loneliness, where I might spin endlessly and founder forever.

Is it any wonder that I crave Forestier's company? Someone who still remembers what's good about being alive, and—as improbable as it is—wants to share it with me, though I have not been warm or kind or in any way worthy.

Let me stick my oar in the whirlpool and record here, in one last, futile defense, that I hardly know Forestier. He has reasons for traveling with me that he has not revealed. I believe he hates Malbosc in truth, but the exact nature of their history together is unknown to me. I need to discover what Malbosc took from him.

When we have accomplished our goal, if I still live, will Forestier use my secrets against me? I should not trust him. I cannot trust him.

In the pocket of my dress sits the sponge. An airy little shape that holds both hope and death. Will it be Malbosc's undoing? Will it be mine? If it reverses or erases magic, to touch it might kill me. My body was not meant to live this long. Without healing, there is a chance I will die instantly.

For years I have known that there is no purpose to my life beyond killing Malbosc. At last I can imagine an ending. I am prepared to pay any price.

But that ending—hope and death, a weightless weight in my pocket—lies in an uncertain future. It has not yet come. I am here and alive in this coaching inn, still hundreds of kilometers from my destination.

Forestier has drifted toward me in sleep. Even as I write, his hand curves over my thigh. It is a gentle touch; it is the point of an arrow that will pierce my heart.

I have not removed it.

ISABELLE DE TOURZIN AND VICTOR BEAUCHÊNE, APRIL 24, 1825

WRITTEN IN A PAIR OF LINKED NOTEBOOKS

I need you to bring your notebook to Dominique so I can correspond with him.

You could open with "Hello, Victor, how are you?" next time. On that note, how are you? Have you murdered Forestier yet, or only broken his heart?

No need to ask after your health. You are clearly well enough to write nonsense on these pages.

I'm not taking the notebook to Dominique until you answer me.

We are in Chalon-sur-Saône. I'm alive. Forestier is alive. His heart is not my affair.

.   .   .

Of course. Absolutely.

Victor—no, I refuse to waste more time on this. I need to speak with Dominique.

I am healed enough to walk. I keep glancing at my leg like I might find some sign of magic, but there's nothing.

Isabelle and I are taking the stage coach again. We left the inn together and boarded together, so she pretty much <u>had</u> to let me sit next to her. It's the least noticeable and memorable thing we could do. Myself, I am sitting next to her because I want to, and I get to indulge all the way to Lyon.

She's less stiff than last time we tried this. Still not enjoying herself, though, which, as her presumed husband, I find offensive. Am I not good to her? Am I not gallant? Are we not traveling for the sole purpose of fulfilling her lifelong dream?

I am the world's most devoted imaginary husband. When her hand cramps from writing, I massage it. When she reads, I kiss her temple. (She bats me away, but I don't mind.) At night she lets her hair down and I wash it and comb it for her. I let her wear the hideous dresses she chooses for some reason, even though she knows I would buy her a dozen silk gowns, or waistcoats and trousers if she preferred. But I am a good husband, and I respect my wife's need to dress like a pile of dirty laundry.

I bring her flowers, and jewelry, and all the little delicacies she likes best. (I don't know what these are. When we eat, she is depressingly mechanical about it. Some mornings, I think I could replace her bread with sodden tree bark and she would chew it as dutifully. Tragic. I must fix this. Even at thirty-two, after years of living in relative comfort, breakfast every day still feels like a luxury to me. This morning, she snapped at me across the table. "We are in public," she said, keeping her voice low. Naturally I lingered over my next bite with even greater pleasure. Banked fury glowed in her eyes. Even now, it warms me.) As her imaginary husband, I wake up early to serve her apricots, and almond croissants, and coffee with a plume of steam that she pauses to inhale like it's perfume. She knows how to do that, as my imaginary wife.

When I tell her the silver teaspoon she's stirring with is stolen, she says "Céleste," scolding but affectionate. I'm too extravagant in my gifts. Always scaling walls and picking locks to drape her in diamonds she can only wear in the privacy of our bedroom, but I can't stop. Otherwise I'd never see the <u>smile</u> she only wears in the privacy of our bedroom. When she tells me—from the warmth of our marriage bed, with an empty breakfast tray still on her lap—that she needs to take the stage coach across France to do a murder, I tell her I'll carry her luggage.

(Isabelle tried to carry her own luggage this morning. I lifted it from her arms and said, "Darling, please let me." We both should have let the postilion do it, but I'm still not used to that. The old widow Mme Drouet, who's asleep across from me as I write, said, "We must give men ways to feel useful, my dear," and I beamed at her for playing such an excellent supporting role in my Husband Comedy. She patted

Isabelle on the arm. Isabelle looked as though she really had taken a bite of some sodden bark.)

This is the first time I've written where she can see, and though she's pretending otherwise, I can tell she's very interested—what do I have to write about, other than her?—but she can't read my code.

We spent all day yesterday in the coaching inn. I slept a slothful amount, even considering my injury. It must have worked because my leg is almost painless today. The whole thing is uncanny, but I'm damn glad not to have a broken leg. Isabelle can be as surly as she likes. She saved me. Twice now.

She stayed with me. She wrote her private writing and brooded while I slept (I'm guessing) and maybe slept a little herself (I'm hoping). She brought me more food. Lavished me with it, really. I can't ever tell her that. She'll stop and I don't want her to stop.

When we were both awake, I asked her questions. At first it was like when Louise and I caught Hermès in the alley behind Les Feuillantines and tried to bathe him. He was so matted with filth we could barely even tell he was a cat, let alone a grey one. Our rescue efforts were met with teeth and claws. He hissed and contorted himself every time we held him near the tub of water. Isabelle just sat on the bed next to me, of course. I managed, after much coaxing, to persuade her to dip her toe in.

"Why don't you ask me a question? There must be things you want to know," I said.

I was hoping for "tell me about that sister you mentioned," but that was pure fantasy on my part. She jumped on the chance to interrogate me. "What was the nature of your relationship with Malbosc?"

"We fucked," I said. "Four years ago. For a few months."

I didn't say "I thought I was in love with him" and she

didn't react to any part of my confession, spoken or unspoken. That bothered me.

"Men fuck each other sometimes," I added. She knew that already; we'd talked about Malbosc and César Duret being lovers. And I wasn't always a man with Malbosc—fatal mistake, trusting him with that—but I was provoking her, not making myself more vulnerable.

She didn't roll her eyes. I'd never seen anything so close to pity on her face. Maybe it was fatigue. "Forestier. I have been alive for two hundred and sixty-nine years."

The thinnest thread of restraint kept my jaw from dropping. I'd suspected some great age ever since Victor had shown me Malbosc's book from 1623, but to have her tell me the number was astonishing. She offered. I didn't even pester her for it.

With effort, I arranged my expression into one of indifference. "So you know about men fucking."

"You concern yourself with curious details."

"Tell me which details I should concern myself with, and I will," I said.

"How did he betray you?" she asked.

"Simply. I trusted him with a secret and he stole it. I woke to find him gone." The very morning after I'd demonstrated how the comb worked, he'd taken it. All the time we'd spent together, every smile, every touch, it was all for that. Nobody can turn shit into gold, but the world is full of people who can turn gold into shit.

"I am... sorry," she said, hesitant and pained.

"You didn't take anything from me." I shrugged. "It's not your fault."

"I also trusted him with a secret. He would have died long before he ever met you if I hadn't." Despair and regret consumed her, and she disappeared within herself, leaving only moody silence behind.

Louise is always telling me how she has to smile for her clients, how they like her best when she's happy, and I do understand that. A good humor is like sunshine. It's natural to want the light and the warmth. Maybe it's my contrary nature, or maybe it's that Isabelle's unfixed stare let me study her solemn, strange beauty at length. Either way, her melancholy drew me in. I wanted to smooth the deep furrow in her brow. I knew she'd push my hand away if I tried.

What seemed a long time later, she said, "You haven't said what he stole. You know what he has of mine."

Her blood. Years of her life. I shuddered. Then I felt small and ashamed. If I did tell the truth in that moment, I'd have to tell this woman who'd lived through captivity and assault at Malbosc's hands, maybe for longer than I've been alive, that I'm sulking because he stole a comb from me.

In my dreams, she hears that and says, "He stole a part of my body, and he stole a part of your body, too." In life, I didn't give her the chance. If she learned my secret and plotted to take it for herself or destroy it, I would never forgive either of us. If she grimaced in disgust, I would shatter.

I said, "A trinket. I'm sentimental about it."

She glanced at our surroundings and my not-broken leg, the material proof of how I'd overturned my whole life to follow her to some unknown place where she was convinced I would die, and said dryly, "Very sentimental."

A silence flourished between us, spreading into every corner of the room.

At length, she said, "You will have to tell me the truth eventually."

"Or what? You'll beat it out of me? Extract it at knifepoint?"

"It's foolhardy to confront Malbosc without sharing all our knowledge," she said.

I scoffed. "And you, Isabelle de Tourzin, born in 1556, have you shared all your knowledge with me?"

"Someone taught you your numbers as well as your letters," she said.

I didn't bristle. There was no point and I refuse to be ashamed. "One of the sisters at the orphanage taught me a little, and I learned the rest on my own."

Her gaze flicked to my face at the word "orphanage," but she said nothing.

"What was it like, 1556?" I asked. "I don't even know who was king then."

"Do you know who is king now?"

I laughed. "Does it matter?"

"Sometimes," she said. "There was no king where I was born, though it would not have made much difference to me. The beginning of my life was small and squalid and desperate, and things remained that way for about twenty years."

I knew we had poverty in common. I knew it. "What changed?"

Her smile was so subtle, and I had seen it so rarely, that I almost didn't recognize its fleeting presence on her face. It was gone by the time she spoke. "I fell in love."

"With Malbosc?" I asked.

"No. That came later. Her name was Laura."

She'd had both men and women as lovers. The note of hope those words plucked inside my heart would have been too loud and exaggerated for even the worst of melodramas, and still I thrummed with it. She might not want me, but the possibility existed. To mute the music rising up in my mind, I thought to myself: she is ruthless and you are withholding the truth from her; you should be afraid.

 It had no effect.

"Women also fuck each other sometimes," said Isabelle de

Tourzin, and if I hadn't already been lying in bed, I would have swooned.

C. F. TO LOUISE, APRIL 26, 1825

POSTMARKED CHALON-SUR-SAÔNE

My dear Louise,

Hope you're well. I'm still alive.

You know how you told me to make a friend or fuck somebody? Just wanted you to know I'm trying my best.

CF

ISABELLE DE TOURZIN AND DOMINIQUE GALMICHE-VUILLEMIN, VICOMTE DE SAVIGNY, APRIL 26, 1825

WRITTEN IN A PAIR OF LINKED NOTEBOOKS

Isabelle? It's Dominique.

Apologies for disturbing your retirement. You were doubtless relieved to be rid of me at last, and here I am again, haunting you. ~~I think I've forgotten how to work without you.~~ No, ignore that. Have you remembered anything about Marie Reynaud? My thoughts return incessantly to that night when I found her and Duret asleep together in his bed. I've been assuming she must be Malbosc, that he must be using some magic to maintain his disguise even in sleep, but what if I'm wrong? Who is she? Perhaps I should write "who <u>was</u> she." Did Malbosc invent her? Or is he possessing her body in some way? Have you ever encountered such a case?

I'm always pleased to receive word from you, Isabelle, even on such dire matters. And I'm touched that you miss me. Are you well? Regarding Marie Reynaud, I've never encountered an artifact that would allow one person to possess another, but magic is vast and unpredictable.

It troubles me that I cannot explain this woman's presence. We know she was not among Malbosc's circle of admirers in Paris; Victor would have met her. Rarely have I wished to remember more of my past, but it chafes to think I might once have known the answer. My mind's own weakness and cowardice conceal it.

I will keep this notebook and write to you when I have something of substance to offer.

Thank you.

I wasn't finished writing. I do not believe the lacunae in your memory result from either weakness or cowardice, as I have never known you to lack determination or courage. I no longer know how many times you saved my life, and you never bothered to count in the first place.

That isn't courage. I was never in danger.

I shall call it generosity, then.

I kept you alive because working with you was always my best chance of finding Malbosc.

Acta, non verba, *and all that. Bad trees don't bear good fruit, Isabelle.*

Stop quoting nonsense at me. I am not a tree.

Say you saved me for my wit, at least. Say the world would be impoverished without my elegance.

No.

Do you know, I can almost hear your voice? What a marvelous magical device this is. When young Beauchêne explained it, I told him I was impressed with his work and the poor thing forgot how to close his mouth. Can you see the ink flowing across the page as I write? If I strike through a word and rip my paper, will yours rip as well? I know these are not the questions you need answered, but they fascinate me.

I cannot see you forming letters. I believe your words appear to me after you pause, which often coincides with the end of a sentence, but not always. If you've tried to rip my page, I don't see it.

You know me well. I did try.

Reckless. You know how volatile magic can be. What if there had been an explosion that hurled you across the room? I am not there to rescue you.

I'm touched that you care.

I never said that. But it would be a shame to make your young man a widower so soon.

I knew you liked him. It's impossible not to.

I never said that, either.

There it is again, your voice. And I can picture your flinty, disgruntled expression. Imagine if we'd had these notebooks when I was chasing after that self-replicating coin in Saint-Malo. Or that time you spent tearing your hair out in Ajaccio. How much easier things would have been! I wish you an easy journey and a swift return to Paris. Quang and I are in good health, as are Sophie and Béatrix, and we all look forward to seeing you again.

There is no need for all this, Dominique.

What do you mean?

Your reminiscing. Your work of fiction about how much you miss me.

Pardon me for enjoying our correspondence. Henceforth I shall lie and say I never think of you, the woman I worked with for thirty years, nor all the cursed artifacts we collected, nor all the unknown harm we might have prevented, nor all the secret accomplishments in which we shared. I don't miss you. I certainly never <u>worry</u> about you.

I don't know why you would.

You cannot hear me sigh, so I must write it.

We're wasting paper. And Victor is insufferable enough without your compliments.

I'll tell him you miss him, too.

PRIVATE DIARY OF C. F.,
APRIL 26, 1825
WRITTEN IN AN INVENTED SHORTHAND

What a strange day, and it's only early evening.

The diligence arrived in Lyon this afternoon. It's funny how a city accumulates around you when you roll in by coach, the little outlying towns clustering together until there's no space between them, the buildings squeezing in close and growing taller. The sound under the wheels changes, too. I'd stopped hearing the rumble of our coach on the packed earth. The clatter of wood on stone jarred me.

Lyon is not as grand as Paris, but it's dense and bustling. I'd almost forgotten what a city feels like, even though we haven't been traveling that long. The smell was a shock. Bodies and refuse and smoke and food. People streamed in and out of markets and factories. The rivers—there are two, and much of the city lies between them—are clogged with boats. The first one still felt vast, though. It was such a change to emerge from the narrow, dim streets into the sudden bright expanse that it made me squint. I'm sure the water is filthy, but the river sparkled. All the old stone bridges had a yellow cast this afternoon, the sun catching on the undersides of their arches. A charming picture.

Isabelle was pointing out streets and landmarks as we drove along the Saône, telling me how old this place is, how it's famous for silk weaving. She probably thought it was all necessary, practical information, but it felt like friendly chatter to me. I was so giddy about the new city, and maybe having the kind of relationship with Isabelle where she likes talking to me, and thinking about how much she knows, and how low and sultry her voice is—I would let her read me a dictionary—that I don't remember anything she said.

We crossed a bridge onto the land between the Saône and the Rhone and disembarked in the Place des Terreaux. The Hôtel de Ville loomed over us. Other people probably think it's majestic, but official buildings make me wary. There was comfort in the crowds milling around, though, all the shops with their painted advertisements and colored awnings. I gave generous tips and said my goodbyes to the driver, the postilion, and the other passengers. Isabelle stood stiffly beside me and nodded. It's like she doesn't know that being taciturn and rude to everyone makes us more memorable, not less.

(In the Husband Comedy that I have continued imagining, they all murmur about how a woman so lacking in manners ended up with such a polite, affable man, and what a strange pair we make, and how could we possibly be happy together. Their gossip would wound me if I weren't so in love. Can a husband not be besotted with his misanthrope wife? Ours is a private sort of happiness, the kind they censor in books because it harms impressionable young minds.)

(It's possible that the Husband Comedy is harming my impressionable mind.)

It was a huge relief to stretch my legs. I'm healed, but my injury still bothers me when we spend too many hours in the coach. Making myself this tall was a mistake. If I live long enough to get my comb back from Malbosc, in my next shape

I plan to lose twenty centimeters of height at least. Travel will be so much easier. For now, I can't say anything about my discomfort because Isabelle will leave me behind with orders to marry a silk weaver's daughter.

I wasn't expecting that we'd stop for the night. I thought we'd board a new coach and continue our journey. We've traveled through the night before. But Isabelle's whims are mysterious.

She wouldn't have slowed our progress for something so minor as my comfort, so I should stop wondering. It's not as though I'd ask her why we were stopping and her face would soften with concern and then she'd cup my cheek and give me a kiss. That's Husband Comedy thinking. In real life she'd snap at me and then sneak off in the middle of the night to do a crime I'm not invited to.

She _is_ doing something secret. I've noticed her writing in two different, but nearly identical notebooks. It's good to remember she's keeping things from me. It tempers my fantasies.

Today in the coach, she snapped one shut with such force, like her own writing had given her a horrible shock. What words could make Isabelle de Tourzin pale like that? All my surreptitious attempts to read over her shoulder have failed. I couldn't ask her in public—not that she's likely to answer in private, either. Shortly after that she put away her papers and pencil and small portable desk. We approached the city and she offered her murmured guidance.

We left the bulk of our luggage in the rented room. Isabelle must have repacked some of hers while I was indisposed because when I came back, she'd attached a leather strap to a particular trunk, a long slender one. She slung it over her shoulder like it weighed nothing and informed me we were going on a walk.

This made no sense to me. On our other stops, we've

never done anything but eat and wash and rest. Still, I shrugged and followed her. I could write that I wanted to see more of the city (I did), or that I wanted to know what was in the trunk (I did), or that I would've been bored in the room (also true), but why lie to myself? The heart of it is that I wanted to be with her.

I'm not so immersed in the Husband Comedy that I've tricked myself into falling in love. I just think she's interesting and fun to tease and that we could have really good sex.

It's an infatuation. A powerful one, with all the life-saving and the caretaking, but that's all it is. No matter how enjoyable, it will pass. I won't be heartbroken when our paths diverge. Either I'll be dead or I'll have my comb back, and if I do, I'll take a hundred different shapes with a hundred new bed partners, and that will fix me. I don't <u>truly</u> want to devote the rest of my life to Isabelle.

I think.

It would be remarkably foolish of me to fall in love a second time after my affair with Malbosc went so spectacularly wrong.

Then again, Malbosc exercised all his charms to seduce and deceive me, and Isabelle hasn't tried any of that. I'd have noticed the merest hint of seduction—I would've said yes so fast we'd both be dizzy. If this is her attempt at charm, she's a failure.

And she's not skilled at deceit.

Her sneaking is excellent. She can stay still in the shadows a long time. She moves quietly and discreetly. And I know she can pick locks and climb in windows. No fear of the law, which is a necessity, and obviously no hesitation about danger, which can be an advantage. But she's terrible at the <u>people</u> parts of crime. Disguise, pretense, any kind of persuasion or influence. If I ask her what she's hiding in those two nearly identical notebooks, she'll be flustered and she'll tell me to fuck off, but she won't lie. It took her some time to tell me the truth about her magic, but all she did was ignore my questions for a while. She's not a good liar. I like that about her.

We took a bridge to cross back over the Saône, not exactly retracing the way we'd come by coach. Isabelle set a fast pace through the streets of the old city, dodging people and animals and carts. I kept up, a little dismayed, not because my leg was bothering me but because I wanted to dawdle. She strode off in singleminded pursuit of her goal.

For a quarter of an hour, I chased her around corners, down alleys, and over a bridge. The streets began to slope gently uphill. Evergreen trees and shrubs crowded out the buildings, soft spring earth swamped the cobblestones, and the city bowed to a forested hillside. Up and up we went. Far below us, the Saône was a ribbon winding under thin bridges.

Slightly out of breath, I said, "I was hoping to guess, but I give up. What are we doing here?"

Isabelle zigzagged up the hill, not stopping until she came to a relatively flat stretch of dirt—calling it a path would suggest that other people had recently walked there, and that can't be true—protected from view by trees. Twenty paces separated us. She measured.

"I think this will do," she said. She put the case on the ground, knelt in front of it, and unlatched it.

Inside were two swords. Rapiers, based on what Isabelle said about the weapons I'd been stabbed with. Long, thin, and pointy.

I couldn't help it. A certain lightness bubbled up in my heart.

"You're going to teach me to use a sword?" A lot of my fellow criminals would've been offended by that kind of offer. I've spent more than half my life winning fights with knives and fists and whatever's within reach. I've stabbed Isabelle herself. I don't need help. But I like Isabelle, and I liked the idea of the swords, and if she wanted to do this, then I wanted to do it, too. "You think this'll be a useful skill when we get to Songecreux?"

"God no," she said. "If anyone other than me comes at you with a sword, you should run. Last time didn't go well for you."

"I don't know about that. I woke up to breakfast in bed." When I earned the glare I was due, I smiled. "So why are we doing this?"

"Because I can no longer tolerate being confined in a coach or a rented room."

Isabelle's inner life is a mystery to me, but that seemed true enough. She was definitely agitated. Probably it had something to do with the notebook she'd snapped shut in the coach, but I needed to wait for a better moment to coax that story out of her.

"You're going to duel me in that dress?"

"'Duel' is a grandiose word for what is about to happen," she said. "My skirts won't pose a problem."

She handed me a sword. My first attempt at holding it displeased her, and her explanation of how to fix it baffled me. She showed me the other sword in her own hand after that, and comparison made it easy to see my mistake, but instead of correcting my grip, I said, "Why do you have two swords?"

"One is a spare."

"Because in a fight, you'll have time to fetch the second one from your case?"

The question didn't impress her. "One might be stolen or lost."

"That one fits in your hand perfectly," I said, nodding at

her index finger and thumb pinching the hilt just behind the guard.

"Yes."

I, in contrast, am big at the moment, and have the hands to match. The sword she'd given me had a thicker hilt and a larger guard. I still wasn't holding it right, but I'd begun to suspect it was selected deliberately.

I wiggled it. "This one's bigger."

"Arrive at your point."

"You brought it for <u>me</u>," I said, smug with certainty.

"It will do you no good if you don't hold it correctly," she said, which wasn't a denial, so I counted it as a victory.

"You wanted to play a game with me," I said. She intended to point a deadly weapon at me, and yet some warm and fluffy sentiment nested in my heart. "Did you haul that sword from Paris? Or did you buy it especially for me somewhere along the way?"

Isabelle ignored these questions, but I claimed yet another victory: she set aside her sword and put her hands on mine in order to correct my grip. I didn't need the help, as I'd grasped where my fingers should rest by then, but I'm always happy for her to touch me.

These were the only points I scored. It has never occurred to Isabelle in her life to go easy on a beginner, and teaching doesn't come naturally to her. When I had the sword in my hand to her satisfaction, she corrected my stance with a few words. Then we simply faced each other. She made some sort of salute with her sword and I copied it.

"These are sharp, aren't they?" I asked, scrambling backward by a step as she advanced. "What if we hurt each other?"

"Though you do occasionally test me, I possess enough control not to stab you," she said. "But if it would grant you a measure of serenity, I will put something over the point of my blade."

"It would," I said mildly. "Not that I don't trust you. But that is a sword."

Isabelle halted like I'd said something shocking. She turned away, bent to the case, and retrieved a wine cork from it. She broke the cork into pieces, selected one of a suitable size, and fit it carefully over the tip of her sword.

As touched as I was by her preparations—she might momentarily have forgotten the cork, but either she'd stolen it at one of our evening meals, or she'd packed it back in Paris, and both possibilities meant she'd been thinking about me—I was puzzled when she didn't hand me a piece for my own sword. "But what if I hurt you?"

"You can't."

As it turned out, she was right. I thought it was a comment on her ability to heal, but with time, it became clear that it was also a comment about my skill. Every time she struck and withdrew, I tried to use the moment of her retreat to land a hit of my own. Every time, I failed. By the time I could think where her sword would go next, it was already there. She was faster than me and seemed to be able to see more, or better, though I've always prided myself on predicting fights. Long practice—maybe a whole century of practice, I remind myself—let her recognize things I couldn't.

She never hit me. Occasionally the corked tip of her sword would pass close to my clothes, and my heart would beat as though her thrust had met flesh. Her avoidance was precise. So was her aim when she knocked my sword away.

She skipped her chances to insult me for being slow and clumsy, for my repeated defeats, though if she'd tried, I would've told her it was her fault for handing me a sword and abandoning my instruction. We went back and forth in silence. She had nothing to say. I was breathing too hard to talk. Even when a person assures me that they're not going to stab me, it's instinct to dodge.

Fighting back was half instinct and half pleasure. If we did this again, I found myself thinking, or again and again and again, maybe some day I could beat her. A drop of sweat ran down my side, collecting in my grimy traveling clothes with all the others. I didn't call her off. I didn't want to.

A sheen of sweat glowed at Isabelle's temples. I couldn't win, or even give her a worthy opponent, but I could lunge back and forth and provide her with a target to not-quite-stab. She seemed to need that. Serving her in this way pleased me—I can't miraculously save her life, and she won't let me bring her apricots in bed, but I can still be useful.

The point of her sword came to a quivering halt alarmingly close to my neck. Cork or no cork, that sent a jolt through me.

"Yield."

"I yield." I let my sword fall, put my hands up, and grinned. "You know, if that was what you wanted, we didn't have to come all this way or do all this pageantry with the swords."

A little suggestive, but I've said more outrageous things to her. I expected an eye roll or a grimace. Or maybe she'd tell me, in ridiculously formal language, to shut up. That's always especially rewarding.

Instead her mouth opened silently. Her face went grey. She spun away from me, her sword landing harmlessly in the dirt. The rest of her didn't drop so lightly. One instant she was standing and the next she was sitting.

I had no idea what was wrong or what had caused it, but it must have been some kind of crisis of the body. She clutched at her chest and folded herself into a tight curl of misery. Isabelle could heal from any wound, but could she have a heart attack? I didn't know. Her breath was labored and too fast.

I went to my knees beside her. I reached for her, as if there might be a knife in her chest or something stuck in her throat. There wasn't. My fingers alighted on the fabric of her dress, just below her collarbone. She didn't rip my hand off. That's how I knew things were dire.

Whatever troubled her, it was invisible to me.

One of the girls Louise and I grew up with, Marie Françoise, used to get like this sometimes. Before she'd come to Les Feuillantines, she'd lived with her father, a violent drunk. He was dead and gone by the time we met her, but every now and then someone would step toward her, or raise their voice, or accidentally move in a way that reminded Marie Françoise of that villain, and she would react as though her heart had stopped. These memories would seize her whole body. We learned to speak softly and move with care so she suffered fewer attacks, but we never discovered how to release her from that terror once it had begun. One of us would sit with her until it passed.

So I sat with Isabelle.

I only touched her for that one moment, since I knew she wouldn't like it once she regained her calm. Last time I'd tried, she'd even said "please" to get me to stop.

I stayed close, though. I put my bum in the dirt right next to hers, within reach if she wanted me, or if it seemed like I ought to grab onto her to keep her from dashing into the trees. We haven't had time to get our clothes laundered while we've been traveling, everything we were wearing was now filthy, and I'd only packed so many changes and I'd already lost one suit on the night I broke my leg—but I didn't consider any of that. Isabelle was locked in some private pain. I wasn't going to loom over her while she was down on the ground having a crisis.

I spoke. Quietly, easily, as if I wasn't worried. Maybe it wouldn't help, but it didn't seem likely to hurt. I told her she'd be fine, she had to be fine, because I didn't know where I was going without her, and we hadn't traveled for days to quit on some overgrown hillside in Lyon.

"And," I said, "I need someone to make aggrieved grimaces at me a certain number of times per day, for my health. If you don't do it, I'll have to find a stranger, and nobody else will have your natural aptitude. Lyon might be a big city, but there's no one in it who could tell me to shut my mouth with such frosty, disdainful panache. Even if they could manage a watered-down imitation, who would stick the business end of their sword near my neck? I'm sure you agree that I also need that—for my health. It keeps my head from getting too big. And I can't let a stranger do it, Isabelle. What kind of fool do you take me for?"

"A talkative one," she said.

I didn't let out a great gusty sigh of relief, or ask her what happened, or tell her how glad I was to hear her usual acerbic tone, no matter how shaky. I'm not that kind of fool, either.

I humiliated myself in front of Forestier after our fencing match, and he was kind enough not to mention it on our long, stiff walk back into the city. How it galls me—not merely to be seen in such baseless terror, but to be treated with tenderness. I wish I did not know this about Forestier, that he will sit in the dirt next to me and chatter about nonsense until the shadows recede. He has already crept too far inside my defenses.

My mind is in chaos. In my need to confess, I have failed to start at the beginning. Let me begin again.

We have arrived in Lyon. Forestier was favoring his bad leg after so many hours in cramped conditions—he is too tall to travel comfortably in a coach—so I insisted we stop for the night. He put up no resistance. He did not even make an attempt at humor. Perhaps pain affected his mood, or perhaps he is unhappy that I prodded him about his secret.

Useless speculation. I confine myself to improving his chances of survival. His mysterious melancholy seems to have dissipated since our arrival in the city, and regardless, it is not my affair.

In the absence of Forestier's antics with the other coach passengers, and his distracting attempts to put as much of our bodies in contact as possible, I was able to think again. The matter of César Duret and his companion, possibly a woman named Marie Reynaud, troubled my thoughts. To dig through my memory is always a painful and frustrating exercise, one that often unearths nothing of value. I spent many hours in the coach turning it over.

In the last hours before we arrived in Lyon, I saw that Dominique had written me a long letter in the linked note-book. I snapped the notebook shut after only a few sentences. The last thing I read was: <u>I am reporting here everything I remember of the night I found you</u>. The diligence was a poor choice for reading, lest the letter provoke some visible emotion in me. The other passengers might notice.

I channeled my restlessness into telling Forestier about Lyon, and then into marching him up the Fourvière hill for a duel. That unbearably clever rascal <u>guessed</u> that I had purchased a sword specifically for him. What a profound embarrassment. I should have known.

I have already recorded enough of the disgrace that followed our bout, and will spare myself further details.

Once we'd returned to our rented room, we washed and changed without looking at each other. Then we could dine in public without drawing so much attention. I had no appetite, but if we remained in private, Forestier might dare to ask what had caused me such panic. I intended to linger at the table until I came up with a suitably neutral explanation.

Unfortunately, due to the late hour, there was no one else at dinner. In the silence, I felt exposed. Forestier spoke only of the meal, and how good it was, something I would not have noticed even if I had eaten any. The main course was breaded and fried beef tripe, I think.

Alphonse always liked tripe. I can't stop thinking of his given name tonight. Sometimes it is useful to remember him as a person. Other times, it is catastrophic when any small human quality of his crosses my mind. The Burgundy he preferred. How he always used to sneeze twice, uncontrollably loud and at odds with his elegance. The way sleep mussed his dark hair. His favorite forest green velvet doublet.

How much he loved fencing.

I rarely won, so Alphonse didn't have many opportunities to yield, and he would never have done it like Forestier. Still, our duels were always charged. Physical, even though we were separated by our swords.

I wanted him. I loved him. That is what hurts me the most to remember: the sweetness, the laughter. All the times he cut me open, or ordered me into docility, those I know only by their absence. There are years and years missing from my memory. What few cruelties of his remain—snide remarks, dismissals, infidelities—I can conjure to mind with no disruption to my breathing. But when I think of the man he was before all that, I crumble.

Outside the murky fog of my thoughts, I was vaguely aware that Forestier was talking about the defrocked priest and nuns who had charge of him in his wayward childhood and what they used to feed him. Bread and soup, mostly. My attention drifted while he spoke. The place he described, a half-abandoned convent-turned-orphanage that became a secret little wilderness in the heart of Paris, sounded like a forgotten dream. I must have missed something.

"I only had sweets if I stole them," he continued. "I think that's what set me on the criminal path."

He was making such a valiant effort to turn my thoughts elsewhere. As a token of appreciation, I asked, "Did the nuns catch you?"

"Not often," he said. "And when they did, I learned from it. So in a way, they trained me to be a thief."

"Did the other children share your proclivities?"

"For stealing? No." The smirk I expected from him nearly coalesced, but some inscrutable sadness took its place. That passed before I could wonder what caused it. He jumped into another cheerful anecdote. "Louise did help me smuggle a cat inside once. By the time we were discovered, Hermès had been living with us for a month, and we were able to argue that, as a fellow orphan, Les Feuillantines was his home too."

"You named your cat Hermès?" I asked, distracted. Louise must be one of the children he'd grown up with. He spoke her name as though we'd already discussed her, but I couldn't remember having done so.

"He was quick and sneaky."

"God of travelers and thieves."

That pleased him, but he didn't say anything. With a tilt of his head, he indicated the young woman who'd brought our dinner. With no other guests to serve, she was slumped in a chair, on the verge of falling asleep. I took his meaning that we should settle our bill and leave, though I dreaded returning to our room.

My hand aches. I will record the rest after a break.

PRIVATE DIARY OF ISABELLE DE TOURZIN, APRIL 26, 1825
WRITTEN ON ENCRYPTED PAPER

Our walk was silent and short. When we'd closed the door to our room at the inn, Forestier said, "Are you... well?"

"You are the one with the injury," I said. "I made you walk up that hill and do all that work."

"Moving around felt good." He waved a hand and bent to unbutton his boots.

I turned away.

Forestier has ruined me; infected me with some fever of sentiment and melted my resolve to feel no tenderness or lust for any other person. It can no longer be ignored that I do not hate his company, and that he is not repulsive in either character or appearance.

And that he has seen me in a low moment and, instead of exploiting my weakness, treated me with care.

Still, to watch him use his long, deft fingers to reveal any part of himself is an intimacy I cannot bear.

There was a time, centuries ago, when carnal indecencies were my profession. I am rusty with disuse. Forestier teases and flatters as easily as he breathes; he does it with everyone, so I cannot be certain that he desires me. He has little reason to. I am, at best, brusque and strange. I have never been a great beauty, my youth faded long ago, and in his presence I have exercised neither cleverness nor charm. Were I to throw myself at Forestier, he might laugh and reject me, and I would still feel too much affection to murder him for it, meaning we would have to continue living with each other.

What a pointless flight of fancy. Rejection is the <u>least</u> painful outcome of this ridiculous infatuation.

It would be far worse if he accepted me; I would have to grieve him when he died.

Forestier stretched flat on the bed with a sigh. His arms and legs were spread wide. Like one of those large dogs that still tries to curl up in your lap, sometimes he has no notion of how much space he occupies. There was nowhere I could sit without touching him, so I remained standing.

He drew his limbs in and patted the bed next to him. "Sit down. You never said what's bothering you."

"You," I said.

That was a mistake. It made him laugh.

He has a nice laugh. Or rather, it's terrible and I fully intend to hate it once I reconquer myself. Instead of subjecting myself to whatever sly amusement was warming his face, I sat on the edge and removed my shoes where he could not see.

"Naturally I bother you," he said. "But I've been here the whole time, and something is especially bothersome to you <u>today</u>. Even before we fenced. In the coach, you snapped your little notebook shut like it bit you. And it was a different one from the one you usually write in. The bindings are almost identical, but one has more wear at the corners. I've noticed you switching."

"Of course you have, you pickpocket."

The attempted insult was another mistake on my part, and a glance at Forestier was a worse one. Must he find everything amusing? His smile slips into places I would rather keep locked.

It faded, and I missed it when it was gone. "Isabelle."

He wanted to talk about the crisis of nerves I'd suffered. But he was too kind to demand an explanation, and I took advantage and turned our conversation toward something of more importance than the frailty of my heart.

I explained how I'd been pondering Marie Reynaud, wondering if I'd met her before. I did not mention that I'd written to Dominique for help. Nor did I mention that his lengthy reply awaited me. After the humiliation I'd already suffered, I could face neither that letter nor Forestier's knowledge of it.

"Does it mean anything to you that she and Malbosc were engaged to be married?" he asked.

"What?"

"It was in the letter I stole from Duret," he said. "I promised to tell you some of what I know at our halfway point, and I'm not going to bother counting the kilometers. Here you go. Duret hated her. It was mutual. He thought Malbosc was marrying her for her money or her property. And Duret's scullery maid said the Baron and his companion were going to her Reynaud family estate somewhere in Ardèche. You heard 'Ardèche' and thought of Songecreux."

"I am sure he's going to Songecreux." The compass still pointed in that direction. I checked it in secret at every opportunity. "It's his fortress. He might even believe I won't follow him. But I don't know why he would marry, and I don't know why he would marry Marie Reynaud in particular."

"You don't think it's for love?" Forestier asked with false innocence.

I snorted.

In a more serious tone, Forestier said, "She killed Duret. I think Malbosc is... wearing his body. Something ghastly like that."

So it was Reynaud who'd killed Duret, and not vice versa. Either version of the story was awful. I knew little of Duret and even less of Reynaud, but I doubt they were murderers before they came under Malbosc's influence. Near him, people's characters decay. Mine certainly did.

One detail caught my attention. "She wrote about killing him?"

"You sound more horrified by the record of her crime than the crime itself."

"I suspected something monstrous had occurred," I said. "The surprise is that she took notes."

"It was meant to be a private confession, and she seemed distraught. I gather none of this—Marie's engagement or the murder she committed—rings any bells for you?"

"No."

Forestier twisted toward me. "There's nothing else to do in this room, so you might as well tell me the story of your life. If Marie Reynaud shows up in the telling, we'll find her." Whatever he perceived in my expression caused him to add, "Go on, it'll be fun! You love fun."

I merely looked at him in silence and he burst out laughing.

"I'll start for you," he said. He was lying on his side with one arm tucked under his pillow, lit up with a kind of adolescent giddiness. "Isabelle de Tourzin was born in Paris in 1556, and even as an infant, she vehemently disapproved of all this."

"The date is correct."

"Not Paris?"

"No, and I wasn't called Isabelle de Tourzin then, either. But that doesn't matter. Nobody named Marie Reynaud lived in the ghetto of Venice, and I didn't get out until I was twenty. We might as well begin in the 1630s. That's when I came to France. Or we could start in the present. She's young."

Forestier raised a finger and made a staccato "Ah! Ah!" sound, as if reprimanding a child or interrupting himself in his own haste to stop me. "She <u>looks</u> young. That doesn't mean anything, as you well know. Don't skip. By your own admission, you don't know Marie Reynaud, and she could be anywhere. And I want to hear about Venice."

"You don't," I said. "It's not like you think, with the dreamy paintings and the music. The churches, the grand piazzas, the tall ships in the harbor, the gondolas in the narrow canals, none of that was part of my life—at least not then. The canals were fetid, we lived on an island where the Gentiles chained the gates at night and made us pay the guards and patrol boats who kept us in, and we starved and died of disease."

"<u>You</u> didn't. You lived," he said. "Do you think you'll scare me off? I grew up in an orphanage, Isabelle. Things didn't get easier once Louise and I were on our own. I know about digging through rotting piles of garbage for anything that might still be food."

I relented. I'd obscured the full picture from him and some remnant of feeling made me correct myself. "Life wasn't so hard for everyone in the ghetto. Other people were happy, educated, rich. There were rabbis and doctors, merchants and poets. Our neighbors came from Rome and Madrid and Berlin. You could have a good life there, even though they chained the gates. It was better than being exiled."

"And you?"

"My father sold rags. My brothers—" My throat closed. I turned away, and swallowed, and Forestier waited. It had been so long since I'd spoken of this. Two centuries was insufficient to vanquish the hurt. "One died when I was little, and the other when I was nineteen. That was a plague year. It took my parents, too."

One after the other, swollen and feverish, all three of them succumbed. The last of my family. The memory of that sweaty, parched winter in 1575 nearly stifled me. Why couldn't that nightmare have been one of the details that faded, instead of the sound of my father's laugh?

I know why. It was an early lesson: I always end up alive and alone.

Forestier regarded me with an expression of such horror, or disgust, or some other wet and unpleasant emotion that I had to turn away. Indeed, that I did not fling myself from the window is proof of my restraint. We are on the ground floor, and even if we weren't, it would not have accomplished much. Wiping a tear from my cheek will not un-cry it.

"I'm so sorry, Isabelle," he said. Did I hallucinate a sniffle? Would a centuries-old account of my misfortune really bring him to tears? I could not look at him to verify. "You've had a hard life. To lose them all, and so young... What a devastation that must have been."

When I found my voice again, I said, "My apologies. You told me of the orphanage. Your loss is far more recent than mine."

"I'm a foundling," he said with careful indifference. "Well, in 1793, they called us 'natural children of the Republic.' Whatever the name, I never knew my parents. Maybe they're still alive and they just didn't want me."

"That is its own kind of suffering," I said, groping desperately for any wiser, kinder comment. "I'm sorry."

"Louise knew her parents," he said. That name again—she must be important. "She was so small when she came to Les Feuillantines that I don't think she remembers them now. But I remember she used to cry for them at night. 'Maman' was one of the only words she could say. So I made her my sister."

"Oh." The story itself was too painful for any adequate reaction. I was acutely aware that a different person, someone who was not me, might have offered a comforting touch. An embrace, even. I felt, curiously, both made of stone and on the point of shattering. I could not move. "I hadn't realized she was your sister by choice."

"She might've wished otherwise a few times, especially over the last four years, but she's stuck with me now," he said, amused. Her memory seemed to buoy him, or his sorrows had already ebbed.

My recovery was not so swift. I was stricken by the knowledge of their bond. "How could you come with me, knowing you might die and leave her?"

He shrugged. "I could've died at any point over the last thirty-two years. Might die tomorrow. Can't let that stop me from living. She knows it as well as I do. That's how it is for all of us."

"No." I bolted upright and stalked toward the door.

"Isabelle."

His pleading tone gave me pause. He rose stiffly from the bed and came toward me, making haste despite his fatigue.

I should have darted out the door. Instead I spun toward him. How could one person hold so many wrong notions— including that I was worth getting out of bed for? I had lured him far from home, far from a sister he might never see again.

He said, "I didn't mean to upset you."

My hands tingled with fury. I curled them into fists and raised them. When he came within reach, instead of hitting him, I clawed both hands into his shirt and yanked him down until our eyes met.

He didn't gasp or swallow in fear. There was something unbearably soft in his expression.

"You shouldn't be here," I said, low and angry. Heat gathered under my skin. "You're going to die."

He lifted a hand to my face to brush a loose tendril of hair behind my ear. "And you don't want me to?"

"Your sister—" I said, having trouble recalling her name. He was playing with the strand of hair, letting it slip between his fingers. His hand curved around the shell of my ear. How long had it been since anyone had touched me like that? I squeezed my eyes shut as though it could block the sensation, and tried again to resist and remember. "Louise—"

"I asked about you, Isabelle."

My name again. He was better at distracting me than I was at distracting him. My desperate attempt to change the subject had failed. When I risked opening my eyes, his were dark and intent. He hadn't moved; I was still clutching his shirt. The linen wrinkled in my fists. My knuckles brushed his chest, warm through the thin fabric.

His fingertips grazed the side of my neck in a slow, lingering touch. I couldn't think of an answer. His question had gone up in smoke. Only one last terrible truth remained in my mind. In a plaintive whisper, I said, "You're going to die."

"Not tonight."

Forestier kissed me. Naturally he did it in the most infuriating way: barely at all. His lips brushed mine. It was warm and soft and over too quickly.

I wanted more.

Was that all it took? Was the fortress I'd built around my heart really so defenseless?

Such gentle teasing didn't merit my surrender. If he was to win—and he had already won—I wanted a hard-fought victory. I wanted conquering. An undeniable onslaught. Surely, after so many years of stony resistance, I wouldn't crumble in the face of one brief, gentle kiss?

I shoved at his chest. Startled, he stepped away. I surged

into the space he'd left and dragged his face down to mine. I captured his mouth. It was rough and artless. Forestier made no effort to escape or to soften the blow. He let out a little breath against my lips. He bent toward me and welcomed my tongue.

Here was the fire I'd been seeking, the all-consuming conflagration. My thoughts burned away. There was only my mouth on his. I cupped his face, then sank my fingers into his hair. I did not want to let go of him. Whatever I demanded, he gave.

Lust overpowered me. I marched us toward the bed and we toppled onto the mattress. This rude handling elicited no complaint from him. He only sucked in a gulp of air, arranged himself to accommodate me straddling him, and invited me to resume.

I besieged him with kisses. He grew hard beneath me, ran his hands over my body, and rolled his hips to meet mine. Mindless with passion, I rutted against him until I was panting.

That same troublesome strand of my hair had come loose again. He brushed it tenderly from my face, tucking it behind my ear.

"I can be whatever you need," he said. "We can go as slow or as fast as you like."

These words, spoken with such earnestness, broke the spell. I reared back. Forestier had sat next to me in the dirt while I had a crisis of nerves. He'd listened to the grim beginnings of my life and responded with almost unbearable kindness.

I did not want another kindness.

Perhaps it is despicable of me, but if he had not spoken, I would have used him to slake my lust. An animal coupling, a physical release, that I could have survived. What he was offering was something else entirely.

I am taking him to his death. He will leave his sister Louise bereft.

Regret curdled in my stomach. I grabbed my cloak and fled the room. He pleaded with me not to go walking alone in the middle of the night—as though the most dangerous thing in the city wasn't already in that bed.

He is still there, asleep. I required an hour or more of wandering to calm myself. He must have stayed awake for a little while waiting for my return. On the desk is one of his perplexing little notes.

C. F. TO ISABELLE, APRIL 26, 1825

LEFT ON THE DESK

Sorry. I shouldn't have done that. You'd had a bad day and you were upset and I made it worse. I swear I didn't mean to take advantage of you. I won't do it again.

I can't promise to forget that kiss, but if you need me to, I can promise not to speak of it. I can act like it never happened.

I can even act like I don't want another. You know I'm a good liar.

—CF

ISABELLE TO C.F., APRIL 27, 1825
WRITTEN AT THE BOTTOM OF THE PREVIOUS LETTER, LEFT ON THE DESK

You, take advantage of me? That is not what happened. You must be remembering a past kiss with some shy and maidenly creature. I am not her.

And how, exactly, would I know your skill at lying? You are concealing the nature of what Malbosc stole from you, but I do not count that as a lie. On occasion, your behavior is a performance—Monsieur de Tourzin, cheerful and devoted husband to his ill-mannered and gloomy wife. This irritating farce, useful as it is, lacks the malice of a genuine lie.

Have you been deceiving me in some other manner?

C. F. TO ISABELLE, APRIL
27, 1825
UNSIGNED, LEFT ON THE DESK

My God, Isabelle, aren't you rich enough to leave me a fresh page? Maybe that's where you've gone this morning—to get more stationery. There wasn't any need, of course. Surely you recognize this paper? I stole it from your house. There's plenty more in my valise.

Anyway, you're avoiding me. And you don't have to be shy or maidenly to have feelings, you know. More importantly, you don't believe I'm a good liar, which is hurtful. I don't think I've ever been accused of that before.

How about a truth instead?

I'm a shapeshifter. Or I used to be. That's the secret.

It feels good to write that. Not telling you was weighing on me these past few days. Ever since you told me you'd had women as lovers, if I'm honest. And then last night we—well, you know.

You told me a little of your childhood, so I'll tell you some of mine. I had a wooden comb that could make me look however I wanted. Malbosc took it; you know that already. Here's the rest.

I made the comb when I was about five, I think. I've

never known the exact date of my birth. Certainly I was living at Les Feuillantines—the orphanage. Not, at that time, a convent, but instead an institution of the virtuous Republic. Louise wasn't there yet. She's about eight years younger than me, so actually, Louise wasn't even born yet.

I'm not sure if the comb belonged to Sister Marie-Agnès or Sister Angélique. Probably Marie-Agnès. She had the longest, most beautiful silver waves. Angélique was around the same age, I think, but her hair was brown like a walnut shell. I can remember watching with envy as they combed each other's hair.

One of them had a little hand mirror. In retrospect, they probably weren't supposed to, but they weren't nuns anymore.

They weren't supposed to kiss, either. They never did it where they thought anyone could see. But I was small and good at hiding.

I used to be small, did you know that? Not only as a child. I've been small many times. Short, thin, tall, fat, weak, strong, male, female, old, young, all of those used to be possible for me. If I'd known diligence coaches were so cramped inside, I would've made myself shorter—but I can't do that anymore.

So one evening, long after they'd tucked me in, I'd wandered out of bed and slipped myself into their wardrobe. The doors were crooked on their hinges and their edges didn't fit together, so there was always a little slit I could see through. After they'd combed and plaited each other's hair and gone to bed, I snuck in and took the comb and the hand mirror.

It was late. I couldn't light a candle for fear of being caught, but it was a moonlit night. Les Feuillantines was a rambling old building with a lot of tumbled-down walls. Even when they locked all the doors, I could clamber into the walled garden. It was an overgrown thicket by then. No money for gardeners or repairs, but that was good for me. I perched on a ruined half-wall, the stone cold beneath my thin sleeping gown. I set the mirror on my knee and started to comb my hair.

It hung down to my shoulders, wispy and straw-colored. I'd always found it disappointing. I thought about Marie-Agnès and her ridiculous abundance of hair, how the comb sank into it, the pale wooden teeth disappearing between gleaming grey strands. With each stroke, mine became a little more like hers. Except for pulling the comb through the thickness of it, the transformation was effortless. I wanted it, so I did it. I don't even think it seemed extraordinary to me at the time. Not any more extraordinary than successfully sneaking around after bed, which I did most nights.

I did have the sense that I'd get in trouble if anybody saw me like this, with silver hair down to my waist, the same way I'd get in trouble if they caught me in the garden when I was supposed to be asleep. So I undid all my work and put myself back to bed looking exactly the same.

I gave back the hand mirror.

Not the comb, though. Marie-Agnès and Angélique searched for it and talked about where they'd misplaced it, but they had another one, and a dozen small children to take care of, so it slipped their minds quickly. I kept the comb in a handful of different hiding places—under my clothes when I could, but if I thought its shape might be noticeable, I'd slide it into a slit in my mattress or a crack in the garden wall where the mortar had crumbled and the weeds covered it.

I didn't get many opportunities to use the comb in those first few years, but just knowing where it was made it easier to breathe. It was mine. It was safe. I was safe. I can't explain how deeply it soothed me. How much I needed it, even when I wasn't using it.

I don't think I'm ready to tell you about Malbosc stealing it. But you know the important parts now: I used to be able to look however I wanted, and now I can't, and that's because of him. You're only the third person I've told. Louise knows, and Malbosc, and now you.

Most of the time, Louise seems like she understands. She works at Florine's, and before that, she knew all my criminal associates, so she's met plenty of people who needed to change their names or their clothes or their bodies to live the way they wanted. Some of them, I've helped. The magic works for people besides me, if they need it. Louise appreciates all that. But she can't see why I've consecrated the past four years of my life to hunting down Malbosc and stealing back the comb. In her defense, I've been a miserable bastard for most of that time. It wasn't until I met you that I started enjoying myself again. Still, enjoyment or not, danger or not, I can't rest until I find him.

I know you understand that.

Louise did ask me why I haven't made another one. Maybe you're wondering too—or maybe you know. I tried. Of course I tried. But magic is fickle, and I am not who I was. Children possess such singular focus and such boundless imagination. I didn't know or care what was or wasn't possible. I knew what I wanted.

And I hadn't been betrayed.

I knew abandonment as a child; I knew what it was to be unloved. That, for me, was a cold and hungry feeling, but it had none of the piercing intimacy of betrayal. Malbosc used my love to get in close. It is sickening—I feel nausea when I think of it, I mean, but also, like a person whose winter cough scrapes and rattles their lungs until easy breathing is a thing of the past, I'll never be the same. He changed me.

That's the ugly core of it, I think, why I can't do it again. I don't trust myself the way I used to before I fell in love with him. Or maybe it's the anger, the spite. I'd rather steal back the one I had than make a new one. I <u>want</u> to take it from him. I want him to suffer. That's all in me, festering.

I think you understand that, too.

In Louise's more candid moments (she <u>only</u> has candid moments) she tells me how bad for me all this is. If my obsession were a boil, she would have lanced it long ago. Instead it's in my mind, where she can't get to it. She's always grumbling that no matter what shape I'm in, I've got a thick skull.

I probably shouldn't bring up Louise. You didn't like it when I mentioned her last night. My imminent death at Malbosc's hands—imminent according to you—was only a minor inconvenience until I had a sister. It's very tender-hearted of you to worry so much on her behalf, but you can save your energy. She's tough and clever and she knows I made my choices. Neither of us really expected to live this long in the first place, not after we lost Marie-Agnès and Angélique and the city took the stones of Les Feuillantines for other buildings.

I don't know how to explain it any better than I already did. Louise and I grew up with death. We've both always known that we might be next. We've talked about it. If Louise dies first, I'll hate it, and if I die first, she'll hate it.

What am I supposed to do, not love her?

I've written all this and you're still gone. I'm too hungry to stay in this room waiting for you, and besides, I don't want to be here while you read this.

Are you furious with me? Do you forgive me for kissing you?

PRIVATE DIARY OF ISABELLE DE TOURZIN, APRIL 27, 1825
WRITTEN ON ENCRYPTED PAPER

Forestier is out wandering the city, no doubt. I returned ready to tell him, calmly and with implacable truth on my side, what a mistake it would be for us to touch each other again— only to find him uncooperatively absent, as if he knew what I had come to say and refused to hear it.

In his place was a new letter on the desk. It rendered me speechless. I suppose it's good he was out.

I had known that Malbosc was employing some kind of magical disguise, of course. I had even suspected that this magical disguise, whatever it was, might be the stolen artifact that Forestier wanted so badly. Learning the details still set me reeling.

This portrait of Forestier as a lonely, misbehaving child— as an angry, wounded adult—as someone with a longing powerful enough to manifest as magic, only to have that stolen—oh, it was a mistake to learn more. I am hopelessly entangled in sentiment.

I am going to kill Malbosc to prevent him from making me party to any more of his evil. It will never be justice. It rights no wrongs. It merely puts an end to something that can have no other ending. I will do it because I have to, because I need to, because I am the only one who can.

But now I will do it for Forestier, too.

When Forestier returned at last, he hesitated in the doorway with an unaccustomed hunch in his shoulders. He made a survey of the room—the brown wool and linen covering the bed, the uneven planks of the floor, the evening light restrained by the drawn curtains, the carefully written pages of his letter spread on the desk, and me.

From my seat in the chair, I said, "Come in."

"You don't seem furious." Forestier took a tentative step into the room and closed the door. "I didn't know what to expect. But I thought you'd be furious because you're sort of always furious, and I <u>have</u> been concealing this from you—"

"Forestier. How?"

He shrugged and sat down on the bed. "It wasn't that hard. You didn't ask as many questions as I thought you would."

"No, not that. I need details. How did the comb work?"

"Well... magic."

Instead of shaking him, I threw my hands into the air. "Stop being dense. <u>True</u>, material shapeshifting is rare. Vanishingly rare. I've only encountered one other case in my many, many years of investigation, and the change required both skill and effort. Most of what passes for shapeshifting is illusory or impermanent or both. It often fades during sleep or even flickers during moments of distraction. Your comb is astonishingly powerful. Am I correct to assume the changes were tangible? How long did they last? Did everyone find using the comb as effortless as you? Did its use have consequences for your health, or anyone else's?"

"They last," he said, as grim as I'd ever seen him.

I tried to remind myself that I hated his smug and awful smile, but it was too late. I hated its absence more.

"I hope you're not scowling like that because you're worried I'm secretly Malbosc and have been this whole time," he said.

"I spent a hundred and sixty-nine years with him. You could deceive me about almost anything, but not about that."

"You think I'm still deceiving you?" He sounded hurt. "I'm trying to tell you the truth."

"Then answer my questions. I asked you several and you've kept me waiting."

"You're not... going to ask who I am? What I 'really' look like?"

"Is it relevant?"

After a pause, he said, "I suppose not."

I wanted him to give me more information about the comb, but he seemed a bit adrift. I should have pressed him, but instead I found myself stumbling through a different line of inquiry. "Do you have another name, or want me to address you as a woman? Your letter had some feminine adjectives, and your first note was signed 'CF.'"

Forestier blinked, taken aback. "Was it? I forgot I did that. I... have a lot of names. I'll tell you about it another time. As for being addressed as a woman—God, I miss when people used to do that spontaneously. I miss so much."

There was some alchemy in that yearning tone and those downcast lashes, that tension in the shoulders and the spine that marked a struggle repressed. Something in the softness of the fading light. I saw her. What man speaks, with such unbearable longing, of being addressed as a woman?

The one in front of me, apparently. After some contemplation, he said, "I don't want it right now. I'll tell you when it's time."

"As you wish."

"Maybe when we take the stage coach home, you can be the husband."

"Forestier."

"I know, I know, imminent death." He waved a hand at me, too cheerful for the topic. "That's why it's so important to enjoy myself now. If I became your wife, would we both be called Madame de Tourzin, do you think?"

"A hypothetical too distant to entertain. I will address you and introduce you however you desire, but we will not kiss again, or touch each other in any... amorous way. That was a lapse in judgment. Right now you are going to tell me everything you know about the comb in order that we might deduce how Malbosc has used it."

"You can answer your own question about whether the changes are tangible," he said. "You've touched me."

This reminder was, I suspect, meant to make me regret my proclamation against kissing. In the note he'd left me, Forestier offered not to speak of our kiss. He never promised not to twist the knife. I did not wish him to see me grimace, or know the depths of my doubt, but he is so eerily perceptive I sometimes wonder if he can read these pages. He can't, though—if he'd read my writings, he'd know I behaved like a wild beast when he was injured, and he would not be able to refrain from commenting on it.

Forestier continued, "You've seen me sleep, too, so you

know it lasts through that. It lasts through everything. As for the comb's effect on my health, there's only the pain of losing it, and that's not a pain I can point to anywhere on my body."

"Does it heal injuries?"

Surprise registered in the width of his eyes and then faded as he thought. "I can definitely get rid of—or add—scars. Same with scratches and bruises, though I can usually still feel them after I hide them. Something more serious, or something internal or invisible, I don't think it could fix that. I wouldn't rely on it for a broken leg."

"Still, it's a powerful artifact. When others use the comb, do they find it easy?"

He shrugged. "I've only lent it to people who wanted it. Some of them were even quicker with it than me. Some were slower, but I don't think anybody found it difficult."

"And they used it on themselves? It wasn't you combing their hair?"

"It wasn't me," he confirmed. "And you don't need hair for it to work. One of the girls I lent it to was bald. She worried it wouldn't work because she had nothing to comb, but it worked just fine. She gave herself lovely blond ringlets."

"It can generate matter?"

He gestured to himself. "You think I was always this tall?"

I'd told Forestier I wouldn't ask about his other forms, but that question provoked my curiosity. I've only known him as a tall man, but for him that was a temporary state—or it had been. An image came to mind of Forestier as a short woman, nestled invasively against me in the stage coach, her head resting against my collarbone. She would have smelled as fresh, and her hair would have been as soft. I banished the vision.

"Is it possible for you to transform someone else's appearance?"

"No," he said. "Louise and I played around with that. She

wanted to be taller, and that's a tricky thing to pull off, so she asked for my help. I couldn't make it happen for her even when she wanted me to. She got it eventually, but then none of her skirts were the right length, so she undid it. That part was easy, at least."

"So if Malbosc did use your comb, he had to be alive and well enough to do it himself."

"I can't imagine that the comb was enough to save him after Victor cut his head off, if that's what you're getting at," he said. "You know more about magic than me, though. Can I ask you something?"

My expression must have been wary because he added, "About magic."

"It's a slippery subject."

"If I could make one magical object, why couldn't I make another?" he asked.

"Some people can," I said. "New artifacts seem to fall from Victor's pockets; they have a talent for creating them, or some affinity with magic. I've never known anyone else like that, though I have met several people who carry their magic within themselves and never disperse it into objects. Regardless, most people live and die without even knowing they could. For those of us who do unlock that door, deliberately or otherwise, it's most common that it only happens once. Either because the exact circumstances are impossible to replicate, or because when you give some part of your life to create the artifact, afterward you have less. You made a singularly powerful object as a young child. Naturally it would be difficult or impossible to produce an identical copy."

"What do you mean 'those of us'? Have you made something?" he asked. "Or no, you haven't, you're one of the people who carry magic within themselves. You must be. But you <u>also</u> disperse your magic—your blood heals other people even if they get it from a vial."

Having talked himself through the question without me, he seemed satisfied. I was relieved to evade any further interest.

"I hate that Malbosc stole from both of us," Forestier said. "I do think of the comb as a piece of myself, but no one's ever put it like you just did, that it has some of my life in it. Not that I've told many people about it."

"What did you tell the people you lent it to?"

"That it was magic. That it could give them what they needed. I appeared to them in different forms, and I never said it was mine, or that I made it—except to Malbosc. What a fucking dupe I was."

"You're a generous person. He exploited your honesty because he's greedy and treacherous and cruel."

"I... thank you."

Forestier appeared so stunned by my words, so warmly vulnerable and flushed with pleasure, that I had an instant of regretting both my former callousness and my vow not to kiss him again. But I have adopted these positions for good reason, and must not waver.

"It's hard for me to imagine Malbosc changing his appearance. He has a very strong sense of himself. He's handsome and vain." I had to pause to brush off the embarrassment that crept up my skin like a beetle. Forestier already knew Malbosc was handsome and vain. They'd been lovers. I had no wish to think of that, but it would be foolish to forget it. I continued, "I expect he'll drop his disguise as soon as he arrives at Songecreux. He probably finds it maddening, having to look like someone else."

"Good," said Forestier brutally.

A little silence crept between us. I considered offering that although Forestier might find his own current form maddening, I didn't. This would have been a step toward violating my vow, and besides, the remark was both unhelpful and false. I suspect Forestier in any form would cause me as many lapses in judgment. Our kiss is too easy to remember. Too easy to reimagine with a different voice murmuring "Not tonight," or another shape beneath my hands. Certain elements remain the same: Forestier wouldn't have been any less generous; I wouldn't have been any less avid.

In the absence of further conversation, we simply went to bed and did not touch, per my own request.

Maddening, indeed.

PRIVATE DIARY OF C. F.,
APRIL 28, 1825
WRITTEN IN AN INVENTED SHORTHAND

I ought to be giddy. I kissed Isabelle. Even better, <u>she</u> kissed <u>me</u> (furiously, ardently, as I always thought she would), and then I finally told her that I'm a man and a woman and she wasn't bothered—at least not by that.

She's bothered by something. I am, too, but in my case I know what the problem is. Isabelle refuses to kiss me again—because I'll die and she won't, I guess? What can we possibly do about that? Besides, as the mortal, I should get a say in what I do with my little eye-blink of a life. I'm the one who's going to die. She can find some other dazzlingly brilliant man-woman to kiss when I'm gone, but I'm only here right now, and I want to take my chance.

I told her I wouldn't mention it, though, so here I am, valiantly shutting up.

There's a chance she feels as frustrated as I do. She must be distraught because we're in the coach en route to Valence and she's not writing in either of her notebooks.

She's not even squinting at mine, or asking where I got this pencil (her house).

The little window next to her is clouded with road dust.

Even if it weren't, there's no way she's so immovably fixated on the hilly landscape out there. Not with that distant expression. The sky is a smear of pale grey clouds today, but I wouldn't be surprised if they darkened into a thunderstorm in sympathy.

Intervening is probably a worse idea than leaving her alone with her thoughts, but I know which one I'm going to do.

I pressed my thigh against hers in a gesture of support and she didn't glare at me or pointedly move away. Her rigid posture's gone all slouchy with despair, so our shoulders are touching, too, and either she hasn't noticed or doesn't care.

Or she wants a hug and this is as close as she'll let herself get. No, that's Husband Comedy thinking again.

There's an idea.

In my most adoring husband voice, I will say, "My dear, you know how prone I am to faults of style. I depend on you. Could you look at this memoir I've been composing of our travels and make some corrections? Perhaps we could work on it together. I do so appreciate your insight."

C. FORESTIER AND ISABELLE DE TOURZIN, APRIL 28, 1825

ORIGINALLY WRITTEN IN PLAIN TEXT IN C. FORESTIER'S NOTEBOOK, ADDITIONS IN BRACKETS MADE LATER

Now we can talk without the other passengers eavesdropping. Tell me what's wrong and what I can do to help.

Naturally you assume you can help.

You help me, then. I'm desperately bored. If you don't entertain me, I'll have to resort to robbery. I bet stuck-up old Monsieur Fanelli across from us has a watch to match his silk waistcoat. Can you believe his wife didn't sit with him? It's so sad when married couples don't like each other. Madame Fanelli being next to me has provided an opportunity, though. Her jewels are paste, but stealing a ring off someone's finger is one of my favorite tricks.

You could not and would not. I refuse to countenance your absurd threats.

Ooh, countenance. I like that.
[ISABELLE plucks the pencil from FORESTIER's hand,

strikes through the word "countenance" in her sentence, and writes "tolerate" in its place. FORESTIER chuckles and murmurs, "Good point, my dear."]

"Tolerate" is the word for you, though you do approach its limits.

Maybe you'd feel more tolerant if you told me what's wrong. If you don't tell me, I'll make up my own answer.

Less absurd. Barely a threat. Go ahead.

First of all, if you don't think I'm capable of waiting until someone is deeply asleep and then sliding a ring down their finger with expert stealth, then why tolerate me at all? I pursue my aims with patience and devotion, and I'm very good at what I do.

Not very good at getting to the point, though.

REASONS ISABELLE IS UNHAPPY
1. Malbosc alive, immortal?, evil
2. More than one lifetime's worth of grief and loneliness
3. Forestier alive, mortal, insufferable
4. Accidentally revealed human frailty (any emotion other than anger)
[ISABELLE grabs the pencil and crosses out the last line vehemently.]

You promised not to talk about that.

I meant the crisis you experienced after we fenced. But if you want to strike it from the record, we can.
[ISABELLE opens her mouth, closes it, and then writes with slow care.]

4. Sudden, incapacitating attack of memory.

[With mild astonishment, in a voice audible to the rest of the passengers, FORESTIER says, "I *have* made a lot of errors in this passage, haven't I?" He touches ISABELLE's clenched fingers with a gentleness that surprises her into letting go of the pencil. She swallows and averts her gaze.]

5. Second, even more secret notebook contains upsetting revelation of some sort

[ISABELLE scans the last written line with mounting perplexity. At last she scans FORESTIER's face instead of the page. There are no answers there, only wry amusement. He resumes writing.]

I didn't go through your things, if that's what you're wondering. All I did was observe you.

This page and pencil are both stolen from my home.

<u>You</u> abducted me. My brief perusal of a few desk drawers hardly registers. They weren't even interesting. Unlike whatever's in your second notebook.

I wouldn't know. I haven't read it.

You haven't read what you yourself wrote?

I didn't write it.

I see. That's why there are two notebooks: one is magic. You're corresponding with someone. The latest entry must be relevant to your goal. Why haven't you read it?

Cf. item 4.

Would you object to me wrapping an arm around your shoulders? It's the best I can do in the coach.

I suppose it serves the ruse that you are my husband.

Yes, pure ruse. No sincere sentiments at all. Certainly not sympathy or concern or reassurance.

Stop writing and do it.

[FORESTIER drapes an arm over ISABELLE's shoulders with nonchalance. Once settled into position, his grip tightens and he draws her against his body. Only the two of them are privy to the weight and heat of this gesture. The other passengers don't remark on it. Perhaps they think it uncommon, but sweet, for a long-married couple to show such affection. Perhaps they don't notice at all.

"This woman saves my life regularly," FORESTIER tells the other passengers with an enthusiasm that none of them reciprocate. "A brilliant wife is something to treasure. I'd never get anywhere without you, my dear. Will you show me your own writings? I know you like to keep them private, so I won't push you, but I'd be honored. I won't be able to make corrections, but maybe I could still be of use to you as a reader."

ISABELLE, who seems rather shaken, burrows a hand into her skirt pocket to retrieve a notebook. She opens it as though its pages are filled with deadly ink. Her hand trembles as she passes it to FORESTIER, who gives her a quick, hard squeeze around the shoulders and kisses the top of her head. He lets go of her afterward with some reluctance.

While he reads, he remains so close that ISABELLE is snug between the coach wall and his body, though there is plenty of room to his other side. Seated next to the gap left by FORESTIER, MME FANELLI has pursed her lips in disapproval of his impropriety. A pair of newlyweds overcome with feeling can be forgiven, but after a certain age, when the pretty young bride has become a wife with neither quality, lingering touch is unseemly. M FANELLI would never flout public decency to kiss her on the head, or be so gauche as to tell a coach full of strangers that she's brilliant. Traveling by diligence really does put one in contact with undesirable sorts.

In six hours, MME FANELLI will depart the coach with her husband, but without the ring on her right pinky.]

DOMINIQUE GALMICHE-VUILLEMIN, VICOMTE DE SAVIGNY TO ISABELLE DE TOURZIN, APRIL 26, 1825

ORIGINALLY WRITTEN IN A PAIR OF LINKED NOTEBOOKS

I am reporting here everything I remember of the night I found you in Songecreux. (I will not call it the night we met; that happened later.)

I do apologize for not coming to your aid sooner, Isabelle. You will say I cannot be blamed, since I was not yet born when you were captured, but still, I should have been quicker. Even in all that chaos.

You know I always found it difficult to describe the ability that helped me locate so many magical items. Never having lived without my sense of patterns, I didn't know what made my experience of the world so different. In its absence, I see now that most people do not feel called to be in certain places at certain times, and would regard this calling—which I always felt as a physical tug—as a terrifying imposition. Most other people have no intuition for probabilities. They do not, by instinct, collect and connect whispers of conversation. They don't remember everything important; they don't experience "importance" as a kind of glow, an inexplicable knowing. The need to pursue important connections doesn't keep them awake at night.

For me it does. It did. I didn't sleep much in the 1790s. With so many great houses having their contents scattered across France, I could turn in any direction and find some dangerous magical item to track down. I kept myself plenty busy in Paris. The city was, for me, a cacophony of overheard rumors, all of which led somewhere.

A horse's unbelievable winning streak sprang from a set of horseshoes that caused ill luck to befall any animal that trod behind it. You know that story; the shoes are in your house. You probably don't know the story about the particularly disliked political cartoonist repeatedly escaping imprisonment. He had a key that would make a door in any wall. I confess I let him keep it, as it did not seem immediately harmful, though I have never been sure if this was the right choice. I confiscated many other items—magical spying devices, undetectable weapons, tools of illusion and coercion.

And sometimes there was nothing to confiscate, as when Paris's most popular new soprano had dozens of admirers vying for her attention, including a few notorious rivals, and she'd managed to get lavish gifts from all of them without a single insult or dueling challenge issued. People began to whisper that the men were bewitched. It was true; that's how I met Béatrix. It's a good thing she's the one who has that persuasive voice, and not someone worse. I couldn't have stopped her. Besides, those young men never missed that money, and Béatrix was funneling it toward abolition. I paid handsomely for her company and suggested that she use her power more subtly, which made her laugh.

This is only a fraction of what I was caught up in. There were so many signs to follow that I inevitably ended up ignoring some; I'm only one man. Ardèche is far from Paris, and that distance made it easier to set aside. I knew, though, by the sixth or seventh tiny thread I'd plucked from the grand tapestry, that whatever was pulling me to the provinces was important. I first overheard the word "Songecreux" at a club meeting, I think, though that detail is lost to me now.

I remember the dreams, though. Never before or since have I dreamed of a place I needed to go. Not when the pattern pulled me toward Béatrix, or Sophie. Not even when my niece needed help in Saint-Malo, where I was to meet Quang for the first time, when his ship docked carrying something apocalyptic. I went willingly and easily to those places, and I approached Songecreux with reluctance bordering on dread. That jagged old stone fortress, curled on a mountaintop like a beast guarding a treasure, loomed nightly in my mind. Something very magical, and very dangerous, awaited me there.

I did not know then that fear comes from Songecreux the way light comes from a lighthouse—a warning. I should have understood that magic as part of the pattern, but I assumed the feeling was my own cowardice.

You may not know this, Isabelle, because you replaced them so completely, but before we began our work together, I relied on a loose, changeable confederation of knowledgeable friends and hired help to retrieve artifacts. They often accompanied me, serving as lookouts or distractions or lending a hand to carry heavy items. When I explained to my usual companions that I'd heard whispers of angry peasants who might drag their seigneur out of his château like it was still 1791, and that I wanted to go to the provinces to investigate, they refused to help. "That's finished," they told me, "there are no more lords. We live in a Republic."

I told them I thought I'd found a sort of lost village, a place untouched by the tumult of the past few years. A seigneur still ruled over Songe-en-Val. The village didn't send a list of grievances to the King in 1789. The peasants didn't bring their lord to court over cruel taxes. Nobody had danced around a liberty tree. No negotiation had happened there, no violence, no change.

There was one notable recognition of the new regime: when France had demanded soldiers for the armies of the Republic, Songe-en-Val had provided men without complaint. Since neighboring towns, those where people were more reluctant to send their sons to battle, had their protests met with drownings and burnings, Songe-en-Val's quiet acquiescence to conscription struck me as strategic.

I'd met one of those soldiers in Paris by chance—an ex-soldier by then, and a beggar—and he was the one who'd given me the fullest picture of Songe-en-Val's strangeness. He had no remaining family and had been only too glad to escape the village. When war had ground him up and spat him back out, scarred and malnourished and coughing up blood, he hadn't even considered going home.

His name was Jean-Marc. I paid him well for his story. (Even in his impoverished state, he required a great deal of coaxing before he would speak of it.) He's retired now, but for years he served beer in a little brasserie near the Sorbonne. Got married, had children. You will scoff that Jean-Marc's life is an irrelevant detail that I am including because of my own softhearted nature, and that is true. But I know your softhearted nature, no matter how well you disguise it. If I did not tell you what had become of Jean-Marc, you would search for him to ascertain his welfare. Let me save you the effort, Isabelle. There is a great deal of suffering in this story, yours included, but some people made it out.

Jean-Marc confirmed much of what I've already written about Songe-en-Val. The villagers feared their lord too much to rise up against his cruelties. The lord's château was haunted, the lord's family and the whole village cursed. The nature of this curse or haunting was vague, and Jean-Marc offered me several versions.

It went more or less like this. Long ago, the lord had been a handsome young man named Jean-Louis-Alphonse Malbosc. Possessed of a brilliant mind and an urge to see the world, he'd traveled to Paris, and London, and Rome, and at last, to Venice to educate himself in that great city. There, he became a celebrated poet and writer of letters. Tragically, as a naïve and innocent youth, he'd fallen prey to Venice's avaricious, duplicitous women and been corrupted. He lived a dissolute life and even brought one of his unworthy mistresses home to live in Songecreux, where she spent all his money and forced him to bedeck her in jewels. Emeralds, specifically. The most polite word his family and the villagers used for her was "courtesan," but they rarely troubled themselves with politeness. Another word was "Jew."

(At this point, Jean-Marc said, "I met a couple of them in the army. Jews, I mean. I thought they'd be different. Well, they don't eat pork, but otherwise they're not that strange. Did you know that? And of course we're all citizens of the Republic now, aren't we, you and me and them." I concurred that Jews were indeed people and promised him I had no intention of accusing him of counterrevolutionary sentiment, and he resumed his story.)

The Malbosc family hated the new mistress. They poisoned her, or locked her in a tower, or the cellar, or threw her from a high window, or forced her to flee, or dragged her corpse into the woods. Him, they married to a respectable woman. Possibly under the threat that this was the only way to save the life of his beloved, or perhaps not. His heart was broken, but the worst was yet to come: his spurned foreign lover, or her ghost, came back to Songecreux. Betrayed and enraged, she killed him. Before he died, he begged for his new bride's life, and the life of the child she was carrying. His furious mistress didn't kill them, but she bitterly cursed his family and all the generations to come.

The château has been a place of misery and death ever since. The ghosts of Malbosc and his lover are seen frequently, so solid they might still be alive. Anyone can feel the evil that has settled over the house. All the sons and daughters of the family live in fear of whatever sudden, brutal death might befall them—and something always does. A fire, a riding accident, a rival's knife, a plague, a fall down the stairs. Because they know they are doomed and have only a short time to enjoy their power, they take whatever they want from the village. The wheat and the barley, the fruit and the wine, the milk, the cheese, the suckling pigs. The pretty girls. The money—though there's precious little of that. They'll cut off a hand for stealing and kill you for trying to leave. No villager who ventures up the mountain into Songecreux ever comes back unharmed, if they come back at all.

The only way to survive, Jean-Marc told me, was to work quietly and try to avoid their notice. This state of affairs seemed inescapable and permanent, as though the village were encased in stone. When the King asked for lists of grievances, of course no one in Songe-en-Val had a word to say. A few years later, when the army demanded conscripts, Jean-Marc thought the seigneur might forbid anyone to leave. When that didn't happen, going to war seemed like a welcome respite.

That was Jean-Marc's story. I needed to know how much of it was true. My usual contacts told me it wasn't possible to preserve a village like that, to pickle it in ignorance or fear or magic. Most of the items we collected were small. The largest enchanted thing we'd ever encountered was that pianoforte in your storage room, the one whose sound lulls people into revealing things they're ashamed of. (I've never touched it in front of you, but I think if I had, some of this story might have come out. I saved you, Isabelle, but I was late, and I failed in so many other ways.) My acquaintances did not believe that a house could be enchanted, let alone a whole village, and thought Jean-Marc's story full of contradictory details—did the spurned lover die or not?—was nonsense. Frustrated but short on time, I left Paris without them.

As it turned out, my erstwhile companions and I were both right.

It is possible to keep people fearful or docile, to separate them from the rest of the world and any popular movements —but not forever. And one night in 1794, a few years later than their compatriots in the rest of France, the villagers of Songe-en-Val lit their torches, raised their pitchforks, and marched up the mountain to Songecreux.

I'd arrived in the region a few days prior. I'd hiked a nearby mountain to glimpse Songecreux by the light of day and confirm it was the place from my dreams.

It wasn't possible to infiltrate Songe-en-Val, as the villagers all knew each other and had only limited exchanges with outsiders. Otherwise I'd have been buying everyone wine in order to hear their stories. This technique worked in the neighboring villages, and what those people told me was to stay away. When I pressed them about why, I received variations on Jean-Marc's legend. I learned two new things as well. First, Songecreux was currently occupied by its lord, his widowed mother, two distant cousins (a man and a woman, both adults), and a passel of servants who were either terrified or bewitched. The lord's son had gone to live in London in 1789. Second, on the day before the mob formed, one of the men in the house had abducted a village girl on the night of her wedding. Her name was Mélanie and she was beloved. The morning after, she returned to her new husband in tears.

Attacking the lord and his family in their cursed home meant death, but that no longer mattered. The villagers could take no more. They marched for Mélanie, for their sons at war, for every lash and cut and tax, for every stolen mouthful.

(Mélanie, like Jean-Marc, still lives, at least as of the last time I had news from the region. She bore her first child more than a year later, not in Songe-en-Val, but in Aubenas, where her family resettled. I don't know if the events I am about to describe brought her any peace, but I hope her suffering troubles her as little as possible.)

From the shadows, I watched the mob coalesce in the village center. Once night had fallen, I joined. No one questioned my presence.

I commend the villagers' bravery in breaching Songecreux's threshold—the urge to turn away was powerful. Magic hummed against my skin. What could have caused this whole place to pulse with such dread? Most magic keeps to a human scale: people carry it in their bodies, or enchant the things they make and use and hold in their hands. I know now that it is possible to imbue something as large as the château of Songecreux with magic, but to do that, the magnitude of feeling—will and desire and fear—must have been staggering.

You and I have never spoken of that. I did not think you would want to discuss it.

I trailed the mob into the house. People flowed in all directions, into the parlors on either side of the entrance hall, up the grand staircase, back toward the kitchens, down into the cellar. Most of the crowd went up, I think, in search of the family. As incoherent as our entry was, that was my last true understanding of the house's floorplan. Once the crowd on the ground floor was more dispersed, only a dozen or so people per room, the house took on a fluid quality. I couldn't say if it was like that for everyone, or only for me. Doors would appear where I hadn't noticed them. Retracing my steps would lead me somewhere I hadn't expected to go.

This was deeply troubling, and I was already terrified. I don't think I took a full breath the entire time I was under that roof. The villagers were furious, stealing what they could and destroying what they couldn't, and I had to dodge their torches and pikes. The fire and weapons were dangers, but it was the house I feared.

Whatever I was seeking—and I had no notion of what it was—had to be there. Usually, once I was close to an artifact, I could simply follow the feel of the magic. A vibration in the air. A prickle against the skin. That was impossible in Songecreux. I'd never been so immersed.

Was the house itself the object of my quest? I didn't know what to do with a house. I hardly knew what to do with the smaller items I collected for safeguarding, either, but at least those I could lock up in some secret place. Back then, I had no idea it was possible to nullify magic. I just stole the nastiest stuff and hid it.

In terror and on the verge of defeat, I failed to see a pitchfork swinging toward my head until it was nearly too late. A gap opened in the wall next to me and I ducked inside.

The house had saved my life.

I still feared it—I'm not a fool—but its magic no longer seemed so malevolent. And letting the house guide me _was_ following the signs, in keeping with my usual method. When I stepped out of the gap, I was in a shadowy corner of the cellar, far from the lone, lit sconce. A thin haze of smoke hung in the air and a knot of people in the center of the vaulted room tussled and shouted at each other, their voices slapped back by the stone ceiling. An old, solidly built wooden rack of wine bottles separated us, obscuring whatever they were fighting over. The room was lined with racks upon racks of bottles, but some had already been looted. Others had been smashed on the floor. It didn't smell like wine, though.

It smelled like wet earth and blood.

One villager broke from the group and sprinted away.

Something green glinted in his clutched hand, and I thought of the detail in Jean-Marc's story: emeralds.

The rest of the crowd dashed after him. If I'd had a partner, I could have followed. That single flash of gem had given me a shock of magic. Even back then, I'd collected enough to know jewelry was a common receptacle for enchantment—people attach great significance to it. Whatever was in that man's hand might well have been the object of my quest.

But I didn't have a partner yet, Isabelle, because you were lying on the cellar floor.

As much as I wanted to chase after the man with the emeralds, decency obliged me to stay a moment and check your vitals. I thought you were dead. There was a pool of blood around you like I'd never seen. I couldn't imagine a person losing so much and surviving. Your hair and clothes were drenched. It squelched beneath my boots and seeped into the leather. I thought the villagers must have throttled you unconscious to get that necklace. Blotches of angry pink ringed your neck.

You were breathing. They'd beaten you, but you'd survived.

I didn't know who you were. A servant wouldn't be wearing emeralds, but you looked the wrong age to be the seigneur's mother. Yet if you were the lady cousin, why had you been in the cellar? It was a poor choice of escape route. My grasp of the house's geography was not good, but I could only see one mundane entry, and if you had the power to pass through the walls of the house, then why hadn't you used it to evade the mob?

Even as I shook you awake and tried to get you to sit up, I worried I was wasting my time saving some villainous member of the seigneur's family. Those emeralds, whatever power they held, became harder to track with every minute that I stayed. I wondered if I ought to have gone upstairs to hunt down the lord himself, to see if he really did have power.

But the house had brought me to you. I needed to know why.

You couldn't speak or walk and could barely train your eyes on me. I hadn't yet ruined my knee back then, so I was able to heave you over my shoulders and carry you a short distance. It was only thanks to the house that we lived—another convenient opening in a wall, an abandoned handcart in the kitchen garden, a quick escape before the fire that caved in the roof.

What a nightmare it was, pushing that cart down the zigzagging path in the dark. We were both soaked in your blood by then. My hands were scraped raw and full of splinters from the cart handles, and my heels and toes were blistered, but in the morning, they looked as though nothing had ever harmed them.

That was my first inkling of suspicion regarding your power. Later, when I was less exhausted, I cast my mind back to the scene in the cellar and wondered if there hadn't been a knife on the floor next to you. Perhaps you hadn't been beaten, or throttled, but killed.

I wanted to reject that notion as too far-fetched, but all my Parisian contacts had told me it was impossible for a whole house to be enchanted. Nothing seemed too far-fetched any longer. There was only what I knew for sure and what I didn't, and I knew very little about you.

It's miraculous that all the villagers survived, as that fire burned explosively fast, which I'm sure was a consequence of the magic in the house. I'll never be able to prove that. I don't know the other details of what happened, only the results. The lord and his mother died that night. The servants were all rescued. As for the gentleman cousin, we lost him for years, but Malbosc resurfaced as you always said he would.

I hired three Ardéchois locals, village men too old for conscription but hardy enough for travel, to help me convey you back to Paris. It took three weeks. I don't know if you remember any of that journey. You didn't speak a word the whole time. I lived in doubt about whether I had accomplished what was needed—except that I'd stopped dreaming of Songecreux.

When we arrived in Paris, Sophie Beauchêne, our angel among frivolous young socialites, took you in. She was the one who eventually coaxed the story out of you—the emerald necklace Malbosc had locked around your neck to cut off your will. How furious you were with me for losing it, and losing him, as you knew he would return and that the necklace would some day collar someone else.

What a great pity that you were right about both of those things, Isabelle, and a great relief that the necklace no longer exists. But I could only spirit one thing out of that cellar, and I am not sorry that I chose you.

I'm sure you remember the rest of those years with Sophie, so I won't bother to record any more. I hope what little I've been able to convey of Songecreux is useful to you.

Here is an addition, several hours later: I dug up my correspondence from the time and have reminded myself that the family living in Songecreux in 1794 had the surname Reynaud, much like your mysterious Marie. I apologize for not thinking to do that earlier, but I've been scattered since my injury.

(It was Sophie who helped me find those letters. As payment, she demanded that I include her remarks here: "I can't say I'm doing this for the memory of the good old days, as we all know the old days weren't good, so you'll just have to tell Isabelle that I'm helping because I cherish her friendship." A provocatrix as always, our Sophie.)

Marie is a descendant of that family, and Songecreux belongs to her. We have not yet had time to research her exact lineage, but we suspect Malbosc is her ancestor by eight generations. More information as we acquire it.

C. FORESTIER TO DOMINIQUE, APRIL 28, 1825

ORIGINALLY WRITTEN IN A PAIR OF LINKED NOTEBOOKS

This is Isabelle's traveling companion, C. Forestier. I don't have her permission to write in this notebook, but I have to thank you for that account.

And thank you for saving her.

Christ, that letter. Isabelle let me put an arm around her in the coach, but she's been distant ever since. We're in Valence for the night. She claimed to be tired (believable) and is lying in bed pretending to sleep (not believable).

I want to hug her so much that it's become a physical ailment.

We have arrived in Valence. I had to wait until Forestier was deeply asleep before writing this, as I knew I would disintegrate under further concerned scrutiny. I have not suffered another attack, nor fallen into bed with Forestier, but both outcomes hover menacingly close.

In an effort to avoid a second crisis of nerves, I allowed Forestier to read what Dominique wrote about me and summarize it, under strict instructions to report only what was relevant to our mission, that is to say, Malbosc, the mysterious Marie Reynaud, and Songecreux itself. Our conversation was brief, which is surprising, as Dominique's letter was long.

Forestier, uncharacteristically serious, said nothing of the letter except what I asked of him. He followed my orders meticulously. I wish he had not. I wish he had been smirking and unkind so I could like him less.

Lest I worry that Forestier has become too virtuous, I found a ring in my skirt pocket. One of Madame Fanelli's imitation diamonds. It only fits my pinky, which is a silly thing to write and to know. I would never wear it.

I am sick of diligence coaches. We have arrived in Aubenas at last and will continue our journey on foot.

I left Forestier at the inn all day while I acquired provisions, that he might rest before we depart. He did not care for this. Forestier is restless like a horse that must be exercised daily. A horse, noble and elegant creature that it is, cannot construct irritating and lengthy verbal arguments in favor of its desires. Much noise was made about his miraculously healed injury and vigorous health.

He did not say so, but I suspect he is worried about me. I wish he would stop perceiving all my weaknesses and perceive instead my need for solitude.

He nearly followed me—out of obstinate concern, or simply to win our argument—and was only cowed by my threat to disappear in the middle of the night and complete this journey alone.

He seemed to believe me that I might abandon him, which is strange, as I did not believe myself.

PRIVATE DIARY OF C. F., MAY 1, 1825

WRITTEN IN AN INVENTED SHORTHAND

We walked all day today. What a relief after the endless coaches and coaching inns. I sat around all day yesterday while Isabelle bought food and whatever else is in this pack I've been carrying. It was almost fatally boring. She wasn't there to glower at me.

She's here now, not glowering but writing in one of her notebooks. I hope she's thanking her friend for his letter, but she's probably writing an account of our day just like I am. ("Forestier talked ceaselessly.")

We left the town and have been on dirt roads, following streams and cutting between pastures. There are tiny hilltop villages surrounding us. I've never seen anything like it. Chestnut trees, little purple and yellow wildflowers, birds. Everything chirps and buzzes and burbles. It smells green out here.

I love it. Isabelle told me I wouldn't once we had to bed down outside, and I laughed in her face. Grass and rain-soaked earth are so much softer than flagstones.

"Do you think I've never been cold before?" I asked.

"I suppose you have," she said. She hasn't been able to

maintain her silence now that it's just the two of us and all this nature.

"It's May," I said, spreading my arms. "It won't even be that cold tonight. A little wet, maybe, but that won't kill me."

She grunted, and I realized I shouldn't talk about things that might kill me. It upsets her. I had to talk about something, though, because otherwise my mind would wander. Worse, my gaze would wander. For this part of our journey, Isabelle has exchanged her terrible shapeless dresses for equally terrible shapeless trousers and frock coats. Even that small and unsatisfying reminder that she possesses two legs scrambles my thoughts. I want to touch her so much.

Out here in the country, she's taken to wearing her sword. A more rational person would see it as a warning, not an enticement.

I once scaled a wall using no tools but my body, silently opened a second-floor window, crept into a man's bedroom, and stole a watch while he slept. Today when Isabelle's arm brushed mine while we were walking, I tripped over my own feet.

It's not just that I want to dive between her legs and lick her pussy until she screams. (Speaking of things that might kill me—but I'd die happy.) It's far worse. She's so foul-tempered and wretchedly brokenhearted that I fantasize about sweetly kissing the top of her head again or making her laugh. That's what Isabelle reduces me to.

I bet Louise is laughing right now and she doesn't know why.

While Isabelle and I were ambling up a zigzagging path toward a forested hilltop, I said, "I've never told you my given name."

"You don't have to."

"You've told me part of your life story, so I want to tell you some of mine." I wish I could blame the birdsong or the cloud-spotted sky for this foolishness, but it's all me. "They named me at Les Feuillantines, but it didn't mean anything. I've had a lot of names and most of them didn't."

"I have as well," she said. "But 'Isabelle' is the one that fits now."

"It's Céleste," I said. "My name. Not many people call me that, but I chose it and it's mine."

"Clever of you, choosing one that could be a man's or a woman's."

I am thirty-two years old and a hardened criminal. Lying and stealing are easy for me. In addition my long list of thefts and deceptions, I've fucked a whole parade of my fellow degenerates in delightfully unspeakable ways. I've stabbed people—including Isabelle.

But when she said, "It's a pretty name," I blushed.

"Forestier," Isabelle said sternly. Her use of my surname disappointed me. "You will tumble down the hillside and break your leg again if you don't watch where you're going."

"Where are we going, exactly?" I asked. "Songecreux, I know. But how long will it take to get there?"

Crisply, she said, "Four days."

That was the end of that topic. I didn't expect more, not after Dominique's account of how cursed the house was—and his implication, not in so many words, that it was Isabelle who'd poured her life into it and made it magic. I didn't report that detail to her when we discussed the letter. She asked very precise questions and I answered them. I can't stop thinking about it, though. There's no easy way to ask her.

Anyway, she'd said my name was pretty and she didn't want me to break my leg again, so I was feeling bold. And we had a lot of hours to fill. "That letter taught me something about your relationship with Malbosc, so maybe we should even the score. Do you want to know about my time with him?"

"Score?" she asked. "I have lived eight times longer than you. If we are trading life stories, there will never be parity."

"You've already won, then. Be gracious and let me take my turn."

"What a victory," she said dryly. "Is there a reason we must talk about your affair with Malbosc? Will it bring you some... relief?"

"Oh, that I was hoping to get from watching you kill him," I said cheerfully. "I don't know why I want to tell you more about it. We have him in common, I suppose."

"Like we slipped in the same shit."

I laughed. "Exactly. Don't you want to hear how I fell? I couldn't tell you the details before because I met him in two different shapes. It happened in a dim, well-loved little place called Brasserie La Fortune."

"I know it."

"You do? I think I'd remember if we'd ever crossed paths there."

"I never go there," she clarified. "But I know it. A few years ago it was rumored to be the favorite haunt of a criminal called Cheats Death. In the end, Dominique and I never pursued that connection. We didn't think he'd know where to find Malbosc, and we didn't want to open ourselves up to robbery. Cheats Death mostly steals mundane items, at least if you believe what you hear, but there isn't much reason to. I'm not even sure Cheats Death is a real person. The stories all border on the fantastic—swooping in to save a condemned man from the guillotine, replacing a lady's diamonds with fakes while they were dancing, that sort of thing. But nobody could ever give me a reliable physical description of him. One source even insisted Cheats Death was a woman."

Isabelle halted so abruptly that I nearly ran into her back.

She turned back to face me. On that steep path, our eyes were level.

"No reliable physical description," she repeated. "Sometimes a man, sometimes a woman."

She gave me a penetrating stare and I let a smile crinkle the corners of my eyes.

"I didn't steal the Duchesse de Périssy's jewels <u>while</u> we were dancing, but we did dance. The guillotine one is true, but afterward I warned all my people not to get accused of murder, because I'm never doing that again. It's too bad you never came to find me at La Fortune. I would have helped you with anything." I emphasized this by gesturing at the wilderness that surrounded us. "And, unfortunately, I knew exactly where Malbosc was."

Isabelle sighed, turned around, and continued her march uphill. "This story is already depressing and you haven't even told it."

"Oh, it gets worse," I said, delighted that Isabelle knew me by reputation before we ever met. "I do miss La Fortune, though. It still exists, it's just ruined for me now. The company was always interesting. It's run by the meanest woman in Paris, a tough, sinewy grandmother named Léonore who would twist your ear for breathing wrong. But she brews good beer. She didn't mind the rumors about Cheats Death frequenting her establishment. And sometimes I could get on her good side. I like a challenge."

"I know."

It was such a brief, understated comment, but it felt much bigger. "I met him in 1821. A miserable March. The brasserie always smelled of wet wool in addition to sweat, beer, and smoke. Some nights we were at the same card table, and I looked a little like I do now. Reddish-brown hair, pale complexion. Skinnier and not as hairy. Kind of raw and young and wide-eyed. Spectacles always slipping down my nose."

"Did you need spectacles?"

"No, they were fake," I admitted. "Though I suppose I could have changed myself to need real ones, but that sounds troublesome. I just wanted the air of a student. They fogged up when I walked in the door, which was a nice touch, like I could never quite see anything clearly. An abstract sort, you know. In need of a haircut. Easy to trick. That's a good way to play cards—either people underestimate you so you win, or you lose and confirm their opinions of you, and then they let their guard down. Malbosc told me his name was Jean. He was the best-looking man I'd ever seen at that table, and the best dressed, too. I told him my name was Guy Desaules. I had no reason not to be sweet and eager. I let him take my money and buy me drinks with it, which he was happy to do. I had a certain innocent, virginal air, and I think it gave him a thrill to manipulate me."

"I'm already planning to kill him, you know," Isabelle said. "No need to throw oil on that particular fire."

Guy and his innocence had been a fiction, but still my heart beat faster to know that Isabelle wanted to protect him —me. Steadily, I said, "Of course, at the time, I thought I was manipulating him."

"For what? Sex? If you both wanted it, that hardly counts."

"Well, I <u>was</u> deceiving him rather extravagantly. He didn't know that some nights I was the woman serving the drinks. Marianne Olivet. Léonore thought young Guy was a fool, but she had a grudging respect for Marianne, who was, naturally, rumored to have the ear of infamous thief Cheats Death. Sometimes one of the bar's regulars could coax a laugh out of Marianne, but usually a tart one. I was a little older in that shape, mostly because I like having wrinkles at the corners of my eyes, but also because it's easier to convince drunk men I'm unimpressed with them if it looks like I've seen their ilk before. I'd made myself sturdy for similar reasons. Having some bulk was useful on the nights I had to chuck someone out the door. I had a single wide streak of grey in my brown hair—for the drama. It causes problems if I make myself too pretty, but I can never resist a little bit of beauty."

"You have... unusual notions of beauty."

"I have excellent taste," I corrected. "Anyway, I'm telling you all this because Guy and Marianne didn't look the least bit alike—"

"But Malbosc recognized you."

"Can we pretend you didn't say that, and then I'll say it, and you'll gasp in shock?"

She cast a glance over her shoulder and said, very flatly, "Gasp."

I'd expected a "no," so that took me by surprise and I snorted. It is such a pleasure to make a direly serious person do something silly, even if she does it begrudgingly or poorly. Isabelle may be sorely out of practice at silliness, but she didn't have to do it at all.

She did it to please me.

No. Wait. Is that Husband Comedy thinking? It feels like simple truth.

Isabelle asked, "Had anyone ever guessed your nature before?"

"No one else ever put it together, at least not that I know of," I said. "But I was careful with everyone but him. He was so much fun—courteous and charming when I was Marianne, wickedly suggestive when I was Guy—that I found myself spending time with him every night. Guy and Marianne never being in the same place probably gave me away long before he revealed that he knew."

"Mm," said Isabelle.

"One night, fairly early on, he asked Marianne to play cards. My reluctance was half for show and half real. I made sure to play differently. Marianne almost never joined anyone at the card tables, but she wasn't as quick to part with her money as Guy. I won, actually. He stayed all the way through closing, and after I locked the door, he kissed me in the empty, darkened street. That was all we did that night. It was all I could do, since Marianne wasn't the type to trust easily. But that kiss…"

"I'm aware that Alphonse is an excellent kisser. You can stop protecting my delicate sensibilities."

"I wish I was less aware," I said honestly, though she was right that I'd stopped my sentence on her behalf. Isabelle said 'delicate sensibilities' with such disgust, and 'protect' like it was a joke, but it wasn't. Not to me.

I continued, "His courtship of Guy was almost equally slow. Guy <u>was</u> the type to trust easily, and it would have been in character for me to follow Malbosc home like a lost puppy, but he didn't push me. The opposite, really. He insisted we go slowly."

"More time to study you."

"It made him seem trustworthy. I was impressed by his patience. He really made me believe he cared for me—so much so that I started to worry about breaking his heart."

Isabelle made a disgruntled noise.

"I had to work hard not to lose my head, you know, to remember that Guy and Marianne would respond differently to being kissed. I must have failed in that, or in a dozen other ways. It was risky and overly ambitious, trying to sleep with the same man while I was two different people. I think maybe at heart I—"

My mind caught up with my mouth just then. I knew all this, but I'd never said any of it out loud, not even to Louise.

Isabelle understood. She said, "You wanted him to know."

"I'd never been caught before. Most of the time, it would have meant prison or death. Even when I wasn't committing crimes—even when I was just passing time with someone I liked, I was afraid of how they'd react. But there I was, flirting with someone in two different shapes, and he liked both. I'd never even let myself think about being whole with somebody. It never seemed possible. But once it was within reach, I wanted it so much. Still, I didn't tell him the truth for months."

"A measure of caution was logical," she said.

"My measure should've been a lot bigger," I said. "I mostly slept with him as Guy. When I take the shape of a woman, I never get courses—years ago, Louise dared me to stay in one shape for a couple of months to find out if they'd come, and they never did—so I can't get pregnant, and as Marianne I looked old enough that it would have been unlikely in any case, but I didn't want to discuss that with him.

"So when I was Guy, we'd get a room at Florine's sometimes, since I didn't want to take him to the room I was renting. I never took anyone there. People would have asked questions about all the dresses and trousers and shoes in a variety of sizes. Malbosc never took me to his townhouse, either. When I was Marianne, he'd sometimes kiss me after I closed the brasserie, but we never went anywhere together. Not until the second time he asked me to play cards. I remember it excruciatingly well. We played a round by the light of a single lamp after everyone else was gone. I won. This amused him, and he said 'How refreshing to see you do something other than lose deliberately.' I said, 'We've only played cards twice and I've taken your money both times.' And he said 'You're very clever, but not as clever as you think, Guy.' While I was frozen with the shock of finally being discovered, he smiled, touched me lightly on the forearm, and said—"

"You flick your wrist very sharply when you deal."

I stopped walking. It took Isabelle three or four steps before she realized she'd left me behind. She turned and came back down the hill until we were standing together. I must have looked ill. She put her hand on mine.

"How could you know—" I began.

"A lucky guess," she said. "I thought you'd correct me and say it was the way you held the cards, or rubbed your index against your thumb while you thought."

"You've never seen me play cards."

"I know him; the rest is, as I said, an educated guess. From the beginning, he was hunting you. He watched you closely and selected a detail to make you feel a little bit wary, but also special. He wanted to intrigue you. As a skilled thief, you probably thought you were beyond that kind of trick, which he would have noticed and taken as a challenge."

"No. I know what Malbosc did and how he did it. I want to know how _you_ know about the way I deal cards."

"I don't. But I've seen you handle cutlery and paper by now. You're experienced with cards. And in everything you do, you move with grace and confidence. You're quick, both mentally and physically. You pride yourself on disappearing into the shadows, but you also crave recognition. You like people who notice how good you are—even when you're not being showy about it. A sharp flick of the wrist is exactly the kind of subtle display you'd make to impress everyone without engaging in too much theater. You'd naturally be especially taken with anyone watchful enough to catch you. Most importantly, even if it's false, even if you deal slowly or clumsily, 'sharp flick of the wrist' has a flattering sound to it. You'd like to think of yourself as a person who deals with such effortless brilliance, as a person whose effortless brilliance is undeniable in any context—to the savvy observer. It was perfect for him."

After a moment to absorb all that—grace, confidence, it would almost have been flattering if it hadn't been about how susceptible I am to flattery—I said, "Next time just get out your fancy sword and run me through."

Isabelle twisted her mouth into the saddest little smile and said, "He used to write me love letters."

"What?"

"I replied in kind, but his held more power over me," she said, admirably ignoring that my eyes were the size of dinner plates. "It isn't a flaw. Wanting to be seen."

"It's a flaw to show your betrayer exactly how your magic works and then go to sleep with it sitting right where he can steal it. Normally I sleep lightly, but I changed so many times for him that I was exhausted. He wore me out on purpose."

We were still standing in the path like we were rooted there. Isabelle hadn't removed her hand from mine, which I think she'd forgotten until surprise caused her to clench my fingers painfully tight.

"So this body—your body—he—I'm sorry," she said haltingly, and I wasn't sure if she meant her grip or what Malbosc did to me. Her expression remained stricken even after she let the blood flow back into my fingers.

It's funny, writing this, to try to capture what I felt in that moment. My body's been marked by his treachery for years. Time has deadened the pain a little. Not as howling or as burning as it was. I've shoved it down and forged it into something cold and hard and sharp.

Still, for some reason—shame, maybe—I never told Louise that detail, that it was Malbosc's desire that shaped me.

Or maybe it was because I didn't want to see Louise look as horrified as Isabelle did.

Having it reflected back to me, fresh, made me want to weep again. I did, a little. Tears sprang to my eyes. But it was also good in a way I don't think I can capture. It hurt her too.

She saw me. She understood.

She held my hand and let me keep talking.

"I don't hate this form so much as I hate being stuck," I started. I wanted to say something about how every time she let slip, in words or glances, that <u>she</u> liked my face or my body, it helped me remember all the reasons I'd chosen this shape. But Isabelle was holding my hand and I didn't want to scare her off.

I gestured at myself. "This was still my idea—he made suggestions, but I'd never let anybody dictate every last detail, no matter how much I thought I loved them. And it's some comfort that he didn't like how I interpreted his request. He thought I'd made my nose too big and my face too weathered, didn't like the lines or the grey hair or any of that. Thought I should've sculpted myself an abdomen like a marble god instead of like a human being who likes to eat. Had some other opinions that I'll spare you. He said 'You avoid perfection because you fear your own potential.' I said 'I avoid perfection because I don't fucking like it.' That was the first time I wondered if I'd made a mistake with him. He clarified that for me in the morning when he was gone."

"Fuck," said Isabelle eloquently.

"I knew something was wrong, but had to allow for other possibilities, so it was a day or two before I was really, truly certain of what he'd done," I said. "I didn't even know his full name. Didn't have a pair of boots big enough for my feet, either, but that was easier to fix."

"Perhaps I <u>can</u> resurrect people, and we can find out after I kill him, so you can kill him a second time."

I shrugged. "I won't mind seeing you end him, but what I really want is my life back. Still, that's very sweet of you."

She laughed. Really laughed. I didn't even mind that she dropped my hand to do it. The sound was better than birdsong or lullabies or Apolline playing her fiddle in the parlor at noon when there aren't any guests and all the girls are sprawled on the sofas and chaises in their dressing gowns. Free, beautiful, all for pleasure. I've never played an instrument, but I imagine that's what it feels like to hit a note just right. Like floating.

Isabelle said, "I don't think anyone has called me sweet since the sixteenth century, and I'm not sure an offer of necromancy and murder should qualify. But I meant it."

I risked nudging her with my elbow affectionately. Miraculously, she nudged me back.

"Let's walk," she said briskly, like she was embarrassed and needed to cover it, even though I was the one who'd been revealing secrets. "We have a long way to go."

PRIVATE DIARY OF ISABELLE DE TOURZIN, MAY 1, 1825
WRITTEN ON ENCRYPTED PAPER

Céleste and I walked and conversed all day. He waited until we'd made camp to ask me a question that must have been on his mind for some hours.

"Will you tell me about Malbosc's love letters? You don't have to, if it's painful. I just—you know, he tricked me, and—"

"It is painful," I admitted. "And I am ashamed. But I'll tell you a little. Exposing myself to a small quantity of the disease might protect me from its worst damages."

"Now there's a comparison for a love letter."

"I wrote to him too, but those were never published."

"Wait, published?"

"It was what everyone did in Venice's intellectual circles at the time," I said. "Social clubs of a sort. We called them academies. Ours was the Accademia degli Sconosciuti. We all wore masks—it blurred the lines between noble and citizen, and made prosecution very difficult, so we could say what we wanted. And it was coincidentally very easy for me to get into spaces mostly populated with men."

"Sorry, I don't—masks? You met up with a club and you all wore masks?"

"And people had debates and published their correspondence," I said. "The masks really weren't that notable. Honestly most of the Gentiles in the city did it between October and Advent, and again from the Feast of Saint Stephen to—"

"What did they look like?"

"You truly don't know?"

"You think the ex-nuns who raised me spent a lot of time educating me about Venice in the... what years are we talking about?"

"We met in... 1618, I think? I had already turned sixty, and by then it was clear how slowly I was aging. I'd risked returning to Venice and taking up some semblance of my old life—Laura's old life—as an honest courtesan. It had been decades since our exile, so we were mostly forgotten, but still I was careful not to associate with people who'd known me then. The masks were useful for that. They were white, with a sort of beak at the bottom that allowed for eating and drinking, and we wore them with black tricorn hats and lace shawls. And capes, usually."

"And why were you going to this club that Malbosc belonged to?"

"They were free thinkers, you know, libertines. It was what Laura would have done in my place, I think, if she'd been alive and allowed back into Venice. She would have wanted poetry and intellectual sparring. And what else was I to do with myself? Time had hardly touched me. Some days I felt more like a tomb effigy than a person. But I was that, too. Still adrift, wrecked by grief. If I had to keep living, I needed the society of interesting people to make it bearable."

"I have a hard time picturing you voluntarily going to a social gathering," Céleste said.

"I was different then." I nearly said that in the decades since my escape from Malbosc, I had lost interest in making my life bearable, but I stopped myself. That might have been true once, but it isn't any longer. I must admit that I do enjoy the society of interesting people. One interesting person, at least.

Tapping his chin, Céleste said, "There was that night in Paris when you came home in that red dress. Were you out in company then?"

"I suppose. You focus on such odd details."

"It was a memorable dress," he said. "So you went to your academy club thing in Venice. Did you stand in the corner and scowl? No, you couldn't have, you were wearing a mask. And pretending to be a man! And getting into arguments with a secret society of stuck-up perverts! Except for the part where Malbosc wrote you love letters, this is all very exciting and romantic. What a life you were leading. I'm picturing you slipping across a grand plaza by the light of the moon."

"You are ridiculous."

"A lonely and mysterious figure. Obviously your black cape is billowing behind you," he continued, undeterred.

"Are you finished?"

He sighed dramatically. That seemed to conclude his fanciful imaginings, because then he said, in a quieter and more serious tone, "You haven't said how you met him, or what was in his letters."

"He approached me," I said. "I liked that he only sought me out for my opinions, and not what I looked like. When we met, we were dabbling in the same sorts of dangerous freethinking, and we often spoke of what a more just world might look like. He gave that up, or was never sincerely interested. He has, as you discovered, a talent for ferreting out secrets. In retrospect, he was drawn to me because he sensed that I was hiding something. 'A lonely and mysterious figure,'

I suppose. I let him guess what he could, but did not reveal my magic for years.

"As for what his letters said, does it matter? I believed it at the time."

"I know how that goes," Céleste said. "Did you want him to publish what he wrote to you?"

"He never consulted me," I said. "They were his letters. I was incidental to the project, really. None of my words were included; what mattered was his literary prowess. In the book, he excised my name—a false name, admittedly, but still the name I'd chosen to give him. The volume was addressed 'to A Lady.' From a certain perspective, there is humor in that."

"Because you were pretending to be a man?"

"Because I'm a gutter rat," I said. "He knew I was a woman. He liked knowing that secret. But I never told him I'd been a street-corner whore who was born in the ghetto. Or rather, I suppose I probably did tell him during the long years he had complete control of me. But when we knew each other in Venice, I kept my origin to myself. He would've held that secret over me, but he wouldn't have <u>liked</u> it."

"I like it," said Céleste. "Being a gutter rat is one of your best qualities."

"That speaks so well of the rest of me."

"I <u>also</u> think you are beautiful, and brilliant, and good with a sword, and terrifying. That's very attractive in a woman, don't worry. And though you will deny it, you're soft-hearted, which is even better."

There was no response to that. I flushed hot in the cool twilight. Though of course he had not been drinking, I said, "You must be drunk. Go to sleep."

Miraculously, he only said, "I'd like to do a little writing first. Thank you for telling me that." Then he left me in peace.

I both want and do not want to arrive at Songecreux. I burn to kill Malbosc this instant—more with each new horrifying detail I learn—and yet I would prolong these spring days of walking with Céleste, whose undeserved, sunny companionship I fear to lose.

ISABELLE DE TOURZIN AND DOMINIQUE GALMICHE-VUILLEMIN, VICOMTE DE SAVIGNY, MAY 2, 1825

WRITTEN IN A PAIR OF LINKED NOTEBOOKS

Do you think it would kill me instantly to touch the sponge barehanded?

~

DON'T DO THAT, ISABELLE. What an alarming question, especially given that you must have written it in the middle of the night. Are you in distress?

No more than usual.

Am I meant to find that reassuring? Last time we corresponded, you lectured me about taking a reckless risk with an artifact. Don't take one of your own.

I am merely contemplating possible outcomes.

Even if I still had my sense of probabilities and could guess how harmful the sponge might be, I would advise you to catch Malbosc and test it on him first.

That is still my plan. I do think things through on occasion.

In the future, if you ask me whether an action would cause your immediate death, could you preface that question with "I'm not going to try this"?

I'm sorry. Should I ever ask you anything similar, I will.

Did you just apologize? No, don't answer that, I can see plainly that you did. Is this the civilizing influence of your mysterious traveling companion? I was surprised to receive his thanks on the previous page; I didn't think you'd let anyone else read these words. He's very polite.

That is one way to describe him. How strange to imagine that a person such as Forestier might have a civilizing influence on me. It would make him laugh, I think. Almost everything does.

You've made a friend.

No, I fear that's not the word.

Then what is the word?
Isabelle?

It was very rude of you to quit our conversation at such an intriguing moment. You've inspired an insight, though. I thought you were asking about the sponge because you wanted to die; I know that particular despair often hangs over you, and it was the source of my

worry. But it just occurred to me that you might have been asking because you want to live.
I hope that's true, Isabelle. I want you to live.

PRIVATE DIARY OF C. F., MAY 2, 1825

WRITTEN IN AN INVENTED SHORTHAND

I have to write this carefully so as not to disturb Isabelle, but I can't wait until later. I am exhausted but elated—but melancholy—but elated. I don't know. This energy has to go somewhere.

We walked all day again. Heavy clouds hung over us, but it didn't rain. After yesterday's conversation about my mistake with Malbosc, I thought I ought to talk about something lighter, so I chose books. Isabelle loves to read. I would've guessed she read serious, tragic, intellectual things, and maybe she does, but more importantly, she has a secret love for the comic and the filthy. She likes Villon and Rabelais and Sorel. Delightful. I feel like I went rifling through someone's pockets looking for a few centimes and instead pulled out a diamond the size of a grape.

When I risked mentioning the title of a certain infamous, banned work, she said warningly, "We should not talk about that."

"But you know it," I teased. "The Education of Young Denise."

"Victor's aunt Sophie," she started.

"Oh, right."

"You don't know what I was going to say."

"Yes, I do," I said, ridiculously pleased with myself. "When I lived in the Maison Laval, I broke into the rooms of all the other residents for my own entertainment. She and Victor had the most _interesting_ books. And Dominique's letter said you used to live with her, so you must know that, too."

"We did live together for a time, or I should say she cared for me when I couldn't care for myself. And yes, Sophie has an enormous collection of illegal obscenities—mostly books."

"She made herself so dull at those boarding house dinners, and so did I. Of course, I couldn't be anyone's friend because I was posing as an officer of the law, and also because I was completely fucking miserable. But knowing about her secret stash of pornography was a bright spot for me. I bet she's wonderful."

Isabelle paused for a strained moment. "She... has been a good friend to me."

"Why did you say it like that?"

"I haven't been a good friend to her."

"What's stopping you?"

She stared at me like I'd spoken another language—or like she knew exactly what I'd said and the answer was too obvious for words. Either way, I had to clarify.

"She's alive, you're alive," I said. "Write her a note and tell her you're sorry, or you'll do better, or whatever it is you need to say. Give her a dirty book or something. Aren't you the one who's so worried about the short lifespans of your mortal friends? If you only have a little time together, spend it right."

Maybe I wasn't only talking about Sophie Beauchêne.

"Hmm," she said, which wasn't nearly as good as "thank you, Forestier, you're so wise, I see now that I _should_ stop repressing my desire to kiss you." Then she surprised me by asking, "Was it your hair-brushing nuns who taught you to read?"

"Yes," I said. "There was a defrocked priest at Les Feuillantines as well, so he took charge of some of my education."

"And they taught you to love books?"

"I don't think anyone had to teach me that."

"Also true for me," she said. "My mother taught me to read Hebrew and Venetian. We couldn't afford many books, but I always longed for more."

"Who taught you French?" I asked.

"Ah," she said. "The rest of my youth. I suppose I should continue that story."

"You don't have to, if it's too painful," I said. "But if you want to tell it, I want to hear it. When we stopped, you were nineteen, and you'd just lost your family, and you were living in Venice."

She said, "By the time they were gone, I had nothing. I took up whoring."

"An honest trade," I said with approval. "Louise is a whore."

Walking side by side, we had one of our rare moments of direct eye contact. She broke it with a blink of those lovely dark eyes. "In the coach with Mme Verville, you said your sister loved her work."

"One of the few true things I said in that conversation. She does."

"I didn't," she said. "Not at first. We had a hierarchy, you understand. The ones on the street corner, like me, and the pampered indoor ones. Some of them were intellectuals. Artists. Laura—I mentioned her—"

"Oh, I remember," I said, smiling. "Your first love."

She cleared her throat and looked away, like it embarrassed her that I had paid such careful attention to her affairs of the heart. To her love of women. As though it weren't one of the most enticing things about her, that she might be able to love <u>me</u> as a woman. Whatever attraction she felt for me—whatever attraction she was desperately pretending not to feel for me—might survive if I changed shape.

"Laura was like that. An honored courtesan. Of course, no matter how much you read or how much money you make or how celebrated you become, when a man is angry with you, or when it's convenient, you're still just a whore to him."

"I've never done that work myself, but I'm familiar."

"The things men said about Laura... they were jealous, of course, male poets who wanted the patronage she was receiving for her art and her charms. They thought she was their rival, and that it was cheating for her to be beautiful as well as gifted. There was never any rivalry. She was their superior. Every man who complained about how she used her face or her breasts to win fame for herself, not a single one of them ever produced a sonnet half as good as what she used to write for a laugh, while drunk. We all knew it. They couldn't play against her and win, so instead they wrote her out of the game entirely."

Cautiously, I asked, "Wasn't she your rival?"

Isabelle shook her head. "Never. She rescued me. I left home after my family died. I couldn't bear to stay there, so I ventured into the city, where I spent most of my time frightened and hungry and lost. She found me on the street, took me in, kept me from starving, and taught me everything she knew. Laura continued my education. She taught me to write and to converse. Latin and a smattering of other languages. She taught me social graces, and how to dress, and how to sing, and how to prevent pregnancy, and who to charm and who to avoid. It was a project of hers, lifting up other women. Most of them thanked her and went on their way. I never wanted to leave her."

"A legendary beauty, a poetic genius, and a generous

heart." I was outclassed by a woman I'd never met. One who'd been dead for two hundred years.

"You make her sound like some insufferable saint," Isabelle said.

The day was drawing to a close then, so we paused to seek the shelter of a stand of trees. Last night we slept on some mats on the ground, covered only by blankets. This evening, under the threat of rain, Isabelle unrolled a square of waxed canvas, perforated at the edges, and affixed it to some tree trunks. I would've helped, but I honestly had no idea what she was doing. During my stint of sleeping in the streets of Paris, I never had <u>equipment</u>. In the rain, Louise and I found nice deep doorways or eaves. Stables, sometimes, if there was an empty stall. Anyway, now that I know what to do with that sheet of canvas, next time I won't just sit and stare.

The canopy wasn't a coaching room inn and breakfast in bed, but Isabelle was taking care of me again. As much as I like it, I itch to do the same for her.

Isabelle plopped down on her mat and withdrew a hard, salty cheese and slightly stale bread from her pack. She broke off a piece of the latter and handed it to me. "Laura loved dirty jokes and cheating at cards. Half her ambition came from spite. She was a vain, petty bitch with a razor-sharp tongue who never forgot a grudge. And it was <u>her</u> stubborn nature that ruined my life."

"What?"

"I was born mortal," Isabelle said.

"How did it happen?"

"I don't know the exact moment, the instant," Isabelle said. "It took me some time to realize I'd changed. When I was grieving her, my mind felt underwater for months. I might have sliced my finger open while cutting an apple and simply not noticed the cut healing too quickly."

"Wait, wait, slow down. You just met Laura, and then you lost her?"

Isabelle shook her head. "That was an elision on my part."

"Well, stop skipping. I want to hear the whole thing."

"I couldn't tell you the whole thing if I wanted to," Isabelle said. "I wouldn't know how. We lived together for fourteen years, from her glory days in Venice to her exile in the countryside after one of her letters got her in trouble with the Inquisition. That exile was most of our life together. A little villa among the olive trees. Sunlight on the kitchen tiles and blue curtains in the bedroom. All the books we could afford—she lost her patron when she fled the city, and the Inquisition seized most of what she possessed, but I had my own money by then. Our only real expense was the thick stacks of paper she went through, corresponding furiously with all her old friends and enemies. Sometimes we had visitors, but it was mostly the two of us. Our solitude didn't trouble us, but occasionally I returned to see our friends in Venice. It was my fault Laura fell ill. I went away for a few days and came home with some kind of fever."

"That's not your fault," I protested. Her tone had been so fond until she'd mentioned the illness. I'd been happy to hear her reminisce about something nice, even if her eyes were misty. She'd spoken her last few words in a halting tremble.

Isabelle regarded me wordlessly for a long moment, and then said, "We weren't young then, but we weren't so old that we thought seriously of dying. We should have; humans are frail creatures. The sickness hollowed both of us out, but I had the worst of it. Not true plague, with buboes, but something else. I ached all over, and coughed bloody phlegm, and felt my body failing. There was a long, trembling night where she held me and begged me to recover, to live. In the end, I did. But she didn't."

I wanted to hug her. No. I wanted to gather her in my

arms and rock her for an hour while she cried, or while we both cried, since tears were already beading on my lashes. Life is so hard. Too hard. And Isabelle has lived through so much of it. But she didn't cry, and nothing in her posture invited an embrace, and I wasn't sure she was done yet. The love of her life dying was <u>an</u> ending, but not <u>the</u> ending. So I bit my lip instead of saying "let me hold you," and clenched my fists instead of reaching for her, and comforted myself that at least, this time, she hadn't fled the room yet.

We were both still seated under the canopy. I angled myself toward her. Maybe I could surreptitiously edge my mat closer to hers.

Eventually, Isabelle said, "I loved her. I love her. I forgive her. She couldn't have known what was to become of me. She saved my life when I was twenty and again when I was thirty-four, and every day in between. She made me want to live. It was her nature. I wish it had been mine to save her."

"Maybe you did," I said. "Not that night, not forever—but fourteen years, that's not nothing. That's a gift, fourteen years with somebody you love."

Isabelle turned to me and her eyes filled with tears. It was a slow, silent collapse into crying. I caught her in my arms. She sagged into me, heedless of her weight or her sobs soaking my clothes. We knelt in that awkward embrace until my arms were sore, but I didn't let go. She had nothing more to say. There was only the occasional sniffle or hitch of breath, something I felt as a jolt against my chest.

Louise had cried so loud when we lost Marie-Agnès and Angélique, in great heaving, piercing wails. Even when we lost Hermès the cat. I'd cried for all of them too, with the same feeling but a lot less movement. Holding Louise had meant constantly adjusting my grip.

With Isabelle, it was an exercise in stillness. She hardly moved, so I didn't either. Her tears left a wet streak that spread from my shoulder down my front and back, and it was unpleasantly chilly as the sun went down, but I didn't care. Whatever she needed, even if it was to lean on me silently for six hours while she released two centuries of unshed tears, I was determined to give it to her.

She was so quiet that it took me a long time to notice that no new tears were flowing, and that her sobs had diminished. Her weight rested limp and heavy against me, and I began the painstaking process of shifting into a more comfortable position without disturbing her. With a lot of time and patience, I managed to lean against a tree trunk, slide Isabelle so her head was resting in my lap, and pick my own pocket for this journal and a pencil.

I spread one of the blankets over her, though it was very nearly out of reach. I'm proud of that gymnastic effort. It's not exactly a miracle, or even breakfast in bed, but it's something.

I can't stop turning things over in my head.

Malbosc imprisoned Isabelle and bled her and stole from her body, and maybe he left marks, but Laura marked her, too. Changed her. Or maybe Isabelle had some hand in it, maybe the two of them did it together. That's not how Isabelle explained it, but it's not possible to know for sure. If magic were easy to understand, to reproduce, I'd have made myself a new comb and been a hundred different shapes by now. I never would have come on this journey.

What matters is that Isabelle's been living in the aftermath of Laura's love, walking around in it, carrying it with her everywhere, breathing it, the same way I've been living in the aftermath of Malbosc's betrayal. I feel strangely envious—at least <u>one</u> of the two transformations Isabelle was subject to came from love. It was done to give her power, instead of to take it away. I can't say the same of my own. But I don't think I can ever express that envy to

Isabelle, not with how much she's suffered for her long life.

Laura never meant to hurt her. She meant, I think, to make sure Isabelle could never be hurt. But that's not what happened.

You can't ever really promise a person you'll never hurt them. Even if you love them as kindly and generously as you possibly can, right up until your dying breath, you might still end up leaving them alone.

I wish I believed in Heaven. I might have, if Marie-Agnès and Angélique hadn't felt so abandoned by the church and abandoned our religious education in return. It would be a great comfort to think I could be with them again. I don't know what happens after we die, so I suppose I can't rule out the possibility, but I'm not much for things I can't feel in my body or hold in my hands.

We never really leave each other, though. If we did, Isabelle wouldn't have sobbed herself to sleep in my lap over a woman who died more than two hundred years ago.

I understand why she's afraid to love again. But here we are, me in a body that can't change and her in a body that can't die, hearts still beating.

I have to stop writing. Leaning against this tree trunk puts me right underneath the edge of Isabelle's canopy, and rain is starting to spatter these pages. I've kept her dry, at least.

PRIVATE DIARY OF C. F., MAY 4, 1825

WRITTEN IN AN INVENTED SHORTHAND

<u>FUCK</u>, what a <u>SHIT</u> day. Two days? I don't know. It's dawn.

This'll be unreadable garbage. These pages aren't too warped, and I'm warm enough, but my hands are still shaking. I think my mind is too. Can't fall back asleep so I might as well try to record what happened. Maybe someday it'll be a funny (?) story for Louise.

I felt so relieved after Isabelle finally let me hold her. It seemed like she needed it, and obviously I needed it. So I didn't care that it rained all night.

We got up in the rain and packed our (at that time, only slightly damp) things. We kept walking in the rain. It wasn't as easy to chat, and we were climbing some steeper sections of the path anyway. On a clear day, the scenery's probably awe-inspiring: distant peaks against the sky, their thickly forested slopes descending until they're split by the shining curves of the river. Isabelle told me that somewhere around here a natural stone arch bridges the water, which must be magnificent. We haven't seen it.

Yesterday I didn't see much of anything. Isabelle was just a cloaked smudge ahead of me on the mounting path. The rain was so hard I could only get occasional glimpses down into the valley, where the river roiled and swelled its banks.

The path was slippery muck. Our boots sank in, sometimes above the ankles, and my thighs got sore from pulling my feet out of it. Deep puddles pooled in every depression and overflowed to make a few new ones. There was water fucking everywhere.

Then—

At first I thought the noise of the rain had intensified. The sound <u>was</u> the rain, but it was the ground too. A sudden river opened up in front of me. The earth from above slid down, took the path with it, and kept going. The mud rushed downward, uprooting every little plant and even some small trees. Under the roar of the rain was the slurping, sucking rumble of a whole slick section of the mountain sloughing off.

I jumped back, terrified. I clung to the biggest, most solidly rooted tree I could find.

Only then did I realize I couldn't see Isabelle.

The mud might have caught her. Overtaken her. It was moving fast. If she'd shouted, I hadn't heard it over the water. I yelled for her, but heard no answer. There were so many indistinct, dark shapes in the flow. I had no way of knowing which one might be her. Even if I knew, how could I help her? I'm strong, but not against a goddamn <u>landslide</u>.

As fast and overpowering as the flow was, it had formed into a narrow rapid. I'd avoided being drawn into it, and my tree didn't so much as tremble. That was good—at least one thing was steady. It certainly wasn't me. I quivered in fear and shock and cold and blinked rainwater out of my eyelashes and looked for Isabelle until I was dizzy with it. My throat hurt from shouting, but I kept trying every few minutes.

My brain chased its tail, thinking "what if she's dead?" and "she can't die" over and over.

She couldn't die, but she could be buried.

I couldn't let that happen. I had to find her. Powerless against the rain and the earth, I had to wait until things slowed. Hours passed. It felt longer. My hands went numb from the cold. I couldn't feel the tree bark underneath my fingers.

The storm quieted before the ground stilled. When, at last, the mud crawled to a halt, I detached myself from the tree and walked a few stiff paces so I could peer down the slope. Isabelle wasn't in evidence. Had she been carried all the way down to the riverbank, or into the water? It would take me ages to get to her—if I could find her at all.

Without Isabelle I had no notion of where I was, or in which direction Songecreux lay, but that didn't occur to me until much later. Nothing mattered except that she might be trapped in the dark, or underwater, suffocating or drowning forever.

Was that even possible? It didn't seem possible. I didn't want to find out either way.

Keeping my distance from the depth of the debris-clogged mudflow, I began the most uncertain, exhausting walk of my life. No sane person would've descended the way I did, alternately picking through masses of sodden leaves, sticks, and rocks, or slipping and falling in ground that wanted to swallow me. It's a miracle I didn't break another bone. If I hadn't needed to find Isabelle, I would've just plopped down under a tree and sobbed or slept until the world dried enough to be navigable.

But I couldn't leave her alone.

The mudflow had carried so much matter into the river that the water was coursing around the new intrusion in a fast, narrow channel. Even the wider, unobstructed parts of the river were churning, and I could see no sign of the usual riverbanks. Any flat stretch of sand had been flooded, leaving only the steep, rocky mountainside.

I found her pack, splattered, but not submerged. The straps were broken. It must have been ripped away from her by the other debris. Only one apple had escaped. The fall had flung it a short distance away and it was half sunk into the mud. The ground looked treacherous, so I didn't bother retrieving the fruit, but the pack was easier to get. Soaked, it was even heavier than it had been, but I heaved it onto a large rock. After a second to think, I put my own waterlogged pack beside it and continued my search.

Her sword, still in its scabbard but trailing a length of leather belt, was tossed onto a broken branch a little further down. I collected that too. Yelling her name hadn't produced anything, but I kept trying. Her things were evidence. She'd passed through here.

If she'd been shoved under the gargantuan pile-up of mud and rocks and logs that amassed on the side of the river, I couldn't see how I'd ever find her, let alone dig her out. But maybe after her pack had been ripped away, she'd been dragged further.

I needed to go downstream to check, but the makeshift mountain was in my way. I opted to clamber over the mound of logs and rocks rather than ford the mud alone. It wasn't to save my clothes, as I was entirely slathered by that point, but to save my tired legs. The muscles I'd been using to pull myself out of deep muck were screaming. Finding handholds in the entangled mass felt both novel and like using an old skill, even though it had little in common with scaling a nice, dry, civilized work of masonry.

After a tricky descent, my ruined boots squelched into several centimeters of water and more mud below. Even though I was wet all over, it still made me grimace.

I scanned the river and yelled for Isabelle again. Detritus from the mudslide was strewn everywhere. I've never seen a battlefield, but I imagine they must have the same feeling.

Some great, roaring violence subsides at last, but even in the quiet, everything is disturbed. Nothing is in its right place, chaos surrounds you, and yet it's too empty.

Scared, I picked my way along the edge of the water until I came around a curve.

The first thing I saw was a yawning black gap in the mountainside—the mouth of a cave. It was just high enough above the water to have remained relatively dry, and a few overturned shrubberies scattered around it suggested that it might have been hidden until the storm and the mudslide uprooted everything.

The second thing I saw was a boot.

It was Isabelle's boot, lying in the shallows at the base of one of the haphazard pyramids of debris. Mud coated the soaked reddish brown leather. The force of the landslide must have wrenched it from her foot.

That my gaze fell on it was sheer luck. It didn't look that different from any other lump.

The boot was the closest I'd come to a clue. I splashed over to it. When I lifted it, water poured out. I tossed it gently to land on a slightly drier section of the rocky slope, and began to examine the pyramid. The giant mass where the mudflow stopped up the river had disgorged a few dozen of these smaller mounds, like a pummeled fighter spitting out loose teeth. Eventually the river would win that fight. Until then, these piles of muck and rock and branches dotted the shallows. This one was as tall as I was, and there was too much mud at the bottom to tell if it hid anything else.

My pulse pounded and my throat went tight. I had to try.

Dragging the topmost branches away was rough, nasty work, but I could do it with the strength of my body. Then I came to a branch so heavy it required a lever. Finding one didn't make my task go much faster—I kept slipping in the mud, and if Isabelle was under all that, I was scared of accidentally making everything worse. What if I dropped the branch on her and crushed her? Cold and bruised and more tired than I've ever been in my life, I panted and tried again. And again.

With one last effort, I heaved it into the river. It fell with a splash. Then I was down to the sticks and the gravel and mud. My hands were bleeding from little cuts all over, but I didn't stop to dig my gloves out of my tightly packed knapsack. I plunged into the mess.

A couple handspans down, I found her. I thought it was her, anyway. It was a body.

Through the mud and the layers of drenched clothes, I couldn't tell if there was any heat left in it. Any life.

She was pinned under the mud. It would take me a long time to dig her out and I was terrified, yet relieved. To <u>see</u> her, to know where she was, felt like such a gift. She'd been invisible. I could have missed her. She could have been kilometers down the river, or trapped in its impenetrable depths.

I scraped frantically until I'd uncovered her shoulders and head. She was lying on her belly, not quite facedown. Her head was turned to the side, unmoving. Probably unconscious, I had to remind myself, when my heart screamed "dead."

When I felt the contours of her face, I forced myself to move more with more precision. I cleared the mire carefully away from her nose and mouth until I was sure she could breathe.

Crouched down so close to her, I nearly collapsed backward when I saw the first stirring of breath, like a second storm had rolled through and blown me over. I gulped in air like I'd been the one suffocating.

"Isabelle." I brushed my fingertips over her eyelids to swipe away the mud. The tiny, gentle motion made me recall doing Louise's makeup, and it was so jarring—so different from the panicked, urgent way I'd been using my hands—that I choked on a sob and mumbled, "Fuck."

Isabelle's eyelids fluttered, her eyes opened, and then she closed them.

My heart lurched. I wiped a dirty hand across my face, like that might help me see through my tears. I kept digging. "You'd better be alive," I said, blinking furiously. "I'm too tired to bury you again after all this, so you'd better be alive."

When I freed her arm and lifted it, Isabelle woke more fully, observed my efforts, and mumbled, "Hurts."

"I'm sorry, love," I said. "I'll get you out, I swear."

She didn't say anything else while I finished, and it took me a long time. She lay still even after I'd dug her out, so I scooped her into my aching arms and carried her into the cave.

She was in bad shape, trembling and bruised and bleeding all over, and probably with worse injuries I couldn't see. But her mysterious nature meant there wasn't anything I could do for her health that she couldn't do for herself, so I lay her down and took care of other things.

Collecting our scattered affairs and finding enough dry sticks to start a fire took me ages. Peeling myself out of my ruined clothes was unpleasant, but getting Isabelle undressed was worse.

"This is <u>not</u> how I wanted this to happen," I told her, even though she was barely conscious and in response she only shivered. Convulsively, I mean, not in the good way. She wasn't present enough to protest or complain or even to lift her arms when I pulled on her sleeves. When I finished, I was too exhausted to feel much of anything. I lay us both down, curled around her to warm her up, and went to sleep like I'd been bashed in the head with a rock.

That was a few hours ago, I think. I woke up to tend the fire—everything's still so fucking damp, it's almost impossible

—and wonder what I'll do if Isabelle never comes back to herself.

She's not shivering any longer, at least, and she's breathing normally. She'll probably be fine and I'm worried over nothing. I hope she wakes up and tells me it was absurd to panic. Wholly unnecessary to undress and share body heat. Ridiculous to cling to her, to press my face into the crook of her neck and splay my palm over her heart to feel it beating.

Will she be angry that I removed our ruined clothes? I acted from concern, not lust, but it's her right to be furious. I'd welcome it, I think—if she got mad at me, I'd know she was herself. She might not even mention our nakedness, as though it's beneath her notice.

"What a lot of trouble you've gone to," she'll scold me, "when you know I cannot die. You should have saved your efforts."

Some of that's a little bit true. I know I didn't need to contort myself so I could keep touching her while I wrote this, but I did it anyway.

PRIVATE DIARY OF ISABELLE
DE TOURZIN, MAY 4, 1825
WRITTEN ON ENCRYPTED PAPER

The haze in the cave matched my state of mind when I drifted awake. Everything emerged slowly: the damp, sputtering fire; the arch of rock overhead; the clouded midday sun whitening the distant entrance; yesterday's events; my bruised, naked body; the warmth of the body clamped protectively around mine.

Céleste had saved me.

Not my life, perhaps. I shudder to think how it might have continued, had he not dug me out. How long would I have lain dormant, buried under all that debris? In the wet, airless darkness, I had a brief enough moment of consciousness to know that consciousness could not be borne.

From the moment that the earth overtook me, tumbling me headlong down the mountain, there was only pain and terror in my awareness. Of my many near-deaths, the landslide was one of the worst. The abrupt chaos of being swallowed and dashed against unseen rocks, the agony, the helplessness. Coming to rest in the mud seemed, for an instant, like relief.

And then I was buried, and my relief with me. The mire

overwhelmed me. I was in too much pain to struggle free, if such a thing had even been possible. The suffocating burden of the mud extinguished all hope of escape or discovery.

It was like being at Songecreux again, with Malbosc's emeralds locked around my neck. My mind remained intact, but my will was lost to me. No matter how much I wanted to, I could not move. At Songecreux I could see and hear and know what was being done to me, and that was a torment. In my muddy grave, I could do none of that, and that was a torment, too.

I let my mind go. That was easier to do in the grave than at Songecreux, thanks to the lack of air. Whether long unconsciousness differs from death, I cannot say, but I welcomed both indiscriminately. To be alive and trapped was unbearable.

Writing this, I feel the urge to say my last thoughts were of Céleste, that I regretted not kissing him again. That is not true; with the shredded remnant of my mind, I did very little thinking. I felt pain. I felt fear. I wanted release from my prison.

But I <u>wish</u> it were true, that I had thought of Céleste.

Anyone who would race down a mountain in the wake of a dangerous mudslide deserves that kind of devotion. Who would search when there was so little chance of finding me. Who would heave away branches and dig barehanded in the muck until he found me.

I am not sure <u>I</u> deserved such a laborious rescue, but I remain full to the brim with gratitude and admiration. My doubts will have to wait.

While it is not true that my last thoughts were of Céleste, my first thoughts were. He'd saved me from something unimaginable, and now the solid heat of his body was wrapped around mine. His hand was splayed over my heart.

I'd almost died without this. I'd almost lived without this.

I did not want to do either anymore. I could not miss another chance. It was the simplest thing in the world to take his hand and slide it down to cup my breast.

It startled him. He withdrew his hand by a centimeter and said, sleepy and confused, "Isabelle?"

"Céleste," I said and firmly replaced his hand.

He couldn't resist a squeeze, and with it, he loosed a dreamy sigh. His skin was hot against mine. He caressed me, brushing his thumb over my stiff nipple and sending a little shock through me. He ran his hand over me in slow and thorough exploration, like he was committing me to memory.

At the curve of my hip, he slid his hand down and brushed the dark hair between my thighs. His uncertainty returned, and he let go of me to ask, "You... want this?"

I twisted to face him. As stiff and bruised as I was, the movement cost me, but it would have cost me more not to press him flat to his back and kiss him. The long tangle of my hair curtained our faces. He'd made, I think, some effort to rinse both of us in river water, but we were a long way from clean and sweet-smelling. I did not care. In all my years, I have never felt more naked—more stripped to my essence—than I did in that cave.

He parted easily beneath me, letting me taste the heat of his mouth. In return I poured myself into him. They were urgent kisses, hot and hungry, and still he broke from me to ask one last time, "You're sure?"

With a slight sharpness I couldn't dull, I said, "I am, but I begin to suspect you're not."

A smile split his face. "That's good, that makes me feel like it's really you. Could you scold me a little? Tell me how irritating you find me. How unreasonable."

He took my hand and put it between his legs. His cock had thickened and was already wet at the tip.

"I find this eminently reasonable," I said, running my fingers along it.

"Is that a comment on the size of my cock, Madame de Tourzin?"

"Only your state of readiness," I promised. I swung a leg over him, sat on his hips, and gave him a slow stroke. "Though I imagine many people with your ability would have... exaggerated."

"Exactly," he said, managing to affect disdain even though his breath hitched. "People utterly without finesse."

I laughed and confessed, "I might have exaggerated, given the chance."

"Now <u>that</u>," he said, "is a very interesting idea."

"Laura and I had a collection of a variety of sizes," I said, surprising myself with a piece of information I had never imagined sharing with anyone. For a moment I worried about my misstep, mentioning an old lover when I was straddling a new one, but he looked so openly delighted that I found myself smiling back. Céleste makes things easy, even when they aren't. It's a gift. I bent down to kiss him for it, and gave him another stroke. "Yours is lovely."

"Thank you," he said warmly. "It's only part of my collection. We women must be prepared for every occasion."

When I'd asked whether I ought to address Céleste as a woman, she'd said <u>I'll tell you when it's time</u>. I'd thought she was awaiting the return of her long-lost shapeshifting, but apparently the time had arrived. As smoothly as I could manage, I said, "And is this one of the occasions you're prepared for? Awaking in a cave, entangled with another naked woman?"

"Yes," she said and pressed her lips to mine.

We lost ourselves in kissing for a while. Finally certain of my desire, she ran her hands over my body, lingering appreciatively on my hips and backside. She traced up the flare of my hips, around the curve of my belly, and then brought her hands to my breasts. Though our presence in this cave served as testament to how durable I am, she cradled their weight as though they were fragile. I shivered. It had been a long, long time since anyone had touched me with such tenderness.

It had been a long, long time since I'd allowed it. Our first kiss had ended disastrously because Céleste had wanted to be kind to me, and I couldn't permit it. She still wanted that. The thought of accepting more made me freeze.

I think, had I been driven to behave as a devouring beast, to shove her and bite her as I had last time, that she would have given herself up to me and enjoyed it. That might even have been her preference. She had, after all, let me climb on top of her. But Céleste is adaptable. She perceived my hesitation. This time she said nothing so earnest as "I can be whatever you need," or "We can go as slow or as fast as you like."

Instead she grabbed me by the hips.

Lying beneath me made it difficult for her to lift me—Céleste is strong, but I am heavy, and further weighted with an instinctual resistance to being seized—so we tussled for a moment before I relented and let her drag me toward her face. Flush with triumph, she kissed my cunt. The heat of her mouth shocked me.

That first taste of pleasure so dazzled me that I let my body go soft and pliant, making it easy for her to rearrange our position. She put me on my back and herself between my spread knees, then scooped her hands under my bottom and brought me to her mouth again. All the air seemed to have gone out of my lungs. She plunged her tongue into me and I found myself gasping. From the spark of her touch, she kindled a fire inside me. I felt it in my breasts, my belly, my cunt.

In that position, I could do nothing but feel. I wasn't helpless—I know helplessness well enough—but she had put me here, and I had granted her that power. Céleste's unmistakable desire was an overpowering force. She gave me what I needed, in the way I had not known I needed it. There, under her rough enthusiasm, I took it until my legs shook.

When I was nearing the edge, she lay me down so as to have one hand free, then slid two fingers into the slick, soaked channel of my cunt. A few thrusts had me shouting and then sinking my fingers into her hair and gripping tightly. An orgasm pulsed through me in hot waves. I clung to her, and it was only after the sensation receded that I realized I was trapping her in place and keeping her from breathing.

I said as much and apologized.

She wiped the back of her hand over her mouth and said, "Who needs to breathe?"

Ready to wrest back control, I smiled, sat up, and pushed her flat on her back. "Not me."

I kissed down her chest, grazing her nipples with my teeth and making her arch toward me. Céleste is pleasingly responsive and—naturally—unafraid to be loud. She sighed when I nuzzled the softness around her navel and gasped when I bit the inside of her thigh. I licked a long, salty stripe from the root of her cock to the tip and heard her fingers scrabble for purchase on the rocky floor of the cave.

When I took her fully into my mouth, her hands flew up and came to clench in the damp mass of my hair. There was no effort to push me one way or another, only a need to hold onto something. I let her. It pleased me to have put her in such disarray; I had hardly begun. I wanted to make it worse. I wanted the sound of her moans to echo for hours.

With wicked deliberation, I ran my tongue over her slit, slowly back and forth, and slower every time I felt her hips twitch or her hands spasm. She groaned extravagantly the whole time, so much that I wondered if she was performing. I dragged my mouth up and down the length of her until she was so wet I could only slip, and then felt satisfied that her desire was genuine. When I briefly pulled away to suck two of my fingers into my mouth and then coat them in her slick, I felt it drip down my chin.

"Isabelle," she said, panting and lifting her head to catch my eye. "You're... really good at that."

Crouched between her spread thighs, I gave a small shrug. Then I pressed the wet tip of my finger to her hole in a silent question, and she said, emphatically, "God, yes, please."

I put my mouth on her again. As ever, I proceeded slowly with my finger, more from a whim to prolong her squirming, shouting condition than from caution, but that was a benefit. She welcomed me into the hot, tight embrace of her body. I could feel, as I licked and sucked her, a certain rising urgency in her movements.

I did not want this to end. What might happen next, where we would go, who we would be to each other—all of that loomed over me, and I wanted to block it out. To remain in this moment and to think only of Céleste. So I made it last. It was easy to slow, to still, to withdraw.

At the loss of my touch, she blinked and mumbled, "What's wrong?"

"Nothing."

With endearing petulance, she said, "I was close."

"I know," I said and resumed, causing her to make a short, choked gasp. She lifted her hips toward me and pulled my hair, and I declined these invitations to move faster. Still, very little time elapsed before she neared orgasm again, and I stopped.

"Oh my God," she said. "You're mean. Of course you're mean. I knew you'd be mean. Stingy. Cruel. Awful. Wicked. I hate you."

Mildly, I said, "Would you like me to stop?"

"Fuck no," she said. "I want you to keep going."

The only possible response was to lick her slit and suck her again. She did not go silent, but what emerged from her mouth was impossible to transcribe in words. We repeated this pattern twice more. Whenever the end approached, I would remove my hands and mouth and smirk at her. In the flickering shadows, down on the cave floor between her legs, I probably had something of the demoniac about me.

Or at least, the last time I stopped, she shuddered and laughed shakily and said, "Go to the devil."

She was red-faced and wild-eyed, perhaps even on the verge of tears. Lovely. Already I missed the taste of her in my mouth. Each time I returned, she accepted me more eagerly, letting me slip inside her body and glide my tongue over her skin. It took almost nothing to coax her back to readiness. She strained toward me.

I toyed with the idea of keeping her suspended there—it was beautiful, how much desperation and desire curved every line of her body. It had been so long since I'd done anything like this, and she'd surrendered herself so willingly. I was moved.

"You'd let me do anything to you," I said.

Another ragged laugh. "Thought that was obvious."

I stroked her with the tips of my fingers and she shivered. My other hand still had two fingers buried inside her, and these I slowly slid out and back in. She closed her eyes and sank into the sensation.

"Could you come like this?"

She nodded mutely, minutely.

"Good girl." My touch stayed light and gentle, skating over her wet, swollen sex, and I worked my fingers steadily inside her. She raised her hips, craving more. Before I'd even offered it to her, an orgasm seized her. She came spectacularly, writhing and moaning and sobbing and splattering both of us with her release. Hot drops of it slid down my skin while I watched in awe.

Afterward, she collapsed like all the spirit had spilled right out of her. I crawled on top of her and kissed her, heedless of the mess. Then I fit her thick thigh between mine, ground down a few times, and came with a silent shudder.

I lay my head in the crook of her neck and listened to her catch her breath.

"Fuck," she murmured. "Am I dreaming? Was that real? Are we still alive?"

At that word, the world outside our cave crashed in all at once, a landslide in my thoughts. Songecreux, and Malbosc, and everything that awaited us there. An unknown ending, but an ending all the same.

I pushed myself up, ignoring the protest in my stiff joints, and said, "My pack. Was it lost?"

"What?" she asked, still dazed. "No, I put it over there. I'd show you, but I'm never moving from this spot ever again. Why? You need something?"

"Good," I said absently. I could have told her about the sponge, but I know so little, and she, at least, was still enjoying her reverie.

"I deserve more cuddling than that," she said, so I lay back down and luxuriated in the softness of her skin and the warmth of her body and the quiet, thudding vibration of her heart. It was a pleasure to give her what she wanted.

It's been hours. We washed and ate and slept. Céleste is sleeping still. I will lie next to her again when I finish writing this. I must touch her as much as possible while we're both still alive.

❦ III ❦
SONGECREUX

1825

Originally written in a pair of linked notebooks

Dear Dominique,

You have been a good friend to me for many years. I owe you the life I have, though I have scarcely allowed myself to live it. You were a loyal and brilliant partner. There is no one I would rather have stolen dangerous magical curiosities with. It is a difficult thing to make the world a better place, but I think, in our one small way, we have managed. The ledger of lives saved and harms not inflicted is an invisible one, so it falls to me to recognize your efforts, and I have been negligent for years. You are a good man, Dominique. The best of men. You have earned your happy retirement of losing at chess to your beloved and your dear friends.

Certainly you have made me a better person, though it was a thankless task. Thanking you now cannot repair all that in one letter, and this one, in its shocking inadequacy, also contains a few requests. I am leaving this notebook in the hands of my traveling companion, Céleste Forestier, who may write to you for assistance. Please give it if you are able.

Being headstrong and reckless, Céleste will ask you for directions to Songecreux. I would ask that you delay these answers by three days. Songecreux will not be safe by then, but it will be safer.

Should Céleste come to you or Victor in Paris, in need of money or shelter or anything at all, give her everything she wants. I leave her what remains in my bank accounts, and anything she wishes to take from my library, my wardrobe, or my desk drawers. (The house at 9 Rue Branoux and its other contents are still technically yours, I believe, and you may destroy or distribute them as you see fit.)

I am also appending a few notes to our other friends, and I would be grateful if you would convey the messages accordingly.

To your young man Quang, please tell him that though we are hardly acquainted, I think very highly of his character, and it gives me such contentment to know that he and you have found each other. I wish him a long and happy life with you.

To Béatrix, surely the greatest soprano in all the history of the world, and the most beautiful, and the most beloved, with the fiercest commitment to justice in her heart, who had nothing in common with me but an abundance of magic in the body, and still managed to be a friend: thank you. It made the years a little less lonely, knowing you also understood what it was to be set apart in this way. You and Sophie make each other so happy. Please accept my apologies for being rude to your wife.

To Sophie, who cared for me when I had no will to do so myself, who showed me what it was to be alive—a lesson I could have learned better—if I filled a whole book or even a whole library with thanks, it would not be enough. You would find that library very dull, so I will spare you. If I had more time, I would track down every peddler of illegal books in the city and buy them all for you, and I would let you drag me to ruin a dozen parties with my gloomy expression. We could go to one of Béatrix's performances together. I'm sorry we never have. You were a better friend to me than I was to you. Even in the coldest, bleakest conditions, you and your kindness persevere. It is a marvelous quality. I wish I had spent more time in your radiance. Do try to keep the worst of Victor's reckless impulses in check.

To Victor—in retrospect, it was sweet that you tried to get me to go for a walk, or out to the theater. I wish I'd gone with you. I think I find you rather adorable, though I'm unaccustomed to allowing myself such feelings. You have no need of another aunt, but I confess I envy Sophie and Béatrix that role. I'm two hundred and sixty-nine years old, by the way, and Céleste Forestier is devastatingly beautiful. Your youthful bad taste prevents you from holding the correct opinion on the matter. Happy early birthday. Be careful.

Your friend,
   Isabelle

ISABELLE DE TOURZIN TO DELPHINE DE TOUSSERAT, MARQUISE DOUAIRIÈRE DE QUENNETIÈRE, MAY 7, 1825

WRITTEN IN PLAIN TEXT, LEFT FOLDED UNDER A COMPASS IN A BRASS CASE

Dear Delphine,

I regret that we did not have more time to know each other; in our brief acquaintance, I very much admired your practicality as well as your rage. Those will serve you well, I think.

Enclosed with this note is your beloved compass. Thank you for lending it to me. I did, both fortunately and unfortunately, find my quarry.

I promised to return the compass to you. While I cannot do so in person, I am arranging for the device to make its way back to you, as I did with the other thing you were looking for. That one has likely found you by now, or will soon, and I hope everything is as you wished it would be.

Your friend,
    Isabelle

ISABELLE TO CÉLESTE, MAY 7, 1825

WRITTEN IN PLAIN TEXT, LEFT ON TOP OF THE LINKED NOTEBOOK

Dear Céleste,

I woke with your long hair tickling my arm and saw you had dreamed yourself a different shape.

You make a lovely brunette.

[A rough erasure scars the paper.]

I think you will make a lovely brunette even if your expression contorts with rage when you read this. You will have discovered my absence before this letter. In the event that you do not tear this page to pieces or throw it into the river, or both, here are some of the things I wish you to know. (If you do destroy this letter without reading it, I have shared all the most crucial information with others, so you will not be entirely without help.)

First, I have left in your possession all the money and food in my pack. The food is not much, but the money should suffice to pay for stage coaches back to Paris, provisions, lodgings, and more. It may even be enough to keep you in the style to which you are accustomed.

Second, there is a village half a day's walk downriver from here. I have drawn you a map. From there, it should be simple to make your way back to the stage coach route, for which I have left you the brochure.

Third, I have left you the enchanted notebook. I do not know whether it is Dominique or Victor who currently holds the other half in Paris. Either of them will help you if you write to them.

Fourth, I am leaving in your care a compass. It cannot tell you which way is north, but it is of sentimental value to a friend of mine, and I would be grateful if you could return it to her in Paris. Her name is Delphine de Tousserat, and she is the dowager Marquise de Quennetière. You once investigated a suspicious death in her townhouse, though you did not encounter her, as she had already fled. I have faith in your ability to find her and deliver the compass and the enclosed note.

Fifth, I have left you one of my dresses, should you wish for a dress. Your old trousers may not fit. A simple glance between your feet and your boots was enough to know that they did not match, so I have left you mine, which are smaller. You have a longer walk than I do, and going barefoot in the woods will not kill me.

Sixth, and seventh, and on and on forever, I am sorry. I will spare you the full litany of my regrets, as my feelings do not change what I have done—taken you far from home and abandoned you. It was never my intention. Indeed, early in our journey, when I cared for you less, I thought to use you to gain entry to Songecreux. The house might like you better than me. I thought we might cross that threshold together. You are, after all, not bad in a fight.

Then again, the house might have punished you for accompanying me. There is no telling.

Regardless, I cannot take you to Songecreux, Céleste. You are wonderful, and I cherish you, and I cannot subject you to that torment.

You no longer have need of your comb. Last night you changed in your sleep without the aid of an artifact. You are free. Malbosc has no hold over you. There is no reason for you to come with me. It would be a senseless risk. Go home. Embrace your sister. Live your beautiful, clever, unpredictable life. I will finish this alone.

You do not owe me the time it will take to read the rest of this letter, and I am stalling and should depart. But writing this allows me to spend a few more precious minutes in your sleeping company, and I can comfort myself with the fantasy that I am satisfying your ever-curious mind.

You are familiar with the magic of small objects, which can be quite powerful. Your comb, for instance, and the way it materially alters a person. Not all magic is transferred into objects—some lives in the body, like mine, and now yours, too.

A body can become an object, in whole or in part. That is what Malbosc did to me.

You read Dominique's letter, so you saw his mention of the emerald necklace, which he glimpsed on the night he found me. Malbosc created it, locked it around my neck, and used it to make my will his own. I could do only what he commanded, and only he could unclasp the necklace. It is a horror to me that I cannot remember most of the century and more that he kept me that way, but I think it would be more of a horror to know. Malbosc undoubtedly had me do villainous things; the villagers who attacked Songecreux sought me out deliberately, and I am sure I deserved their vengeance.

The mob that attacked me that night beheaded me, but lying in a pool of my own blood, I survived, or, I suppose, involuntarily resurrected myself. Dominique found me and, against all sense, rescued me—you read that part of the story already.

Most enchanted artifacts, disastrous in the wrong hands, are each the work of a single human being. We imbue objects with our will, our desire, our great passions, even our malice and fear. Most creations occur all at once, whether it takes an instant or an hour.

Songecreux is not a small object. It is not the work of an individual or a single instant. That house is soaked in the collective suffering and hatred and fear and yearning of many, many lifetimes, more than one of them mine. I seethed in captivity there for more than a century. Malbosc bled me and hurt me and used me. He was no kinder to his family or to the villagers. The house absorbed all of that. It is a place of nightmares, and I choose that word deliberately: it conjures things in the mind to make you afraid. It twists its stairs and its hallways to confuse you. It blocks its doors to trap you, or it passes you through its walls, or it spits you from its windows.

You will wonder if Songecreux has a will of its own. I don't know. The magic of small objects lies dormant without human intervention—touch, regard, wishing, and so on. Songecreux may be big enough and old enough and magic enough to have become something else. It may have lain still and quiet in those uninhabited years after it was ransacked, but magic is hard to undo. Malbosc's arrival has likely revived it.

The house does respond to the will of its owners and its makers, which is a shifting and easily blurred distinction. Though I was a prisoner, I number among them. We made each other. Songecreux would never have become so powerful without all the fury I poured into it, all the blood I spilled into its floors. It loathes me—as I loathed it. But it has also, on at least one occasion, responded to my need. I speak of the night Dominique entered with the mob; he would not have found me without the aid of the house. I cannot say whether the house meant to save me or simply to expel me.

I am sure Malbosc sought out Marie Reynaud, last descendant of his terrorized family, because he thinks marrying her will bolster his power over the house. He went to Songecreux to reclaim it, to rule as a lord in the old days, as violent and rapacious as he pleases. Knowing that I hunt him, he hopes to entrap me there, that he might live forever.

I will die before that happens.

I <u>expect</u> to die. Now you have the last of my secrets: this whole journey, I have carried with me an artifact that undoes magic. Its touch will either kill Malbosc or render him mortal. I do not know what will happen if I touch it. The odds that I will manage to attack him without finding out seem vanishingly small, as do my odds of survival. If my life is the cost of ending him, so be it. I must pay.

Thus, this letter is a farewell. Is this warning a kindness? It is intended as one, though it feels like a cruelty. My departure is meant, in part, to spare you any gruesome spectacle. Whatever must happen requires no witnesses. Ever since Dominique carried me from Songecreux, I have known my only purpose is to kill Malbosc. I will die fulfilling it. He will never hurt anyone again. There is no need to search for me or wait for me or even to mourn. This is what I wanted.

It is not the <u>only</u> thing I wanted, here in these last few weeks, but it is the only thing I can permit myself to have.

Do not think I left because you changed shape. Your new shape is as beautiful as your old one, and I regret that I will not be there to know the rest of them. It is a foolish thing to confess that to you in this goodbye, but I will not have another chance.

A few weeks together, that's not nothing, right?

Still, you deserve better, so you must live long enough to find it. I know some day you will meet someone who loves you whole.

Isabelle

PRIVATE DIARY OF C. F., MAY 7, 1825

WRITTEN IN AN INVENTED SHORTHAND

Was overjoyed to wake up in a different shape and <u>crushed</u> to find Isabelle gone.

Even more disappointing than her leaving me while I was asleep, just like he did, or all her goodbye-forever letters that scare the shit out of me, is that I can't seem to change at will. Spent so long trying I got dizzy. No idea how I changed in the night. Now I'm just stuck differently, and none of my clothes fit.

Her boots are a better match for my feet than my old ones. Putting them on made me burst into tears. How can she be so thoughtful and so thoughtless at the same time?

She hasn't listened to a goddamn thing I've said. Obviously I'm going after her.

CÉLESTE FORESTIER AND DOMINIQUE, MAY 7, 1825

WRITTEN IN A PAIR OF LINKED NOTEBOOKS

So you're going to tell me how to find Isabelle, right?

I'll do my best, but I don't know exactly where you are. Songecreux is northeast of the river. Do you have a compass?

She left me one. It belongs to the Marquise de Quennetière, apparently. Isabelle said it doesn't point north, which is strange, because I'm sure I saw her consult it on our journey.

Wait. It doesn't point north, but I can use it to track her. I'll be in touch.

PRIVATE DIARY OF ISABELLE DE TOURZIN, MAY 8, 1825

WRITTEN ON ENCRYPTED PAPER

I arrived at Songecreux exhausted, my feet chilled and covered with cuts. The pain was useful. I spent most of the ascent consumed with dread, my mind dredging up gory scenes half-remembered and half-invented, times Malbosc had sliced me open or ordered me to enact some cruel whim of his. Stepping on a sharp rock was a welcome interruption.

The house was much diminished. Holes gaped in the roof. What remained of the walls still bore scorch marks from the fire. The earth pressed a poultice of greenery to the wounds, covering them with ivy and brambles. Some of the weeds had been cut away, however, and lay on the overgrown lawn in shriveling piles. Portions of the house had fresh carpentry and masonry, and outside lay evidence of more to come: stacks of stone blocks, a few beams laid out. Malbosc and his new bride were paying for repairs. Yet the workers were absent, or had already quit from fear.

Even in decay, Songecreux loomed over me. The sprawl encompassed different eras. A few remnants of the medieval fort, including the lone round tower where I'd once lived, sat jumbled with grander Renaissance expansions and other, later, even more fanciful additions. It had never been a beautiful house, but no one could doubt that its owners had lived in luxury—until the fire.

The heavy wooden main door had been replaced. It still smelled of sawdust. I didn't expect it to be unlocked, or to open for me without the slightest resistance or screech of protest, but it swung like it was weightless. My entry made no sound.

Songecreux had allowed me in. I didn't know what to make of that. The house might have been responding to Malbosc's desire to trap me, and now that I'd stepped inside, the door would slam to keep me here.

It hung open behind me, as unresponsive as any door. The foyer amplified my thudding heart, as there was no other sound to bounce from wall to wall. Under my feet, the cold stone was almost a balm.

Malbosc and his bride were not there, but someone had been. The first step of the staircase had writing finger-painted all along its width.

YOU LIED YOU NEVER LOVED ME

More disturbing than the message was its medium. Not bright red and wet, but brown and tacky. The pit in the bottom of my stomach told me it was blood. I felt no recognition, but at a guess, it was mine. Blood spilled at Songecreux usually is.

He'd had more of it, then, and perhaps still did. Victor had tried to force a confession of all Malbosc's secret stores, but in February this house hadn't technically belonged to him. It had been Marie's.

I should have known he would plan this way: devious, paranoid, infuriating. So many years spent in his company, both willingly and not, and yet I had failed to foresee this. My fear of returning to Songecreux had made me ignore it. A mistake.

Standing in the foyer, shivering in the silence, I cast a wary glance around. As disturbing as it was to come here, to be greeted by a message in blood, I had to clear my head. I had to <u>think</u>.

What might more of my cursed blood do to this already powerfully magical house? Nothing good.

I'd pulled on a pair of gloves before I entered—thinking wistfully of my own survival for the first time in years, that vanishingly slim chance that I might live to see Céleste again —and I considered the sponge in my pocket. My fingers twitched. I could clean the stair with it and nullify the magic in the blood, if not the whole house. But what if the blood and the sponge caused some unexpected alchemy? Magic is a strange and volatile thing. I decided against it.

I bent, cautious of the sword hanging from my belt, and used the sleeve of my coat to wipe the stair. Some of the blood came away in sticky clots, but some soaked into the cloth. No odor arose. My mouth seemed to taste of copper from proximity alone—or memory. I sealed my lips shut instead of spitting.

As I cleaned, the house seemed to settle around me, to sigh. Houses cannot, should not do that. Songecreux did. I felt it in the air, suddenly thinner and easier to breathe. A shudder ran through me.

I stilled myself, then straightened.

Malbosc was unlikely to have authored the message. He must have bitterly disappointed his young bride, or the house had gotten to her. It was already getting to me.

What mattered was where they were hiding. Why was it so quiet?

The floor rippled under my feet, a sickening and impossible shift in the stone. My stomach flipped. I glanced down in alarm, but found myself unharmed. The house had merely dragged me a centimeter or two to the left. A distance so small I could almost convince myself nothing had happened. I knew better.

Left, then. That way lay the master bedroom. It was as good a place to search as any. I wandered, one hand on the hilt of my sword, through the large parlor and into the corridor beyond it. The doors opened at my approach, beckoning me nearer. It happened twice before I arrived at the bedroom, and still I jumped when that door swung wide for me. It may be possible to accustom oneself to a house moving on its own, but not for me. Not in this house.

As distressing as I found the house's behavior—if I can apply that word—it was preferable to the visions I'd been expecting. The nightmares I hadn't wanted to subject Céleste to. I hate having my mind invaded.

For a brief, dizzying moment, I almost thanked the house aloud for not forcing me into a dream. How absurd. Then I thought that Céleste would talk to the house, if she were here, and she would laugh, and I felt hollow inside and said nothing.

The bedroom door hung open, waiting. I craned my neck to check for an ambush, but could detect no one. This room, unlike the others I'd passed, was lavishly furnished. A bed, two small tables, a wardrobe, a wash basin, an armchair, a rug. I recognized some of it from César Duret's Parisian townhouse.

A pale wooden comb lay on one of the bedside tables.

I stepped into the room.

A piece of paper skidded out from under the bed and came to rest at my feet.

THIRD NOTE BY MARIE REYNAUD

DISCOVERED AT SONGECREUX

Our wedding was a hasty, private affair. Alphonse promised me all the gowns and jewels and flowers I wanted afterward, once we'd arrived at Songecreux to make our life together, but instead all we've done is hire laborers to move furniture and repair the ghastly damage. The house is in appalling condition. Crumbling and freezing and lonely. I hate it here.

I wouldn't be writing—I shouldn't be writing—except I have no one to talk to, not even Alphonse. He's been distant since the first morning we awoke here. As cold as the house.

I thought we'd make love every night like we did the night of the wedding, when he was finally free to look like himself again. Oh, it was marvelous to see his true face again, handsome though he's still sickly and weak. He tried to achieve his former height, but he must not have the constitution for it yet, as that magic never lasts. Over the course of the day he shrinks. It leaves him in a snarling fury.

He blames me for botching his revival. When he woke, he was livid that I had to use all of the blood, and wouldn't listen when I said I used all of the blood precisely <u>because</u> I wanted him at full strength. How was I to know it wouldn't be enough to restore him?

But now it's all gone, and since the morning after we were married, he barely speaks to me.

I'd be upset, too, if I lost my beauty. He uses that comb twice a day, but the effects fade quickly. He's tried to hide that from me—both the fading and the use—but once I caught him hurling the comb to the floor in anger, and after that, I paid attention. He does it while I pretend to sleep.

I do a lot of pretending. I've cried in secret. He can't see that, or these pages—God, the risk I am taking. He's right about me. I really am a fool.

He was never so cruel to me before we got here. Maybe it's just the stress of discovering the house in this state. Maybe he'll go back to telling me how pretty I am.

I love him so much. I've been waiting my whole life to arrive here. He was always so handsome and gallant. I thought it would be wonderful to be his wife and to live together in our ancestral home.

It isn't. At exorbitant expense, Alphonse hired an old woman and some girls from the village to come daily to cook and tend the fires—some of the hearths in this old pile don't even have proper chimneys because so many nasty little peasants have been here to steal stones over the years! Frightful. They don't respect our family at all, which I can tell because the cook and her girls didn't come yesterday. The crew of laborers gets smaller every day, too, because these country people are foolishly superstitious and they think this place is haunted.

The house is magic, according to Alphonse, but it should be a good kind. Our family owns this house and controls all its magic. He thought coming home would lend him strength, but it hasn't worked yet. He's hardly been in our marriage bed because he's so plagued by nightmares. He tosses and turns and then gets up to wander the halls.

I don't know why. Is he searching for something? It's cold and empty out there. We have hardly anything. I've had nothing to do but take inventory of this place, but that hasn't kept me occupied for long. Ashes in the library. Smashed wooden racks of wine bottles in the cellar. We've managed to stock the kitchen for a very lean, lowering sort of existence, which I suppose suits the rest of our miserable life here.

I miss Paris. I hated Renard Bertin's awful family and his dull cow daughters but at least their house was comfortable.

The only room I haven't explored is the one at the top of the old round tower. The door is locked and none of the keys work, though Alphonse has told me over and over again which one to use. I would ask him to try it himself, but I feel too ashamed. He'd have such scorn for my failure.

There's something you should know. I don't know if Isabelle told you about the sponge I gave her.

I'm catching my breath while dragging myself up a goddamn mountain, Dominique whoever-you-are. I'm trying to stop Isabelle from killing herself. I don't have time to write you gossipy notes about the sex we're never going to have again.

Not that kind of sponge.

PRIVATE DIARY OF ISABELLE DE TOURZIN, MAY 8, 1825

WRITTEN ON ENCRYPTED PAPER

As I came to the end of the first page of Marie's diary, a tremor ran through the house. A fine rain of dust fell from the ceiling and the wash basin rattled in its stand. I shoved the pages into my coat pocket. I wanted to dash for Céleste's comb and pocket that as well, but it was a selfish, foolish desire to hold some part of her close in my last hours. She no longer needs the comb to change, but if she wants to retrieve it purely for reasons of sentiment, I will not force her to search my remains.

Another tremor made me scan the room for threats—thinking, in error, of what might fall on me if the house collapsed, instead of the man in the doorway whose sword was already drawn.

Malbosc. He'd found me.

I drew my own sword, but his tiny instant of advantage allowed him to press me into a retreat. I nearly backed into the bed and had to swerve around its corner.

"Wonderful to see you again, Isabelle," he said, and there was a ghost of his old charm lingering in his smile.

I knocked his thrust away and lunged at him, but he parried easily.

In the narrow space between the bed and the wall, the long window cast an oblique gold rectangle of light on the floor between us. Our swords' shadows sliced through it as we fought back and forth. Such a familiar rhythm, even after decades apart.

We'd sometimes fenced even when I was his captive. The house seemed to echo with his old orders—_it will never cross your mind to do me harm_—and I flinched at the memory. For so long, he'd been able to slip inside my mind and turn my thoughts any way he wanted with only a few words. The instant of distraction cost me. I had to leap back from an attack.

But the weight of the necklace was no longer locked around my neck. I did not have to obey.

Doing him harm had indeed crossed my mind. I thrust my sword toward his chest.

He parried again, but with a fraction less speed than I expected.

As Marie's note had said, he was sickly. Even in such a deathly state, handsomeness still clung to him. He'd been barely thirty when I'd shared my secret with him. While I had acquired a few silver hairs and crow's feet over the course of the centuries, aging in tiny, gradual increments, he'd preserved the beauty of his youth. His pale skin and honeyed brown hair had remained unblemished until now. His hair was still brown and his skin was unwrinkled, but both were dull and waxy. There was a sort of malnourished, grey cast to his features. The skin of his neck was oddly mottled.

He noticed my gaze. "Yes," he said in a nasty tone. "You'll be fixing that for me."

Fixing it for him in the sense that he would no longer care what he looked like after I killed him, but to say so would have been a waste of breath. I attacked again, but he knew me too well and saw it coming.

Caught in our old pattern, my body remembering all the duels I'd been ordered to lose, I wanted to scream. Frustration goaded me into another useless thrust, and he profited from it to puncture my shoulder. I shouted with pain. The wound was just below my collarbone. Blood ran down into my armpit and I stumbled to the side.

The wall swallowed me and spit me out.

I landed on the ground below, the mud softening my landing, but not so much that I didn't grunt and curse. I dragged myself away, bruised and bleeding, to hide in the woods and recover.

I need time to heal, but I am not sure I will have it.

As I collapsed against a tree, some pages rustled in my pocket. Marie's diary. That is not what I wish I had brought from the house.

Céleste's comb is still on the table in that room. I left it there deliberately, and yet I feel bereft.

FOURTH NOTE BY MARIE REYNAUD

DISCOVERED AT SONGECREUX

I've begun to have nightmares just like Alphonse.

Well, probably not like his. I don't know what he sees.

My dreams show me people living in this house. Sometimes they're wearing hose and doublets and that sort of thing, and the house looks splendid, so it must be a long time ago. They don't resemble me, these people, but in that way of dreams, I know they're my family. My ancestors, I suppose.

And Alphonse kills them.

They all live in the house together, Alphonse and my various ancestors, and then at some point they quarrel over why Alphonse has all the power, when he's just some cousin and really the house belongs to <u>them</u>, and why must that strange woman live here, can't he keep her locked in the tower or down in the cellar or something, and when is Alphonse going to share his magical secret like he's been promising—that part is dreadfully familiar—and then he kills them. He suffocates them in their sleep or trips them down a flight of stairs or poisons their food. I've seen so many different murders.

Why am I so sure these dreams are true? This dreadful old house is scaring me out of my wits.

Papa told me that my grandfather died in the attack on the house in 1794, though, and I saw that happen in one of the dreams. So I think that one is true, at least. What an awful night. A mob from the village marched up here, armed with pikes. They smashed up everything they didn't loot and then set fire to the place. They killed everyone but Alphonse, who fled into the night.

I haven't dreamed about my parents, but my father left this house when he was nineteen. He lived in London for the early, awful years of the Revolution, and couldn't return to France until 1795. He and Maman always wanted to come back to Songecreux, but it was ruined and they didn't have the money to fix it, so we lived in Paris with Cousin Alphonse's generous help until they died in 1816.

A carriage accident, he said.

Alphonse held me while I cried over them. For all the years afterward, he took care of me. So often he was away on mysterious business and I pined for him. He was so handsome and kind—if I did what he wanted.

I suppose a sixteen-year-old is easier to manage than her parents.

Oh, God. <u>He killed Maman and Papa</u>.

Is he going to kill me?

He needed me to save him from his enemies in Paris, and he thought he needed to marry me to reclaim Songecreux—but why? It was sitting empty and ruined, and he could have come here alone. He could have returned years ago, unless he really did need me.

Was he afraid? Does he think the magic of this house rightfully belongs to me? If it does, I don't know how to use it. This place is ghastly. It's clear that it troubles his sleep. It troubles mine, too.

My dreams have all been violent and bloody, but one wasn't a murder. I saw Alphonse and the woman—Isabelle de Tourzin, his demon bitch, who must be the cause of all this horror—down in the cellar. She's in almost all the dreams. Most of the time I don't even notice her, she's so much a part of the house. Except sometimes she's the one who kills my ancestors, but it's always on his orders. He made her do all the messy ones. It doesn't matter if she's slitting a throat or blending into a wall. Her face is always blank.

The emerald necklace she wears must have cost a fortune. It's bizarre to see her wearing it with her cheap, dirty clothes. Wearing it while killing. Like putting a lace cravat on a slavering beast.

In the dream where they're in the cellar, she didn't look like a monster, just a plain woman with a vacant expression. She hardly moved or spoke, just stood there while he cut her open and drained her blood right into a wine bottle. He had a blade and a funnel especially for that purpose, like he did it all the time.

"You won't remember this, of course," he said to her as he finished. "It hardly needs saying these days. You're long gone."

But her eyes cut toward him, and I don't think she was.

After that, instead of adding the bottle to one of the racks in the cellar, Alphonse buried it under the floor. I wonder if it's still there.

God fucking damn it. This puncture in my shoulder isn't fully healed, and that will cost me in a fight against Alphonse—funny how reading Marie's diary inclines me toward his given name—but I have to go back to the house.

If I spend too long here among the trees, he will come find me, and might devise some way to imprison me again. Then I will not only have failed, but also have made everything far worse.

Of course he had one last secret cache of my blood. Marie might have found it and used it to leave her message on the stairs.

Is she still in the house or did she make her escape?

The one tiny relief in all this is that I have gleaned this information by reading, rather than the house assaulting me with visions. It sounds as though Marie only experiences them as dreams, and perhaps Alphonse as well. When I was last here, they came at any hour, regardless of my wakefulness. Though I could hardly have been said to be fully awake even in the brightest of daylight. My body was under

Alphonse's control, and even my mind did not fully belong to me.

Reading Marie's diary has left my sense of reality intact, for which I am grateful.

The house, by contrast, seems less and less intact. From my hiding place among these trees, I have heard pieces of slate slide off the roof and shatter. All the wood in the house is groaning, all the stone scraping against itself. What could be making the house shake?

PRIVATE DIARY OF ISABELLE DE TOURZIN, MAY 8, 1825

WRITTEN ON ENCRYPTED PAPER

Naturally I had a vision on entering the house the second time. It was too much to hope that I could escape them altogether.

I have tried to record it here.

VISION

AS RECORDED BY ISABELLE DE TOURZIN

A bedraggled young woman carries a lamp into the dim cellar. This must be Marie Reynaud. She's pretty in a pale, delicate way. There's something familiar about her, which I suppose comes from me living with her ancestors for more than a century, though I don't remember much of that time.

The cellar floor, formerly packed earth, is pockmarked with holes. A rusty shovel lies between them. Marie picks it up and picks her way between the holes. With careful precision, she deposits the lamp on one of the few undisturbed patches of floor. In the faint circle of illumination it casts, she strikes the earth with the shovel. It takes her several tries to break ground.

Digging makes her dark hair slip from its precariously poised pins and stick to her neck with sweat. With each new shovelful, a shower of dry earth dirties her skirt. She's obviously unaccustomed to such labor. Her determination carries her through the task. After a long time—so long it seems Marie might faint before she uncovers anything other than dirt—the blade of her shovel bites into an old wooden box.

Freeing the box from its burial takes more time and more effort, and her arms tremble when she finally pulls it open.

There is, of course, a single bottle inside. It looks like a wine bottle. Marie and I both know it contains no wine.

Alphonse charges into the cellar with his sword drawn. All the holes he dug make it hard to find good footing, and his first rage-driven thrust fails to find Marie. She leaps out of his way. He's so slow—so weakened, even though his eyes are wild—that she has time to scoop the shovel from the floor and swing it.

She hits him in the head. The metal thunks against his skull and he falls limp.

Marie grabs the bottle and runs.

The cellar blurs and fades. Now Marie is in the foyer, sweaty and frantic, looking nearly as feverish as Alphonse. Thin daylight slips through distant windows. She begins to paint the stairs with blood. YOU LIED, she writes.

I want to grab her by the shoulders and shake her. "Run," I want to scream. That hit to the head felled Alphonse, but he isn't dead. He's shouting in the cellar, pounding on a door that won't open. The house rattles and booms around Marie. Right now it's protecting her, but how long before Alphonse wrenches back control of Songecreux's unpredictable magic and escapes the cellar? He will find Marie eventually, and when he does, he will kill her. I want to haul her through the door and tell her to get as far from here as she can.

But this is a vision and I do not exist.

Marie, furious scorned bride, was determined to dig up that bottle, and now she's determined to have the last word. Though I fear for her, I can almost admire the spite. Alphonse wants that blood—my blood—desperately, and here she is, flagrantly wasting it.

YOU NEVER LOVED ME, she writes, and I know that

feeling intimately well. We both wish we could write the reverse, tell ourselves we never loved him. If that were true, neither of us would be here.

To Marie's right, a door swings open of its own accord, inviting her into the unused wing of the house.

Bottle in hand, she goes.

When the vision receded, I thought I was trembling, but it was Songecreux. Or rather, the house and I were both trembling. I straightened from where I'd slumped against the main door, still redolent of newly sawn wood. With every roll of thunder through the house, it jolted against its hinges and the stone where it was set. Everything around me thumped and creaked.

How long since Marie painted those words and hid somewhere in the empty wing? Alphonse had freed himself from the cellar, clearly, since he'd attacked me in the bedroom a few hours ago. When he'd lost me, perhaps he'd gone in search of her.

Songecreux had been curiously helpful to me so far, my distaste for visions aside. It had protected Marie from Alphonse, and had intervened in my fight when Alphonse had stabbed me. The house seemed to have chosen Marie over Alphonse, and as I was certainly Alphonse's enemy, it seemed to have categorized me as Marie's ally. If I found her, she might feel the same.

The thought of allies made me miss Céleste, but I'd abandoned Céleste and would now have to make do with a stranger. I did not know, like, or trust Marie, but if she would help me kill Alphonse, I would let her.

I followed the path I'd seen Marie take in the vision, heading to my right. The door swung open for me just as it had for her.

It did not matter that the vision had stopped there. I knew where Songecreux had led Marie. My feet carried me almost as though I were still under magical coercion to lock myself away.

This medieval tower was the oldest part of the house that still stood. A staircase, its stones worn down in the center from thousands of footsteps, many of them mine, spiraled up to a lone bedchamber. Marie's note had indicated it was the one part of the house she hadn't been able to enter.

My cell.

It had been furnished comfortably enough. Long ago I might have mistaken that for kindness on Alphonse's part, rather than his need to keep up the appearance, for successive generations of his family, that I was a distant widowed cousin whose overpowering grief had caused the loss of her reason— someone for whom he provided and cared. Not his prisoner, his blood supply, his personal monster.

He would always tell them some of the truth: he was powerful and blessed with enduring youth. Then came the lie: he would share his magic with them when the time was right. In exchange, they would protect him and his secrets, permit him everything, and never question him, not even about the strange woman who lived in the tower.

I mounted the first step. The whole structure shook alarmingly. Far above and outside, something tumbled from a height. Slate from the roof, or a stone from the window arch.

When the rumble subsided, voices echoed down the stairwell.

"No! I hate you! You never loved me!"

That shriek would be Marie.

Alphonse's more subdued response was impossible to make out. There was another sound, though, one that I thought might be fists pounding a wooden door.

The house was still resisting him, protecting Marie. He was battering down her door and demanding control of the magic. If neither Alphonse nor Marie let go of their claim, the walls were going to crumble. The whole house was going to break apart.

The top of a tall tower was a remarkably unwise location to have such a fight. That truth seemed to have escaped their notice. It did not escape mine, but I had come here to kill Alphonse and to die. If the walls came down on us, so long as we had both become mortal first, I did not care.

Alphonse's fists slammed rhythmically into the door above. The tower swayed.

In such chaos, it was easy to move silently. The stone chilled the soles of my aching feet. I climbed.

As I approached, it became easier—no, it became possible to hear his voice. Not easier, not easy. Merely possible.

"Open this door or I will bring this tower down!"

"And kill both of us?" Marie asked. "I don't believe you, you lying roach. You want to live. That's all you want. What a coward you are, scared of death! Let me introduce you!"

The hinges creaked as the door opened. Something heavy scraped across the floor and slammed into a wall.

I heard no shout or grunt from Alphonse, so either he'd died instantly (too much to hope for) or he'd dodged whatever Marie had pushed at him. She was too small to move such a great weight, so she must have worked out how to use the house to do it.

Something came crashing down the staircase. As the next few stairs brought me around a turn, I stepped over splintered chunks of an armoire. I recognized it and its contents, all disgorged down the stairs: half-rotted, moth-eaten dresses, and one disintegrating book.

A couple of stray pages slipped down the stairs. In large type, the Veneto word <u>Lettere</u> stared up at me. Alphonse's published love letters to an anonymous lady. The long-ago origin of our catastrophic romance, printed in a language I'd almost forgotten, kept in that armoire as a memento. Or a punishment. Had they held any true sentiment?

It no longer mattered. I stepped over them.

Quickly but cautiously, wary of more hurled furniture, I took the stairs. Alphonse had breached the threshold of the room by the time I arrived. His sword was pointed at Marie. The bed—its wooden frame, rather, the mattress and linens draped across it in ragged decay—blocked his advance. Marie was across the room, her palm planted on the wall, staring him down. Dressed in the same clothes she'd been wearing in the vision, now dirt- and sweat-stained, with exhaustion dragging at her features, she looked like spite alone was keeping her upright. Against the pale grey stone of the wall, her brownish red fingers stood out.

Her other hand was wrapped around the neck of a wine bottle.

Any time Alphonse moved left or right, the bed shifted to block him; the floor rippled like water and pulled it along. Alphonse made a choked noise of rage in the back of his throat, and the room shook. Outside, more debris clattered against the tower wall and landed in the muddy ground below with a muted thump.

Marie could have glimpsed me if she were not so transfixed by Alphonse. Perhaps it was taking all of her concentration to keep him away. The floor shifting and buckling beneath him every time he moved unsettled me. My mind revolted against what it deemed impossible, and I could not look for more than an instant.

He paced to the wall, slapped a hand against it, and roared, "I am your master."

Whether the house could hear or understand that was unclear to me. He jumped on the bed. The last of the mattress gave up, and so did the wooden slats beneath. They cracked and dropped him to the floor. He withstood the shock.

Marie bit her lip and closed her eyes. If it was a silent plea to Songecreux to send Alphonse crashing through the floor, it went unanswered. Jumping to the center of the bed had brought him within range. She was backed against the wall as if trying to sink into it. The house had saved me like that earlier, but Alphonse must be preventing it now. He drew back his sword arm and made a straight, unstoppable thrust through her belly.

She screamed. Red wet the edges of her dress around his sword. Then she opened her eyes and began to laugh. It was a gasping cackle. She shook with it, and so did the bottle in her hand, and so did the tower.

"A nightmare for you, too," she said to Alphonse and then grinned at me.

He whipped around. The sight of me startled him, but he couldn't attack. Marie was still impaled with his sword.

She gripped the blade with one hand, heedless of the blood and the pain, and pulled it out. Some of her came with it. The metal glistened with viscera.

Alphonse, who'd never taken his hand from the hilt, stared down for an instant, disgusted. Then he swept the blade through the air, leapt over the bed frame, and attacked me.

This time I was ready to parry.

While we fought, Marie collapsed into a slow slide down

the wall. Once supported by the floor, she pressed her bloodied hand to it.

"House," she said, and pain had blurred her edges. She closed her eyes. "Songecreux. My blood's not much compared to what you're used to, but it's worth something to me."

I couldn't watch her. I had to watch Alphonse. Her voice was quiet under the click and scrape of our swords, but she did not stop speaking. What had happened to the bottle in her hand? Was it empty?

"So here, with the last of this blood that connects me to the family that built this place, that lived and died here, as their final heir and the rightful owner of this place, I command you to help Isabelle de Tourzin." This said, she dragged an exhalation from her throat, then added, in the barest wisp of a voice, "I think you were going to anyway, but now you have my permission."

I had suspected Songecreux was helping me, and still it stunned me that Marie had perceived the same thing. A roar rose in the back of my mind and a sudden awareness prickled all over my body, especially through the bare soles of my feet. The house. The walls and floor and roof, the stone and mortar and wood, all of it pulsing with magic.

I could feel Alphonse, too, pulling it away from me. Choking it.

That power coursing around and through us distracted me, and he nearly speared me in the gut. The wound would not have killed me, but spilling more of my blood in this house—or within his reach—would do other kinds of damage. I could not fence and control the house's magic at the same time, and I only knew how to do one of those things well.

<u>Do what you will</u>, I said to Songecreux in a silent prayer, and let go.

Alphonse felt it, I think. His eyes widened. He stumbled

backward a step. In better condition, he could have seized all the power I'd relinquished. It was too much for him. Our swords went still as the air around us shivered and exploded. A dam broke and the room filled up with magic. Invisible, but tangible as tremors. The stones in the walls began to crumble and even to melt. (Writing this, I do not know if that was a vision or the truth.)

In a panic, I thought: I chose wrong. I shouldn't have unleashed this. This house I'd always hated and feared, how could I expect it to protect me? We were all going to be flattened in the rubble. I'd never know for sure if I'd definitively ended Alphonse's life. It was too late to regain control.

Alphonse recovered from his shock and lunged for me, and then we were fighting again. He scored wounds in my chest and my belly. The pain overtook me for a moment, a screaming, burning thing. I retreated farther than I meant to —something was wrong with the floor. Then my next attack had to cover more ground, but I must have misjudged the distance. I arrived too soon, and off balance, and he batted my sword away with ease.

A low quaking rumble gathered above us. A rafter crashed down. It nearly hit Alphonse and me, but we both threw ourselves out of its path just in time. Marie yelped—my only sign that she still lived. A chunk of wood hit my cheek. It could have come from the beam itself or the bed frame; the rafter had crushed it. Those beams look so much bigger, lying on the ground.

Had I caused that? Had he? Was the house simply falling to pieces? I couldn't tell. There was no time to think further, not with Alphonse's sword hurtling toward me.

It was a difficult, nasty fight, made worse by the scattered lumber and the floor, sloshing beneath our feet like water, thickening and thinning. The strangeness made me wish for my boots, little though they might have done to protect me.

At least my feet would have been free of the unnatural, sludgy sensation of the stone. I glanced down once and glimpsed the stairs below.

Alphonse snarled in frustration. The house was making itself an obstacle to him—slowing his steps, sending each attack ever so slightly astray—and he always hated to lose.

Let me get close enough, I begged the house in my mind. _I will be in your debt_. What it might mean to indebt myself to a magical house with its own inscrutable will was a problem for later. I would be dead by then.

My bargain was inadequate or unheard. The house did not deliver me sword-first into Alphonse. We danced back and forth, the tower rocking like a ship. My fingers ached from gripping my sword, and my gloves had grown damp with sweat. Either I would exhaust his strength or the tower would fall. He would not win.

He bent as if to lunge. Marie popped up behind him and smashed the wine bottle into his head. Drops of blood flew from the open neck, but the heavy bottom of the bottle did not break. Alphonse's eyes rolled back and he wobbled. I seized my moment and buried my sword in him.

Marie collapsed backward. Her body fell softly and passively. It made no sound as it met the stone that cradled it.

I speared Alphonse and pinned him against the wall. The stone might have been sloughing off in thick layers of grey ooze, but it was solid enough for my purposes. All I needed was one instant of stillness.

He recovered consciousness as I dug in my pocket for the sponge. "Do you really think that will kill me?" he rasped. "Others have tried. You have tried. Maybe I've drunk so much of your blood that we're the same now. Maybe we'll both live forever. Why kill me, Isabelle? You used to want forever with me. We still could. Kiss me. Let me bite your lip."

"You wanted forever, but not with me," I reminded him. I squeezed the sponge hard. Its weight was so slight and my gloves made it impossible to feel its texture. I needed to know it was real.

"That was a mistake, Isabelle. I missed you, you know. I loved you. I still do. Nobody else has ever compared. We could have it again—our life in Venice. We could go back."

"That wound might not kill you," I said, almost close enough that he could realize his threat of a kiss and a bite, "but this will."

I dragged the sponge across his neck—following that strange, mottled discoloration where Victor had cut him— like I was wiping away blood.

The tower heaved like a battering ram had run into it. Shock ricocheted through all my senses.

Alphonse greyed, went cold and limp, slumped backward, pinned between my sword and the wall. His head sheared off his neck and fell forward onto my hand. I yanked my arm back in fear and revulsion. His head thumped to the floor. The sponge bounced silently after it.

There was less blood than there should have been. It feels strange to describe that small detail as unsettling, when the whole affair was more than one lifetime's worth of horror, but it was as horrible as the lifeless weight of his head landing on my hand. The dull press of his corpse's lips against my glove, a mockery of courtly charm.

Bile crept up my throat. I shuddered, sickened and relieved, my mind and body in terrible confusion. My pulse did not slow.

Less blood than expected, and less difficulty, too. My gloves had been a trivial precaution, and yet they'd permitted me to use the sponge without touching it. I'd thought they would be slashed or torn in the fight, or that I'd have to resort to trickery, like losing the duel and hiding the sponge between my breasts or my legs. Never in all my imaginings of this fight had I included my own survival.

That thought made me turn to the other person who might have unexpectedly survived.

Marie had not yelped in terror when Alphonse's head had landed. She was prone on the floor a few steps away, the glass bottle she'd wielded so precisely still in her hand. I crouched to check her pulse, though there was little need. She was gone. I knew she was gone.

Tears sprang to my eyes.

She'd done terrible violence for Alphonse, but so had I. With more time away from him, more life, who could say what she would have become? A better person, perhaps even a good one. Such hope felt foreign and unnatural in my thoughts—she might well have lived to become a worse person—but I could not deny its presence. If she retained the barest trace of life, if it had been within my power to revive her, I think I would have offered her that chance. She'd helped me.

Had I learned nothing? Would I make my worst mistake a second time?

Marie prevented me; her skin was cooling. Too much time had passed for me to help her. I could not know what further life she might have lived, and it was not my choice to make. There was both sorrow and relief in that.

I pried the bottle from her hand to turn it upside down, but not one drop slid out.

The tower was trembling continuously now. It groaned painfully and began to lean. The room slid into a dizzying, perilous tilt. I needed to run. Far behind me, another rafter struck the floor. The reverberation nearly knocked me over. To catch myself, I threw out my arms and planted my heels.

The sponge squashed under my bare foot.

PRIVATE DIARY OF C. F., MAY 9, 1825

WRITTEN IN AN INVENTED SHORTHAND

I was sweating and panting by the time I finally stomped up to Songecreux in Isabelle's boots. The whole climb, I'd kept that compass in my hand, its quivering little needle pointing the way. That had to mean she was alive, I kept telling myself. It was entirely possible that the compass could and would lead me to her corpse, but I couldn't think about that. It wouldn't help me get up the hill. Hope was as good as fresh air in my lungs.

Delphine, wherever you are, I love your compass.

The house was a falling-down old pile of stones, no matter the new front door and repairs to a few sections of the roof, if one could even call it a roof. Huge swaths of the building lay open to the sky or to the green-brown tangle of vines crawling through. It was a worn-out, lonely place, settled on that hilltop like a toothless old mastiff curling up to rest his aching bones.

This state of abandonment endeared Songecreux to me immediately. It reminded me of Les Feuillantines, crumbling profaned convent, secret wilderness in the heart of Paris, sacred hiding place for rule-breaking nuns and shapeshifting orphans. The city tore out the overgrown garden and reorganized the stones into something cleaner and squarer and easier to categorize. I've never stopped missing it, and I suppose now I have a soft spot for ruins.

Even ones that are rattling like the lid of a pot about to boil over.

It wasn't natural. The hillside trembled beneath my feet. It should've been the earth shaking the house, even I knew that much, but it wasn't. The house was the origin. Anybody in possession of their reason would've sprinted the other way. Unfortunately for me, my head and heart had a crack running right through. Delirious affection for this malevolently haunted old château aside, I was furious and exhausted and driven by a consuming need to find Isabelle. Like hell I was going to let her die.

As I stepped up to the door, the house boomed like thunder. I could hear creaks and slams from within as the whole place swayed and groaned. Before I even touched the front door, it swung open.

The entrance had a new roof and was dark inside. All the stirred-up dust made me sneeze. There was a hint of something metallic in the air. At the base of the grand staircase, a tremor nearly knocked me down, and that was as good a time as any to sink to my knees. I put my hand to the floor and, since this entire endeavor was a flight of fancy, talked to the house.

"Hello," I began softly. "You let me in."

My eyesight went all blurry and dark and I think maybe I fainted for a second. My head hurt. I woke up face-down on the stone with a new piece of knowledge lodged in my brain: my comb was lying on the floor of the master bedroom, at the end of the wing to my left. The tremors had sent it clattering down from the table next to the bed.

The house had given me a vision of sorts. Isabelle had

said it would give me nightmares, but this wasn't that. If it was true—and I believed it was—then it was useful information. Receiving it had knocked me flat, which didn't bode well for future conversation, but I wasn't done asking questions.

Dizzy and hoarse, I said, "Yes, that's mine. You recognized me."

I wanted the comb badly. Last night's unplanned change of shape and this morning's discovery that I couldn't shift at will had only sharpened my desire. My whole body ached with yearning. I could almost feel myself running through the hall to sweep it off the floor and clutch it to my chest. The house had shown me exactly where to go. I'd lost years of my life searching for it and traveled hundreds and hundreds of kilometers to arrive here.

But the comb could probably be dug out of the rubble intact, if it came to that.

I wasn't so sure about Isabelle.

"Thank you for showing it to me." My voice shook. The floor vibrated beneath me. Somewhere off to my right, I thought, something heavy fell. To prevent myself from hitting the floor face-first again, I lay my cheek against the stone. "But I need to find Isabelle. You... hurt each other in the past, maybe, but I think you saved her once before, on the night of the fire. Would you help me?"

Another distant crash.

I lost consciousness anew and dreamed in brief glimpses: Isabelle wiping blood from the foyer steps, Isabelle walking through doors that swung open before she touched them, Isabelle climbing a spiral staircase with her sword in hand. A round tower. To my right, where all the violent crashes were coming from.

"Thank you." I pressed both palms into the floor and pushed myself up, blinking to clear my vision of dark spots.

My skull felt like a drum. I staggered to my feet and sprinted toward Isabelle.

Where there were doors—where the wood hadn't been scavenged or destroyed—they hung as open as the roof above my head. Evening sunlight lit my way. Dead leaves littered the stone and rustled with every quake of the floor. There were endless lengths of it, room after empty room. The house was too big and I was flagging.

My body no longer felt new after the long walk from the cave. After such grueling practice using my legs, they didn't feel foreign. They did feel short, though. If I hadn't spent months wishing to be shorter, if I'd kept my height and my long legs, would that tiny advantage have carried me there in time?

It's no use asking that kind of question. If I hadn't changed in my sleep, Isabelle might not have left me there. Maybe she would've done that regardless, but seeing me change without the comb made her think I didn't need it anymore.

She thinks I don't need her, either, and she's wrong about that, too.

The house was rolling from side to side like a riverboat in a storm. Here and there stones would fall from the roofless walls. I never had to dodge one. The house protected me, I'd swear to it. I ran and the rocks tumbled down behind me.

Sometimes the stone under my boots or in the walls ahead stretched or shifted or melted, which is impossible, but so am I. Dominique had told that story about the house absorbing him and pushing him into the cellar to find Isabelle, and she had some idea that the house responded to its owners and makers. As I ran, it was being pulled in different directions. Isabelle had counted herself among the makers. She must be fighting Malbosc for control.

Songecreux had helped me so far, but it was falling apart. Whose orders would it obey in the end?

The next shock through the house tripped me. The fall ripped a side seam in my poor, overworked trousers. My knees poked right through the threadbare stuff. Normal stone would've scraped and bloodied them and my palms too, but it was like falling into mud or wet cement. I pushed myself to standing, hitched up my clothes, wiped stone sludge from my hands, and finally arrived at the base of the round tower. A few broken pieces of wood and chipped stone had been cast down the stairs. Dirty footprints followed them up.

Isabelle.

I made it up fourteen steps before the tower jolted and I was thrown against—no, <u>through</u> the wall.

The house expelled me. It spat me out so hard that I flew horizontally, for long enough that I had time to realize what had happened and spread my arms and legs. My landing in the soft slope of the hillside didn't break my bones, but it did punch the air from my lungs. The unobstructed sky, once I'd rolled over and blinked enough to see it, felt like a vision.

And then the tower came down.

I was far enough away—and well enough to run farther— to see it. The conical roof caved in. The top, already leaning, slanted dangerously to one side. A storm of masonry and lumber pelted the ground. First a few identifiable pieces and then suddenly an uncountable onslaught. The sound was so huge I heard it through every pore in my skin. A burst of stone dust clouded the air and my nostrils.

Afterward there was nothing left where the tower had stood, not even a little ring of foundation like a hollow stump. The spot was flattened. All the stones had been dumped in scattered heaps.

I'd watched for bodies in the fall but couldn't make out anything. When I walked closer to the wreckage, the first thing I saw was an unidentifiable pulp. A smear of wet, pink meat, held together in some places by scraps of skin or clothing, but no longer shaped by any recognizable bones, mostly buried under an immovable heap of rock. It smelled like blood and shit. I managed not to heave, but barely.

Nearby lay another, smaller pile of stone, with a similar, smaller mess of bone and blood under it, except this time there was more greyish pink spread through it. Sickeningly dizzy and detached from the carnage in front of me, I thought: a head.

Beyond that was a woman's body, but not Isabelle's. Marie Reynaud was remarkably intact. I could tell she'd been killed with a sword, and I wondered who had wielded it.

Two bodies. Heart in my throat, I wended my way through the debris. Would there be a third? I thought of the landslide, and wondered if I had the strength left to dig Isabelle out again. I would find it if I had to.

And then I stepped around a towering mass of broken beams and stone, and there she was. Not in pieces. Not buried.

It turned out I still had the strength to run.

I dived toward her. Her chest lifted with slow and difficult breath, but it lifted all the same. She was filthy with blood and dirt, unfocused and unmoving, but she was alive.

It was then that I noticed how bizarrely clear it was around her. Stones lay almost in a circle, none close enough to touch. Nothing but muddy grass was beneath her.

I glanced up at the house, intact but for its lost tower, as silent and still as any old building.

"Céleste," Isabelle rasped. Her eyes were closed. "I didn't want—you to see this—"

"You fucking left me!"

My shouting had no effect on her. Doggedly, with the remnant of her voice, she continued, "The sponge—"

"I know, I know, Dominique told me," I said, still angry but unable to shout at her while she was wounded. "Are you too hurt to move? Christ, you're bleeding everywhere— Isabelle, why aren't you healing?"

"The sponge, you—find. Don't touch."

Her face went slack. That was when I put it together: Isabelle had touched the sponge. Just like she'd said in her awful letter. She'd touched it and lost her ability to heal. Now she was severely wounded and didn't expect to survive. That was what she hadn't wanted me to see.

She thought these were her last words.

I was moved to tenderness and anger at the same time. She was using her last breath to protect me. But I didn't want it to be her last breath. There were some words she hadn't said to me, not even in her goddamn goodbye letter, that I was still yearning to hear.

"Isabelle." My voice broke into a sob as I said it. I dashed tears from my eyes. The sponge wasn't anywhere I could see, and I didn't have time to check every last centimeter of mud and overgrowth. I threw my pack down and tossed clothes and knives and food and journals on the ground until I found the little leather case I was looking for.

Two tiny vials of her blood. I poured them into her mouth and she coughed and didn't argue. I hoped they were enough.

We sat in pained silence. Either a little color came back into her face or I was hallucinating. That made me wonder about the house, about how far its power extended—if it still had power.

When Isabelle's limbs twitched erratically, the way some people's do in sleep, I finally let myself cradle her head in my lap. I'd been waiting for her to heal a little before I moved her.

Also I'd been doubting and fighting myself, because I wanted to touch her and comfort her and tell her I was in love with her, but I was so fucking angry, and if she told me she didn't deserve any of that, my love or my anger, I'd probably burst into tears and start a fight, and I was too tired and she was almost dead. So instead, once I was sure she couldn't argue, I held her in my lap until the night air chilled us both, and then I carried her into the house.

It would've been smart to hunt down my comb and get a lot bigger first. Also to light some candles and map where we were going. As this journal proves, I'm not smart. The only thing in my head was not leaving her. So I scooped her up and started walking. In my short, ungainly way, stopping every so often to shift her weight and gasp for air, I managed the journey without further damaging either of us.

If Isabelle ever asks me how she got into bed, I'm going to tell her I moved with grace and confidence. My usual effortless brilliance.

The house took care of the brilliance—it's definitely still magic. The floor pulled me right along and I didn't trip once. The candles in the bedroom were lit before we arrived.

As for the bed, there was only one in the place. I knew who'd been sleeping there, and I felt more disgusted about touching those fine sheets than I ever have about sleeping in a doorway or a cave. But it wouldn't be the first time for either me or Isabelle.

Besides, he was dead.

When Isabelle was settled, I checked the floor for my comb. It was exactly where the house had indicated.

"Thank you," I whispered.

The house didn't answer.

The wood felt so small and light in my hand. Flat against my chest, it probably left parallel lines pressed into my skin from how long I held it there. The temptation to shift almost overwhelmed me, and if I hadn't been so tired, I'd have done it.

She opened her eyes when I crawled into bed. Sleepy and confused, probably still in terrible pain, with only a single candle lit and me in a shape she'd only seen once, she murmured, "Céleste."

That recognition made me feel tender—soft in both sentiment and flesh, bruised, defenseless. I couldn't think of anything to say except, "Yes?"

"I'm sorry—"

"You should be," I said. "I would rather die than wear one of your dresses."

We are both alive.

Glad to hear it.

Could you do me a favor? I need you to go to a brothel called Florine's and ask for Louise Dubois. Tell her "Céleste cheated death again."

I'm not in the habit of going to brothels, but I'm grateful to you for saving Isabelle. I'll find this Louise of yours.

Thank you. She's not—she's my sister, you understand?

*An interesting message to send to one's sister. You don't, by chance,
frequent Brasserie La Fortune?*

I used to. Tell Louise I'll be home in a few weeks.

PRIVATE DIARY OF ISABELLE DE TOURZIN, MAY 12, 1825
WRITTEN ON ENCRYPTED PAPER

My head hurts. Unnecessary precision: all of me hurts. But the ache in my head has prevented me from continuing my account.

My last entry stopped after I stepped on the sponge. The tower collapsed after that. I should have died, but Songecreux and Céleste conspired to keep me alive.

A thousand wordless sentiments churn within me; recording them seems impossible. I was initially relieved to see Céleste. Happy. It was a pure and thoughtless reaction, occurring first in my wounded body and arriving gradually in my blurred mind. Uncontaminated by past or future, wrong or right, living or dying, it floated free in the present: Céleste is here. I like it when Céleste is here.

She'd kept the shape she'd made for herself while asleep in the cave, the one I'd gazed at while writing my farewell. I did not think of my letter while lying on the ground; I did not think of anything but what was right in front of me, which was Céleste with a frizzed halo of brown hair. The length of it had once been braided, and half still retained that shape. The rest was windblown or plastered to her neck with sweat. Her cheeks were pink from sun and exertion. She had eschewed my offered dress and worn her own clothes, though the trousers were splitting at the hips, ripped at the knees, and rolled several times at the ankles. Her shirt, formerly white, would have billowed, hung to her knees, or slipped off her shoulders in other circumstances, but it was trapped under her suspenders, the straps of her pack, and the strained waistband of her trousers. The damp linen clung to her unbound breasts. It was rude of me to stare, but I was half dead. Etiquette was beyond me. So was stopping.

She stepped closer, her boots sinking into the ground. My boots, I thought, and felt a wash of obscure tenderness. The exact sequence of events that had led her to wear my boots was lost to me. I knew only that it was Céleste, who warmed me like the sun, and something of mine was touching her. Whatever had happened, a simple truth lay at its core. If Céleste needed boots, then I would go barefoot.

Barefoot—that brought it all back. I'd stepped on the sponge. It was like opening a door in a gale and letting the howling wind of pain back into my body, the outlines of which were unclear to me. I remembered the sensation of the sponge under my heel, but could not seem to locate my heel, or my foot, or my leg, or move. Anything beyond mute and immobile admiration of Céleste was agony. A last glimpse of beauty and a quick slide into oblivion was better than I deserved, and as much as I yearned for the latter, I knew I had to warn her about the sponge.

Speech disturbed my wounded torso. It was blazingly painful.

She shouted at me, I think. My memory is hazy. She poured those two vials of my blood—a gift for her, never meant for me—down my throat, and then I lost consciousness. She must have carried me to the bed where I now find myself.

Perhaps her need to carry me explains her change in shape. When I woke, she looked as she had during the rest of our journey: tall with short auburn hair. The same hard-used linen shirt covered a flatter chest and broader shoulders than yesterday's.

"Céleste?"

A pair of strong arms lifted me until I was seated nearly upright, supported by a mountain of pillows. Moving, or rather, being moved brought all my aches to the forefront of my mind. I leaned back and willed the pain to subside so I could participate in the conversation that was flowing by.

"You're awake. It's finally my turn to bring you breakfast in bed. The larder's surprisingly well stocked. Maybe not surprising, if you're accustomed to luxury. The house told me Malbosc hired some servants when he and his bride first got here—I would've known that anyway, there's no way he cleaned that kitchen himself—but it only took a few days before everyone quit in fear."

I only half-listened to that and spared not a glance at the tray. "You changed... back?"

"Did I?"

My mind was cobwebbed. Was Céleste's voice different? Was anything else? I squinted. "You shaved?"

"Saved myself the trouble," she said, dragging a finger along the smooth skin of her jaw, then yanking down the open collar of her shirt to show me her hairless chest—and the beginning of a slight curve that might have been muscle or breast. "I'm a woman. Unless any strangers come by. Act like I'm a man then. I only have the one set of clothes that fit, so I'm working within that constraint."

She poked at a rip in the side seam of her trousers, briefly exposing a flash of skin.

A moment from last night returned to me. "Because you

would rather die than wear one of my dresses. Do you wear trousers regardless of your shape? Do you not like dresses?"

"I <u>love</u> dresses," she said. "That's why I can't wear yours."

"Last night, I was trying to apologi—"

"Neither of us has the constitution for that right now, Isabelle," she said, sitting on the bed. "We're both exhausted, and I have to go do something about the remains."

"Marie," I murmured. Her life, so shaped by Malbosc's control, had been cut short. "She... helped me, I think."

In every shape, Céleste is expressive: her brows lifted, then furrowed. She chewed her bottom lip. After some consternation, she said, "I'll bury her, if you want."

"Thank you."

Céleste nudged the breakfast she'd brought me. "You need to heal. Don't argue. Eat."

From the tray, I learned a great deal. First, Céleste had been awake for some time. Second, Céleste could cook. Third, something was still very wrong with me. My arms were heavy, my grip weak and trembling. I would have dumped a full cup of coffee on myself if Céleste hadn't caught it.

The coffee splashed her, but was no longer hot enough to burn. She brought her hand to her mouth to clean the base of her thumb. The gesture looked very much like a kiss, but I tried (failed) not to think about that. Céleste did not want an apology from me, so it seemed highly unlikely she wanted anything else. My body was in no condition, besides.

Why had she bothered to save me? Alphonse was dead, my task complete. I could have died quietly, without disturbing anyone, if she had only left me alone. Now I was alive with no aim, and worse—or it felt that way in the moment—I was an inconvenience to her.

"Let's try that again," she said and, to my horror, held the cup to my lips. When I kept my mouth closed, she must have assumed ignorance of her intent, rather than outright refusal, because she said, "Drink."

Lips sealed together, I shook my head.

"Isabelle," she said. The cup clinked against its porcelain saucer. She picked up a fork and a knife and began to slice the omelette she'd made into small, precise bites. "You fucking turnip. I am <u>angry</u> with you. I understand if you haven't figured that out yet, due to almost dying yesterday and still being a mess today, but that's why I'm telling you now. You have two choices. One, you can continue to be difficult, in which case I will not fuck off and leave you, because I don't do that to people I lo—like. Not when they're in trouble. I'll stay, even though both of us will be a foul mood. Or two, you can accept that I came here to save you, and I am still doing that, and you can <u>let</u> me. You'll be in bed for a while yet, so you'll have some time to think about what it means that I dragged myself all this way for you even though I'm very angry and you are, like I said, a fucking turnip. Maybe you'll figure it out."

While making this speech, she methodically dissected the entire omelette. She stabbed a piece with the fork and then brought it to hover in front of my face. A challenge.

She was angry. She had every right to be. I'd abandoned her. Still, a feverish chill raced over my skin at being told her feelings so bluntly—and at what she was asking me to do. Nothing, essentially. She'd rejected my first attempt at an apology. Instead she wanted me to lie here—as if I was capable of anything else—and open my mouth.

It did not feel like nothing. That feverish chill turned warm and slow, climbing inexorably up my neck and cheeks. My body, a swamp of pain and exhaustion, experienced a brief, passing ripple of something else.

She was disarmingly handsome. This close, I could appreciate everything she'd kept the same, like the lines at the corners of her eyes and the strands of silver through her auburn hair, and what she'd changed, like the smooth line of her throat and her beardless face. The signs of age meant more to me now that I knew how she cherished her version of beauty—the particular, the irregular. Though her lips were pressed together in impatience, I could guess that she'd preserved the tiny gap between her front teeth.

I wished she was asking me for sex. Even as tired and weak as I was, if she'd demanded that I spread my legs or put my tongue between hers, I would have done it. No matter how physically difficult, that would have been easy. Sex, I understood. I could make amends for having wronged her; I could take care of her.

Instead, she was asking to care for me.

Even though I'd left her. Even though she was angry. She was right that I didn't understand why she had come. In Paris, there would be younger, prettier, easier, sunnier, sweeter, more amusing lovers. Less troubled, less violent, less brooding.

But here she was. And if Céleste needed boots, I would go barefoot. If she wanted me to eat, I would eat.

With as much meekness as I could muster, I parted my lips for her. She fed me. She was a good cook, I think, though it was hard to sense anything other than the burning of my cheeks. I hate being incapacitated. The physical state might be temporary, but it served to underline my newly permanent uselessness. My goal achieved, what purpose was there to my life? Céleste should be on her way back to Paris to see her sister. She had better things to do than sit beside me and hold a fork to my lips.

Her behavior gave no hint of that. Patient and utterly at ease, she lifted my chin with a caress of two fingers. This gesture had no discernible necessity. She touched me. It changed the angle of my face so our eyes met. There was unexpected warmth in hers, though I could not reasonably expect her anger to have dissipated in mere minutes, or for my own status to have been raised from the ignominious depth of <u>fucking turnip</u>.

Having touched me, she could not seem to stop. She tucked a strand of hair behind my ear, where it joined the wild mass crushed between my head and the pile of pillows. She brushed the cap of my shoulder and pushed aside my loose collar to examine the pink, fading trace of the puncture Malbosc had given me during our first, interrupted fight. The wounds I'd suffered in our second duel were not in such an advanced state, but they were healing. I could, both fortunately and unfortunately, feel all of my body. Those last two vials of my blood had saved me. Céleste did not lift the sheet or ask to see under my shirt. Her fingertips were cool against my flushed cheek.

"Fuck." She blinked away tears. "I'm so glad you're alive."

I felt new, different shame at that. Because my survival had been such a remote possibility, it had not occurred to me that Céleste might feel such relief. Leaving had seemed an acceptable trade—saving her life, but making her sad and angry in the process—and I had tried, in my letter, to liberate her from the burden of grief. We had enjoyed each other's company, but she did not owe me that. She did not owe me anything.

And yet here she was. Crying.

"I—" I began, as though I knew what to say to rectify my error.

"No," she said fiercely. She wiped at her eyes once more and then fed me another bite to prevent me from speaking. "No arguing, no apologizing, no justifying yourself until you've eaten. I'm making the decisions now."

Chastised, I nodded and accepted another forkful. No longer embarrassed at my own weakness, but instead ashamed that I'd hurt her, being fed transformed for me from a humiliation that I was grudgingly enduring into an act of contrition. Though if Céleste had wanted to humiliate me further, I would have let her. If my discomfort had brought her satisfaction, I would have made every effort to return to it, to prolong and increase it.

She did not seem to want my suffering, merely my compliance. It became easier and easier to offer that, to lean forward and wrap my lips around the fork or the rim of the cup. It became easier, too, to notice the scent of the coffee, the richness of the omelette, the closeness of her fingers to my mouth. Over the course of breakfast, she settled more fully on the bed, letting her hip touch my leg. She canted toward me. I savored her presence. The inviting brown warmth of her eyes, the faint constellations of freckles on her cheekbones. I had not thought I would see her again in any shape.

By the end we were within kissing distance, though we did not kiss. I had not earned it, I knew. But if suffering wasn't the solution, and compliance wasn't sufficient, then what did she want from me?

After the last sip of coffee, I said, "I might be well enough to feed myself the rest."

"Maybe," she allowed, and it was the first time I'd seen her smile since I'd woken. It was wickedly sharp. "But I'm enjoying this. A powerful woman at my mercy."

I had not thought I would live long enough for her to tease me again. In that light, even the inevitable heat in my face was welcome. And her words did confirm for me that I was not alone in thinking longingly of the sex we were not going to have. Céleste, as a man or a woman, is an incorrigible coquette. Being angry with me was not enough to stop her.

"You're mean," I told her, repeating something she'd said

to me in the cave. My imitation of her voice was poor, but recognition sparked in her eyes. "I knew you'd be mean."

"Don't get too excited. After breakfast, I'm going out and you're going back to sleep."

"Céleste," I said in a more serious tone. "I regret leaving you in the cave. I really am sorry."

"Good," she said, though my cursory apology had crushed our fragile rapport. She edged away from me so we were no longer touching. "But that's not all I need to hear."

She picked up the tray. Instead of standing, she placed it in her lap and fiddled with the handle of the empty coffee cup. The plate was empty as well. So was the glass of water. There was nothing of importance, nothing to study, and yet she did not lift her gaze.

"I will stay until you are well," she said, as though she had come to a decision. "After that, if you... Well, sometimes a silence speaks for itself. So I might—I might have to go."

Whatever she needed to hear, if I did not say it, she would not stay. I swallowed and blinked away some sudden wetness. It was good that she was not looking at me.

I had prepared myself for a future in which Céleste returned to Paris to live free of Malbosc's long shadow—to find someone who could love her whole, as I'd written. It was what she deserved. I had not thought I would live long enough to see it.

Here we were. Both alive. It would be best to let things take their natural course. I did not know what to say to make her stay, and there was little point to investigating. She needed to leave to begin the rest of her life. I should let her.

"Of course," I said. "I am grateful for your rescue, but you have no obligation to me. Do as you see fit."

She hit me with a swift, stinging glance, but said only, "You should rest."

After breakfast, she put my journal within reach and left. I am not sure whether I was telling the truth about being grateful to her for my life. It did not seem, at that moment or at this present one, that I had much to look forward to.

PRIVATE DIARY OF C. F., MAY
12, 1825
WRITTEN IN AN INVENTED
SHORTHAND

I buried Marie Reynaud for Isabelle.

I thought I would have to hike down into the village to steal—borrow—a shovel, but luckily I found one in the abandoned tools and materials in front of the house.

It rained early this morning, so there's less of Malbosc. Some vultures were circling. I decided to let them pick at what's left instead of burying it. Feeding vultures will be one of the only useful things he's done with himself, and I'm tired. I did strip what clothes I could find and search the area for anything he might have been carrying, in case he had other stolen artifacts, but all I found was the sponge.

I almost missed it. It was under a pile of stones. All the other stones had, I think, retained a little of the house's magic, and they were weirdly easy to move. Lighter than they should have been. The only way I can think to explain it is that the house was still helping me, even though the tower was in pieces. The magic is more of a whisper than a shout now, and I haven't had any visions. It made tidying up and checking for remains and lost artifacts go a lot faster, and it was sort of... companionable, even if the house wasn't saying anything. I made stacks when the rocks were flat enough to allow for it and hardly broke a sweat.

This pile, though, was heavy. It was foolish to be alarmed by rocks—unmagical rocks—but I had a suspicion of what might have left them that way.

Isabelle had warned me about the sponge when I'd found her, but it hadn't fallen anywhere near her in the wreckage, and I'd only had time to check around the two of us. I'd been too focused on saving her to do more. I don't know what would have happened to me if I'd touched it. An involuntary shape change, maybe, but to what, I couldn't say. From the time I created my comb to the moment Malbosc stole it, I lived in flux. Sister Marie-Agnès and Sister Angélique called me a boy's name as a child, and I was blond, but the idea of that person, grown to adulthood without magic, is unthinkable. A stranger. I can recognize myself in dozens of different shapes, but not that one.

I picked up the sponge with the shovel, keeping it a good distance away.

Even though I have the comb now and could likely heal myself, it makes me feel sick to contemplate getting tricked and trapped again, or touching the sponge by accident, or enduring any change that wasn't my choice.

Isabelle understood that. She saved me.

The tenderness that wells up in me when I think of that —Isabelle using what she thought was her dying breath to spare me pain—drains away quickly enough when I remember that she didn't protest or plead at all when I told her I might have to leave. She accepted so fast it hurts. No indication that she'd miss me, or that she'd ever want to see me again.

"You have no obligation to me," she said, like we've only

ever been tied together by need and not want. She wanted me in the cave, as a last fuck, but I want more than that.

I can't stick around to pine for somebody who doesn't love me back. As soon as she's well, I'll disappear.

PRIVATE DIARY OF ISABELLE DE TOURZIN, JUNE 12, 1825
WRITTEN ON ENCRYPTED PAPER

How strange that I was seized with such a fury to record my life when I thought it might last forever, and now that I have a fading future ahead of me, I have let a month pass without a word.

There has been nothing to say. I have felt as I did after Dominique dragged me from this place in 1794 and placed me in Sophie's care. Alive, but lifeless. Melancholy fogged my mind, but at least there was Céleste. She suffered a sort of melancholy, too, I think, though she did not say so. She was still energetic in taking care of me, and kind, and even charming. It is only that sometimes she seemed to regret it, and would withdraw into herself.

Now she has withdrawn entirely.

Quiet had pooled in the pitted floors of the house when I awoke. It hung so heavy in the air I could nearly taste it.

Yesterday evening Céleste and I took a walk around the grounds, our first where I did not feel faint or stumble into her arms, though I should have. She would still be here if I needed a steadying hand. I could have lingered in that closeness, learned it by heart, used that memory as a comfort in her absence. The ones I have are not enough.

It is unbearable naïveté to think that one more memory, or a thousand more, might soothe this ache, rather than make it worse. I must accustom myself to it, as Céleste is gone.

There is a note I have not read.

Songecreux's silence has another element: I have not had a vision since Malbosc died. The house has not twitched or trembled. Its magic is much subdued. Songecreux seems to have suffered the collapse of the old tower as a grave injury, and has, I think, been fading ever since. The sponge touched its stones, so it is a wonder that all the magic didn't leach out instantly.

"You were a powerful old beast," I found myself saying to the walls today, pressing a hand to the worn surface of the stone. "And now, here you are, much diminished, but not demolished. I knew you as my prison, a place that gave me nightmares, and couldn't see beyond that, but you were more. You had life, of a kind. A will. You saved me—once a few days ago, and once when Dominique came looking, and maybe more times than I know. Thank you."

That it was bizarre to speak to a house did not stop a certain quiver from creeping into my voice. I took a breath, but it was no help. "Well, whatever you are, only a little remains now. Hours or days or years, there will come an end. You'll only be stone and wood. Someone might live here, or no one, and these walls might stand another five centuries or fall down tomorrow. You won't know. Once, you knew everything. A torment, but also a power. To lose it is a strange sorrow, but also a relief. It was worth any cost to rid ourselves of him."

I packed my few possessions, including the sponge and Céleste's letter. My steps were light. Would it really be so easy to walk out of Songecreux? It was something I had never done under my own power.

The house was the site of so much misfortune. I will not —cannot—miss it. My departure should have inspired only relief. The thought that I would never return, or that I might not live long enough to return, and even if I did, the house as I knew it would be gone, held me at the threshold for a moment. The occasion warranted an adieu.

I laid a hand on the doorjamb and said, back into the emptiness, "To be stone and wood, or blood and bone, to know only what we can know, to last as long as we last and no more, to fall silent—there could be peace in it. For both of us."

Songecreux made no response. I closed the door behind me.

CÉLESTE TO ISABELLE, JUNE 11, 1825

WRITTEN ON THE BACK OF ISABELLE'S LETTER DATED MAY 7, LEFT ON THE BED

My turnip,

I shouldn't be telling you any of this. It's like when Sister Marie-Agnès was teaching all the kids at Les Feuillantines how to write and I let Louise copy my letters. I'm giving you the answer and you won't learn anything. But I'm impatient—even though I got us both more time.

You see that, right? He's dead and we're both alive. We could do a lot with that.

And you're mortal now. Just like me.

I keep thinking about you and Laura. How she sacrificed herself and kept you alive without asking whether you wanted that, and how that's exactly what you tried to do to me (without the immortality, though, and I do appreciate the difference). Am I doing the same thing to you now, rescuing you when you so clearly planned to die? I don't care. I'm selfish enough to want you alive. I love Laura because she let you live long enough that I could meet you.

I'm sorry I never got to meet her, but I never would've known she existed if not for you, so in a way it's like you introduced us. I hope she would've liked me. I'm vain and petty and you <u>know</u> I hold grudges. I love nothing better than dirty jokes and cheating at cards, and all my favorite people are whores.

Anyway, I see why you left me while I was asleep. It's shitty, but I have to do the same because if I wait to say good-bye, either I'll never leave or I'll never stop crying. (As you can tell from the state of this page, I've already made a start on the crying.)

So, since I'm already reminiscing about Sister Marie-Agnès and her lessons, here's a little problem for you to work out:

1. Isabelle slept with Céleste because <u>Isabelle thought it was the last fun she'd ever have before she ran off to heroically sacrifice herself</u>.
2. Céleste slept with Isabelle because ___.

Just kidding. Like I said, I did all of Louise's assignments for her, so I'll do yours, too. Let's make it even easier.

Isabelle wrote "I know some day you'll find someone who loves you whole" in a letter to Céleste, but Céleste thought he had already found that person. Who is it?

If you meant it about wanting to know the rest of my shapes, I'll be in Paris. You figure it out.

IV
PARIS AND VERNEUIL
1825

ISABELLE DE TOURZIN AND DOMINIQUE GALMICHE-VUILLEMIN, VICOMTE DE SAVIGNY, JUNE 13, 1825

WRITTEN IN A PAIR OF LINKED NOTEBOOKS

I have departed Songecreux and should arrive in Paris in two or three weeks.

> *Thank you for keeping me informed. I must say I was not expecting it, though I am relieved to know you're alive. Please call on us when you arrive. But I note that you've written "I," not "we." Is Céleste well?*

He left.

> *I'm sorry to hear that. Are you well, Isabelle?*

No.

> *I'm <u>very</u> sorry to hear that. It must be serious. Do you want me to ruin his life?*

No.

Quang has just read this page over my shoulder—nosy of him—and he said, "Oh, that's bad. Really bad. We're not prepared for this. Get Sophie." So I think I shall do just that.

Not necessary. I have no more to say on the matter.

Not to worry. Sophie will have enough to say all by herself.

*Oh, Isabelle. My Isa. Dominique tells me someone called Céleste broke
your heart, and I am terribly sorry for you. It must hurt very badly,
and there has been too much of that in your life.*

Sophie. Is anyone else reading our correspondence?

*Well, we (myself, Béatrix, Victor, Dominique and Quang) are all
gathered at Dominique's, and everyone is vibrating with eagerness to
know what you will say, but I will deny them a dramatic reading if
you wish. As for whether Dominique or Victor will read what we
write later, you can make them promise not to.*

NO READING ALOUD. And what use would a promise
be? I don't trust them.

*As well you shouldn't! V is a known book thief, and I'm informed that
our Dominique has spent some years spying on his peers and might
even have committed a little burglary. Can you believe that?*

If you mock me further, I will close the notebook and continue my journey.

In perfect earnestness: where are you? Have you eaten?

I am in Aubenas, and not in such bad condition that I require hand-feeding.

Now you are engaging in mockery—I never hand-fed you. I merely sat next to you during the worst of your melancholy and chattered until you shoved food in your mouth to avoid answering a question. But if you are eating even in the aftermath of your heartbreak, I find that very comforting.

Don't call it heartbreak.

What should I call it, then?

Nothing. There is no word for it, for something that could have happened but didn't.

Oh, I think there are many words for that, heartbreak among them. Would you like to tell me what did happen?

Only to rectify the account before the lot of you unleash your imaginations. Feel free to read this aloud. Céleste and I undertook a long journey together. We both had reason to hate Malbosc. After some time, it transpired that we did not hate each other. When we neared Songecreux, it came to me that there was no need for both of us to die, so I left Céleste and went to fight Malbosc on my own. I did not expect to survive.

I haven't forgotten your farewell notes to us, and I don't intend to let

*you forget, either. You wish you'd "spent more time in my radiance."
You promised to go to one of Béatrix's performances with me. And
twelve parties, Isabelle! A ridiculous offer. You must have been in
great distress; I won't hold you to it. I am so, so very glad you did
not die.*

That is kind of you.

*If you mean about not dragging you to the parties, fine. If you mean
that it's "kind" of me to be glad you didn't die, no it isn't. It's a genuine
sentiment. I like you, Isabelle. I always have. Even at your gloomiest.
You not believing me doesn't change the truth. It's not within your
control: I would be sad if you died.*

I will some day. I touched the sponge. I'm sorry.

Should I apologize to you for my mortality?

Of course not.

*Then neither should you. That's life, Isabelle. We love other people
even though we lose them. But now I have a pressing question. If you
touched the sponge, you can no longer heal yourself. Are you injured?*

No. Céleste did not leave until I recovered.

Céleste saved your life and cared for you, you mean.

Yes.

I haven't met Céleste, but

You have, actually. You rented rooms in the Maison Laval
at the same time. You knew him as Forestier.

I know. V told me. But I simply cannot imagine you falling in love with someone so horrible—a cop, Isabelle!—so I am choosing to believe I haven't met the real Céleste. He must be good, though, because he wanted to save your life and you let him.

I remain amazed that you can imagine me falling in love, period. We've known each other a long time.

Well, if you didn't, that must be why Céleste left. If I'd performed such an act of devotion—saving your life, risking my own, caring for you —and you felt nothing for me, I would need to leave, too.

Sophie, I'm sorry

It feels very rude to begin writing when you have clearly paused mid-sentence to think, much ruder than interrupting a conversation, but I can't let you apologize, Isabelle. It was one rejected kiss, thirty years ago, and you were correct that we weren't right for each other. You were in such turmoil, and I should never have done it, but you were remarkably gentle about my mistake. I am in love with Béatrix and honored to be your friend. But you understand that I needed some time away from you, back then? And you away from me, I presume.

Of course. But this is different.

Is it?

I will not write an account of the differences.

You don't need to, my friend. I understood when you wrote "we did not hate each other."

The purpose of this exchange is to stop you from inventing falsehoods and exaggerations.

Something I have yet to do. I have, however, deduced a great deal. Does your renewed mortality trouble you, Isabelle?

No. It is welcome.

And the fact that you survived the fight with Malbosc—is that welcome?

There is a certain melancholy that descends after having outlived one's purpose, but if you're asking if I plan to end my own life, the answer is no. I will let it run its course, though the emptiness of that course does trouble me.

As cheerful as ever. Isabelle, what is the purpose of _my_ life?

What sort of question is that? To be Sophie Beauchêne.

Can't you permit yourself the same thing you permit me? That the purpose of your life is simply to be Isabelle, and thus, by definition, you can't outlive it? You fulfill it by living.

Sophie Beauchêne's life is replete with love and companionship and good deeds accomplished. People are better for having known you. They smile when they open your letters, or when you walk into a room.

I am delighted to know that you smile when you open my letters. I will send you more of them. Perhaps you could send some of your own. Love and companionship are yours for the taking, Isabelle, and I know you've accomplished many good deeds already. Don't argue, or I will bring up how you kept Anaïs alive through so many years of her illness, and I will cry. (Damn. Too late.) If you think the only purpose of your life was to kill your tormentor, what does that mean for my beautiful sister—_V's mother_? Does it mean nothing to you that your intervention allowed her to live longer?

Of course it is not nothing. But whatever good I've done, how could it ever outweigh the evil?

Anaïs's life, how many grams did that weigh?

What?

You seem intent on measuring. So let's measure. We'll use the metric system, naturally.

This is absurd.

Now we agree.

What is your point?

Instead of stewing over impossible calculations, you should come home. You and your heart that you insist is not broken. We'll live, and I'll be Sophie, and you'll be Isabelle. All our friends and loved ones will be themselves too (you know no law or force of nature could stop Béatrix, and it has never even occurred to V not to be V).

You are aware that I am already on my way back to Paris.

I mean back to <u>us</u>, Isabelle. And if you still need to, then we'll look for this person you "don't hate." We'll do it slowly, so you'll have plenty of time to come up with the words you really meant, and say them out loud when we find Céleste.

PRIVATE DIARY OF ISABELLE DE TOURZIN, JUNE 21, 1825

WRITTEN ON ENCRYPTED PAPER

Despite Sophie's instructions not to stew over impossible calculations, I did. My journey was on foot, and then on horseback, and in the abundant solitude, her words were my companions. She seemed to agree with Céleste that I should say—should already <u>have said</u>, even—that I was in love. Sophie had not gone so far as to say I was too late, but the implication haunted her scolding.

She did not have to say it. I knew.

I had chosen my silence with just such an end in mind. I had left those words unwritten in my farewell letter; they would only have worsened whatever Céleste might feel upon learning of my death. Nor had I spoken them aloud after my rescue or during my period of recovery in Songecreux. Why should Céleste bear that burden? "I love you" is a gift if it comes from a worthy person. I did not want to hand Céleste the moth-eaten rag of my love, not when he deserved silk and cashmere. I set him free to find it with someone else.

That this decision made both of us unhappy was unfortunate, but temporary. For me, everything is now temporary. If

I miss Céleste for the rest of my life, there will be an end to that. For Céleste, the hurt will pass.

Sophie's words buzz like a fly at my ear as I write this. <u>It's not within your control: I would be sad if you died.</u>

I suppose Céleste's feelings toward me also fall outside my control, which is fitting, as my own seem to as well.

I fell victim to sentiment in Lyon. Every step of my journey, I'd told myself I was only going into that city to change horses, to find myself lodging for a night, but when I stopped by the stage coach office, I had to confront the truth at last. Though there was little chance Céleste would be there, I <u>was</u> looking.

In the plaza outside, I encountered a pretty young woman whose brown hair was neatly pinned under her bonnet. She was neither embarking or disembarking, but simply standing and waiting. Despite the mild weather, a grey wool cloak draped her from shoulder to ankle. Perhaps if she'd been less covered up, or holding her child, I would have recognized her more quickly—we'd spent hours together on the stage coach. She was the young widow who'd flirted with Céleste. When she locked eyes with me and her lips began to curve upward, I realized I'd been staring.

Her enjoyment made me bristle.

"You don't remember my name, do you, Madame de Tourzin?" she asked.

Céleste would've smoothed this over with a smile, an earnest apology, and a few light remarks. I wished I did not miss him. Stiffly, I said, "I regret that I do not."

"Véronique Lachance," she said. "My son is at home with my family."

I hadn't asked about the baby. Céleste would have.

"I hoped I'd meet you here," she continued. "I saw your traveling companion, and he said you'd been separated. He was very concerned for you, and he entrusted me with a letter for you in case our paths crossed. I waited here yesterday and the day before."

"He... what?"

She'd already withdrawn the letter from the folds of her cloak. I took it without a glance. Its slight weight and thickness disappointed me—only a single page—though I couldn't say what I'd been hoping for. A book of love poetry? Surely not.

"Why did he tell you to wait for me here? He must know I would never take a diligence without him," I said.

The question seemed to embarrass her. "I believe he hoped—he thought you might be looking for him."

That embarrassed me, as it was entirely true, so I scowled at the letter in my hand. "I didn't think Céleste had anything left to say to me."

"Well, I can't say what it's in the letter, but I can tell you he was worried about you," said Mme Lachance. "Forgive me if this remark falls outside the bounds of politeness, but I believe he missed you."

Though she spoke gently, there was a fine thread of amusement winding through her words, and it infuriated me. My gaze snapped to hers.

"This is a private matter."

She offered me a sad smile. "Of course. My apologies. I should not have commented. I haven't been sleeping well, and it's made me forget my manners. You know how maddening the stage coach was, being trapped in such a small space for hours—life with a baby is a little bit like that. I'm quite desperate for novelty. I promise to look for it elsewhere."

A smile, an apology, a few light remarks. Everyone else repairs things so easily. If I hadn't driven Céleste away, I wouldn't need to worry about conversation, because he'd do it for me. But I did drive him away, and I don't know how to repair that, either.

"Are you... well, Mme de Tourzin?"

"What business is that of yours?"

Taken aback by my sharp response, she paled, swallowed, and then forcefully straightened her shoulders and lifted her chin. A brave little thing, or at least one who wanted the appearance. "I can apologize for my nosiness, but not for my concern. You know, Forestier stayed a night with us. He seemed quite—" She paused to reconsider her words. "Well, he played with the baby very cheerfully. I'm sure he's fine."

"I'm sure he is," I said acerbically, though my chest tightened at the thought of Céleste being so melancholy that someone like Mme Lachance could perceive it.

She drooped a little. Before Céleste, I wouldn't have felt any guilt about being rude to this kind stranger. After Céleste, I did my best.

Even more hesitantly, Mme Lachance said, "If _you_ need lodging—"

"No," I interrupted. I fished a coin from my pocket and held it out to her, and she blinked, perplexed. "For your troubles in delivering the letter."

"Oh, I don't want—I did it for him. It was a personal favor."

I took her hand, firmly placed the coin in her gloved palm, turned on my heel, and stalked away. I made sure I was out of her sight, and took several small side streets, before I stopped in a shadowed alley and unfolded Céleste's letter with trembling hands. What I wanted to read, I could not say. Céleste could have no solution to the questions that troubled me. Was my life worth living? Was I a person worth loving?

Sophie would have made more arch remarks about worth and grams. She'd already written her lines about how love and companionship were mine for the taking, that she liked me regardless of whether I believed her. _It is not within your control_. I wanted Céleste to write the same thing, or to send me some treatise specific to my exact condition, some proof that solved all my impossible calculations. Not that Céleste's previous correspondence tended toward the philosophical. The math, he had left up to me.

I wanted the letter to say "I miss you." Selfishly, wrongly, I wanted it to say "I'm sorry I left." I wanted instructions for fixing both myself and the rift I'd created between us.

The page was blank.

My heart seized and my hand clenched. I crumpled the page. I nearly threw it into the gutter.

The page was <u>my</u> stationery, stolen from my home in Paris, and it had not one single mark on it, because the message had already been delivered. <u>Sometimes a silence speaks for itself</u>, she'd said at Songecreux.

But she hadn't been silent in Lyon. She'd been Véronique Lachance.

She'd been right in front of me.

<u>I believe he missed you.</u>

I shoved the page into my coat pocket and sprinted back the way I'd come, regretting all my clever twists and turns. I scanned the Place des Terreaux for a pretty young woman in a grey cloak, and failing that, for anyone at all in a grey cloak. Céleste could change her appearance within minutes, but she couldn't get new clothes so easily. That might explain the cloak—whatever she'd been hiding under it might not have been appropriate dress for a young woman.

There was no one in a grey cloak, and no one who looked like Véronique Lachance. I caught my breath. My feet had carried me, landing on a decision before my mind could. But I knew then that I had to find her. Among all the doubts I had about myself, about my life and my worth and my future, about what I could say and do to make things right, there was one certainty: I wanted to see Céleste. I discarded my idea of keeping apart from her, of saying nothing, of letting her go to find her happiness with someone else. Perhaps she still would, but I had to try.

There would be no instructions. No map. She could be anywhere and look like anyone. Clearly she intended to make my search difficult—even to taunt me—but I welcomed it. It felt like having a purpose again.

PRIVATE DIARY OF ISABELLE DE TOURZIN, JULY 9, 1825

WRITTEN ON ENCRYPTED PAPER

If I encountered Céleste a second time on my return to Paris, I failed to recognize her.

Most of my journey was solitary. It was a slow trek, nothing like the relentless pace I set on my last return to the city, with Delphine's compass heavy in my coat pocket and Malbosc weighing on my mind. That kind of travel is no longer possible now that I must sleep and eat regularly. My strength is still diminished. After Lyon, I chose to walk to reacquaint myself with this new-old, fragile body.

Spring was unfurling into summer, green and abundant, and it is a wonder how easily sunshine and fragrant air can carry away melancholy. I did not know what I would do with the remainder of my life, but what had seemed insurmountably bleak from my sickbed became a bearable condition on the footpath, and besides, I supposed it put me in the company of most of humanity.

I missed Céleste, and regretted driving her away, but she missed me and had asked me to find her, and on sunnier days —and days when my blisters were less numerous—it seemed possible that I might.

Though I spoke only briefly with other people—innkeepers, guests, travelers on foot—I was kind to all of them, and polite, not only because each of them might have been Céleste, but because that is how Céleste would have approached them.

She might also have cheerfully stolen their money, or their imitation diamond rings.

I still have the one she gave me. It has been a long, long time since I voluntarily wore jewelry. This piece is not especially beautiful or valuable, but it fits my little finger, and it makes me think of her. No one remarked on it. I think if I had encountered Céleste, she would have noticed.

It is here in Paris that I have the best chance of finding her.

I did not immediately set about the affair. I had no compass prompting me in the right direction, and I was dirty and exhausted besides. Céleste spent weeks chiding me to eat and sleep in Songecreux; she would not begrudge me rest before I began my search in earnest.

And, if I force myself to be honest, I harbored a hope that she might be waiting for me at the house.

It was one of those summer evenings where even the city breezes carry birdsong, and it seems like the sunlight will last forever. A perfect moment for young lovers. I was surprised to find Victor still at work, valiantly curtailing the chaos of the study. They were equally surprised to see me in the corridor, though I'd made no effort to silence the squeaking floorboards.

"Good evening, Isabelle."

They stepped forward with open arms as if to embrace me, something we had never done before. It would be both bold and sentimental on Victor's part, and—if this were not Victor in front of me, but Céleste—sly in a way I found embarrassingly endearing. I let it happen. Victor, for a small person who spends almost all their time indoors and hunched over books, gives shockingly tight hugs.

Or perhaps they're not shocking, and it's simply that I've received so few that any squeeze is bound to feel ferocious. Certainly I felt out of practice as I returned the embrace, wrapping my arms more loosely than theirs.

"I can't believe you're letting me do this," they said, still clinging to me. "I wish I'd tried it earlier, but it took me until now to marshal my courage. You said I was adorable and wished me happy birthday, and then you didn't die, so I thought I should risk it."

It must be Victor, then. Céleste would not know what I had written in that letter. I released them, feeling a curious mixture of relief and disappointment. It would be intrusive and unsettling if Céleste posed as someone in my life, but I wanted to see Céleste so badly that I would have accepted any disguise.

In Céleste's absence, though, it was good to hug Victor. Strange, but good. In the wake of their touch, I felt like a creature without its shell: exposed, soft. The world was bigger and louder, and for a moment, I took in so much of it that it knocked me off balance.

Imagining Victor attempting to embrace me at any other point in our acquaintance was bizarre. I asked, "What do you mean, you wish you'd tried it earlier?"

"When you were here this morning," they said.

My heart kicked in my chest.

Céleste had come here. As <u>me</u>. A taunt, but I did not take it for cruelty. To pose as Victor—or another of my few confidants—and converse with me would have a certain edge of wickedness. To disguise herself as me was so clearly an amusement, like stealing a ring from a sleeping person's finger. She'd wanted me to discover the ruse.

We were playing a game. Interest sharpened my focus, and

I straightened my spine and said, as evenly as I could, "I need you to tell me everything I said and did."

To their credit, Victor answered without bursting into questions or hypotheses, though that restraint must have cost them. "You came in and said hello in, uh, your usual way?"

"Coldly?"

"Something like that," they agreed sheepishly. They paced back and forth a step or two and made some untranslatable hand gestures, unable to think without fidgeting. "I said I was glad to see you alive, and you seemed uncomfortable, which struck me as normal. You asked what you had missed, what you needed to know from the past few weeks, which I thought was strange, because we had the linked notebooks during your journey, so you could have asked any time. I also thought..."

"Yes?"

"Well, you were dressed nicely. Not like..." Victor lifted and dropped their hand to encompass my current travel-stained dress. "Like you never want anyone to look at you."

"You remarked upon this."

"I didn't <u>comment</u>! You would have given me one of those death glares," they said. "Or maybe not, since clearly it wasn't you. Was it Forestier? With some kind of illusion? It was convincing. I'd love to know how that works, and I bet Julie would too. I noticed you switched from 'he' to 'she' with Forestier, but I didn't know there was magic involved."

I ignored this digression, but the detail about the dress was interesting. Had Céleste broken in and gone through my wardrobe? She wouldn't have worn the dark red evening gown, not so early in the day. It would have stood out as unusual, and Victor would have mentioned it. But my collection of dresses included nothing else Céleste would accept.

"Tell me more about this conversation," I said and walked to my bedroom to examine my clothes. Now that I knew

Céleste's opinion (<u>I love dresses, that's why I can't wear yours</u>) and Victor's (<u>Like you never want anyone to look at you</u>), they did all strike me anew. They were practical garments, meant for moving through the city and its residence unseen, but there was an element of deliberate, defensive hideousness that I had not perceived until now. A depressing collection. A fitting portrait of the life I'd been leading.

I pulled out an unfamiliar fabric, a muted red linen in a much finer weave than I usually wore, but still without trimmings, so not entirely out of place among my other clothes.

Victor had followed me into the room. "That's the one. It suits you. Other than that one burgundy evening dress, I didn't think you owned anything in color."

"I don't."

"So this is, what, some kind of reverse theft? Oh my God, Forestier gave you a dress." A sparkling sort of mischief spread across their expression like hives. "An expensive, flattering dress. This is a flirtation. I thought she broke your heart, or vice versa. Probably vice versa, now that I think about it. I mean—pretend I didn't say that. But what is going on between you two?"

"I asked you to tell me the rest of your conversation."

"You—<u>she</u> asked what had happened in the past few weeks, so I talked about acquiring Maximilien Taillefer's collection, and how hard Julie and I have worked at identifying artifacts for her to nullify—you know that will go so much faster if you still have the sponge and we can use it instead—and then I mentioned there was some correspondence from Delphine. She was interested in that."

"Is it still here?"

"It is," they said and left.

When they returned a moment later with the letters, I was still holding the new dress, running my fingertips over the smooth weave. Their reappearance startled me. I felt as though I'd been caught fondling something obscene. I set the dress on the bed, but it was too late. Victor was all knowing smiles and repressed commentary.

Delphine's letters were too numerous and lengthy to read while standing there with Victor, but a quick scan revealed that Delphine had asked for my help, and I had not been there to give it. My stomach twisted with guilt.

Victor offered, "I haven't read those—I can't, they're encrypted—wait, do you think Céleste could read the encrypted text? Since she looked like you? That's an interesting question, I hadn't really considered—"

"Victor."

"Right, sorry. Anyway, whatever's in there isn't the whole story. A lot has happened with Delphine since you last saw her. Her troubles are, uh, resolved. She just left the city with the writer Camille Dupin and this man named Ari, you wouldn't know him—"

"I know who he is."

"Oh," Victor said. I had never told them about orchestrating Ari's exit from prison. I had never told them quite a lot of things. "Well, the three of them went to Verneuil. Camille's country estate. You—I mean, Forestier was very interested in it this morning. Wanted to know how far away it was, and whether I thought you'd be welcome there."

"And you said?"

"I don't understand what's between you and Delphine, but she wrote you all those letters, and I know you wrote back at least once, and you <u>hate</u> letters. So you two must like each other. And Camille loves Delphine. So you could probably get yourself invited, if you wrote and asked. Forestier asked for Camille's address after I said that. Why does Forestier want to see Delphine?"

"I entrusted her with a delivery, and I suppose she's honoring my request," I said. Céleste still had the compass.

She could use it to find me—or to avoid me, if that was part of the game. Her visit this morning was as good as writing a letter telling me her destination.

"And Forestier's impersonating you because... ?"

"To get information out of you."

"I would've helped her if she'd looked like the person I know," Victor protested. "You said to help her in your letter. She knows that, right?"

"There are further advantages to impersonating me. Camille Dupin is unlikely to invite a stranger to Verneuil, and Delphine knows me."

Céleste's true motivation was her own amusement, or to provoke me to catch her, but those were the same thing. That knowledge felt thrilling and intimate, and I wanted to clutch that secret to my chest for as long as I could.

Victor made a thoughtful little hum. "That's so disappointingly logical. I was hoping it was—well. So you're going to let Forestier pretend to be you?"

"It will take her time to secure an invitation and travel to Verneuil," I said. "I plan to find her long before then."

I did not write to Delphine, as I wish to see what Céleste will do, but I have seen no evidence that Céleste has done anything. She no longer resides at the Maison Laval and left no new address. She is no longer employed as an agent of the police. I suspect she made these arrangements before our departure, though we never discussed them.

Each day I have either passed by, lurked near, or spent time in Brasserie La Fortune, but have not yet discerned whether anyone there might be Céleste, or, failing that, who I might ask about Céleste's various personas.

I have spent every evening and several afternoons in company. Sophie and I went to a recital of Béatrix's, and fêted her appropriately afterward. Dominique played his Pleyel for me (and the rest of us, though everyone else had heard it before) on many nights. Once I consented to play cards and chess with him, though I enjoy neither, and found both pastimes pleasant enough until I won. In theory, I had known such an outcome was possible. I must have looked stricken; Dominique patted my hand. I recalled, months ago, Victor scolding me for my inadequate sympathy. <u>Isabelle. He gave up his magic. For you.</u>

"I'm so sorry," I said.

"For beating me at chess?" he replied lightly, though of course he knew what I meant.

I understood then that it would always be between us, his sacrifice—and that it was only one stone among many, and what they built was not a wall, but a bridge. We had worked together, and saved each other, and suffered, and lived. Dominique did not need me to apologize endlessly. He did not require a payment of some imaginary, reciprocal sacrifice on my part. He just wanted me to come over.

So I did. For lunch, for dinner, for morning walks, for no reason at all. With Sophie and Béatrix, or by myself. We ate and drank and I permitted him a few limited reminiscences. His memories were, I think, less crystalline—he used to be able to tell me exactly what he'd worn on any given day, and the number and street name of any house we'd visited—but his version of events still accorded with my own.

When I'd had enough of that, I let him recount in astonishingly vague, disorganized terms the plot of a long novel he has been reading in his new life of leisure. Though based on his account, "plot" is a generous assessment. He also spent a lot of time singing Quang's praises—kind, thoughtful, generous, steadfast, that sort of thing—even when Quang was with us, though evidently being complimented in public does not discomfit him.

"I like that Dominique doesn't start his list with 'handsome,'" he said. "Everyone else starts there."

At this point, Dominique felt the need to add "handsome" to his list, and there was some nudging of shoulders and probably more giggling than was merited. In thirty years of acquaintance, I don't know that I have ever seen Dominique giggle.

All I could think was that Céleste would have loved it. If Dominique and Quang had been a pair of strangers we met on the stage coach, they would have been more restrained, but she would still have been charmed. She probably wouldn't have emptied somebody else's coin purse on their behalf, as I suspect she did for Véronique Lachance, because she would have known with a glance that neither of them needed money. She would have said, in some subtler language, how endearing she found them.

I lacked her finesse, and did not wish to embarrass all three of us by saying something clumsy, so merely smiled.

"Enjoy that," Dominique said to Quang while tipping his head toward me. "She likes you. It's an uncommon sight."

"I do like you, but I'm smiling about both of you together," I corrected. "You're happy. I'm happy for you."

This rendered them speechless.

Neither of them remarked on the ring I have been wearing, but naturally Sophie and Béatrix noticed right away.

"I've never known you to wear jewelry," said Sophie, while Béatrix said, in her direct way, "I didn't believe it when Sophie told me you were in love, but I do now."

Béatrix and I have never been close, but we have—or had—a certain understanding, as two people in possession of powerful magic that puts us on a lonely path. Hers is in her voice, which she can use to compel people. She must take great care not to do so by accident.

How strange that I have just written that. I have no need to explain something I already know. It is as if I expect Céleste to read these pages some day, though they have been enchanted to be illegible to anyone but my destined readers—a group I thought included only myself.

I wonder, if she broke into my house and found this diary, could she read it? Have I unwittingly granted her access to my most private self?

I know she could read this ring I've been wearing. Béatrix and Sophie could, and Céleste would have the advantage of recognizing these paste gems. This fantasy—Céleste reading my diary or seeing the ring and coming to an instant understanding—appeals because it relieves me of the burden of further explaining myself. It is a little like Céleste doing Louise's writing exercises for her.

Well, Céleste, if I imagine you reading these pages, I hope you see that I am practicing my own penmanship, as clumsy as it is. When Sophie and Béatrix accused me of being in love, I could not bring myself to speak of you, nor the many hours I have spent scouring Paris for any trace of your presence—but neither did I deny it.

ISABELLE TO CÉLESTE, JULY 17, 1825
LEFT IN THE CARE OF LOUISE DUBOIS AT FLORINE'S, RUE BLANCHE

Céleste,

This is as close as I have come to finding you. I miss you and wish to see you again. Would you permit that?

Isabelle

I could have gone to Florine's days ago if I'd had more courage. I knew Céleste's sister worked there; Céleste had asked Dominique to deliver some news, and I had shamelessly read their correspondence. Dominique would have given me the address, but not knowing the address allowed me to delay going.

I was afraid to meet Louise. She might judge me unworthy of Céleste, which would be correct, or excoriate me for having treated Céleste poorly, which would be deserved, but in either case I dreaded hearing it. If she did neither, and welcomed me warmly, that would be worse. My guilt would suffocate me.

However she might react, the simple idea of Louise herself—her face, the few childhood stories I knew—rooted me to the ground with terror. So much of my journey with Céleste had been dreamlike, outside of time and life, separated from everyone we knew. Even without Céleste by my side, as long as I searched for her, I could preserve that dream. Meeting Louise would thrust us into a new world. The dream might vanish as though it had never happened. I did not want to lose it.

But I wanted to find Céleste more, and Louise was the person most likely to know where she was.

In a low moment, I confessed my anxiety to Victor.

"Louise? I know Louise," they said, still seated at the desk in the study, but having long since ceased to work. Their eyes were bright with the prospect of meddling in my affairs. "I can't believe she's related to Forestier."

"By choice," I clarified. "They grew up in the same orphanage."

"Still," Victor said. "Louise is delightful."

This remark was obviously calculated to make me protest that Céleste was also delightful, but I was more interested in Victor's acquaintance with Louise. "Are you offering to speak to her on my behalf?"

"No. Louise knew me as Horace and thinks I have withdrawn from the city," Victor said. Some color rose in their cheeks. "If you marry Forestier and we end up celebrating holidays together every year, I'll tell her the truth."

"What?"

"Lying to her was unavoidable, but I was a paying customer, and I did my best to treat her right, so maybe she won't hold my deception against me," Victor continued.

"Marry?" I said. "Holidays?"

Victor shrugged. "Never known you to do either of those things, but this is a whole new life. You could be different. Go talk to Louise."

When I failed to depart quickly enough, they added, "Besides, I am trying to work. You're just haunting this place and distracting me."

Florine's establishment was on the upper floors of a building in the Rue Blanche, not even ten minutes' walk from my home. What a thicket Paris is, to hide so many things.

Céleste and I might have passed each other on the street in prior years, never knowing each other.

It was early evening when I arrived. Florine herself was not in evidence, and the whole place had an air of just having woken. They would have been more ready to receive me at night, and I considered leaving and coming back later, but this was cowardice on my part. Louise would be working later. A child led me to the parlor, and there I waited.

The child must have informed Louise of my presence, but she took her time. It was not for pinning her hair up or lacing herself into evening clothes. She entered the parlor in shocking dishabille, with her hair loose and her silk dressing gown held closed with a brooch.

Louise's appearance caused something to twist painfully in my chest. She looked like her sister. The shape I'd seen Céleste assume in her sleep, the brown-haired woman with sun-tinged white skin, that was Louise's older, plainer sister. It must have been purposeful, the choice to resemble Louise, but not quite as beautiful—her nose and brows less delicate, her lips less full, her hair less glossy, her figure less abundant.

I stood to greet her, but she dismissed me with a wave of her hand. "You're Isabelle. I'm Louise. Sit down."

"It's a pleasure to make your acquaintance," I said, clinging to the ritual she'd tossed aside.

"We'll see about that. Why are you here?"

I withdrew a letter from my skirt pocket.

"Apolline! Catherine!" Louise shouted, causing two other women to dash through the corridor and half-tumble over each other in their hurry to get into the room. One was slender and brown-skinned, with a luxuriant fall of black hair down to her waist, and the other was plump and milk white with blond curls piled on top of her head. Like Louise, they wore dressing gowns.

"This is Isabelle," Louise said. "Apolline, Catherine. Isabelle wants me to deliver that letter to Céleste. Read it."

"Opening your sister's mail?" asked the black-haired one, who was Apolline. She sounded uncertain, but crossed the room, held out her hand, and waited until I placed the letter in her palm.

"Has Céleste been with you all this time? No, that can't be it, otherwise you wouldn't need Louise's help. I'm sorry, we've only just met, I shouldn't pry or speculate," Catherine said. "It's just that we miss her."

Not knowing when they'd last seen Céleste, I could not answer.

"The years away weren't Isabelle's fault," Louise said firmly, which was more than I'd expected from her. "Read the letter."

Apolline unfolded my letter and read it aloud, then passed it to Catherine, who did the same. Louise nodded thoughtfully. I was relieved to have kept the text brief. That Louise might read it had occurred to me, but that she might have two strangers read it aloud had not.

"Not much of a letter. Still, I'll give it to Céleste if you stay with us this evening," Louise said. "Maybe tomorrow evening, too. None of us have appointments until later."

"Stay with you and... do what?" I asked. "Is this a punishment?"

She laughed. "I suppose you could make it one, for me or for you. I just want to chat. Play games or music. The things people do to get to know each other. I can't tell what kind of person you are yet."

"And a game of cards will teach you?"

"It will tell me something," she insisted. "For instance, whether you're too stuck up to play cards with whores."

"If that were the case, I couldn't even play solitaire," I said, surprising laughter out of all three of them.

"You?" Louise asked. "Really?"

"I'm old and I've come a long way in life," I said, and then, leaving out the dates, I told them about Venice, and Laura, and Malbosc.

It was easier than I had imagined, or than I would have imagined, since the thought of telling strangers had never crossed my mind. Céleste had made it easier. She had listened. She had cared. The version of my life that I offered at Florine's was much abridged from what I had told Céleste. I skimmed lightly over my childhood and the loss of my family and my time on the streets, but still had the feeling they understood. I mentioned Laura only briefly—the woman who had educated me, with whom I had eventually fallen in love—and her death only in passing. "After she died..." I said, and did not cry, though still I wished Céleste were holding me.

The women were so rapt we didn't end up playing cards. Apolline and Catherine both brimmed with physical affection and sounds of shock and sympathy, laying comforting hands on my arms while we all sat on the sofa. They let me speak without interruption. Louise sat in an armchair across from us, and her sharp gaze never wavered. I could almost see her fit together the pieces—I had been a cruel man's mistress, and a cruel man had broken Céleste's heart—but I hadn't given her quite enough information.

I concluded by telling them that Céleste and I had met because we were searching for the same man, but that we had parted ways and lost touch once we found him.

"I see," Louise said. "You skipped over the parts that are of most interest to me—your relationship with my sister—but I suppose I shouldn't be so nosy about Céleste's affairs. Thank you for telling us so much of yourself. I'm sorry for all you've suffered. It wasn't my intention to force you to speak of it."

"You did no such thing," I said. "It was freely offered."

"Louise is right that we all want to know more about you and Céleste," Catherine said. "You must be good friends—or perhaps even lovers?—to come here looking for her, but I have a hard time imagining it. You're so bold and experienced, and she's such a timid creature. I was surprised to learn there'd been any man in her life, and am even more surprised to learn that she went looking for him after he broke her heart. When you say you found him..."

"He won't trouble her or anyone else ever again," I said firmly. "You think Céleste is timid? That is... not my impression."

Louise shared a private smile with me. "My sister doesn't come here often. She likes us, but our work makes her blush. Years ago, before I realized how unsuitable she was, I tried to persuade her that she'd get more rest and live better if she joined us, that this work was easier than working in the laundry, but she refused."

I stopped myself from murmuring "laundry" like I was taking notes. Apolline and Catherine think Céleste is a shy laundress. They do not know she is a shape-changing thief who gets in knife fights and lies to strangers on the stage coach and thinks everything is funny.

Belatedly, it occurred to me that Céleste's story of modesty and inexperience and heartbreak would arouse protective instincts in these women, and that they regarded me as a potential threat. Though Céleste is neither shy, nor modest, nor inexperienced, this is not so different from how I regard myself. I cannot reconcile my desire to see her with the knowledge that some day we will surely make each other unhappy; I have abandoned myself to wanting her.

"It's for the best. Two sisters working at a place like this, that gives the men ideas," Louise said. "Less risk of pregnancy at the laundry, anyway."

"Could you tell me which laundry? I'd like to see her again."

"She'll get in trouble if you bother her at work," Louise said smoothly. "I'll see about getting your letter to her. Why don't you come back here tomorrow night?"

After I agreed, she insisted I stay for some music and more lighthearted conversation, which I did. That was last night, so I have all of today to anticipate seeing Céleste again.

It was a very different evening at Florine's last night. No guests were in the parlor when I arrived. Apolline was playing her fiddle and Catherine and her young daughter Zélie were singing. They paused to greet me with kisses and tell me how glad they were to see me, then resumed making music once I'd sat taken a seat on the sofa.

Louise came in, singing along, dragging Céleste behind her.

They looked like sisters.

As I had guessed upon meeting Louise, their family resemblance let Louise shine. She was drawn with a bolder hand, all her colors brighter. Where Louise's hair was deep, glossy chestnut, Céleste's was merely brown. But knowing that this was by design—that Céleste had chosen every washed-out shade and mediocrity to slip into her sister's shadow—reversed it for me, and made me want to look at Céleste, modest laundress.

Her dress, though it fit her well and was a flattering blue, was as carefully plain as her face. I would never have noticed it had she not so thoroughly rejected <u>my</u> dresses, but because she had, I was struck by its simplicity. She deserved lace and ribbons, embroidery, flounces, whatever fashionable people were putting on their skirts and sleeves these days. I only wear clothes not to be naked, but I wanted, with sudden urgency, to gift her a dozen dresses and any sparkly thing she took a fancy to. Or suits and waistcoats, if she'd rather.

I thought of the red dress she'd left in my wardrobe, how it was a daytime echo of my one evening gown—the burgundy silk one I was wearing. Perhaps it's not true that I only wear clothes not to be naked. Last night I put that dress on because Céleste had once admired it.

I stood when Louise brought Céleste toward me.

All I wanted to do was take her in my arms and kiss her. My invitation to do so had been rescinded weeks ago. Dammed desire and frustration hummed in my body, a low note under a higher, simpler, happier melody, one that sang: <u>Céleste is here, Céleste is alive, Céleste agreed to see me</u>.

It sweeps away everything, being in love.

Louise greeted me first, brushing her cheek against mine and saying, "You'd better be worthy of her."

As that is Céleste's to decide, I made no reply. She stepped away, and I waited for Céleste to take her spot, which did not come to pass. Céleste remained in her place and offered me an uncharacteristically shy smile. To greet her, I would have to move. We had not seen each other since our meeting in the Place des Terreaux in Lyon, where she had been Véronique and I had been too slow to realize it.

Still overpowered by the song in my head—Céleste, Céleste—I felt slow in Florine's parlor. That was an advantage, I think; the person Céleste was in that place would have been startled by haste. The other women pretended to be caught up in their song, but they were watching, wary of me. Céleste had accepted this meeting with unspoken terms. I could not reveal her to be other than what Apolline and

Catherine thought she was, and that meant I had to tread carefully.

They suspected that we were lovers—in their profession, they were unlikely to be surprised—but to them, she was neither bold, nor experienced, nor sly, nor teasing. No matter how downcast her gaze, to me she was all of those things.

I thought of Céleste's suppressed laughter when we'd been trapped in the servant's stairs at César Duret's. We'd been in real danger then, and still she'd found it amusing. How could this be any less entertaining? Here we were again, keeping a secret together. Instead of our intrusive presence in the Baron's house, it was the truth of who were to each other. Instead of the Baron's servants hunting thieves, it was Céleste's sister and friends hunting for any threat I might pose to her. There should have been less to fear this time. Louise was unlikely to stab me and dump me in the Seine.

But if I failed at playing the game, Céleste would be disappointed. A stabbing would be preferable.

So if she wanted me to court her as if she were some naïve girl with her family scowling over her shoulder, I would do it.

I reached for one of her hands, which she lifted and placed in mine with some reticence. Touching her skin sent an undeniable spark through me, and brushing the lightest of kisses across her knuckles doubled it. A tremor ran through her hand. She stilled it, but I knew.

One glimpse of her face confirmed that we were playing. Her eyes were bright.

"Céleste," I murmured, saying her name solely for the pleasure. "I did not know if you would come."

"I didn't know, either."

It struck me then that while this was certainly a game, it was also real. Céleste was not a modest laundress, but she still wanted the protection offered by her sister and friends. Caution drove her to meet me in a place with stringent limits on what we could do and say. When we had last been alone together, and free, I had not done or said the right things. However inadvertently, I <u>had</u> hurt her. My miserable convalescence had prevented me from seeing any future for us. I needed the present—the long walk home, these weeks of seeing my friends, these nights of meeting hers—to help me remember how to live.

I'm a long time out of practice.

"Sit down, you two, you're in the way," Louise said. She pushed me gently back to the sofa.

Céleste sat a respectable distance from me. As soon as we were seated, the other women took up their playing again. It was louder and less precise than the music that Béatrix and Dominique made—bawdier, too—but there was joy in it. I was content to listen and be next to Céleste for two whole songs. We traded glances, and once I caught her smiling.

To be heard over the music, I had to raise my voice or lean in close. I chose the latter, but tried to respect the distance she'd put between us. "They know you as Céleste. And your last name?"

"No one here is concerned with 'real' names," she said with a shrug. The music allowed us a measure of privacy. "I'm Céleste Forestier when I come here in this shape. Apolline and Catherine probably think Louise and I are half-sisters with different fathers, but they've never asked. I used a false name when I came here in my other shape and I always ensconced myself with Louise so I hardly saw anyone else. I missed this." She gestured to encompass her friends and their music.

"I'm glad you have it again. What I meant was… you're Forestier, she's Dubois," I said, tilting my head toward Louise. "Forests, woods. That must be deliberate."

"Of course. She's my sister."

"And the aliases you mentioned—Marianne Olivet, Guy

Desaules—olive trees, willow trees. Do you also go by Alder and Pine?"

"No one's ever noticed before." Solving the puzzle earned me a genuine smile. "My little family joke."

"Connecting your names is a foolish risk," I said.

"You know I like those," she said and dipped her head so our brows nearly touched. For all the times I'd accused her of foolishness, recklessness, her tone was remarkably warm. That single quiet phrase sent a shock of heat rolling through me.

No one was paying attention to us, or if Louise was watching, she was discreet. Still, I wanted to ease into my own foolish risk, so I changed the subject to something safer.

"Do you know this song? Do you sing?" I asked.

She shook her head. A little color came into her cheeks. I was disarmed by it, though I had thought myself unarmed to begin with. She did not sing and was embarrassed to try. There were things about Céleste I did not know. What better future could there be than discovering them?

She shuffled closer on the sofa. Not close enough to touch, but close enough to whisper. "I only do the ones where everybody shouts the chorus. This one's too pretty for me."

I dared to trace the warm pink curve of her cheek, feeling very much like the kind of ill-intentioned seducer her family should throw out. "You listen beautifully."

Her blush rose as if my finger were painting it. Neither of us was thinking about singing.

The sofa was the well-worn kind that slumps into its usual shape no matter what, and we had both fallen toward the middle. Our hips pressed together. It was a warm evening, and Céleste was warmer, but still I aligned the length of my thigh with hers. She was soft in this shape. There was a pleasing give to her flesh that made me think of other places I could rub and squeeze.

That was not what I had come here to do—I had come here to see her, to speak to her, to spend time with her and her friends and family, to be part of her life, to prove that we could be something other than two people forced together by circumstance, abandoning ourselves to lust in a cave. I wanted her, of course, but I could wait. I thought I could wait.

Then she shifted. Squirmed, really. Clenched her thighs together. With sudden clarity, I knew she was having the same argument with herself. She had not come here to sleep with me, but she wanted to.

It would have to be Céleste who made the advance. I would not fall on her like a ravening beast in front of her friends. If she wanted something other than the delicious torment of our nearness, she could choose it. Or if all she wanted was to tempt me and send me home alone, she could choose that, too.

My long experience denying myself should have been of more use. Perhaps I was only good at denying myself these past decades because I had not yet met Céleste.

I redoubled my determination to appreciate the music and the company—not only her, but her friends—and drank the wine that Louise offered us. So did Céleste. The time passed in a warm haze of song and laughter, such that I felt a pang when the gathering dispersed. Apolline and Catherine excused themselves to take Catherine's daughter to bed.

Louise stayed behind to kiss my cheek. "How gallant you are."

Céleste, who had not done anything all evening that might contradict what Apolline and Catherine knew of her, rolled her eyes. "I don't need this, Louise."

Louise dismissed her with a hand gesture. "She never brought anybody else here, you know. The last few years, she barely came here herself."

"Céleste is with us. I will not discuss her as if she is absent."

"That's good, you're putting on a good show," Louise said. "All I'm saying is, she was absent a lot. She had her heart broken and I don't want to see that again. Whatever she told you, my sister's a good girl."

I cast a sidelong glance at Céleste. "Is that so?"

"Well," she said. "Sometimes."

"Be wise, you two," said Louise, giving her sister an extravagant number of goodbye kisses and departing in a flutter of silk.

We were alone in the parlor. Céleste walked with me the few steps to the door that led to the stairs, then touched my hand.

No, not my hand—my littlest finger, where I was wearing the ring she'd stolen for me. Writing this, I have no doubt she had noticed earlier in the evening. It was only once we were alone that she drew my attention to her gift. What pleasure it brings me to imagine her nurturing the flame of that little secret for hours, sitting next to me and holding her silence.

Our eyes met.

"I don't want to be wise," Céleste said and kissed me. The heat of her mouth, the urgency, was the same as what she had shown me in the cave, no matter that now she was shorter than me. Different in almost every physical respect, and yet I knew her.

It seemed to me that I knew her reactions before they happened, though this is an exceedingly rare magic, and not one I have ever possessed. But what need did I have to foretell the future when I was making it myself? My fingers tangling in her hair produced a low hum of surprised pleasure in the back of her throat. My tongue sweeping into her mouth, a softening of her body against mine.

I caught her around the waist and guided her to lean

against the door. It was the one that led to the stairs. No one could enter Florine's so long as we had our weight against it, though the parlor's other door, the one by which Louise and her friends had departed, was unlocked.

My hands found the delicious, fat curve of her bottom, hidden under her skirts, but mine to squeeze. Next to her ear, I murmured, "Someone could walk in."

"I don't care."

She punctuated this with a fierce kiss. The sharp edge of her teeth sank into me, and I discovered that I didn't care, either. Or rather, I did care—the risk of getting caught with Céleste enticed me.

"They think you're a good girl, but I know you're not," I said, and when she only sucked in a quiet breath in response, I bit her neck to elicit a true gasp. "If I lift your skirts right now and slide my hand between your thighs, my fingers will come away dripping. You've been wet for hours, sitting next to me, squirming, trying to pretend."

"Do it."

I kissed her again. Traces of me were everywhere, in her brown hair loose from its pins, in the red, bitten flush of her lips, and in the fast rise and fall of her chest. Anyone who looked would see my imprint. I wanted more. More of her, more evidence of my presence. The neckline of her gown was frustratingly high—appropriately modest, not the kind of sensual, shoulder-skimming audacity she deserved—and all the buttons were in the back. I reached for them, but the patience to slip each one from its buttonhole was beyond me. Instead I ripped her gown, pushed down its bodice, and bared her breasts to my mouth.

She was as soft as a dream, warm and heavy in my hands, and she clawed one hand into my hair when I sucked her nipple. Her other hand opened and closed helplessly on my back. I only felt the graze of her nails when I pulled up her skirts, as promised, and pressed a hand to the apex of her legs. The fabric blocked my view, so I lifted my face to watch hers as I found my way by feel. I was eager to discover her, as any form of Céleste's would please me. My fingers combed through her nest of coarse hair, and then traveled down to the dimpled flesh of her thighs. I nudged them open and at last touched the sweet slickness of her lips.

"You need this," I said, skimming my fingertips along that seam without dipping inside, though she was so wet that her lips parted at my first touch. "Right here."

"Right here, right now, right <u>there</u>."

I thrust two fingers inside her, but her cunt was so slippery with want that it was more like sliding into a warm pool, gliding stroke by effortless stroke. Not warm—hot. Shockingly hot. I welcomed it like I'd been cold all my life. She clenched around me and I pressed deeper. When I brushed my thumb over her clit, she shuddered.

I did not think she had flushed so easily in her other form. In this one, whether it was modesty or honesty or some mingling of the two, I kissed the warm, pink spread of desire under her skin, from her cheeks to her mouth to her throat to the tops of her breasts to the peaks of her nipples. Her low groans of pleasure and keening sighs called me back, and I captured her mouth with mine. All the while my fingers moved inside her, soft but audible, not stopping.

I broke our kiss to catch my breath and pressed my forehead to hers. "You need this," I repeated. "Sweet, needy girl. Nobody knows how much you need this but me. I'm here to give it to you."

She gave a helpless little moan that jolted through me, making me acutely aware of the heavy, swelling ache in my own body. My breasts pressing against the confines of my clothes. The throb in my cunt. Everything I'd been ignoring so I could attend to Céleste.

"Will you come quietly? Or do you want them to hear?"

"I—" she said and halted herself with a ragged breath. She met my eyes and there was only lust-dark pleading in hers.

"You don't have to tell them anything," I said, deciding. "I'll keep your secrets."

I swallowed her next sound, and the sound after that. Waves surged through her, and she clung to me, digging one hand into my hair and the other into my backside. Anyone could have seen her come, pressed between my body and the door, with her breasts bare and her skirts pulled up, her whole body trembling. But only I did.

"Isabelle," she murmured. "Isabelle, can I—"

There was a pounding on the door behind her. It was loud and aggressive, suggesting we had, perhaps, missed a more polite knock.

Céleste's face could not flush any pinker. Her eyes widened. She grinned and pressed a hand to her mouth to stifle a laugh.

I slid my hand out of her and adjusted the fall of her skirts. Her bodice was unsalvageable. I tugged it to cover her breasts. She was less bare, but she did not look any less fucked.

"Open up," shouted the disgruntled person on the other side of the door. "I have an appointment with Mademoiselle Dubois."

"Coming," Céleste called, as though she were far away. It was a good imitation of her sister's voice. Her eyes lit with mischief. She lifted my hand to her mouth, sucked my fingers clean, and then wiped them across her ruined dress. With one of her own fingers, she made the sign for silence. A tilt of her head indicated the other door, the one that led to the corridor and the bedrooms. Then she pushed me away, gave me one last kiss, and scurried out.

Was I meant to follow her? Surely there was no space for

us in those rooms. The night's work was beginning. It would be better if Céleste borrowed some clothes and returned, that we might go somewhere else.

The pounding on the door happened again.

Louise appeared instantly, opening the door and greeting her client as if nothing were unusual. I suppose it was neither the first nor the last time that Florine's parlor has reeked of sex.

I stepped into the stairwell and strode down to the street. Louise's goodbye echoed after me. She was puzzled by my departure, I think.

For a time, I waited outside in the darkness and the dissipated heat of the day, fantasizing that Céleste might emerge in a new dress or a new body to accompany me. When that failed, I walked home, wondering if she might go some other, more shadowed route to surprise me in my bed.

She was not there; I slept alone. I found a note in the foyer this morning.

CÉLESTE TO ISABELLE, JULY 21, 1825

LEFT INSIDE THE FOYER AT 9, RUE BRANOUX

Sorry for leaving so abruptly last night. I suppose I thought you would follow me, but I didn't extend much of an invitation, did I? I wanted to continue what we were doing, but also to talk. By the light of day, I can see it's unlikely we would have done much talking.

I can't seem to think in your presence—usually for enjoyable reasons. Still, that wasn't how I wanted our reunion to go.

[*The note is signed with a crude drawing of a pine tree.*]

ISABELLE TO CÉLESTE, JULY 22, 1825
WRITTEN ON THE SAME PAGE, LEFT INSIDE THE FOYER AT 9, RUE BRANOUX

Which part did you find objectionable? Should I have used my tongue?

CÉLESTE TO ISABELLE, JULY 23, 1825

WRITTEN ON THE SAME PAGE, LEFT INSIDE THE FOYER AT 9, RUE BRANOUX

Yes, but not in the filthy way you're suggesting. I think you know that.

Look at you, leaving obscene notes in plain text where anyone might see. What will young Victor think if he stumbles across these? I fear for his innocence.

You fear for Victor's innocence? You've seen Sophie's personal library; that ship has sailed. Besides, they and their lover have left for Verneuil. That's Camille Dupin's country estate, but you don't need that explained, do you?

More importantly, I would very much like to speak with you—face to face, alone.

CÉLESTE TO ISABELLE, JULY 25, 1825

WRITTEN ON THE SAME PAGE, LEFT INSIDE THE FOYER AT 9, RUE BRANOUX

Ah, Isabelle, how I hate to deny you, especially as I owe you a certain debt now, but if we see each other in person, alone, I will fall into your arms again like a fool. Write me a letter to make me feel less foolish.

You're right that I don't need Verneuil explained. I'll be traveling soon, and have only taken temporary lodgings in the city, so you'll have to leave your correspondence with Louise.

ISABELLE TO CÉLESTE, JULY 26, 1825

WRITTEN ON THE SAME PAGE, LEFT INSIDE THE FOYER AT 9, RUE BRANOUX

Last time I brought a letter to Louise, she had both Apolline and Catherine read it aloud. Do you want our correspondence to be so public?

CÉLESTE TO ISABELLE, JULY 27, 1825
WRITTEN ON THE SAME PAGE, LEFT INSIDE THE FOYER AT 9, RUE BRANOUX

As discussed, these notes in your foyer are not private. Besides, what do you have to say to me that cannot be said in public?

Taking the stage coach isn't nearly as entertaining without Isabelle, so here I am, scribbling to entertain myself. Was it cowardice to flee Isabelle like that? Decidedly yes. I'd do it again.

I feel too much for her, and can't let myself until I know her true feelings for me.

Until then, I will pass the time making this delivery. The coach route doesn't go all the way to Verneuil, so I'll have to walk the last few kilometers. Delphine sent me directions.

She thinks she sent them to Isabelle, and it's Isabelle she'll see when I arrive. The guilt I feel over this deception weighs on me, which comes as a surprise. I am merely returning Delphine's compass. If anything, it is a good deed.

One with risks, though. Delphine is one of Isabelle's few friends, from what I can tell, and I don't want to undermine their friendship. Delphine might recognize me as a fraud. I tried to read the letters she wrote to Isabelle to learn more about their history, but the text all looked like chicken scratch. I'm sure it was that same enchantment that Isabelle has on her diary. That in itself is telling. Isabelle likes

Delphine enough to provide her with magical paper. Still, I'm missing a lot. Any conversation longer than a few sentences might reveal me to Delphine. After I return the compass, I'll make some excuse to return to Paris as swiftly as possible.

Perhaps by then Isabelle will have written to me.

PRIVATE DIARY OF C. F.,
AUGUST 10, 1825
WRITTEN IN AN INVENTED SHORTHAND

I knew I was fucked when I got to Verneuil. A woman saw me sweating through my dress and said, "Isabelle? I thought you were going for a walk in the woods. It's much too hot to be out of the shade."

The woman spoke like she knew me. While I'd never met the dowager Marquise de Quennetière, I'd asked around Paris until I acquired a description that would help me recognize her: twenty-five, fat, auburn-haired, pretty.

"Delphine," I said, hiding the chaos of my thoughts with a polite nod. Of course Isabelle got here first—she knew where I was going, and she didn't have to take the stage coach. The diligence is fast, but she might have departed before I did.

So I'd miscalculated, and now there were two people who looked like Isabelle de Tourzin at Verneuil.

Delphine let go of the child whose hand she was holding —Octave, that's his name—and left the shady grove of trees where they'd been playing. She was beautifully dressed in green, and far less crumpled than I was, though still touched by the heat. As she approached me, her brow creased. "It's a very hot day. Are you well?"

I gave her a wobbly smile. "I don't have the hang of this place yet."

That gave her pause. Isabelle would have said it all stiff and formal if she ever admitted any such weakness in the first place. Shit.

The smart choice would have been to hand Delphine the compass and leave as soon as she was out of sight, so of course I didn't do that. Isabelle was somewhere near. I wanted to find her.

Delphine either knew that Isabelle was newly mortal and frail, or had never known her to be anything else. She was worried. I took advantage of my sweat-sheened flush and acted like I was short of breath. "Remind me where my rooms are?"

She nodded with no indication that such a menial task was beneath her. The way people talk about her in the city, she's either an irresistible seductress or a hideous hag, but definitely a vile, selfish spendthrift monster who wasted the fortune her son inherited from his late father. People also love to speculate about how Delphine's husband and Maximilien Taillefer both died in her house.

Her son seemed cheerful. A few picked flowers were wilting in his clutched hand. I wanted to crouch and chat with him, but Isabelle probably wouldn't.

Delphine took Octave's other hand and the two of them led me through the halls of Verneuil, which is a rich person's country house, not especially rambling or complicated, so it hardly made sense that I would need help finding my rooms.

Luckily, Delphine was too concerned about my health to suspect me of fraud. She didn't ask how heat exhaustion could possibly have made me forget the single turn and flight of stairs required to arrive at my room.

My luck was even better than that: the door opened to

reveal an empty bed. Wherever the real Isabelle was, she hadn't ruined my ruse yet.

"You should rest," Delphine said. "I'll have some refreshments sent up."

"No need," I said. "I'll... ring for some later."

Delphine didn't look convinced, which was wise of her, because I was fucking thirsty. But I couldn't sit in that room waiting to be served—and found out. I needed her to be on her way.

"I wish you a swift recovery. I hope I'll see you this evening?" she asked.

My confusion was not feigned. "Hmm?"

"At dinner? Or in the salon afterward?"

"Oh, ah... the salon, perhaps." If Isabelle was here, she could attend the salon as herself. I had to change shape before it got too hard to lie my way out of trouble. Finding new clothes would require a discreet act of theft.

Isabelle's presence had caught me off guard. Why had she come here? The answer that floated to the surface of my mind was <u>to look for me</u>, but I'd told her to write me a letter.

Delphine took her leave and I closed the door. My brief dream of leaning my forehead against the cool wood and taking a moment to curse myself was shattered in an instant.

Isabelle was standing in the corner.

I almost jumped. She would've been smug about that, so I held myself still and took in the amused lift of her eyebrows. Without making a sound, she was laughing at me.

It <u>was</u> pretty funny. And I was relieved that she wasn't angry or perturbed by my use of her appearance.

I asked, "Do you hide in a dark corner any time you hear a rustle outside your door?"

"Don't you?" She stepped toward me and cupped my face. Her hand should've been uncomfortably warm against my sticky, heated skin, but it was a light, cool touch. "You've made me prettier than I really am."

"I didn't." I have an impeccable memory for faces and never get a likeness wrong. "You just like me better than you like yourself."

"True," she agreed. "And looks aside, you're nothing like me. I made no promises to go to the salon, and would never have submitted to Delphine sending me to my room for a nap."

"She didn't—"

"She did," Isabelle interrupted. "You should take one, since you're attending the salon this evening. Delphine expects to see me there, and I have other plans, so it will have to be you."

"What other plans? You look shifty. Are you stealing something? Can I come?"

"No."

"You know if you make me pose as you this evening, I can make your life very annoying," I said. "I can say yes to so many invitations. People will be agog at how strangely Isabelle de Tourzin is behaving."

"In this house, the only people who know anything of my character—other than you—are Victor and Delphine. Both of them have accepted and will likely continue to accept all manner of oddness from me. Victor will probably guess your imposture, as they know you deceived them once already. I doubt they will act on that knowledge. As for making my life more annoying, you are welcome to try to outdo yourself on that count, but there are limits to what is possible. There's an evening gown in the wardrobe, and Delphine's maid Amélie can help you, if you like."

"You're leaving?" I asked, feeling even more like a spoiled child. I didn't stamp my feet, but it was a near thing. I only like to keep secrets if Isabelle and I both know what they are.

"Lie down," she said, softening. "I'll stay for a while."

I stripped to my shift. It was too hot to press against each other on the bed—and that is exactly the sort of thing I've told myself not to do, not to want, not until she clarifies her intentions toward me—but she stroked my back until I fell asleep.

When I awoke, she was gone. In the damp clutch of my hand, leaving tooth marks in my palm, was my comb. Isabelle must have retrieved it from my discarded dress, but how she'd slipped it into my grasp without waking me was a mystery. I was startled that she'd gone hunting for it, and found it, and <u>could</u> have stolen it, all while I was asleep—but of course she hadn't taken it. She wouldn't. She knew how much that would hurt me. She'd even carefully placed it where I would find it upon waking.

A page crinkled under my hand.

ISABELLE TO CÉLESTE, AUGUST 10, 1825

LEFT IN THE BED

Céleste,

Forgive me for borrowing from you without asking permission. If I caused you any distress, I do regret it, and hope you will find the ends worth the means.

There is a box of jewelry in the wardrobe. I merely paid for it with money, rather than stealing it from a sleeping person in an act of astonishing skill and audacity. Nevertheless, it is a gift. You have my promise that it is mundane and harmless, or at least, it was mundane and harmless at the moment of purchase. I hope it suits you.

Isabelle

So much happened yesterday. Have to write it all down before I forget it.

To pick up where I left off: Isabelle thought she could pacify me with rubies, and she was absolutely right.

I've stolen a lot of jewelry in my life, but I've never had anybody <u>give</u> me any. The necklace caught the sunlight through the window, redder than red. It was heavy in my hand. Each metal link held a faceted gem. With earrings and a bracelet to match, I knew it represented a small fortune.

She'd also had her evening gown retrimmed with black velvet ribbon. I have to imagine she did that for me; she seems perfectly satisfied never to think of her own clothing. All of that, as well as her borrowing of the comb and talk of "other plans" for the evening, spoke of some scheme long in the making. The thought sent a thrill through me. As much as I wanted to know what was to come, it was exciting just to know Isabelle had been thinking of me.

I feigned a lingering malaise from the heat and had a cold dinner sent to my room, then asked Delphine's maid Amélie to help me dress for the salon. I could have done my own hair, but Amélie was nice to talk to, in addition to being skilled at setting curls. She'd attended a few salons and enjoyed them, but was not going tonight, as she preferred the evenings with music and theater. "And besides," she added, "I like to spend my time with... well." That intrigued me, and I could only ask a couple of oblique questions without being too rude. I never found out who she liked to spend her time with. She wouldn't tell me any really salacious gossip about anyone else in the house, either, though I did my best to ferret it out.

Isabelle wouldn't have tried, but Amélie doesn't know that.

The salon was a more intimate gathering than I had expected. I recognized Delphine, and could guess that one of the two people next to her was our host, the writer Camille Dupin, and the other was Ari, the father of her child. Victor was there with a tall, handsome, long-haired person in a grey suit. The artist Morère, I supposed. I'd heard their given name as both Julien and Julie. There were six other guests I did not know, any of whom might be Isabelle, except that they all responded quite smoothly and cheerfully when we were introduced. Isabelle could probably do that in the right circumstances, with effort. I took the liberty of playing her role as though she could.

A few chairs had been added to the room's sofas and armchairs, all the furniture arranged loosely into a circle. Victor patted an empty seat, and I joined them.

"I'm glad you came," they said.

"Why?"

"Everyone's so curious about you," Victor replied and then spoke to everyone assembled. "Good evening, welcome. We have a reading tonight, something a little bit unusual, and I'm just waiting on—there you are!"

I walked into the room.

Or rather, the shape I'd taken when Isabelle had first met me, the scruffy, square-shouldered redheaded man who'd fought her and hidden with her in a stairwell and taken the stage coach across France with her, <u>he</u> walked into the room. Except he was Isabelle.

Amélie had equipped me with a paper fan. I raised it to my mouth to hide my smile. Isabelle wasn't as good at likenesses as I was, and she'd unknowingly made me prettier, smoothing out some of the rough edges, but it was a flattering sort of accident, to see exactly how doe-eyed she'd found me. I was pleased that she'd kept the scars and the crows' feet.

Her suit was borrowed, but couldn't possibly have been Victor's. Camille was also too short. Ari, perhaps, or Julie, though either way, the frock coat's seams strained at her shoulders. I wondered how Isabelle had arranged for the loan, what exactly she'd said. Did Victor know? Did anyone else?

"This is Céleste Forestier, an acquaintance of mine who, ah, finds lost things," Victor said. "I'll let Céleste speak now."

"Good evening." The body might be different, but I could see Isabelle in that stiff, uncomfortable posture. Victor had offered her a chair, but she remained standing. She must be doing this despite a distaste for public speaking, or public anything, and that spun the twist of tension running through me even tighter. Why had she chosen to do this here and now?

With determination, she continued, "I recently came into possession of a cache of letters. They're two centuries old. I needed help to make out the handwriting and translate the text and understand the circumstances of their creation. The person who helped me doesn't wish to be named. But these are Venetian. While they're love letters, and thus personal, they might have been intended for publication, or at least to be read aloud at a salon something like this one. I don't have the whole correspondence, and this first one is evidently a reply to some earlier letter. The language makes clear that the writer is a man and the recipient is a woman. Other than that, they're... anonymous."

Her gaze flicked toward me. I lifted my fan again. It didn't matter. There was no hiding from her.

I had no idea what she intended—the disguise, the story about these old Venetian letters, none of it made sense. All I knew was that Isabelle had something to say to me. I wanted to listen.

She cleared her throat and began to read.

ANONYMOUS LETTER, UNDATED
READ ALOUD AT VERNEUIL

You asked me, my lady, to solve a certain problem. Here I reply with regret that I have not solved it, for there is no solution. Perhaps you will call me a turnip again. Please do me the courtesy of reading the rest regardless.

I do love you, of course, with all my heart; I can no longer imagine not loving you, and if my love is unrequited, I would rather bear that, and bear the memory of what little time we have shared, than to deny the sentiment itself.

Why, you will ask, did I not simply say so in an earlier letter? You are right to accuse me thus. I am not ashamed of loving you. I have no wish to conceal the truth from you, or to keep you a secret from others—not unless you wish for the thrill of a clandestine affair, in which case I will oblige. Regardless, there is no defense for how long I have tarried. However unfortunate my circumstances, the flaw lay in my character. My own inadequacies constrained me from divulging my heart in previous correspondence.

You know I had to undertake a dangerous task, one I feared might kill me. I reasoned that it would harm you to know my love only in death, and did not wish to condemn you to mourn me, as unworthy as I am. I see now that this was no reasoning at all, but cringing cowardice. To call myself unworthy of you is to take from you your choice; to hide my love is the same. If I love and esteem you, as I say that I do, then I must grant you the choice to love me. You may deem me worthy or unworthy. You may love me and mourn me when I die, or forget me long before then.

When I departed without a word of my love, I intended to spare us both as much suffering as possible by excising myself from your life, an act I thought would deal more harm to me than to you. I erred. I was wrong in leaving you and in thinking that my absence would cause you no distress. I had no right to decide for you. For this I apologize.

When I completed my task and still spoke no word of my love, it was because, in expecting to die, I had buried my heart. How surprised I was, weeks later and far from you, to discover it weak and bruised, but beating. This was not the moment I knew I loved you; I already knew. I had known for some time. You are brave and joyful, clever and loyal, and I am drawn to the light of your anger. It burns as bright as mine, and never once did you tell me to extinguish that flame and stop seeking vengeance. This is not first among your qualities, and I hope we will have less to burn in the future, but still it warms me. I feel immense gratitude for everything you have done. What a fool I would be not to love you.

When at last I unearthed my heart, I discovered I wanted to live—to tell you the truth, yes, but also simply to live. You saved me. You changed me. You forced me to ask: if I love and esteem her, and she once found something in me worth loving and esteeming, however briefly, might it still be there in her absence? Might I find it myself?

My search is fruitful some days and not others, but I continue to undertake it. You made me believe it a worthwhile endeavor. A long quest cannot deter me, as you well know.

Repairing the hurt I have done you and regaining your affections may be an even longer quest, and perhaps one that you will forbid me. What do I have to offer you? Material goods—rubies, dresses—I would buy for you, but I know you can easily acquire such things by your own means. My long-buried heart, fragile and charred like something dug up in the ruins of Pompeii, seems to me a poor gift, but that is for you to judge. It is yours if you want it. You can have the rest of my life.

Still it troubles me, this knowledge that in inviting you to love me, and in allowing myself to love you, I have opened the door to future grief. Heartbreak, if we tear ourselves apart. Mourning, if we live happily until one of us dies. Whatever our end, it will come. There can be no joy without pain, but as I have learned very slowly, and over the course of many, many stubborn years, eschewing joy offers no protection. There will be pain regardless.

I will die some day, my love, and so will you. I wish us both to know joy before then, whether side by side or apart. Were it my choice, we would live and die together, but it is only half mine. I can live more easily now, knowing I have told you the truth and left you your choice. Even if the brief time we have already passed together is all we are granted, I cherish knowing you. Any happiness I could give you would be the honor of my life.

Our attention, the dozen of us listening, was a quivering, palpable presence in the room as Isabelle concluded her reading.

Isabelle touched her lashes gingerly, collecting the few tears that had gathered there, and I did the same. We were not the only ones moved.

Julie spoke first. "Was there a reply?"

Isabelle had failed to anticipate her effect. Her ruse faltered. She shuffled her pages as though they were real letters and their text might reveal some answer. Eventually she said, "It has not been translated yet."

"Please write to your translator," Delphine said. "I would love to know what happened next."

"It's me," I said and stood, causing everyone's head to turn. "I'm the translator. Let me see those, and I'll tell you the reply. It won't be as... polished."

There was such pleasure in being a great deal shorter than Isabelle that I wanted to stand next to her for as long as possible, even in the airless heat of the evening, even as she radiated hot panic in her ill-fitting suit. She relinquished the papers with some reluctance. It seemed impossible to me that she didn't know what I planned to do. I found her nervousness touching, though it feels a bit cruel to admit it. I would let her loom awkwardly over me forever. I could only bask in it for a moment.

The sheaf of pages was covered in Isabelle's handwriting, all of it in pencil, and none of it enchanted to make it illegible. I flipped through it with great care. It was exactly what she'd read aloud. At the last page, I nodded.

She'd read me a love letter. Out loud, in public, in our strange, masked way, where only I could decipher the full message. It was an entertaining scheme, and though the real Isabelle wouldn't be smiling so wide, I couldn't keep my grin at bay. And then I thought of how she'd had to look at her own face while writing of her efforts to love herself, and I wondered if it had helped.

To the salon, I said, "Here is how she answered."

And then I dropped the pages to the floor and kissed Isabelle.

She didn't expect me. I might've moved too fast, grabbing her by her lapels and pulling her down. We collided. Isabelle righted us, tilting her head just so and scooping me toward her with both arms. As hot as she was, I matched her. She welcomed my wild enthusiasm, capturing it, taming it, and when she eventually exhausted her tolerance for spectacle and let me go, I felt exercised, and had to keep from panting openly.

"I see you two have made up," Victor observed, lifting a page that had landed near their feet. No doubt they recognized Isabelle's handwriting. "And this anonymous Venetian letter? Was it a ruse?"

It was me Victor was looking at, not Isabelle. I didn't learn until afterward that Isabelle had told Victor almost nothing; she had appeared as Céleste Forestier and asked for an introduction at the salon. Whether or not Victor guessed her identity, they complied. The suit was Ari's, and she had stolen it. This made me love her even more.

To Victor, I said, "It's all true."

WRITTEN IN AN INVENTED
SHORTHAND

Our swift departure from the salon was rude, but everyone seemed amused. We hardly paid them any attention in our rush to get upstairs and close the bedroom door.

I dragged Isabelle down into another kiss—a much lengthier kiss—and only stopped when I caught myself grinding against her thigh.

"Do you want to change back? Or do you want me to change? I appreciated your show in the salon, but maybe you didn't intend to continue the... play in private," I said, faltering a little as I gestured at our bodies. I'd made my own readiness clear enough. Even with the centimeters of space I'd put between us, lust was audible in my voice. I cleared my throat and forged ahead. "I'm given to understand that other people get very attached to one particular way of being, and find it disturbing to be another way. So if you don't want to, ah, make love to me—"

"Céleste."

"Or if it's uncanny for you, seeing your own face—"

She took my hand and pressed it to the bulge in her trousers.

"Oh."

"It's endearing, the way you become shy at the most unexpected moments." She spun me around and bent me over the bed. "I think I will find, if I lift your skirts," she said, doing exactly that without waiting for permission, "and slide my fingers between your thighs, that you want this very, very much. Is that so?"

"Yes," I groaned, extravagantly loud even though she'd barely grazed me.

"Then I want it," she said. "I want what you want. And next time—I'm still speaking of tonight, you understand—I will take my usual form, and you can be any shape you like, but you <u>will</u> fuck me. Hard. It will not be the sort of act anyone can describe as 'making love.'"

Her fingers were slipping steadily in and out of me, relentless and wonderful, so it was a challenge to speak with righteous indignation, but I did my best. "Yes, it will. I'm going to call it that when I write about it."

She let loose a low rasp of a laugh, so I had to keep going.

"'Isabelle de Tourzin and I made love to each other all night long,'" I quoted. "'And even when it was hard—and sweaty—and <u>animal</u>—it was still, at its heart, very beautiful and tender, because we wanted it that way, and she wrote me a secret public love letter, and I'm wild about her and—'"

I was going to say something about wanting to be her husband and her wife, I think, but to be honest I don't remember if I managed to get those words out. She really did fuck me deliciously hard.

I did my best to return the favor, of course.

Anyway, for later, when I teach you to decipher my shorthand and you read all this, what matters is that Isabelle and I made <u>love</u> to each other all night long.

ISABELLE TO CÉLESTE,
SEPTEMBER 15, 1826

WRITTEN ON ENCRYPTED PAPER, APPENDED TO ALL THE PRECEDING PAGES

Having compiled our story, I find myself unsure how to end it. An inevitable and wonderful problem: from my perspective, it has not yet ended.

This volume is meant less as a gift for the Céleste of the present than as a memory for the Céleste and Isabelle of the future. Certainly it is no gift for the Isabelle of the present, as I am thoroughly sick of recopying pages, though I did enjoy drafting the stage directions for our scene of secret dialogue in the coach. I hope we live together long enough to forget some of these details, to rejoice or shudder or groan at rediscovering them.

In that light, on which subjects might our future selves wish to reminisce? You will be disappointed, perhaps, to discover that I was too sleepless and overjoyed to record my version of the night that followed our kiss at the salon, though _my_ memory is vivid, and I could refresh yours, if you need. It will be no exaggeration.

Most of all I wish I had captured that morning, the first time I had ever awoken entangled with you and heard only breath and birdsong, as the persistent hum of dread in my mind had at last gone silent. To feel your body—a new one, but familiar because it was yours—and luxuriate in your touch without fear was, for me, a rare and perfect moment. The experience has become less rare, but no less perfect.

We stayed at Verneuil for several more weeks. I resumed my usual shape, at least in public, and you were a man until you needed not to be. Since everybody in Camille's circle was accustomed to Julie's changing nature, the only thing that surprised them was how quickly you could shift.

Camille was quite taken with your dashing story, and asked if she could write a book using you as inspiration, which you flatly refused. I am privately smug that I have been allowed. What an intimate privilege, to read your diary.

On our return to Paris, we told Louise we planned to live together, and Apolline and Catherine that you could change shape, and incidentally that you had once been, and might be again if the whim took you, an infamous criminal called Cheats Death. Catherine's eyes widened enormously and Apolline laughed until she was breathless. When you asked what was funny, she said it was because she could not reconcile the idea of a dangerous criminal mastermind "blushing at a glimpse of titty." You replied that people are complicated, "me especially," and by then she had caught her breath enough to thank you for the long-ago loan of your comb.

The whim did take you, as it happens, and you took up stealing again within a few months. Our house was nearly empty of dangerous magical artifacts by then, Victor and Julie having nullified almost the whole collection, so you took it upon yourself to seek out more of them. It was a different kind of theft than what you'd committed in your youth, motivated by poverty and desperation, or even what you'd done as an adult, shoring up your legend. You had a partner, for one.

Our work resembles what I used to do with Dominique, but without his sense of where to find artifacts, it's less urgent and more occasional. It also often requires following rumors to no avail. I find this frustrating, but have never known it to bother you. As long as you get to sneak around and whisper secrets and break rules, you are utterly content. I do my fair share of slinking through shadows as well, but with a great deal more caution, lest you scold me for endangering myself, though you rarely have occasion. I am careful now. Because our days are spent together, I want them to be numerous.

It is my fondest hope that we both go on like this until our days quiet, as we grow too old to scale walls and hide in servants' stairs, and diminish. I hope we will look upon these pages with wonder, as though this was another life, and marvel at how much we have lived, though death makes life scarce and precious. And when I die, or when you do, though it still pains me to think of that future, we will miss each other, and mourn each other, and it will hurt, and that too will be love.

Until that ending, here we are, mortal and alive. I love you, Céleste. Let these pages, and all the days to come, be a record of how much.

Yours,
  Isabelle

THANK YOU FOR READING

I hope you enjoyed *The Anonymous Letters of C Forestier*. If you did, please consider posting a review or recommending it to friends who might like it. Word of mouth makes a huge difference for indie books like this one.

For more of my writing, you can find me online at FeliciaDavin.com. Sign up for my email announcements to find out about new books, sales, giveaways, and bonus stories.

ACKNOWLEDGMENTS

Dear Esteemed Reader,

Thank you for reading *The Anonymous Letters of C Forestier*.

This book is much better because Skye Kilaen read the manuscript and made many brilliant observations, most of which I responded to by saying, very eloquently, "oops." Or occasionally, "oh, damn, you're right." It is a gift to be read so attentively; I am so grateful for all her work.

This book and my life are also much better because of my beloved, who endures many rambling one-sided conversations in which I try to explain the feelings of fictional characters. He offers practical solutions to their problems, and also to my problems, because he cooks and parents and repairs our house so I can write.

When I started writing what would become this series, it felt like something I was writing for myself alone—a feeling that was confirmed when some literary agents very kindly declined *The Scandalous Letters of V and J*, gently explaining that it was too niche.

Historical *and* fantasy *and* nonbinary *and* epistolary—in this economy? With weird jokey little tributes to/thefts from [checks notes] Honoré de Balzac? Get the fuck out.

That is an outrageous paraphrase, lest I libel these poor people who were really quite professional and, it must be said, making a sensible decision. This is not a series destined for massive commercial success.

Luckily, as an indie author, I don't have to be professional *or* sensible. I wrote the books I wanted to write. It turned out some of you loved them. Trust me: me and these books, we love you back.

Please accept, Esteemed Reader, my regards,
    Felicia Davin

ABOUT THE AUTHOR

Felicia Davin (she/they) is the author of the queer fantasy trilogy *The Gardener's Hand* and the sci-fi romance *Nowhere* series. Her novel *The Scandalous Letters of V and J* was described as "a string of natural pearls, each a luminous gem on its own but even more exquisite in sequence" by *The New York Times*.

She lives in Massachusetts with her family. When not writing and reading fiction, she teaches and translates French. She loves linguistics, singing, and baking. She is bisexual, but not ambidextrous.

She writes a biweekly email newsletter about words and books called *Word Suitcase*, which is available at feliciadavin.com.